Hounds of Dawn

Hounds of Dawn Book One

H.S. Torben

SIMPLY ABSURD
PUBLISHING

DEDICATION

For Mom, who drove forty miles round-trip to the nearest library
every week to introduce me to magic.

ISBN: 979-8-9863141-0-5 (ebook)
ISBN: 979-8-9863141-2-9 (print)

FRIDAY

Paranoid But They Are Still Out to Get Me

@ShinySilverHats

Three missing people suspected of being unregistered Sovaj. Has @CahladPrime gone full evil or are the Hounds of Dawn finally stepping out of the shadows?

#ItsAllAConspiracy #TheHoundsOfDawnAreReal #MagicUnderground

Cahlad Prime *@CahladPrimeOfficial*

Don't forget to register for the free @EmmettOBrien concert taking place this Tuesday. Tickets are going fast

1

BLUE

"Woo!" The collective battle cry of a half dozen frenzied bachelorette parties reached her ears through the hastily barricaded rooftop door.

Bam!

The door shuddered violently under an impressive impact, but held. Another high-pitched roar of "woo!" made the hair on the back of her neck stand up. The next loud bang and shudder of the door told her she needed to hurry this up. Blue wasn't sure how long the improvised barricade and the rusted lock and hinges would hold.

She rarely left the house without her gun. But since she'd anticipated drinking heavily tonight, it was locked up at home. Probably still the right decision. She had two throwing knives strapped discreetly to her legs, and they would do no good against a horde of crazed, dildo-wielding, "woo" bitches.

She stepped from behind the industrial-sized chiller and approached the terrified man currently leaning over the waist-high brick wall that separated the roof from a four-story drop to the crowded sidewalk below. He peered at the ground as if it was his best option. A drunken shoving match in the middle of the street below drew the attention of most of the people on the sidewalk. They were too busy recording the slugfest with their phones to notice the chaos erupting above them. High-pitched choruses of "woo!" were as much a part of downtown Nashville as potholes and country music these days. Annoying but easily ignored.

Blue couldn't entirely disagree with the idea of jumping, given the absurdity of the situation. Those women were terrifying. They hadn't started the night with a ton of decorum anyway and were now unnaturally amped up. He had an advantage he didn't know about yet. She was here, and this was not the strangest situation she had found herself in lately. Extraordinary situations were her accidental specialty. They were also the reasons she left the house today, intending to drink until she temporarily forgot some of them. Alas, it was not meant to be. The forgetting part, anyway.

Blue tried to stifle a hiccup. Usually, she didn't consume enough alcohol to lose feeling in her teeth before her strange situations, but she could still pull this off.

Stepping as quietly as she could, which wasn't very quietly at all, she registered the nightmare symphony of sirens converging on the building mixed with classic country tunes wafting up from a half-dozen, open-air honky tonks. All were punctuated by the aggressive assault on the door in rhythm with the "woos" of the bitches.

Lucky for this fellow, a sneaky little birdie left a flier for a singer/songwriter showcase on the third floor of this multi-story entertainment mecca. Happy coincidence that it coincided with the time her well-meaning, yet clueless, best friend set her up for a blind date. Seizing the opportunity to evade an awkward dinner with the latest warm body Devon met at a PTA meeting or in a public toilet, she dressed herself up and ventured downtown to listen to a talented set of musicians. That was the great thing about Nashville. Even the terrible music was better than the good music anywhere else.

She had been here for hours. Surrounded by bachelorette parties. Sober. Sometimes the little notes and clues turned out to be nothing. The sneaky little birdie liked to screw with her occasionally, sending her to places where nothing magically interesting happened. Midget drag queen mud wrestling had been one of those times. Figuring the sneaky little birdie was just having a bit of fun with her again, she gave up around hour four and started drinking. Heavily. There was only so much "woo" a sane person could take in one sitting. Truth be told, she would much rather be in a basement pub a few blocks over favored by locals exactly because it didn't attract people who screamed "woo" on a regular basis. Also, the potatoes au gratin and lamb sliders were divine.

She had a little fun fabricating proof of the date she falsely claimed she was on by taking a duck-lip selfie with the hottest guy she could find in the place. His name was Doug. He didn't want to be here, either. Bless his heart. The selfie cost her a very expensive bottle of whiskey offered as a sacrifice to the hot man's very disgruntled

4

girlfriend, Melissa, who was in the bathroom when Blue approached him. The sacrifice worked until she made a joke about their names and if there would be wooden kids' toys at the wedding.

In the middle of getting as far away from scary Melissa as she could and texting the offending picture to Devon so that the matchmaking nonsense would stop, a ruckus erupted in the stairwell next to her. A herd of people clomped up the narrow stairs, some spilling out of the exit on her floor.

A quick check of her favorite downtown Nashville social media accounts told her a dueling piano player belting the *Dawson's Creek* theme song on the floor below her was now trending on social media big time. He whipped a bunch of bachelorettes into a piranha sex frenzy. There were already two injuries, and police were on the way.

Piano man fled for his life up the stairway Blue was standing next to as they mauled him. Someone at the bottom of the stairwell was still live-streaming the coordinated "woo" and shove effort that served as the pre-matrimony debauchery version of heave and ho to bring down the door. That stairwell, the one she could not get through conventionally, was now directly behind her, and packed tighter than a sardine can.

As regrettably visible as this event was, she might be able to prevent the tall beanpole of a man in baggy blue jeans, a faded black tee-shirt, and black Chuck Taylors from being eviscerated by a pack of rabid drunks in tutus and tiaras. His shirt was already shredded, and his arms sported bloody claw marks. This guy would not last long if that mob got to him again.

His head, a combo disaster of male pattern baldness and a long overdue haircut, was blinding as it reflected the full moon. She planned to rely on the cacophony of noise surrounding them to distract him until she could get close enough to make the grab and get out of here. If she could get her hands on him, this was going to be easy. If she couldn't, this situation would get interesting in the wrong way really fast.

A cracking noise rang out behind them as the ancient door lock lost the battle. The only things standing between Blue and an army of woo bitches were an ancient milk crate and an old cylindrical street ashtray.

Bean Pole's head whipped toward the sound of his impending doom with panic on his face. He saw Blue, his eyes widening with surprise and terror at her proximity. She put her hands up in a placating gesture to reassure him, but it did no good. Baldy turned, and with one quick but ungraceful leap, he hurled himself over the wall.

"Jesus!" Blue yelled, lunging for him and catching his upper arm. He was much heavier than she thought a skinny man should be. Her feet dragged across the grit-covered roof, unable to gain traction as he pulled her over the edge with him. She stopped their momentum when her stomach slammed into the ledge. His dead weight almost popped her shoulders from their sockets.

She really needed a firm grip on at least one body part and their momentum to be zero. She couldn't do this if she had to calculate velocity and deceleration. She simply could not math right now.

She admitted to herself at that moment she was extremely drunk. Drunker than she thought when she involved herself in whatever this was shaping up to be.

Half dangling over the brick ledge that was sanding the skin off her stomach, she looked down the four stories to the crowded sidewalk below. She didn't like the view. Turning her head slightly, she saw two large black SUVs screech to a stop a block away, where the street was barricaded for the weekend honky tonk crowds. She counted four occupants charging out of each vehicle before her head spun and she felt her dinner coming up. The goon squad wasn't dressed in civilian clothing. They weren't waving weapons, but they looked militarized. She didn't know who they were, but she bet they were after her boy here, who suddenly developed a sense of self-preservation and clawed at her arm. She took a deep breath to settle her rolling stomach and prevent some unsuspecting soul below her from having a dreadful night.

"Nope. No, you don't," she grunted as much to herself as Baldy. Soon cops and a mystery goon squad would mix with the woo bitch army. She wanted to be long gone before that powder keg exploded.

Using every ounce of strength she could muster, she hauled the kicking and screaming man back over the wall. They both flew through the air in a tangle of limbs before he crashed on top of her, bumping her nose with his forehead.

He continued screaming and thrashing wildly as her eyes watered. She took a knee to the crotch, and he put all his weight on a strand of loose hair, sending sharp little stings down her scalp and ripping a few strands loose.

"Calm down, man!" she shouted, finally sitting up and kicking at him with her feet. This was not her most graceful moment.

"Leave me alone!" Baldy shouted, followed by several loud and incoherent noises. "I didn't mean to."

"Chill, Baldy." She waved at her outfit. She certainly was not dressed like one of them. "I'm not with..." The door exploded. The crate in front of it sailed through the air, and the ashtray spiraled violently to the side. "Oh, boy."

A tiara-topped army of exposed cleavage decorated with tulle, rhinestones, glitter, and the occasional fringe poured through the door "Woo-ing" in triumph and wielding various penis-shaped party favors. "Dear God," she exhaled.

A short woman sporting long hair in a shade of blonde only found in the south, a denim jacket with leather fringe, shorts so short the pockets were showing, and a bedazzled "Bride-To-Be" sash, led the charge toward them. "He's mine!" she roared, bounding faster than a woman in heels should be able to manage.

"Gah!" Baldy shouted, scooping up a handful of dirt and sediment from the rooftop. Instead of hurling it at the charging Bridezilla, he slung it directly into Blue's face and crab-walked himself into an upright run.

"What in the actual hell?" Blue screamed, wiping at her eyes. She heard his feet slapping away and hoped he wasn't jumping over the side again. She couldn't see anything. Two hands buried themselves in her hair and yanked. She sighed and reminded herself to take it easy. They were just drunk woo bitches.

Feeling lazy, she let the person pull her up by the hair and forced her eyes open. The mob of women were trampling each other with their shiny new cowboy boots, chasing Baldy as he fled. A few tripped over the crate and the now erratically spinning ashtray in the chaos. It slowed most of them down enough that Baldy was outrunning them. He picked up a small outdoor table covered in empty soda bottles and cigarette butts and limply tossed it into the wall of crazed estrogen pursuing him. It did nothing.

Doing her best to ignore the scratch and sting from the roof grit in her eyes, she turned herself toward whoever the poor soul was that had her hair. It was Bridezilla. She violently shook Blue's head, lips twisted in a maniacal sneer. Blue calmed her stomach again. Hanging upside down and being shaken while drunk wasn't great for the old stomach. She belched loudly in the woman's face, leading to an indignant "Ew" from Bridezilla.

"Sorry, sweetheart." Blue slammed her palm into Bridezilla's cute little button nose. She giggled, then yelped as a chunk of her own hair was ripped loose.

Cursing, she sprinted after Baldy, shoving tulle-ringed women aside, roller derby style. Lacking the common enemy of the door, the mob turned on itself. Hair, tiaras, mixed drinks, tutus, shoes, and dildos flew through the air like surreal confetti. The women brawled with the single-minded focus of preventing the others from reaching the bald man, who was desperately searching for a way off the roof.

Blue hurtled a downed lump wearing a "Same Penis for Life" sash, almost tripping when her foot destroyed a plastic tiara. Those not brawling gained on Baldy as he neared a fire escape.

Overwhelmed momentarily by the absurd chaos of it all, she paused and put her hands on her hips. She took a deep breath of pleasantly cool air and looked around her. She liked the country song playing on the street below them. Women bumped into her from all sides, but sometimes you just had to stop and appreciate the exceptional moments in life. This moment, for better or worse, was exceptional in so many ways.

A hiccup that threatened to be more ended her zen moment. She resumed her charge through the Woo Mania main event, watching as a pretty redhead wearing a penis-shaped balloon crown and a toddler's skirt caught Baldy by the collar and dragged him back toward the mob.

Blue shoved aside two more sash-wearing women in matching shirts and grabbed Baldy's arm. "Gah!" he shouted at her again. His eyes were wide, and he had apparently lost his ability to use actual words.

"Sup?" She nodded and head-butted Red. The woman let go of Baldy, flying backward and confirming to everyone on the roof that she was not wearing underwear and liked to wax. He still fought, and Blue couldn't grip anything but his shirt — the wily bastard.

"Stay still, damn it!" she screamed, yanking his shirt with one hand and trying to catch his wrist with the other. She could grab his ear, but it might rip it off.

"GAHHHHH!" he screamed. The smell of stale beer and onions hit her in the face. Her stomach flipped, and she clamped her lips shut as bile rose in her throat. She gave serious consideration to letting it fly.

"NOOOOO!" a primal scream erupted behind her. She turned and immediately caught something hard with her face. It stung. Badly. She couldn't let go of Baldy, which meant she was defenseless when her new bestie, the now bleeding Bridezilla, swung an oversized dildo like a baseball bat, striking her across the cheek and making her momentarily see stars.

"Heifer, did you really...?"

"She just hit you with a giant dick," Baldy pointed out unhelpfully.

"You mother..."

"Everyone, put your hands behind your head!" Two uniformed officers, guns drawn, burst onto the roof. Just great. The goon squad wouldn't be far behind them.

Blue ducked the third dick bat swing. Baldy caught it across the nose and produced a satisfying cry of pain. She closed her eyes and caught Baldy's now still wrist. She focused on the arctic cold in her veins and the prismatic plasma that filled her vision. Ozone filled her nose, and she was skipping across an electric trampoline, clutching Baldy for his dear life. The nightmare rooftop symphony faded and was replaced by the creaks and groans of ships rocking on their moorings.

They tumbled ass over teakettle into the tiny galley of her vintage houseboat. Baldy, still recovering from a dildo to the nose, went down hard. Blue blamed the last three shots of whiskey for her ungraceful landing.

She raised up as he regained his focus and realized he wasn't on a roof surrounded by a main event of murderous woo bitches, cops waving guns, and a mystery goon squad.

He opened his mouth to speak, scream, or sing the *Dawson's Creek* theme song. She wasn't sure which and didn't care. She punched him in the face.

His head lolled to the side. She collapsed on top of him for a moment and just laid still, trying to calm her stomach. Finally standing, she resisted the urge to kick his ribs. It wasn't his fault he was an out-of-shape, chaos-causing, dumb-ass.

Pulling a small bag from the pantry, she fished out a bottle and a syringe. Crouching over him, she eyeballed his frame, guesstimated his weight, and added about thirty pounds. This guy was heavy, and she wasn't taking any chances on whatever that was in the bar happening in her boat. She eyed the skullet and wondered if those women would feel dirty tomorrow.

She plunged the syringe into his neck, needing him to stay quiet and still for a while tonight. She needed a moment after all that nonsense.

Blue contemplated trying to move him to the couch or the bed. He sprawled across the entirety of her tiny galley. She was cold and hungry. Her cheek needed ice. She needed a good puke. He could stay where he was. She danced through the obstacle course of his arms and legs toward the boat's head, only stepping on one of his phalanges in the process. She pulled her phone from her back pocket and was glad to see it survived the chaos. There was already a text waiting.

Mama Bear: How did it go? Do I get to meet him?

Me: Not a keeper. Still need me Tuesday?

Mama Bear: Yes. Greenlee says 8:30.

2

BLUE

F resh off a puke, showered, and starting on her rally, Blue climbed out onto the sun deck of her boat, wearing Daffy Duck slippers and a fluffy wool cardigan. The night was calm in a way only nights on the water surrounded by the creak and groan of ropes and the gentle lapping of waves against hulls could be. It was in stark contrast to the surreal chaos that had surrounded her a mere forty-five minutes ago. The stars gleamed so brilliantly that if one were so inclined to believe for a moment; they were using the glass-smooth water as their own personal mirror. The dock was mostly empty tonight; the summer crowds fled for the season when the weather turned chilly. A few people were about, cozied up in their boats or relaxing on the fingers between casting an occasional lure into the dark water.

With an exhausted sigh, Blue blew on her hot tea and gazed out at the night, trying to absorb some of its calm. Failing, she took a sip of her drink to see if she could help the calm along, or at least appease her rebelling stomach. This had been a hell of a day, even by her standards. She reached up and freed her hair from its binding, letting it get caught in the breeze and pile around her shoulders in a damp, tangled mess.

Climbing to the flybridge where a well-loved outdoor couch awaited her, she took a moment to rock back and forth with the waves and buttoned her cardigan, which was too warm for the current weather. She reveled in the feeling of warmth seeping into her skin and reflected on what tomorrow would hold.

Sleeping Beauty was her problem until she could get him resettled somewhere. He couldn't go home. His face was all over social media and the Cahlad, the official governing body of all things magic by international treaty with almost every non-magical government on the planet, already released an official statement that he was wanted as an unregistered Sovaj and considered dangerous. That meant a Stalker unit, the Cahlad's version of an investigative strike team, was tearing his life apart, trying to find him right now. She still did not know what that goon squad that had rolled in on a crowded city street was about. They were a worrisome new player.

Mr. Hank Schooner, who should have considered locking down his social media accounts or at least using some filters, was internationally famous in the least desirable way right now. TikTok videos of his face when the woo bitch army descended upon him had millions of views and shares already. They all contained the hashtag #thenova, tying him to the unexplained magic surges happening across the Southeast over the past few weeks. Between the Cahlad press releases and social media coverage, Mr. Schooner was in dire need of a makeover.

She would go shopping tomorrow and pick up some clippers, hair dye, nice clothes, and Clark Kent glasses for him. Devon could help her with the rest. She and Devon were a well-oiled machine when it came to making magical fugitives drop off the face of the earth. Greenlee wouldn't need to be involved in this one. Mr. Schooner was a fairly low-level magic user in the grand scheme of things.

Mr. Schooner would not be happy. None of them ever were when she explained they essentially needed to ghost their personal lives and shelve their magic if they wanted to stay alive and out of a literal or figurative cage. Worse, she had a sneaky suspicion that Mr. Schooner hadn't even known he was a Sovaj, much less that he needed to register to comply with the Sovaj Registration Act of 1978. He had no idea he was expected to submit his life to the invasive pseudo-governmental oversight; the act required to appease the fear and concern of two important demographics of people: a non-magic populace struggling to deal with the concept of people who could do things they didn't understand and couldn't explain, and the vast majority of magic users who could only channel magic using rare and heavily regulated artifacts. The man currently drooling on her galley carpet likely thought hot women were interested in him because of his sloppy mom's basement fashion and awesome hair. Not whatever it was that had set the Woos off.

Most of the Sovaj, the name for magic users that didn't need to rely on an artifact to channel their magic, knew what they were.

If they found themselves in need of Blue and Devon's unique set of services, they usually fit into one of two buckets. Either they had remained hidden and unregistered but had screwed up, or they had never been without oversight and were trying desperately to disappear into a normal, non-magic life. Occasionally, they dealt with a magic user that used or owned an unregistered artifact. But the penalty for that offense was peanuts compared to being an unregistered Sovaj. So those cases were few and far between. They were never happy people, but most of them understood how they had gotten to where they were. That would not be the case with Baldy.

Hot spots of powerful magic anomalies had popped up across the region recently. Artifacts were misbehaving and registered Sovaj were experiencing unexplained and often dangerous surges in power. The Cahlad and government were keeping a tight lid on the details for the moment, but Blue followed a few reliable sources in the form of well-placed listening devices and key loggers that told her the cat was almost out of the bag. She suspected Schooner was an unfortunate victim of whatever was causing those strange magic surges.

The spikes seemed to move every three to four days. Then there would be periods without activity. Chances were, Mr. Schooner could perform the Dawson's Creek theme next week to a room full of "same penis for life" obsessed women with no ill effects. He would not get that chance now though because he was on the Cahlad's radar. She felt a little bad for him, but she still hadn't fished all the roof dirt out of her eyes yet, so it was an exceedingly small bit of bad.

Tomorrow. Tomorrow she would need to move the heavily drugged and unconscious man from the galley of her ship. As far as she knew, no one that had made it onto the roof while she wrestled with Baldy, Bridezilla, and Red were taking pictures or recordings. The frenzy overrode the need to share every moment of their life on social media. But it was late, and she didn't want to assume. She and Baldy needed to lie low right now.

She would advise snoring-beauty to undertake some cardio training or ballet. He was slow, clumsy, and heavy out on that roof. He was joining the wonderful world of living as a fugitive. He needed to be quick and nimble now.

"Neighbor!" she heard a gruff, slightly slurred voice call from a few slips down. She glanced to her right and lifted her tea toward a behemoth of a man in just a tee-shirt and Tabasco-branded boxers teetering unnervingly from side to side while urinating into the water of an empty slip. He lifted his hat with his free hand and nodded his head when she met his gaze.

"Mister! How's it going?" she turned to face him.

"Got some grilled shrimp and salad left over from dinner. It's yours if you want it." He tucked himself back into his boxers, tripped slightly on his flip-flop, and wobbled wildly again. Blue grimaced. She wasn't sure how he didn't end up in the water. But he never did.

"I appreciate it, man, but I just ate. I wish I had waited." She was lying. She couldn't eat right now if she wanted to. She regretted that fact immensely because Mister was an incredible chef who took it upon himself to make sure that the entire dock was fed. Grilled shrimp and a tossed salad covered in one of Mister's divine home-made dressings would have been a lovely dinner if she could have managed it.

"Another time then." He smiled and turned back toward his floating accommodations. But something stopped him. He turned sharp brown eyes toward her and grunted, "I didn't hear you walk down."

Nope, he hadn't heard her walk down the rickety old dock to the boat she called home a few nights each week or when she was too beaten up to risk Lexi seeing her. Nor had he heard her heave the dead weight of a surprisingly heavy for his size thirty-something bald man into the boat. The extra padding under the carpet was a wonderful investment. She gave him a dazed smile and twirled her hair a bit. "I didn't want to wake anybody. Such a peaceful night."

"Hmph." He peered at Blue for a moment before he turned again. "Let me know the next time you are coming in. I worry. You all by yourself out here. I'll walk you down."

"Thank you, Mister." She smiled genuinely. Mister deserved better than churning his life away on a lonely dock without contact with his family. Most days, she was confident what she and Devon were doing was right. That it was helpful, even if it wasn't perfect. On days like today, she questioned everything. She wanted more than anything in the world to blow a hole in the entire sordid system. She let her head fall back to stare up at the stars. A girl could dream.

TUESDAY

Save Down Nashville *@SaveDowntownNashville*
What a spectacle. Something must be done! Hey bachelorettes. Welcome to Nashville. Y'all go home now, you hear?
#NoMoreDildos #NoMoreWoo #DoSomethingMetroCouncil

Paranoid But They Are Still Out to Get Me
@ShinySilverHats
Anybody else see the Mystery Goon Squad in Nashville this weekend? They are following the magic. @USSenatorNolanMiller has finally gone over the edge and taken matters into his own hands.
#ItsAllAConspiracy #TheNovaStrikesAgain #TheyAreComingForYouNext

Cade Rhodes Biggest Fan *@CadeRhodesBiggestFan*
Cade Rhodes is the new performer for the Cahlad's

Free Concert tonight. And I have tickets! Time to meet my future husband.

#FurtureMsCadeRhodes #AmericasBeard #MagicAintSoBad #ILove-

FreeTickets #EmmettOBrienSucks

Cahlad Prime *@CahladPrimeOfficial*

Please join us for the dedication of the Greenfield Greenspace today at 10 a.m. in honor of the victims of the horrible events of ten years ago. Made possible by the generous donations of @ClayGreenfield and @LydiaGreenfield.

3

BLUE

B lue raced down the steps to the curb, where Finn waited in his shiny silver Audi. She yanked open the door and flopped inside, apologizing for running late, even though she knew he expected it. No doubt he would make up the time on the way over. His car had every bell and whistle available and several less-than-legal after-market modifications. It surprised her when he handed her a coffee and a bagel with honey cinnamon spread, like he wasn't worried she would ruin the softest leather ever made. She was also grateful because it was early, and they both needed caffeine and calories to get through the task ahead of them. Leave it to Finn to be responsible. She rode in silence until they arrived at a new park. In two hours, people arrive for the park's dedication ceremony and a viewing of the sculpture Greenlee created to be its centerpiece. Neither she nor Devon understood why he had entered the call for submissions, especially considering the whole site was a trigger for all of them. She didn't intend to stay for the ceremony; she was not emotionally capable of holding it together in front of an audience. But the least she could do was show her support for her friend's amazing talent.

Blue took in the recently completed green space featuring a butterfly garden and modern playground as she climbed from the car. Finn climbed out of the driver's side; his face was somber. She followed his gaze to a familiar black work truck. Somehow, they still beat the others. Greenlee helped Devon down from his truck and took her hand and led her toward a large object covered with a sheet in the center of the park. Her shoulders were tense. Like Blue, Devon didn't want to be here, but was doing her best to support Greenlee. "You ready for this?" Finn asked her quietly as they walked together to join their friends.

"No," she answered him simply. She would never be ready for this. She hated this place. Her hands shook, and if Finn hadn't fed her, she would be vomiting now. His expression grew darker.

Today the statue Greenlee created for the Cahlad would be unveiled. The park where they now stood was the location of a devastating explosion that occurred ten years ago. The official story from the Cahlad maintained the bombing was part of a coup to take over the organization.

Devon, Blue, and Greenlee knew better. They met on this spot ten years ago on the day of the supposed bombing. It is also where the body of Devon's son, Gage, was found days later in the rubble of the building where they had all been held. Her husband, Alexander, was murdered trying to keep his family from being captured and brought here. Devon did not know Gage was in the building when she fled for her life. She had never forgiven herself for leaving him.

Greenlee kissed the top of Devon's head and moved toward the covered statue that was the focal point of the park. Blue and Finn stood on each side of her friend. She met Finn's eyes one more time over Devon's head. Alexander was Finn's stepbrother, but they didn't remember a life without each other. Their parents married when they were both toddlers. Gage was his nephew. His pain was etched across his features as he wrapped an arm around Devon's shoulder. Blue wrapped her arm around Devon's waist. This was a rough day for everyone, and being here wasn't making it better.

"I wanted you to see this. And I wanted you to have a moment before everyone else got here," Greenlee told Devon. Blue thought he was second-guessing himself. He looked at her when Devon didn't respond. She nodded, and he gently pulled the cloth from the statue.

Devon gasped and shuddered. A moment later, she erupted into anguished sobs, curling in on herself. Blue's vision spotted, darkness creeping in at the edges as painful steel bands clamped on her chest, and she fought for breath. Greenlee appeared in front of them. "I'm sorry. I'm so sorry. I wanted the world to remember your beautiful boy the way you do."

Devon fell to her knees, Greenlee going with her and holding her against his chest. He extended his hand up toward Blue, who stood numbly staring at the statue, and she took it. Finn stood perfectly still, jaw clenched, and his face turned to the ground. The statue looked just like Gage. The boy sat on his knees, pushing a toy train across the ground. The expression on his delicately crafted face was innocent and joyful. Greenlee hadn't told them this was what he was making. It was supposed to be an abstract piece of artwork.

"It's my baby," Devon sobbed. "It's my perfect boy."

Blue rattled in a breath and turned her head away. "It is amazing, Greenlee," she choked out.

She pulled away, but Finn reached out to stop her. She shook her head at him. "I can't. You take care of them," she whispered as he tried to pull her back.

"What about you?" he asked with a gruff voice, arm still extended toward her.

"I'll be fine." She hurried away, rounding Finn's car and sitting on the ground with her back to the emotional scene behind her. She gulped in air and saw images of the horrible things that still haunted her nightmares. She felt the panic taking over. If she didn't get herself together, she would lose herself in it. She leaned her head back, listening to Devon's sobs. The car door was cold.

She was lying on something cold. Quiet sobs filled the air from somewhere far away.

"Come on, woman. Wake up." Blue turned her head to get away from the annoying tapping on her forehead. She cracked open an eye and stared up into the frantic brown eyes of a Hispanic woman with chin-length hair. She wore pink scrubs and dark-rimmed glasses and only stepped back slightly when Blue swatted at her. The lighting in this room was bright, and whatever she was lying on was hard.

"I can't keep them down much longer. The shift changes soon," the woman kept speaking. When Blue didn't respond fast enough, the woman resumed tapping her on the forehead with her index finger. "Now."

Blue swatted again, confused. The last thing she remembered was decimating her coffee table and seeing Rhodes' panicked face hovering above her. She sat up and spotted a drain on the floor below the table. Blood splattered the concrete. She shuddered and looked down at herself. She wore a pair of black scrubs that were stiff with blood. It crusted her skin, but she seemed uninjured. "You are?"

The woman huffed and placed her hands on her bright pink hips, drawing Blue's attention to her stomach. Very definitely a baby bump. Great. "Esdevona Irving. But people call me Devon. And you have to move your ass."

Frustrated, she hopped off the table, her feet hitting the cold floor. Of course, she didn't have socks. She bent her knees and stretched her arms, taking inventory of what worked and what didn't. She reached out for her magic and felt the prickle and fizz at her belly button. That was a good sign.

"Ass moved. Give me something I can work with." Blue peered around. No cameras. Door open.

"Just teleport me out of here or whatever it is you do. They said you could. That's why they kept you knocked out. I've flushed the gas from your system and the room. You can take me out of here."

Blue shook her head, a sad smile crossing her face. Devon's face grew angry. Blue pointed at the baby bump. "Your baby won't survive. You OK with that?"

Devon's face grew pale, and she placed a hand over her stomach. "What do you mean?"

"I can take you. But the babies don't survive. Sometimes it causes issues for the mother. But it's your choice." It was a lesson she had learned the hard way and wasn't eager to repeat. Blue waited for Devon's answer as she pilfered through the drawers that lined one of the walls. Saws, scalpels, torches, sharp things she couldn't identify. This was a torture chamber.

"Shit." Devon wailed.

"Don't want to go with me?" Blue plucked two scalpels out of the drawers and turned to watch the woman.

"I can't." Devon shook her head, and tears filled her eyes. "You are going to leave me here."

"I'm leaving. But how and with whom remains to be seen." Blue leaned back against the cabinet and leveled her gaze at the woman who might be useful yet. She tied her hair into a knot at the top of her head and stuck the scalpels through, crossing each other. These scrubs did not have pockets. "Who is down and how are you doing it? Talk to me."

"The guards. Three of them in this hall. One on the other side of the door. This is the overnight shift." She pulled a set of keys from her pocket and jingled them. "I've been a good girl. They let me out on work release. I'm pregnant, so I'm not color coded. They don't know."

"OK. Night shift. Four guards. You have keys. Why are you here with me? Walk out the damned door." She needed useful intel. Like where the hell they were. Who was keeping them? All she knew right now was that she had a pregnant lady to bust out of a psycho house of horrors. No pressure.

"They are only to doors in this hallway." Devon told her as she pointed toward the end of the hall. "That door. Someone on the other side lets them out. I knocked them out, too. The keys don't work on that one."

"Getting somewhere. How do they do that? How are the guards down? And what's color-coded? Us?" Blue looked quickly out into the hallway. To her right were four doors on each side and a dead end. Each door had its own large window in the wall next to it. One of them stood open. To her left was a large blast door with a console on the wall. She might be able to do something with that. A camera blinked at the dead end of the hallway.

"Basic radio call to a goon on the other side. That panel is so basic. They are all men, so it will be obvious if we try. I put them to sleep for the duration. We have maybe an hour and a half, tops." Devon followed her.

"What color would you be if you weren't pink?" Blue squatted and put her head in her hands. "How many friendlies are in this hallway? How far do we have to go if we get out that door? Are they armed? With what? Did you do anything about that camera before you walked in here, or do they usually let you into the torture chambers?"

"Black. Like you. Black for extremely dangerous. Blue for moderate. Green for harmless. Pink for preggers. Everyone in this hall right now is black or pink." Devon stood above her, watching with growing panic etched across her features. Blue could tell she wanted to do more than chat, but she didn't have weapons or backup. All she had right now was information. She needed to gather that resource and use it wisely. Devon continued, even when Blue kept her head in her hands. "I used their computer to loop the cameras. I think there are two levels. We are in the basement. There is a lab somewhere. Pretty advanced. Some dude is asleep at his desk. That is the only movement I have seen. The facility isn't very big, or they don't have good visual coverage. I've never seen any guns."

Blue lifted her head and looked hard at the woman. She liked her already. "Nice. Friendlies? Not just this hallway?" Blue was no longer feeling so good about this.

"Four women in the last two rooms. One man in the first room." Devon winced as she mentioned the man in the first room. "They brought someone new in early yesterday. They are in room three. Whoever is in there is giving them problems. They haven't fed them yet. I have no idea what is on the other side of that door as far as friendlies. There aren't any cameras in the rooms."

"So, best-case scenario, eight people. And we are flying blind once we get past the first obstacle." Blue nodded and stood. "Here is what is going to happen. You are going to take those keys and unlock all the cells. Get them ready to move. I'm going to skip to the other side of that door and open it. Then we are going to run like hell."

Devon was silent, staring at Blue in disbelief. "That's what is going to happen?"

"Give or take." Blue nodded.

"Fuck. Me." Devon looked toward the heavens.

"You have a better idea?"

Devon looked like she wanted to say something, but thought for a moment. She shook her head, coming to the same conclusion Blue had just seconds before. This was crazy, and she was probably going to get killed trying it. "OK. Let me get the doors open."

Trusting that the woman knew what she was doing with the cameras, Blue exited the room with her, and they both walked toward door number 1. Two bodies lay in the hallway in plain black uniforms. No holsters. No radios. Nothing.

When Blue looked into the room, her lunch almost came up. A gigantic beast of a man covered only in his own blood lay on a table like the one she had just been on, restrained with absurd numbers of leather straps. His dark skin held a grayish tinge; his face was beaten so badly she doubted his own mother would recognize him. Blood covered every inch of the floor. She looked closely at his hands and feet. She could see fingers jutting at odd angles, and he had no nails whatsoever. Someone cut his torso in random patterns. A rolling cart with a battery and lead sat next to the bed. "Gods." This was the source of the sobbing.

Devon did not look in the window. Blue suspected it was because she already knew what she would see. She hunkered over the door-knob, trying each key and shaking her head. "None of them work."

"Let me try." Blue took the key ring and went through the same process with the same results. "Shit." She looked back into the room and her heart twisted. He was massive. And he wasn't moving under his own power. Not in that condition. He might not even survive. "Leave him."

"What?" Devon turned to her in shock. "We can't leave him."

"Four pregnant women, plus you?" Blue asked her rhetorically. "And some unknown in door number three. I can't carry him and protect eleven other lives. We need to be fast. He will slow us down. I don't have any good choices here. I'm going with the numbers. If I can, I'll come back."

Devon was silent, staring at her for a moment and placing both hands over her chest. Blue understood the motion. It was hurting her, too. The dark-haired woman took the keys back and turned away, continuing down the hallway. She unlocked door number three and continued to the room at the end of the hall.

Blue moved to the window next to door number three. The lights were off. She couldn't see into the room, but she could see her reflection, and it stopped her dead in her tracks. Her hair was dark and straight, about shoulder length. Her eyes were brown and her features were far sharper than they should be. Even her body was different. She reached up and touched her cheek. Her hair should be red. Her eyes hazel. Did Rhodes do this?

She would deal with her makeover if she lived through the next hour. She had to move. She placed her hand on the doorknob, but pulled it *back when it started to heat and glow red. She could work with this. Whoever was in here still had magic and lots of spunk.*

"I'm not here to hurt you. Open the door." She spoke as loudly as she dared into the glass window. She tugged on her black scrubs, trying to convey she wasn't one of the bad guys. "We need to hurry." She glanced back down at the doorknob. She could skip into the room, but that seemed like an amazingly bad idea. If that person attacked her, the five women behind her would be on their own. It was math. She would leave two if she could save ten. And she would deal with the chunk that was carved out of her soul later. Always later.

Four women in pink scrubs hustled by her as she batted at the knob with her fingertips quickly to see if it was still hot. It was warm. But it was also turning. She stepped back slightly and put herself between door number three and Devon's pink ladies. She hoped door number three was a friendly. She really did. But just in case, she held her scalpels at the ready.

A tall figure cloaked in shadow appeared in the crack of the door, regarding her without words. "Come on." She jerked her head and backed away, watching as a tall blond man in black scrubs like her own emerged. Bruises marred his face. He was filthy and walked with a limp. He was also barefoot and looked like an actor off one of those Viking shows if you dropped him into a modern-day medical drama. She took a moment to assess him. He didn't appear hostile. Even if he didn't help them, she had done what she could for him. She turned away and walked back to the door, where Devon and the women, two heavily pregnant, waited for her. "Anything we can use in that office? Weapons? Radios?"

"No. A porn collection and some granola bars. Radio is stationary. Video is still looping." Devon looked back toward the man walking up behind them warily, then at door number one.

"Granola bars?" he rasped, as if it hurt him to speak.

"Yeah, I'll get them for you," Devon offered, and jogged quickly back down the hallway.

Blue placed her ear to the metal door and listened. She couldn't hear movement on the other side, but the door was thick, and there were no windows. There could be a three-ring circus over there. Or twenty armed men waiting to torture her to death. Only one way to find out.

Blue gave herself one more deep breath. In the next very cold breath, she was looking at the other side of the door. A large body lay on the ground next to a stool. It snored. Devon was right. The panel was simple and dumb. Radio only. She squatted next to the man as he let out a rumbling snore and felt around his waist. Coming up empty, she dug in his pockets. Pay dirt. She extracted a set of keys and quickly tried them in the lock, one by one. Halfway through the key ring, she found it and threw open the door, hoping there wasn't a code or a biometric she had missed. To her relief, no audible alarms sounded.

"Step two: let's run like hell. Stay right behind me," she ordered, taking another look at her little band of escapees. She let out an exasperated sigh. Five pregnant women, a Viking gnawing on granola bars, two scalpels, and no socks. What a shit show.

The women filed through. Hovering. The Viking stopped and glanced back. "I can't just leave him."

"There is nothing we can do for him right now. I need your help." Blue pointed toward the five pink-clad women. "We have to go now. I will come back for him once we have this bunch clear."

He hesitated, looking between her and the door Devon had not been able to open.

"Him or us, man." Blue turned her back on him and took the lead. The women followed her without comment. She felt Devon fall in directly behind her.

"I'm Andersen Greenfield," the Viking said from the back of the group. Perfect.

"Nice to make your acquaintance, Green," she answered back quietly as she checked each door they passed.

"If I don't make it out of here. Can you tell my parents that they were terrible, and they can go fuck themselves?" he called from the back.

She stopped and turned to look at him. Three of the five women did the same. "Yeah. Sure." She shrugged. The Viking had mommy and daddy issues.

The next door was marked as a stairwell. They were passing cameras. She couldn't believe an alarm hadn't tripped. Devon must have looped video for the whole facility. She expected a small army to be on the other side of this door. Stopping her group, she took another deep breath. Devon's hands snuck up along her side and pointed outward. Blue understood the intent, but she couldn't stop the warning of "don't hit me with whatever that is," that escaped her mouth as she grabbed the handle and pulled the door open. She entered carefully. The stairway only went up. The large letters painted on the wall next to the door indicated they were on B1. Good sign. "Shut that door behind us quietly, Viking dude."

This seemed too easy, but she didn't have better options. Up they went. She heard the Viking helping the very pregnant ladies.

They reached the top of the stairs without incident. Devon's hand peeked around her side again. It made her feel marginally better. Even if they hit resistance on the other side of the door, she would prefer to just have them go sleepy time instead of attacking them with her pilfered scalpels.

"Here we go, ladies." She looked back over her shoulder to make sure that everyone was ready. Frightened faces looked back at her. She would really like a fully equipped team and a set of eyes in that hallway. But with four unconscious guards, it was unlikely they would get a second chance at this. The Viking at the bottom nodded. "OK." She opened the door slowly and observed the portion of the hallway she could see.

Nothing visible. "Give me sixty seconds. If there are no gunshots, explosions, or screams, follow me." She whispered to Devon.

The woman's face was incredulous. "We are going to die."

Blue ignored her and stepped into the hallway. It was empty, and the doors were closed. It appeared to be an office facility of some sort. The carpeted floor silenced her steps as she crouched low and moved quickly to an intersection. She looked around the corner in both directions. One hallway was dark. The other led to a small foyer. She could see *a walk-through device that looked like a metal detector flanking the entrance of the hallway and a man in a black uniform sitting at the desk, clicking away at his computer. Past the desk and through the glass doors, a parking lot loomed, with several cars sitting under lights. She sat for several more moments, waiting to see if anything changed. When nothing happened, she hustled back to the stairwell where Devon waited. "One guard. Exit to a parking lot." She took in a deep breath. "Can you knock him out before we move the group?"*

Devon nodded and stepped out of the stairwell. "Stay here," Blue instructed the rest before turning to go back down the hallway. The two women exited together, and Blue watched the way the pink-clad woman moved and took in what was around her. This was not the first time she had snuck through a dark building. They reached the intersection and Blue checked the dark hallway one more time, just to be safe.

Devon zoned in on the guard and extended her hand outward. She glanced at Blue. "We ready?"

"I really hope so," Blue responded. "When he goes down. You stay here. I'll check to make sure it is safe."

Devon nodded and turned back to the guard. A second later, he slumped forward, and his head fell into the keyboard in front of him with a thud. "Have at it, Leroy Jenkins."

"I like you. We should grab coffee later." Blue crept up the hallway. She looked over the metal detector. She wanted to keep her scalpels, so she skipped the two feet to the other side and walked behind the desk where the security guard lay. She shoved him the rest of the way onto

the floor and glanced around. His calendar was open on the computer screen. Holy shit. She had been here for four days. And she had only been awake for a few minutes that entire time. Her skin crawled.

She didn't want to think about what could happen to a person in four days, so she stooped to check sleepyhead's pockets. She found a set of facility keys clipped to his belt and a set of car keys in his right front pocket. She pulled his wallet out and grabbed the small handful of cash out of habit. All they had were pajamas and a strong will to live. Cash wouldn't hurt. She found nothing else of use except a door button next to a console with a black-and-white image of the parking lot. No weapons or even sharp objects.

She stood and nodded to Devon, lifting the pilfered car keys. "We are looking for a Ford. Let's go." She saw Devon turn and wave behind her. A sea of pink followed by a Viking rounded the corner. Blue moved to the windows to check for movement in the parking lot. The sky was still dark, and there was no activity. The place was deserted. At least this wasn't a 24/7 torture facility.

The metal detector chirped once quietly behind her, and Blue heard a thump as something far more powerful than a magnet clicked into place. She spun, taking in Devon and one of the other ladies, a small woman with dreadlocks on this side of the metal detector. They were staring in horror at the ceiling above them. Green gas billowed from a vent just above the metal detector and similar click-thumps sounded down the hallway behind them. The doors were locking, trapping them.

"Get that door open!" the Viking man yelled as he pushed the three remaining women out of the hallway and into the foyer. Blue raced to the door system on the guard's desk and smashed the button. It just blinked red. No doubt, someone off-site knew about what was happening now. And the damned door wasn't budging. The gas fell toward the floor, toward them. Blue mashed the button again. "It's in the hallway too," the Viking man announced, no doubt thinking about going back the way they came to find fresh air. A tall, black-haired woman with high cheekbones who looked like she could pop out that baby at any minute collapsed, jerked, and her nose started to bleed. "Oh shit," the Viking said as he caught her before she hit the ground. He dragged her the rest of the way through the device at the end of the hallway and crouched. "Get down. Try not to breathe it."

"It's not opening. We are trapped." Blue told them, looking around one more time for an override switch. Anything.

"Get out of here," Devon ordered, as she helped another woman crawl toward the door. "You are the only one who can. Go!" A second woman collapsed, her body jerking just as the first.

"She isn't breathing," the Viking she had nicknamed Green told them as he placed both hands on the woman's chest and pressed down. The two conscious women cried and crawled.

"Damn it!" Blue screamed, letting the cold of her magic wash over her. It was barely there, and she had to fight to get to the other side of the glass. She could see the group huddled in front of the guard's desk. His foot twitched. Devon's sleepy time wasn't working anymore. Her new friend crouched next to the two women who were still conscious,

speaking to them. Green performed CPR with a frantic look on his face. As he counted out compressions, he glanced toward the vents, still billowing gas. There was so much now that it obscured her vision of the group. The second woman that had fallen unconscious was no longer jerking. Her body was unnaturally still. "Damn it!"

She scanned the parking lot and looked up. She didn't have a clear view of the roof. Didn't matter. Two Fords. One a small hatchback. The other a gigantic truck on lifted tires with KC lights and lots of chrome. That guy looked more like a redneck conveyance kind of dude. Bemoaning her lack of socks as her feet grew icier, she fell into the rainbow once again and appeared on the other side of the black truck, somewhat shielded from view of the facility because of its sheer size. Pushing the button on the key fob, she caught her reflection in the glass of the passenger side door and blinked. Half her hair was red, the other half brown. What was going on?

The truck beeped open with a flash of headlights, and she scrambled in and across the seat, dropping the wad of money she had taken out of the guard's pocket into the floorboard. She climbed over the console and stuck the keys in the ignition. The thing roared to life as a security guard rounded the corner of the facility. This guy was dressed like an average rent-a-cop and had a weapon. She floored the gas pedal and arced wildly in a squealing circle through the parking lot, leaving smoke and black marks in her wake. She shoved her palm into the steering wheel, letting loose a persistent scream of the horn as she hurtled toward the windows of the office building. She steered the truck toward the small seating area across from the desk. None of her people had been in that proximity when she jumped away. Letting out a shout, because this was not her first head-on collision, she threw her arms in front of her face as the truck jumped onto the sidewalk and smashed through metal and glass. She slammed on the brakes as chairs crunched under the tires. Miraculously, the airbag did not go off.

She threw open the door and jumped out, letting out a string of curse words as bits of glass poked her feet. They weren't large shards, just rock-like chunks of shatterproof glass. But they were still uncomfortable. Green was no longer trying to give the woman CPR. He wrestled with the now awake front desk guard. It was a brutal fight, and both men were bleeding.

She heard shouting and saw the security guard from outside racing through the wreckage. His attention was on the fight happening in the lobby and the two obviously dead pregnant women laying on the floor. Blue was so done with this. She pulled a scalpel from her makeshift bun and stepped out despite the glass. She jabbed the hand holding the scalpel out. No more grace. Anyone associated with this place was on her shit list. Who gassed pregnant ladies? She caught the man under the chin and sliced. He uttered a surprised shout, then a gurgle. She easily knocked his hand holding the weapon down and shoved him back out the window. He fell backward. It only took seconds for him to bleed out from his jugular. She waited a few of those seconds, followed him out, took his gun from his weak grasp, and crunched across the glass into the lobby, leaving him to die.

The truck still ran, and her feet were numb. She could see her bloody footprints, but she was so cold she could no longer feel anything. It was the first time in her life she was grateful for the strange side effect of her magic. "Get them into the truck," she shouted at a shocked Devon as she advanced on the two wrestling men. Blue glanced down at the fallen women and suppressed a horrified shudder. Their faces were green and their eyes bloodshot. Froth leaked from both mouths. Whatever that gas was, they were beyond help. Fortunately, it was dissipating out the window. She had no idea why they were dead, and the rest of them were still standing.

She raised her pilfered weapon and took careful aim, waiting for something to happen between Green and the front desk guard. This is why Devon couldn't help; they were too close to each other to get a clean shot. Green was big, but he obviously wasn't a trained fighter. The guard was beating the shit out of him. But Green wasn't giving up. She took another step forward. Nobody was throwing magic around. She reached for hers and realized it was weak at best. This was beyond messed up.

With a grunt, the front desk guard pushed Green backward, flinging him over the rolling chair and upside down onto the ground. She fired once with her stolen weapon, watching as the back of his head exploded. All three of the surviving women screamed. They weren't moving. "Go!" Blue shouted. She rushed toward the hallway, stopping to shout at Green, who was regaining his feet and ready to attack. "He's dead. Help them." She jerked her head toward the women who were struggling to cross the sea of glass toward the still-running truck.

"Where are you going?" he demanded, ripping the boots off the body in front of him. "I'm going for the big guy." She sniffed the air.

41

It was no longer putrid. She could feel a stronger prickle of magic. Whatever that green stuff was, it worked as an anti-magic field. They were obviously rigged for "experiments" here. What were they going to do with five pregnant women and babies? Fury rushed through her. Fuckers.

The man in front of her nodded without hesitation and offered her the boots. "These won't fit me. Your feet." He waved at the bloody footprints she was trailing.

"That's sweet," Blue said as she reached toward him. But she didn't take the boots because they were gigantic and would just trip her. She grabbed his wrist instead and skipped. They landed in a contorted pile in the passenger seat of the truck. Her face smashed up against the window, his butt under her chin. His face, still shouting in surprise, was shoved into the floorboard by the console, but his feet weren't sliced to shreds. "You are welcome." She told him. Two crying women scurried into the back seat of the cab as Devon ripped open the driver's side door and took in the scene in front of her.

"Scoot over," she ordered without hesitation as she climbed in and shoved his face aside. She put the truck in reverse before she shut the door.

Blue looked around the man's head at Devon even as she shoved Green's butt out of her face. "Get as far away as fast as you can. There is money in the floorboard. Then ditch this thing."

The woman gave her a feral smile. "I've got this, sweetheart. Good luck."

"Wait," Green commanded, twisting to face her. She watched in confusion as he stuck his fingers into his mouth and twisted. A moment later, he handed her a still-wet tongue bar.

"Ew," she said when she realized what he had deposited in her hand.

"Say mango. It will melt anything. It's the only one they didn't take," he instructed. "What's your name?"

"OK." Blue nodded slowly and closed her fist around the small piece of metal. "My friends call me Blue."

"I've got this lot," Devon told her as she threw the car into reverse and Blue began her skip. "Go if you are going to."

Green buckled his seatbelt as the rainbow-colored her vision. "Don't die Blue."

"Blue." Someone shook her. "Blue? Come back to me, sweetheart." It was Greenlee, his eyes concerned and red-rimmed. "Come on. Finn and Devon wanted a minute with Gage. He has a meeting with a client, but he'll bring Dev home." His big hand palmed the top of her head and shook it. "Look at me." He waited until she focused on his face, still not saying anything. "You're with me. Let's get you home."

4

SAM

S am fidgeted in his suit, the first he had worn since he was a
boy. It was a very nice suit. Custom made at Nisha's insistence
because she said nice suits for men six feet seven inches tall did not
come off the rack. As nice as it was, it felt like a straitjacket. Nisha
stood in front of him, arms extended as far as she could reach to
adjust the damned tie.

They stood in a tent in the center of a park, waiting to be called to
the stage. Their group represented the highest ranks of the North
American Cahlad, which was also Cahlad Prime since it was the
Paragon's home base. The morning was clear. The sky was beautiful.
Flowers were blooming.

And he would appreciate it if he didn't have to go out on that stage
in less than ten minutes and make a speech. On top of that, magic
surges were happening all over the area. Unregistered Sovaj were
disappearing, and unknown para-military operators were showing
up in both cases. He suspected the people behind the uptick in

disappearances were the Hounds of Dawn, a criminal organization operating deep in the shadows that had thwarted the Cahlad for the better part of eight years. The military operators weren't their usual M.O., but they might be expanding or growing bolder. The media relations team was barely keeping a lid on all of it. He was so grumpy; Mitch and Ivan stood on the other side of the stage, eying him warily, leaving Nisha the only member of their group brave enough to be near him. "Let me fix your tie. And the Hounds of Dawn are an urban legend. There is no proof it exists."

He swatted at her hands. "Why do you care? You leave in two weeks." He was still pissed about that fact, too. He needed Nisha at his side now more than ever. "How are people disappearing without a trace from crowded rooftops?"

His best friend smiled brightly and swatted right back. She grabbed his tie and tugged it into place with more force than necessary. "Subject for a different time," she told him. "You need to get your head in the game."

She smoothed his tie out and motioned for him to lean down so she could look closer. He huffed in frustration and leaned down to compensate for the foot difference in their heights. "This is important, Samuel. We need the good PR publicly and politically. And there are people out there with loved ones we are memorializing. Now put on your big boy britches and prove Mitch was right to appoint you Regent." The charming quality of her accent, a mixture of her native India and the southern drawl of Nashville, eased the harshness of her statement.

Sam frowned. Few people would have the courage to say that to his face, charming accent or not. The reputation of his temper preceded him. But she was right, as usual. The Cahlad had spent years trying to repair its image after the attack. They needed the public to see them as the good guys again. That was why his team looked like it did. Stalker Prime used to be a brutal enforcement unit, but since he took over and Nisha joined, their focus was on diplomacy and mediation. Nisha was a pacifist at heart. Their unit still had the most kills of any Stalker Unit, because sometimes it couldn't be helped. But that was no longer the preferred method for dealing with unregistered Sovaj and people who broke the rules established by the Cahlad for magic users. The head of the Senate Magic Relations and Regulation Committee was also out for blood this session, perpetually undermining the Cahlad in any effort it made to work cohesively with the non-magical authorities.

"I know I'm right." She stepped back and swiped her hands in satisfaction. "And I can't stay."

"We will talk about that after I live through this hell." Sam shoved his hands in his pockets and refrained from telling her to stay out of his head. He must be projecting if she was reading him so clearly. That wasn't her fault. He also felt naked without his sidearm. Apparently, diplomats didn't need weapons. And Nisha said it would ruin the lines of the suit.

"There is nothing to talk about."

He glared and pulled the speech he worked on with the media team from his pocket to read it carefully once more. They already hated him. Writing a speech without direct statements was a challenge. Welcome to every day of his life. He handed the paper to Nisha. "Can you double check this and make sure I'm not going to tell people to riot or give their firstborn to the friendly neighborhood drug dealer?"

She gave him a rueful smile and took the paper. "Yes, I will read it. Again."

He stared at his shoes as she read, focusing on the purpose of the event to calm his nerves. Today they were dedicating a park to the victims of the bombing ten years ago. The explosion, caused by a radical group called the Sovereign that believed in the superiority of magic users, killed six children and ten adults. It coincided with an incident at Cahlad headquarters that killed eight staffers and Mitch's daughter Amber.

Sam, Nisha, Mitch, and his wife—though they weren't legally married—Zella survived the explosion at headquarters. Not all of them unscathed. It had irrevocably changed the course of their lives. Today was personal for many of them as well.

The Cahlad purchased the bombing site and turned it into a green space. A call for artists resulted in hundreds of applicants to create the statue at its center. Ultimately, a metal artisan from right here in Nashville, Greenlee Anders, won the bid to create the sculpture. Today, they unveiled his work.

What no living person other than the people standing backstage with him knew was that the Sovereign was a splinter organization of the Cahlad itself, led by the former Regent, Larson Battle. The

Regent was the Cahlad's title for the Paragon's second in command, much like the US government's Vice President. If anyone outside of Mitch's inner circle found out about what happened and how high up the power structure it originated, it would have been disastrous.

The shopping center they demolished was a front for an underground laboratory where Battle and his cronies experimented on and tortured magic and non-magic people alike. The explosions were an attempted coup by Battle. One of the Cahlad's Zenith, or elite magic soldiers, named Indigo Vale, aided him in his efforts. The children that died at this site didn't die in an explosion. Their deaths were much more horrific and prolonged. This charade was the Cahlad's attempt to protect itself.

"The firstborn are safe. Chances of a riot are also very low." Nisha handed the paper back.

The event's MC announced their group. They all filed to the steps leading onto the stage.

Mitch, Paragon of the Cahlad, went first. His long shaggy hair, a mixture of blond and gray, fell into his eyes over his glasses. He swept his hair to the side. "You are ready, son." It spoke to the importance of the event that the Paragon was in attendance and his faith in Sam that he wasn't making the speech personally. Usually, Zella would be by his side for an event like this, but Ms. Z declined. Today was the tenth anniversary of her daughter's death, and Sam couldn't blame her for not attending.

Ivan followed Mitch up the stairs, tugging at the custom-made suit Nisha inflicted on him. He grunted. That was Ivan-speak for this suit is bullshit.

"The suit is not bullshit," Nisha grumbled, ascending the stairs in front of him and tripping. She recovered gracefully at the top with a toss of her hair and took her place on the stage. Sam wiped sweat from his brow and took a breath before following.

Hundreds of people, magic and non-magic alike, along with a dozen members of the press, waited. Sam took his place at the podium and delivered the speech without a misstep. He instructed the event organizers to unveil the statue and breathed a sigh of relief. He had completed his first official public speaking engagement as Regent without a disaster. The event staff dramatically whipped the sheets from the statue and silence fell over the assembly. A metal statue of a child sitting on his knees gleamed in the mid-morning sun. His face was tranquil and happy. In one hand, he pushed a toy train across the ground. In the other, a shower of sparks erupted. This is not what they commissioned. The park's financial benefactors, Clay and Lydia Greenfield, stipulated an abstract piece of artwork. But this was one of the most realistic, reverent, and moving tributes he had ever seen. He was speechless. He hated every single person who had anything to do with Larson Battle and his murderous quest to wrest control of the Cahlad from Mitch to pave the way for the ridiculous concept of magic supremacy.

He looked at Nisha. Her eyes watered as she gazed at the child. Even Ivan and Mitch looked touched by the artwork. Sniffles floated on the air, mixed with a sound he couldn't identify. The sound grew louder. He stepped away from the microphone. "Nisha?"

"I don't know," she told him, tears still streaming from her eyes. She was having trouble keeping it together. He knew the thoughts and emotions in the crowd were overloading her senses. He admired her more than she would ever know for putting herself through this.

Scanning back across the crowd as he searched for the source of the noise, Sam did a double take. There, in the center of the uneasy crowd, was a tall woman in a red sundress. She sat primly with her long legs crossed at the ankles. She had stick-straight black hair, but Sam got the impression that it was a wig. It cascaded down her shoulders, and her bright red lips turned up in a small smile. Large sunglasses covered her face. She wiggled her fingers when their gazes met. She was looking right at him like she had known exactly when he would look. She raised her other hand and flashed something small and red, then she held out her arm and dropped it onto the ground. A scream pierced the air, but Sam's eyes stayed glued to the lady in red. She disappeared just as a rolling wave of birds dove at the chair she was sitting in, knocking it over and causing the people near her to flee.

His eyes snapped back to the statue and the audience in general. The source of the noise became clear. A flock of birds so large the sky turned black and covered the crowd in its shadow descended upon the gathering. The smaller group that had dive-bombed the chair rejoined their avian kindred and dove as a group toward the audience. Attendees leapt from their chairs, dashing in all directions.

What was this? Mitch stood and pointed to Sam in warning as a wave of energy hit them, picking the stage and everyone on it up and hurling it through the air. Sam landed hard on his back, covered in the splintered wood he had just been standing on. Nisha's scream joined the crowds as she flew away from him. He couldn't see Ivan or Mitch. Shoving boards aside, he stood and took in the chaos. A horde of birds strafed the crowd. Many audience members were already bleeding. Magic users threw a barrage of effects into the attacking sea of feathers and beaks. That was a problem and probably the reason the stage was a pile of rubble. None of the people here were battle trained. He had already seen friendly fire injuries. The sky grew suddenly dark overhead, and thunder rolled.

"This is just fantastic," Nisha groused, dusting herself off and looking around. "I swear by all that is holy, Sam, I am not dying in a Hitchcock movie!"

"Source?" Sam demanded.

"The bird lady doesn't know how to stop it. They aren't listening," Nisha told him. "But we have other problems. Lightning, fire, telekinesis, and ice at a minimum." She rattled out the incoming threats.

Mitch called for Ivan, who emerged from the wreckage uninjured, unsurprisingly. His suit, however, was ruined. Sam looked at his own. It wasn't faring any better than Ivan's. "Incoming!" Nisha screamed, covered her head, and dove back beneath the rubble of the stage. Sam ducked but didn't fully crouch.

Foot-long shards of ice flew through the air in a vortex, twisting its way across the clearing. He heard Nisha yell in exasperation, "Is that an Ice-nado?"

Wider at the top, it shredded birds like a Made for TV blender. Their bodies hit the ground with gruesome thuds. It was, however, problematic for the people unlucky enough to be near its narrow tail on the ground. Sam watched in horror as the tail headed directly for Mitch and Ivan. "Look out!" he shouted, and both turned immediately. "Move!"

The command didn't arrive in time. A shard impaled Mitch just above his left hip, knocking him to the ground. Ivan pulled the Paragon out of the tornado's path, putting himself directly in harm's way. He faced the tail of the ice vortex straight on, his clothes shredding like they were being cut with scissors. Ice shattered and flew to the side. Sam felt a rush of blistering heat pass by. Seconds later, a fireball burst around Ivan, knocking him back several feet and causing his jacket and pants to erupt into flames.

Ivan stood, his hands on his hips, with a stunned and irritated look on his face, glaring at his smoldering clothing. Who thought that was helpful? Were they trying to melt it? Sam eyed the crowd incredulously.

"Sam!" Nisha cried, sprinting past him as a bolt of lightning scorched a play set thirty feet to their right. She tossed him a black metal object and continued to Mitch, sliding to her knees beside the wounded man. Instead of putting pressure on his wound, she covered his ears. "Ivan! Sam has the floor!" she screamed. Ivan placed his hands over his ears. Confused, Sam looked at the object Nisha threw him: a cordless microphone. Brilliant woman.

A shock wave flew toward them, grazing Sam and forcing him sideways. It slammed into Nisha head-on, flattening her on top of Mitch. Ivan stumbled backward under its force.

He regained his footing, thumbed the switch, and brought the microphone to his mouth. "Stop using magic!" The ice fell, and the sky cleared. Thank God the speakers survived. People who had not cleared the area continued to scream as crazed avians harried them.

"Get them down, son!" Mitch shouted. He stood shakily over a crumpled Nisha, clutching the hemorrhaging wound in his side with one hand. He held a small golden pocket watch in the other. His eyes glowed a golden color, and his hair waved like a strong wind blew only on him.

"Everyone but the Paragon get down," Sam ordered, using the microphone, and watched people drop like stones across the park. Seconds later, hundreds of circular golden disks catapulted from the center of Mitch's chest and flew toward the flock of birds. The disks hit the birds, unleashing a cacophony of whatever a bird did when it screamed, covering everyone in the park in a fine mist of blood, feathers, and gore. A beak without a bird bounced off his shoulder. Dear God. It looked like a scene from Carrie.

The park grew quiet. People still huddled, some sobbed. Many moaned in pain. Sam heard sirens in the distance. A man sprinted from the crowd, speaking rapidly, and ran up to Mitch, who stepped back with trepidation. He had survived numerous attempts on his life as Paragon and remained perpetually cautious. "What is he saying, son?"

"He says he can help you with your wound." Sam translated the Mandarin.

Mitch waved a hand and shook his head. He pointed toward Nisha, who still lay unmoving at his feet. He nodded to the man, silently directing him in her direction. The man bowed slightly and hustled to her side.

Mitch clutched his wound. Sam could see it was already healing slowly. He raised an eyebrow at Ivan, who stood in only his boxer shorts and the singed and shredded remnants of his dress shirt. Both his jacket and pants were piles of ash beneath him. A reporter moved through the chaos, stopped in front of Ivan, and took a closeup. He growled at her.

"Tell them to help each other, Sam," Mitch told him.

"Assist who you can; help is on the way," Sam said into the microphone one last time. He dropped it and climbed over the debris separating him from Nisha. She lay very still. "How is she?" he asked the man, crouching over his friend.

"Many bones broke. Concussion. I can't heal her all." He spoke in broken English.

"Thank you for trying," Sam told the man as he kneeled next to Nisha. Mitch shuffled over gingerly; his face etched in pain.

"I can help. Help me down, son." Mitch extended a hand, and Sam kept him steady as he struggled to his knees with a pained groan. Mitch channeled the golden energy from his pocket watch into Nisha's broken body.

A moment later, a pained "I quit" reached his ears. She had not opened her eyes, but she had managed to speak. Relief washed over Sam.

"I will buy you a lifetime supply of tea and give you my salary if you don't leave me alone in this madness," Sam replied.

"No," she said again, and her head lolled to the side.

Sam frowned at Mitch. "It's normal. She needs her energy to heal. She will be fine," his boss, mentor, and friend told him. Leaving him to literally work his magic, Sam wandered into the destruction to help whoever he could. First responders followed by police appeared on the scene, and he gave his statement.

Curious if he had actually seen a woman in red disappear before his eyes, he walked over to the area where she had been sitting before the avian chaos. He moved aside toppled folding chairs and helped a few people to their feet. Just as he thought he had probably imagined it, a small metal object in the grass reflected the sun. He reached down and plucked it from the dirt, glancing at it quickly. It was a metallic red USB drive and had somehow survived the stampede.

"You OK?" Ivan grunted as he came to stand at Sam's side, surveying the still somewhat chaotic scene.

"Yeah. You?" Sam answered, quickly sliding the USB drive into his pocket. He didn't feel like explaining how he knew it was there just yet. But Ivan and Nisha would need to know about it soon. "Want to debrief when we get everyone taken care of?"

Ivan just grunted, which probably meant yes to both questions. He walked toward a woman, trying to gather the scattered contents of her purse from the ground. He knelt next to her and began helping.

He and Ivan helped clear debris and load people into ambulances. Before he knew it, thirty minutes had passed.

Mitch still sat by Nisha, his watch glowing. Sam wandered back over. "Letting the attendees go first?" he asked. Mitch just nodded. He looked tired. She must have been hurt far worse than Sam had first realized. Nisha's arm was thrown over her face to keep the sun out of her eyes. She looked pale.

Mitch's cell phone rang. He looked at the screen and answered the call. "My love. I'm sorry I didn't call. I'm fine. Sam's OK. Nisha is hurt, but I have it under control. Of course, Ivan is fine." He paused, giving the person on the other end an opportunity to speak.

Sam knew it was Zella, and that she hadn't spoken a word even though she had initiated the call. It was a dance Sam watched Mitch and Zella do hundreds of times, and he knew it tore a piece of Mitch's soul out every time.

"Some of the attendees were hurt. I swear this place is cursed." Mitch blew out a stuttering breath. "I am going to go to the hospital with Nisha. They want me to get checked, too." He paused again, waiting for a response that didn't come. "I'll be there for you soon. I love you."

Sam sat down next to them, wishing he could do something to help. He shoved his hands in his pockets, as was his habit when he was stressed. His fingers brushed against the small, smooth USB drive. What did it contain, and who was the woman who left it?

5

DEVON

Devon glanced up from the papers she graded and scowled at the annoying sound echoing through the house, telling her someone was ringing the doorbell on Greenlee's workshop. His business was appointment only, and he never had anything delivered to the shop. Why was someone ringing his bell? She was not in the mood for this today. This morning was rough, and she needed quiet. Her eyes were still puffy, and her sinuses were clogged.

She slapped on the pair of flip-flops she kept under her desk, stuck her favorite red pen behind her ear, and padded out of her office. She slipped out the back door and across their small fenced yard to the detached garage. Hustling inside, she slapped at the light switch. Trying to cross Greenlee's workspace in the dark would be suicide. As the fluorescent lights flickered and the God-awful clown horn doorbell dinged again, she dodged hunks of metal, a sheet-covered tattoo chair, boxes of random objects, and a fifty-gallon trash bag full of yarn to get to the door.

She shook her head as she passed the six-by-six-foot canvas hanging on the wall to her right. It showcased four dogs of various sizes resting on a grassy hill overlooking a sunrise. Her favorite dog was the beagle, second to the right. Devon always thought he had big-dog energy. Lexi liked the husky on the end. The thing lived somewhere between pretty incredible and hideous. The story behind it made a sad smile briefly cross her face.

"We are closed," she said as she snatched open the back door of the shop that faced the alley and a small parking area.

"Is this the Sundry?" an average-height white man with a raving case of dad bod inquired with a greasy smile. He wore an ill-fitting suit. His buzzed light brown hair did little to hide the fact that he was going bald, and his blue eyes were too small in his face. His tie, she noted, also fell a little short of acceptable, as if perhaps it had shrunk, or the wearer had gotten bigger. She didn't like this guy; it was a complete and immediate impression. She raised an eyebrow.

"It is. But we are open by appointment only." She pointed at the sign next to the door. He probably cheated on his wife and reported people to the HOA for having grass that was three-quarter inches high instead of a half inch. This guy emitted an aura of douche-nozzle just by breathing. He glanced over her shoulder into the workshop with curiosity. His eyes flicked over the general disarray, then she saw his eyes harden.

He gave her a half-hearted smile and straightened the too-short tie. "Might I inquire about the Hounds of Dawn?"

Devon stood straighter and eyed the man a little closer. The Hounds of Dawn were an urban legend. Rumored to be an underground railroad for unregistered magic users. Many people looked. But the only way to find the Hounds of Dawn was if they found you. Why was this guy looking here?

The afternoon had just gotten more interesting. In what way, she wasn't sure. "The Hounds of Dawn? I'm sorry, sir, I can't help you with that. I don't know what that is," she lied as she began shutting the door. "If you would like an appointment for a commission, call the number."

He frowned. "Let's try again. I need information about the Hounds of Dawn." He raised up to his full unimpressive height, puffed his chest out, and rammed his hand into the door. "A representative? A name?"

"You need to leave," she told the man, refusing to be cowed by his intimidation tactic. She smiled sweetly. It wasn't hard to smile. She found him entertaining. He was trying so very hard for big dog energy, and the beagle in Greenlee's painting had him beat by a mile. The sweet part of the smile was a struggle. "Are you talking about that painting behind me? I think he got it at a flea market. It doesn't have a representative." She pushed on the door again. He wasn't overly large. She could probably out muscle him.

To his credit, the man looked at the painting, studying its surroundings closely. With the hand not holding the door open, he reached into his jacket. "Listen. I don't have much time. I know..."

Devon's smile grew wider the farther he reached into his jacket. She could use a distraction this afternoon. Just as she was getting ready to handle things herself, she heard the click of the door she had just walked through.

Blue, her hair in a ponytail revealing her undercut, wore yoga pants and a blue tank top proclaiming, "Do No Harm. Take No Shit." Tattoos covered her arms and a small nose ring graced her face. She was barefoot and sweating. "Who the hell interrupted my Destroyer of the Universe pose?"

Devon looked back toward the man who oozed a terrible respect-my-authority or my-employer-is-a-low-level-crime-boss vibe about him. Devon had a lifetime of experience with both options. Neither of them was going to work out well for him here. Blue's appearance and interruption obviously frustrated him. Devon began gathering her energy. "He was just leaving," she replied.

"I'm looking for a representative of the Hounds of Dawn," he announced yet again, as if just by asking three times they would appear like the Bell Witch. He forgot his mirror. One look at Blue, and Devon knew they were on the same page.

"Oh. Of course." Blue played along. "Mister...?"

"Richard Mann."

"Mr. Mann. Welcome to the Sundry. Please follow me." Blue extended her hand in greeting, leading him into the shop when he removed his hand from his jacket and took it. Devon closed the door behind him and threw the deadbolt.

"Excellent." He smiled. Obviously, he had no concerns about two women who weren't even five-and-a-half-feet-tall, locking him in an unknown space. He would learn. Devon had to stop herself from laughing as the man kept talking. He had no idea what was about to happen to him. "Hello. I'm here with—"

Blue didn't let go of his hand and turned toward Devon as he spoke. She nodded once. Devon nodded back, and Mr. Mann crumbled. Just before he hit the floor, Blue and Mr. Mann disappeared from the room. It did not appear that Blue would cushion his fall at all. Devon rolled her eyes at the things her friend found amusing.

She smoothed her hair back. Discharging her energy usually made her hair frizzy for some God-forsaken reason. Pair that with living in the South, and she sometimes wondered why she even tried to manage her hair. She took one last look at her favorite beagle and resigned herself to a few more hours of grading papers before Lexi got home from school.

6

BLUE

B lue lounged in the folding camp chair, sipping whiskey from the bottle as she waited for the sleeping man on the concrete floor in front of her to wake up. His hands were zip-tied behind his back and his feet were similarly bound. A single 100-watt light bulb hanging from the ceiling illuminated his predicament. It wasn't moving back and forth like in the movies. She always wondered who went around hitting light bulbs to make them swing. Seemed risky. What if the bulb broke? Glass would get everywhere. Or maybe it was just the seismic activity in Hollywood that made the bulbs swing like that. Who knew? She was glad her light was still.

She reached into the duffel bag that she kept in this unit and pulled out a set of clearance rack, brown, sherpa-lined boots that were a size too small, and a neon yellow sweatshirt. She shoved the shoes on her frozen feet and tugged the sweatshirt on. She sent herself a text to remember to restock this bag.

Mr. Richard Mann moaned in a distinctly non-threatening way as he rolled back and forth on the concrete floor. Blue wondered how on earth he knew to find the Hounds of Dawn at their house? That had never happened before. He knew just enough to be dangerous, because he obviously did not know the proper way to contact the representatives of a shadow organization specializing in making people disappear. Which was not to at all.

It didn't matter; this unit was in the middle of nowhere and surrounded by a cow pasture on all sides. She would find out what he knew one way or the other and nobody would be the wiser, no matter how much noise he made. It might disturb some cows from their grazing. That was a risk she would take.

His phone currently crashed against the rocks of a lovely beach on the California coast. If it was still transmitting a location, it wouldn't be for much longer. She had checked for any other communication equipment and found none. Both of his weapons were currently in her duffel bag, out of sight. She had given his wallet a quick once over and found a badge. He hadn't led with, "Hi I'm from the FBI and have a few questions," like a normal agent would have. So here he squirmed. Now she waited for him to wake up and the fun to begin.

Gibberish fell from his lips as he slowly woke back up. Sleep talker. Charming. "Where am I?" he finally muttered something coherent. Coming back from one of Devon's twilights felt like waking up the day after an epic tequila bender.

"That isn't important," Blue informed him, sitting her whiskey on the floor and rising to her feet. He couldn't see her at the moment because he was facing away from her camp chair.

"Do you have any idea how much trouble you are in right now?"

Blue choked on a laugh that ended in a snort. She reached up and bumped the light fixture, making it sway. Ambiance. "Do you Dick Mann? That is your name, right? Agent Dick Mann. You are currently the one tied up on a concrete floor." Blue walked counterclockwise, placing herself at his feet.

The man huffed. He had obviously heard that joke before. He twisted violently, trying to get a good look at her. "I'm with the FBI. This is a felony. I just wanted to ask some questions."

"A felony, right? OK, dick man. Why were you asking about a hideous painting?" Blue continued her trajectory and squatted down where he could see her. "And can't you buy longer ties? Does your wife know you leave the house like that?"

"Are you serious?" He continued to wiggle on the floor to loosen his restraints. He would not get loose. But Blue gave him props for trying. "I don't have a wife."

"Girlfriend?"

"What? No."

"Husband? Never mind," Blue muttered. "The painting. Why were you asking about it?"

"I'm not asking about a painting. Could you untie me so we can talk?"

Blue's phone rang once, followed by a small noticeable pause before ringing again. Devon's answer-me-now call sequence. "Hold that thought, dick man. I gotta take this."

She strolled over to the camp chair and picked up her phone. Dick man tried valiantly to keep her in his line of sight as she moved. "Ja?"

"Do you still have the fat guy with the short tie?" Devon asked as soon as Blue answered.

"Ja?"

"Finn is here. Apparently, that guy is with him," Devon said.

"Really?" Blue asked incredulously. She could hear Finn in the background. She eyed Dick Mann skeptically, having a hard time believing this guy was associated with Herne Tactical in any way, shape, or form.

"No, wait. He is very loosely affiliated with a case that Finn is working," Devon said. "He's an imbecile." Devon paused. "A putz." She repeated, then paused again. "Dead weight." Blue could hear Devon covering the phone and saying something that sounded like what. "And you don't have to bring him back unharmed, but in one piece would be great."

Blue laughed out loud at that. "Does his phone have to come back in one piece? That could be a problem."

She heard Devon pass along the question before replying, "He doesn't give a shit about the phone."

"Awesome. Could Finn run grab me something hot to drink? He knows what I like. I'll have Dick Mann back shortly."

"She wants coffee," Devon repeated, and she heard another deep rumble. Finn did not sound happy.

"God, Blue. He is hot when he's angry." Devon laughed.

"Don't I know it? Meet you guys where I left you in ten."

She turned back to Dick Mann, who had oriented himself to face her. The effort untucked his shirt. It now bunched around his ribs, exposing his paunch.

She placed her phone back on the chair and moved toward him. "Let's fix that, yeah?" She pointed toward the shirt. "Why didn't you just lead with the FBI thing? Surely that is not how they trained you to approach people."

He scowled at her, but made no sudden moves. "What did you do to my phone?"

Blue didn't respond. She reached down and pulled his shirt back into the correct position and stepped back. "It seems Finn Torrin would like for me to bring you back. Mostly unharmed. You probably should have opened with that if not the FBI thing, you know? Hey, I'm here with Finn Torrin. Not that wannabe spy shit you pulled."

Dick man growled again. He didn't like her. That much was clear. "I'm not with Finn Torrin. His company is assisting with my case."

"Interesting. That is not what he says." Blue sat down crisscross applesauce across from her charge and put her elbows on her knees and her chin in her hands. "What is he working? A K and R?" Kidnap and Ransom cases were usually what Finn brought Blue in on. He located the target; she extricated the target without a lot of bullets flying around. He was one of the best in the business at getting people back safely, and she was his secret weapon and occasional medical evac.

"You need to take me back."

"Finn hasn't had time to get my coffee yet. Did he tell you about the ugly painting?"

The man's beady blue eyes narrowed and his jaw set. Blue sighed. He would not tell her anything now that he knew his fingernails were going to stay attached.

"Ugh. Fine. But we have to talk about your tie. Want me to show you how to tie it so that it is long enough?"

Fifteen unproductive minutes later, Dick Mann landed in a heap in the middle of Greenlee's workshop. His hands and feet were still secured with zip ties, and his tie was arranged at the proper length. Devon sat on top of a pallet of boxes, swinging her legs and sipping a drink from a local coffee shop famous for a petrified bagel shaped like a nun. Finn leaned against the closed door. He too had a coffee in his hand, probably black. He let out a deep breath when his "associate" landed.

Blue let go of Dick Mann before he hit the ground, letting him catch himself with bound hands. She turned toward the workbench to deposit the man's belongings.

"Oh. That one must be for me." She picked up a large steaming cup from the workbench and sniffed. Devon waved toward a small space heater in the corner that was already turned on and set to the highest heat setting. Blue skipped to the heater, taking a sip of her coffee. "Extra whip and cinnamon. So good. Thank you, Finn."

"No problem," he said and turned his gaze back to Mr. Mann.

"Untie me, Torrin, and I won't arrest your friends," their visitor barked.

Blue and Devon exchanged a look. Finn's face remained impassive. No one said anything. The silence was comfortable for everyone as they sipped coffee, except the man still laying in a tied heap on a different floor. At least this floor didn't have stains on the concrete. The silence stretched for several minutes more.

"Just untie me. This was a misunderstanding. Nobody is getting arrested."

Finn took another sip of his coffee. "That's better." He sat the cup down on a nearby shelf and squatted to cut the zip ties.

"Dick man tells me you are assisting him with a case," Blue supplied when Finn stood back up, closing his pocketknife and placing it in his pocket. Mr. Mann had the decency to look embarrassed as he rubbed his wrist and got off the floor.

"Is that so?" Her friend eyeballed the FBI agent with disgust.

"Missing persons. The FBI hasn't had much luck, so the family engaged our services," he filled in for Blue.

"I figured. You have anything yet. "

"Can you turn that thing off?" Mann barked, pointing at the heater, pulling at his freshly corrected tie, and wiping sweat from his forehead. He was a sweater.

Devon sniffed at the man and turned toward a row of boxes piled on shelves scattered across the back wall of the room. She pulled boxes out and sorted through the contents as if the conversation wasn't happening behind her. She muttered something derogatory about Greenlee's organization skills under her breath.

"Not yet. Just took the case yesterday. Knowledge transfer with this guy was my afternoon meeting."

"Just a missing person? Nothing exciting?" Blue asked as Mr. Mann continued to try to get someone to let him in on any conversation that was happening in the room. He was very unpleasant background noise. But at least he had lost some of his bravado.

A box slammed to the ground behind them, and Devon began climbing the shelves, reaching for the top shelf. "Damn it, Greenlee!"

Finn made a move to help Devon, glancing at Blue with a question. It wasn't in his nature not to help. Blue gave him a wave to say he should leave it alone. He turned slightly, but monitored Devon's precarious ascent. "Just the targets, but the family wants them back quick. I could use your help."

"You got it."

"That easy?" Finn grinned. As if the answer had ever been in doubt. Neither she nor Devon would tell him no without extenuating circumstances. To Devon, he was practically family, her deceased husband's step-brother. That tossed him squarely into the inner circle for Blue as well.

"Of course." Blue shrugged.

"I'll have my team contact you directly when they confirm the location and secure the site. It will be Tanner or Hale." Finn had finished his coffee and started looking around for a trash can.

"I'll be ready. Why is dick man asking about our bad artwork?" Blue nodded toward the FBI agent, who was standing below Devon with his hands in the air, as if he would catch her if she fell.

Finn waved at Mr. Mann. "Bastard dug through the last locations on my car's GPS when I was pumping gas because he thought I already had leads I wasn't sharing. Trix clued me in on where he was headed."

"Found it!" Devon shouted, waving a pouch she plucked from a heavily taped box on the top shelf labeled Jenga. She let go of the shelf and pushed off, landing softly while Mr. Mann screamed.

"Ah ha." Blue nodded, crossing her arms over her chest. That was concerning information. "Why did he ask about the Hounds of Dawn here?"

"I don't know. But I'll find out."

"Appreciated."

Devon began pulling small stones on leather straps from the pouch in her hand. She shook a large turquoise stone in her left hand. "Big one?" Her other hand held a small black stone. "Or little one?"

Blue raised her eyebrow at Finn. The decisions were his. She and Devon would be covered either way.

"Dinner?" he asked her.

"She can't. She has to help Lexi with her homework so I can get caught up on work." Devon chimed in.

"Shit." Blue glared at her friend. "Rain check?"

"Brunch? At the house. Mimosas. Those qualify as fruity drinks. Tomorrow?" Finn offered.

"Spending the night, Finn?" Devon had an evil grin on her face.

Finn shrugged. "I owe you breakfast, lunch, my firstborn, and fruity drinks after what you did for Hale." His face turned serious, and he scowled. "Probably a lifetime supply, actually. You saved us in Kinshasa."

"He's hot when he scowls." Devon chimed in. "You should say yes."

"My God, woman!" Blue cried in exasperation. Devon would not rest until she set her up with someone. Apparently, at this point, it didn't matter who. "Seriously. The man is your brother-in-law. Are you allowed to call him hot?"

"Well, he is. Just like his brother. Runs in the family." Devon shrugged and bumped into Finn with her hip. He wrapped an arm around her shoulders and squeezed. Blue was glad that Devon was finally at a point where she could mention her late husband, Alexander, without a cloud falling over the room.

Finn laughed out loud at Devon's antics.

Blue rolled her eyes. She couldn't believe he heard or remembered her throwaway comment about fruity drinks on a beach in the hellish chaos of the burning building in Kinshasa where Hale had been trapped.

"Mimosas, you say. But no beach?" Blue sent Devon a glare that could have scorched skin. Devon took the hint and shut her mouth mid-comment. "Sounds delightful."

Finn nodded and reached his hand toward Devon. "Big one. Let me get him out of here."

"I'm not going anywhere until I get some answers. Are the Hounds of Dawn moving the missing Sovaj and artifact users? Are they behind the surges?" Mr. Mann placed his hands on his hips and appeared ready for a standoff. Blue shot Finn a look of warning.

"Grab your guns, Mann. We are leaving," Finn ordered.

"Like hell we are. They tied me up and stole government property."

Finn sighed and walked decisively toward the workbench where Blue had placed Mann's wallet and weapons. He picked them up and handed them to Mann, giving him no choice other than to take them. Finn turned toward Devon. "A little Twilight?"

Small strands of hair waved around her face. Mr. Mann swayed. Finn stepped forward and threw the man's short, pudgy arms over his shoulder. "You really shouldn't drink at lunch, buddy," he said.

"Huh?" Mann grunted, but followed Finn out the back door.

Blue followed them out to the small parking area behind the workshop. Finn's Audi sat across two spots like he had parked in a hurry. She helped him heft the big man into the passenger seat and secured his seat belt. A quiet snore came from the car as she stood back up.

"Anything special about this one?" Finn asked, referring to the large turquoise necklace Devon gave him earlier. It was one of Greenlee's specialty items that they kept in bulk for occasions just like this one. In a few minutes, Finn was going to hold the stone against Mr. Mann's exposed skin and mutter rutabaga. Since Finn chose the larger of the two necklaces, Mr. Mann was going to forget everything that had happened in the past week and undergo treatment for something that looked remarkably like a stroke. But he would live. The smaller stones only erased a few hours.

"Nope. Just like the others," Blue told him as she stepped back.

"Good. I'll see you tomorrow. Enjoy the homework." He winked as he climbed into the driver's seat and pulled away from the shop.

Devon stood at the door, watching as he drove away, her cell phone in her hand. "Did you hear about the shit show at the dedication ceremony? Bird attack like something out of a Hitchcock movie. It's trending all over the place. Ivan Lacroix ended up naked. His abs have their own hashtag now."

"What?" Blue asked. "Let me see," she demanded, and joined Devon in the door to look at the images on the screen. Thirty-five injured, including the Paragon and three kids. Rumors that military personnel were spotted near the scene. Blurry pictures of men who looked very much like the goon squad from the incident downtown. Speculation that the mystery men caused the magic surges. And of course, Ivan Lacroix in his boxer briefs glaring at the world. "Oh, shit."

"No kidding. The place is cursed."

"No. Did you see his abs? Talk about hot when he's angry."

Devon cackled. "I needed that today."

"I need those abs."

"Go finish your yoga. Universe destroyer."

7

RHODES

Rhodes leaned his forehead against the cold shower wall and let the scalding hot water roll down his back. Today was stressful; playing nice with Cahlad dignitaries and their guests in front of the media for the meet and greet was part of this nightmare. People who, if they realized who he was, would take great pleasure in incarcerating him and killing him when they were done making an example of him. He couldn't believe he had let his agent talk him into taking this gig when Emmett O'Brien dropped out at the last minute with an acute case of food poisoning. Even if it was close to home and easy money, it wasn't worth it.

When he wrote "Baby Blue" almost ten years ago, he never envisioned this. He had just tried to find some sanity in this world doing the only thing he ever really loved doing—writing music. That song was an apology, meant to be heard by only one person ever.

But he got drunk and sang the song at an open mic night, catching the eye of a very well-connected industry insider. It hit instantly, playing constantly on radio stations and streaming services across the country for months. He knew she heard it. Everyone not hiding under a rock heard it. She had to know it was about her. He didn't hear a word from her for years.

Four platinum albums, two world tours, and one critically acclaimed movie soundtrack later, he was standing in the shower of a very nice hotel room he didn't need preparing to perform a last-minute free public concert sponsored by the Cahlad Conclave as part of their current goodwill PR campaign. He couldn't get away from these people. They should just cancel given what happened at their park dedication this morning.

The scalding water wasn't helping his stress. Maybe the bottle of very expensive whiskey Harper relented and had delivered to his room would help temporarily. She rarely let him drink anything stronger than a sweet tea these days.

Dragging his hand through his beard, he wondered how many questions about it he had answered today. Why were people so enamored with his facial hair? His beard was trending with its own hashtag, for God's sake. This is not the life he imagined for himself when he told Blue he just wanted a normal life. This was the exact opposite, as a matter of fact. Funny how things like that worked out. In moments like this, he would give anything to be sitting in a tiny condo with Blue, eating one of her limited edition gimmick cereals in front of the television.

He lifted his head from the shower wall, reaching down to turn the water off. Then he reached for a towel and jerked his hand back with a surprised shout, knocking all the complimentary toiletries off their perch in the shower.

A tall woman with black hair covered by a baseball hat sat on the closed lid of the hotel toilet right next to the shower. Her hair was so dark and shiny he suspected it was a wig. She wore large sunglasses that couldn't hide the dark circles rimming her eyes, as if she hadn't slept in days. She lounged, legs stretched in front of her with her ankles crossed. Her arms rested loosely on her lap. She held a half-empty bottle of whiskey he recognized as the one he was just contemplating drinking from. The bottle was full when he got in the shower. She watched him casually, completely unaffected by his shout of surprise.

Even though he was towering over her because of his six-foot height and the extra six inches the bathtub provided, he still felt uncomfortable and very vulnerable. Rhodes' eyes flicked to the doorknob. It remained locked. He purposefully locked it to keep Harper from barging in on his shower. The woman had no boundaries. The clothes he shed in disgust were still piled in front of the door where he had dropped them. Yet here she sat.

He only knew of one person who could appear in locked rooms without opening a door or climbing in through a ceiling tile. He wrote songs about her, and she wasn't here. A familiar energy coursed through his limbs. It was an exhilaration he hadn't felt in years, not since his work at the Cahlad.

His visitor said nothing. For the moment, she didn't seem openly hostile or aggressive. She just leveled a stare at him through her sunglasses. Rhodes had dealt with stranger things than this.

He looked down at his still-dripping body, shrugged his shoulders, and asked, "Can you hand me the towel?"

She didn't immediately move or even acknowledge his comment. The bath wasn't that large, and she was tall. If he got out of the tub and she didn't move, he would have to climb over her. He wasn't climbing naked over this mystery woman unless he had to.

She turned her head to look at the wall in front of her. "I need you to deliver a message. You ignored my last two."

"So no to the towel?" Rhodes frowned. What was she talking about, the last two? "Gotcha." He liked this situation less by the minute. The room was cooling. He wanted that towel. He wanted her out. And he wanted to talk to the one person he knew could make sense of this craziness. He might want to down the rest of that bottle of whiskey, too.

"Ms. Indigo Vale. You know her?" The mystery woman turned her head back toward him as she asked. "Yes?"

Her expression and inflection had not changed. Neither had her relaxed posture, but those words were a threat. Indigo Vale was a ghost. Had been for ten years. He saw to it personally, and it cost him everything. No one alive should be able to dig up that name or tie its owner back to him.

Rhodes didn't answer. He felt a muscle in his clenched jaw twitch and his hands curl involuntarily into a fist. This bitch had just crossed a line, and judging by the change in her expression, she knew it.

Her eyebrow went up at his reaction. "Don't even think about it. I'll be gone before you can get to me." She tossed her hair lightly and smiled. "I rather like this look. I would hate for you to ruin it."

Oh shit. She really knew who he was.

She reached into her pocket, pulling out a small piece of paper that she extended toward him. He could see from here it was a paper napkin with words printed neatly in blue ink across one corner.

"You never gave me that towel I asked for." He held up his still damp hands. "If you want me to pass on that message to the lovely Ms. Vale, you should probably sit it down on the sink over there, where it is dry."

Mystery woman pursed her lips and slowly reached over to the counter to set the napkin on the edge. She never took her eyes off Rhodes.

"How do you know Di?" he asked, using the nickname most people at the Cahlad knew her by.

She graced him with another fake smile and shook her head. "Deliver that soon." She picked up the bottle of whiskey and had another drink, sitting it on the countertop next to the napkin when she was done. She stared at him, weighing her next words.

"Skip the catered meal," she said a single second before she disappeared into thin air.

Rhodes stood silent for another moment. He placed his hands on his hips, then leaned over to take a deep, steadying breath. He didn't smell anything out of the ordinary. The temperature in the room hadn't changed. The lack of environmental change surprised and confused him. There was always residual with magic like that.

He climbed out of the tub, snatched the towel from the hook, and wrapped it around his waist. He snatched the whiskey bottle from the counter. "Shit!" he shouted into the tiny little room, hearing his voice echo off the hard surfaces. He just wanted normal. Just wanted Blue safe. It had all been for nothing. Damn it all!

He needed to contact Blue. But she would show up immediately, regardless of how pissed she was at him. It was possible, even likely, this was a trap. He was bait. He couldn't call yet. He should wait.

He wanted to kill somebody. He snatched open the bathroom door. The only living thing in the room other than himself was Lady Lucille curled up in the middle of the bed, snoring lightly through her stubby black nose. He sat down on the bed, relieved to see she was unbothered, and stroked the Pug's graying head.

He had dealt with many dangerous people in his time. Occasionally, he had not had the luxury of a weapon. But he had never had to deal with them naked and unarmed. This was an unexpected and unpleasant first.

Rhodes shook his head to clear it and sat the bottle down. No mind-altering substances while trying to kill a person or not be killed by one. How had that crazy dude robbed all those banks with his penis hanging out for the world to see so many years ago?

Today had been a long day. Tomorrow would be worse.

8

BLUE

Blue pinched the bridge of her nose and closed the news feed, outlining the magic surges still wreaking havoc on the city. Several people who did not know that they had any magic ability suddenly displayed abilities. An artifact caused an explosion in a candy plant. Another caused a year's worth of rainfall to submerge a suburb to the south of town in less than 24 hours. There were videos of park rangers launching boats on the interstate to rescue stranded motorists. Then the craziness at the memorial dedication. Something weird was happening.

But good news. She had refrained from murdering an FBI agent today, and Baldy from the roof was genuinely excited to settle into his new life. He would start his new journey as a middle school band director in the fall. He seemed relieved to leave the night and weekend gig economy behind. He'd have a hot wife and 2.5 kids in no time. She just had to deliver his official new paperwork. As she suspected, he did not know before the night she met him he had any magical inclinations whatsoever.

Mitch Collins, the Paragon or international leader of the Cahlad, remained hospitalized because of injuries sustained in an ice-nado but was conducting phone interviews from his room. The Cahlad was in full-court press mode, using the grandfatherly looking and sounding Mitch to reassure the public that it was very close to discovering and mitigating the cause of the increasingly strange events. They were even going forward with their free public concert scheduled for later tonight. The government, of course, was in its usual kerfuffle. Senator Nolan Miller, in particular, was very vocal about his lack of faith in the Cahlad's abilities to handle this latest crisis. Blue snorted. As much as she hated to admit it, the asshole Senator was right. The Cahlad wasn't even close to knowing what was going on. If they were, the cause would be dead and buried or being studied in an impenetrable underground lab. She had some experience with their methods from both sides.

If Nolan Miller knew what was good for him, he wouldn't make an enemy out of Mitch Collins. The man might look like a dopey middle-aged nutty professor, but behind the tweed jackets, sweater vest, and elbow patches was a man who had won the role of Paragon in a ruthless magical duel to the death at an unprecedentedly young age, sending the magical world into upheaval. He had defended it decisively numerous times over the years. He maintained loyalty and compliance from every member of the Cahlad Conclave, formed by the other leaders of the various Cahlad campuses around the world. They functioned as a multi-national advisory committee. He did it with diplomacy, surrounding himself with a shrewd team of extraordinarily talented magic users, and with violence when it was absolutely necessary. The Cahlad campus here in Nashville was the Prime campus because Mitch Collins lived here. It had been in Europe for centuries. Nolan Miller had no idea who he was bad-mouthing to the press.

No longer distracted by her news feed, she noticed a pencil tapping frantically on the countertop in the periphery of her vision. She gazed down into big brown eyes, looking up at her. They were brimming with tears and pinched with frustration. She reached down to wipe the escaping tears from young, freckled cheeks.

"Oh, kiddo. You are doing great." She wrapped her arms around Lexi's small, yet strong, shoulders. "Please don't get discouraged. I'll help."

"I hate it!" Lexi yelled from the stool next to Blue, slamming her hands on the counter in frustration.

Blue hated it, too. Reading was a battle for Lexi. Which made it a battle for everyone. "How long have you been at it?" She picked up the book and looked at where Lexi had left off. It was the beginning of a chapter about "The Revelation" and the "Sovaj Rebellion." Blue disliked this on so many levels, not just the fact that it was difficult for Lexi to read it. It was complete propaganda garbage masquerading as modern history. No one should suffer through this, much less someone who struggled this much to read. She should read something fun if she put in the effort.

"Go get us some lemonade, and I will finish reading this to you before your mom gets home." Blue told the girl, using air quotes for the reading part. While Lexi filled two glasses with ice and lemonade, Blue searched on her phone for a wildly popular documentary series that roughly covered the contents of the chapter. It hit big a few years ago because the primary focus of the show was such a train wreck of a man that people couldn't look away.

"Here we go. First episode of Mullet Madness," she told Lexi when the girl brought their drinks. "If you see a penis, don't tell your mom." She sincerely hoped Lexi didn't mention this at all. Mullet Roane was a touchy subject for Devon. But the kid didn't live in a bubble. And the documentary was morbidly riveting.

The smile on Lexi's face lit up the room as they both hunkered over the screen. Blue hit play and the torrid story of the first publicly known individual who could channel magic without an artifact started to play. The opening scene featured a nude Mullet Roane screaming wildly in the middle of a downtown street as bullets halted midair and fell to the ground at his feet. Two police cars hovered in the air in the frame, with terrified officers dangling from windows and open doors. Fortunately, they blurred his penis. His glorious mullet and impeccably applied eyeliner were on full display. Lexi's eyes were wide with disbelief.

Thirty minutes later, Lexi had the basics. Most people capable of magic had to use an artifact to channel it, or they had a really bad day. Death and permanent disability kind of bad day. It took a long time to learn how to use an artifact and most people went to special schools run by the Cahlad for years to learn how to do it safely. Due to the potential danger, artifacts had to be registered with the Cahlad. Owning an unregistered artifact was a grave offense. Recently, in the grand scheme of things, the world discovered some people didn't have to use artifacts. Those people had to register by law with the Cahlad because everyone was scared of them due to the criminal antics of the eyeliner-wearing nudist in the documentary.

She needed a glass of wine. Now. They hadn't even touched on the encroachments to a Sovaj's personal liberties that registration enabled. The catchy theme song rolled as the screen panned into a closeup of Mullet Roane's eyeliner-rimmed eyes. Blue glanced over at Lexi. "Catch all that, kiddo?"

"That was some crazy sh..." Lexi laughed.

"Nope," Blue interrupted. "If Mama Bear hears you..." She pointed sternly at Lexi in warning. "I am done helping that woman dispose of bodies. No more. Not this lady."

"Did that have everything I need to pass my quiz?" Lexi asked as she rolled her eyes.

Blue had skimmed through the chapter quickly as the documentary played. "And then some. You are all set."

"Awesome. Thanks, Tia Blue. I won't tell Mom." She hugged Blue with surprisingly strong arms for a child her size and hopped off the stool. "Can I play my video game now? Tio G said he would play when I finished my homework."

"Sure, kiddo. Go spam kill him when he re-spawns for me."

She heard the door open in the other room as she took the first sip of her second glass of wine. Devon walked in carrying a gym bag and a yoga mat. She raised her well-defined black eyebrow above her glasses and placed a hand on her hip. "You read it to her again. Didn't you?"

Blue was prepared. Mama Bear always knew. So, she walked over and placed a big glass of wine into her friend's already outstretched hand. "Not exactly; I did keep her from saying shit if that counts for anything."

Devon dropped her bag next to the door. "Since you were the one who taught her that word, you had better."

"I'm hurt. Shit is not really my favored explicative," Blue retorted.

"What are we going to do with that one?" Devon asked as she moved to sit at the counter where Lexi had been sitting earlier.

"We," Blue waved between the two of them, "aren't doing anything. She's your daughter." Then she joined Devon in a fit of giggles, knowing that there wasn't a hint of truth in her words. Blue and Greenlee had changed as many diapers as Devon. The surplus gas mask Greenlee used when the poop entered the green stage still hung off the coat rack in the front entryway.

Devon cut Blue a sideways look. "What did you make me for dinner while I was working my magic?" She pulled a tall manila folder from her bag and set it in front of Blue. "One middle school band teacher in a box."

"Thanks! Dinner?" Blue waved toward the sounds of screaming and laughter, but didn't look at the contents of the envelope. "I thought it was Greenlee's night."

"Pizza then?" Devon pulled out her cell phone. "That place in New York by the stadium?" She checked her watch. "I have his card number." Devon tapped her temple and waggled her eyebrows with an evil smile.

"Call it in. I'll grab my shoes."

Twenty minutes later, Blue carried the pizzas into the kitchen. Devon was leaning against the stove, sipping wine. Lexi sat at the kitchen island swinging her legs back and forth, playing a video game.

Devon sniffed the air and leaned closer to the pizza as Blue set the boxes on the island and opened the lids. She closed her eyes. "This pizza smells divine." She snatched a piece and took a seat on the stool next to Lexi. "Thank you for spoiling me."

Lexi grabbed a slice with each hand and settled back onto her stool. Just as she was taking a bite of the first slice, a hand snaked from behind her and snatched the second slice away. "Hey!" she yelled around the food in her mouth.

Greenlee smiled impishly and shoved the entire stolen piece into his mouth, never stopping his trajectory toward the open pizza boxes. His cheeks puffed out while chewing with his mouth slightly open, wearing faded sweatpants and a stained shirt that he had undoubtedly grabbed from the dirty clothes. Blue grabbed a plate from the cabinet and tossed three slices onto it quickly. Devon had many rules about her kitchen. But the only rule anyone paid attention to was that there were two types of people in a kitchen: the fast and the hungry. Today, Blue was going to be fast. Pizza secured, she plucked a fork from the drawer and settled on the stool next to Devon

"Really, Blue?" Greenlee grabbed an entire box of pizza and sat it down in front of an empty stool next to Lexi. He looked at the plate and the fork with horror. "That is blasphemy."

Blue finished chewing and pointed the fork at Greenlee. "Just because you don't know how to use one doesn't make it blasphemy."

"I can use all the forks." Greenlee moved toward the industrial-sized, stainless-steel refrigerator. "Big ones, little ones. The ones on the outside and the inside." He fished drinks out and emptied a packet of hot chocolate mix into a mug he placed under the Keurig. "Pizza should be eaten with your hands." He performed a goofy version of spirit fingers.

"Yes," Lexi agreed, taking a slice from the box Greenlee had claimed for himself. A line of grease rolled down her wrist.

"See that." Greenlee pointed. "That is part of the pizza experience." He placed a glass of milk and a napkin in front of Lexi. He patted her head. "Don't get grease on your shirt, sweetheart. You grow so fast we can barely keep you in clothes. Let's not stain them." Blue always found it amusing when the tattoo and piercing-covered man with a ragged beard and unkept man bun dropped into suburban Dad mode.

"That," he pointed at the grease again, "makes it taste better." He sat a second glass of wine down in front of Devon. "My lady." He bowed grandly.

"Mmmm." Blue glanced at the mess that was now Lexi. The child was completely ignoring the napkins. "Blasphemy," she said as she cut another piece of pizza with her fork. "Tastes so good." She placed the pizza nugget daintily in her mouth.

Greenlee plunked a mug of hot chocolate down in front of Blue just as Devon rolled her amused brown eyes. Blue glanced down at the mug and, yes, he had managed to sneak a dab of cinnamon into it somehow. "You are too good to me, Green."

She looked closer. "Ew. Did you have to shed in it?"

Blue fished a long blond hair out of the mug and held it up for her dining companions to see.

"Oh, Gods, Greenlee." Devon made a disgusted sound.

"Gross, Tio G."

"Adds flavor," he informed them, and went back to his seat with his own glass of wine.

Blue leveled a stare at Greenlee that would have killed a less clueless man.

The banter continued, and Blue finished off her second piece of pizza. She should probably work on eating breakfast, or at least lunch. Binging at the end of the day with only coffee, whiskey, and snacks in between was no good.

Her phone buzzed in rapid succession in her pocket. "See, no greasy hands," she pointed out to Greenlee as she fished it out and glanced at the screen. It was from Rhodes' assistant.

Saint Harper: Drama Llama 911.

Saint Harper: Something about going to the grocery store for butter.

Saint Harper: Says you will understand.

Saint Harper: Something is wrong.

Saint Harper: Call me back.

Blue bowed her head as dread filled her body. She knew what he meant; it wasn't good. She would not finish this pizza. Greenlee or Lexi were going to eat it before she could get back. "Shit. It's Rhodes."

Devon raised an eyebrow, leaned forward, and placed her forearms on the countertop. "Seems suspect."

"You always say that about Rhodes. But it does." Blue nodded.

"I told you, accepting that contract even as a pass-through…" Devon waved a slice of pizza in the air. Greenlee watched them quietly. He usually stayed out of this argument.

"It's fine." Blue replied. Devon held her eyes in a glare that practically wrote the words bullshit across the sky.

"The money is insane," Blue continued. "He doesn't need the level of security I offer. Finn is handling the day-to-day details, so it has been low touch for me. And I never get shot at on this gig." She left off the fact that the message she had just received might change that.

Devon and Greenlee winced. Blue didn't tell them much about the jobs she took and was careful to stay at her boat for Lexi's sake until she had healed up if she had issues. But they weren't stupid.

"Keep your eyes open, Blue," Devon ordered. The woman could hold a grudge like no other. And she was holding one on Blue's behalf. She disliked Rhodes with the intensity of a thousand suns, even though she knew none of the details about why Blue wanted to stay away from him. That was a true friend. "He wears sheep's clothing." Devon shook her head and brought her voice down to almost a whisper as she grumbled, "You should have fruity drinks with Finn on a beach and send him freaking pictures."

That made Blue laugh. "I'll be back down in a moment." She stood from her stool, scooting her uneaten pizza toward Greenlee, the human disposal. "Double shit."

"Not your favored expletive, huh?"

Blue just smiled and pointed at Greenlee as she backed out of the room.

As soon as she was out of view, she stopped and dropped the playful pretense. Heading toward the stairs to grab her travel gear before she returned Harper's call, she waved her middle finger randomly at the universe. She wanted to stay and hang out with her family. Drink hair-filled hot chocolate. She did not want to go see Rhodes.

9

SAM

S am sat in the chair next to Nisha's hospital bed. Thanks to Mitch, her broken bones were already healing, and the worst damage she sported were some nasty bruises from now-healed internal bleeding. Since she had suffered a concussion, they were waiting for the results of her CT scan before she could be discharged. It was already six thirty in the evening. He knew that would be fine as well because it was the first thing the man who had healed her in the park addressed. She slept soundly, curled in a ball in the bed. Magical healing demanded a hefty energy toll, and bone breaks required more energy than anything else.

It was the first time the room wasn't buzzing with visitors or officials since they arrived. He pulled a laptop from the bag of supplies Ivan had been kind enough to drop off and turned it on. The bag also had a change of clothes for him and Nisha, since avian viscera covered theirs. Ivan reported that Nolan Miller was holding a press conference within the hour to address the bird attack at the park dedication, and that there was some problem getting Mitch discharged, so he might have to stay overnight. He eyed the red USB. As soon as they could regroup, he would ask Ivan to review all the footage available of the incident to determine how the woman left without a trace.

But right now, he wanted to know what was on it. Maybe ransomware, but he doubted that was the case. He inserted it into the port and opened the single directory that appeared. It was labeled Project Zenith. The files were all images of physical pages holding the official Cahlad seal printed on red paper.

The very first page held three wallet-sized photos of him taped down the edge. One as a toddler, one in middle school right before he had been accepted into the Cahlad Academy, and his official headshot when he joined the Stalker units. The page itself was a crowded, yet neatly organized, official-looking worksheet containing headings, defining boxes of checklists and minuscule typed print. The headings listed were Exposure Level, Maternal Intake, Maternal Outcome, Paternal, Gestation and Birth, and Follow-up.

He clicked quickly to the next page, scanning. The layout was identical and held similar pictures of Ivan. The page after that was Amber Collins, Mitch, and Zella's adopted daughter. Next were identical pages with pictures of Indigo (Di) Vale and Rhodes Westridge. There were two more pages with pictures of infants, but no other photos.

He flipped back to the first page and started reading. As he read, his heart rate increased, and he began to doubt everything he had ever known about the Cahlad. Zeniths weren't just the three high-ly powered Sovaj Larson and Mitch recruited to receive advanced training. There were more, but only three had received the training.

They had all literally been bred in a top-secret Cahlad facility with the intent to create exceptionally powerful natural magic users. They had tracked the babies their whole lives with the intent of plac-ing them within the appropriate education and training programs to most effectively leverage whatever skills surfaced as they grew. They were monitored into adulthood. Sam included.

Hell, his parents weren't even biologically his. According to the file, the Cahlad orchestrated a swap of the fertilized embryo his parents thought was their own with an embryo fertilized as part of this project. The embryo—Sam—consisted of an egg from a Level 3 Sovaj and a Level 6 magic user. Sam had never heard of either of them. Before implantation, the embryo had been exposed at a level of 9 to something called the Son Sovaj. His embryo was labeled in the file as Embryo 8 of 10. Sam wondered briefly about the other nine.

His scholarship to the Cahlad Academy hadn't been earned. It had been guaranteed because he was a product of the Zenith Project, and they needed to keep an eye on him. His fortuitous rise through the ranks, meeting the right people, being in the right situations to shine — none of it was accidental. They had orchestrated it to place him optimally at the top of the Cahlad's pyramid of power. They had been watching him his whole life. They knew about the incident when he shouted the words "Bite Me!" at Johnny Brigands in middle school and ended up with stitches. They knew his mother had battled leukemia after he started attending the Academy and went into remission.

He flipped to Ivan's page and winced. His mother was a vegetative Jane Doe without magic. The Cahlad found her in a state-run hospital. She was used as an incubation pod and directly and perpetually exposed to the Son Sovaj while pregnant. Sam made a mental note to research the Son Sovaj. His intuition told him it was an artifact. And the fact that its name was so similar to the common name for magic users who didn't need artifacts was telling.

Ivan's father was a Level 8 magic user with shield magic. That made sense. The paternal information indicated voluntary donation. Ivan had two brothers from different fathers. One was listed as a Level 5 magic user and healer. The other was a Level 5 magic user with unclassified magic. Both of the other children died in infancy and were older than Ivan. Ivan had lived in the facility until he was two. Sam didn't realize that. If Ivan was aware or remembered, he never spoke of it. Under the section titled Maternal Outcome, there was an exposure level box. It indicated level 8. The deceased box was also checked, with multiple myeloma listed as the cause.

Sam flipped to Amber's page. Her mother volunteered to be a part of the program in exchange for getting out of a life sentence in prison. Lovely. She, too, was exposed to the artifact intermittently. The paternal information was redacted. Thick black lines marking through the text in the box. Under the Maternal Outcome header, the exposure level was listed as three, with notes that the subject was difficult to keep contained near the artifact due to multiple escape attempts. The deceased box was also checked, listing Waldenstrom's macroglobulinaemia as the cause. Sam had never heard of it.

He swapped to a browser, entering Waldenstrom's macroglobulinaemia and Mycloma into the search bar. His eyebrows drew together. Both of those were blood cancer disorders. Just like leukemia. Had his mother's leukemia been caused by the exposed embryo she was provided... him? Had these people given his mother cancer? Had they known?

He moved on to the next page and scanned with increasing horror. Indigo's mother was a forcible kidnapping, justified by the needs of the particular control being studied. She was the identical twin of Amber's mother. The paternal information was also redacted.

Sam stopped and flipped back through the pages. These were the only two pages with redacted paternity information. He would bet money the father was the same, thus the reason for the identical twin control. This was some Nazi Germany bullshit. How could the Cahlad condone this?

The exposure level in the Maternal Outcome section of Indigo's file was listed as 8, much higher than Amber's mother. The deceased block remained unchecked. He looked further down the page in the follow-up section. The Cahlad lost track of both Indigo and her mother briefly. They found Indigo when she was six at a commune east of Nashville, but not her mother.

He flipped to the page with pictures of Rhodes Westridge. This page had older information, almost eight years before the rest. In the upper right-hand corner, Sam noticed a notation marking this record as part of Study 1. He took a minute to flip back through. His record indicated study 5. Ivan's study 4, Indigo and Amber's study 7. It appeared the Cahlad ran a batch of women and babies through once a year judging by the study numbers and the dates of birth.

He went back to reading Rhodes' record. Rhodes' father was a Level 9 Magic user already working in the Cahlad's upper ranks. His mother, only a Level 2 Magic user, volunteered for the program. She was in the first batch of participants, purposefully exposed to the artifact. The exposure level was rated at 10. The Deceased checkbox was marked with a cause of rapid onset amyloidosis and organ failure. In the follow-up section, Sam noted that Rhodes was born via emergency C-section. The organ failure happened before the end of the pregnancy.

He skimmed the next two records that were less complete. The Cahlad lost track of both subjects in the preschool years.

This was horrific. He kept reading. The last pages of the file held retrospectives for each study and plans for modifications to the techniques for the next phases of the project. For each study, a list of mothers and children was listed. Sam scanned the pages carefully. Most of the mothers died before their children were born. The maternal death rate for the study as a whole was 95% within three years of participation: over 60 dead women. Sam wondered how many were willing participants. That detail wasn't in these pages. He looked at the notes on the children. Some hadn't even been given names. Just Baby girl 4 with a date of death, usually the same day as birth. Many were stillbirths. Only seven children survived into adolescence or adulthood. Indigo was the youngest by a few weeks, and the last, according to this file.

What about the artifact? Was this the whole project file? Was this project still going?

Thoroughly disgusted, Sam closed the lid of his laptop. His knuckles were white as he balled his hands into fists. He didn't know what he felt more of; anger, resentment, or sorrow. He didn't care that his parents weren't biologically his. They loved him, and he was sure they had no idea about this. He did care that his mother might have suffered through cancer because of him. He cared about 60 dead women and dozens of dead infants and children.

Why hadn't Mitch ever mentioned this? He obviously knew about it. His adopted daughter was a product of the experiments. Worse, his signature was at the bottom of each page.

"Regent?" A person in a lab coat poked their head into the room. "We have the results of Ms. Ravi's CT scan." They stepped into the room. "Everything looks fine. I will start the discharge paperwork. As soon as she wakes up, she will be free to go."

10

BLUE

B lue shivered and rubbed her hands together for warmth, taking a moment to inspect the small storage room she found herself in. Deep shelves filled with bulk paper goods jutted haphazardly toward her in the darkness, only broken by a sliver of light peeking under the door. There was more junk in here than last time. The room stunk of cleaners, dust, and stale air. A moldy mop head dangled just inches from her face.

"Ew." Stepping back to avoid a mouthful of mop, her left foot nudged something. Water sloshed in the mop bucket, and the water soaked through her pants. God only knows what delights were in that bucket and were now on her pants. This job was so glamorous.

Patting down her blazer and smoothing out her jeans to make sure she had everything, she took a step toward the door, listening for any noise on the other side. She wasn't exactly dressed like someone who would go unnoticed coming out of a random cleaning supply storage room.

Assured that no one lurked on the other side, she stepped out. As her eyes adjusted to the light, she squinted slightly. She was in a service tunnel in the bowels of Nashville's arena, where Rhodes was to perform a free concert tonight. She had little hidey holes like this one in major event venues across the country. Many of her clients were demanding entertainers that wanted what they wanted when they wanted it. She was better than anyone else at catering to those demands, and her bank account reflected that.

She moved toward the elevator bank like she belonged here. She pressed the button and waited. She had been on edge since she read the words go to the grocery store for butter. He was sending her a message to be careful, but it didn't stop her from replaying the last time he had told her to go to the grocery for butter.

The elevator was taking a while. It appeared to be stuck on the ground level. She could only imagine the chaos that was happening up there. Inactivity caused her mind to wander as the icy knot in her stomach grew. The anxiety she hadn't quite beat back this morning rushed in. Her vision tunneled, and her breathing became shallow. It had been a long time since her last full-blown panic attack. It was a bad day. She went through her mental exercises but found herself visiting a younger version of herself with fewer aching body parts in her mind.

Young Blue stepped onto the chunky pavement of the local grocery store's parking lot and closed the door of her old economy car. Rhodes wanted her to buy something nicer, but this would do for now. Though she was twenty-four, she only had two years of experience driving, and she wasn't very good at it. Before that, she had lived on the Cahlad Campus and never driven anywhere. She only knew how because defensive driving was a part of her training—the only part of her training she hadn't aced, incidentally. So, she kept the beater for now. The passenger side door was a different color because she had to replace it with one from a local junkyard. It sported scrapes and dents on every surface. There would likely be another before the night was out. It had earned her loyalty.

Crossing the parking lot, she inhaled the crisp late evening air. It was a good day. Tomorrow was her birthday, and Rhodes hinted all week to keep her schedule clear. She couldn't remember ever having a birthday party. Rhodes took her out for dinner once, but that was before he realized she had never had a party. Maintaining her surly, indifferent image required that she act like the thought of a surprise party irritated her, but she was secretly excited.

Distracted by thoughts of cake frosting, she stepped through the automatic doors. She waved to the elderly man who owned the store. He worked the evening shift instead of hiring someone six days a week to avoid talking to his wife, who worked the day shift. Blue didn't blame him. Gary was a hoot. His wife was not.

He nodded and returned to reading his gossip magazine. She moved with purpose through the store, empty at this time of night. Rhodes needed butter for their dinner. It would be done before she got home if she didn't hurry. Using cars as primary transportation took so long. She wondered if Rhodes had candles for her birthday. She had never blown out candles.

She stopped to admire the endless options of the cereal aisle. The Cahlad cafeteria only had two or three selections. Restaurants served boring cereal. This selection was delightful. She wanted to try all the cereals. She picked up a box with a strange pink Frankenstein on it, knowing Rhodes would feign aggravation and eat most of the box. Smiling, she continued toward the dairy coolers at the back of the store.

Then she felt it: the sensation of being watched. The second it registered, instinct kicked in, and she stepped toward the right side of the aisle to put her back against the shelves. She heard a click, then felt a lance of fire pierce her upper thigh with such force it knocked her to the ground.

She scanned her surroundings. This was bad. Four individuals advanced from different directions. Two pointed guns at her. One stood in front of the dairy cooler with no weapon. The other held a gun-like object attached to a line. She followed the line to her leg. Shit. It was a fucking harpoon. They had harpooned her like a damned whale. What in the actual fuck!

Somehow, she'd held on to the cereal box when she fell. Confusion swept over her briefly. This was a Cahlad stalker unit. She recognized the people. Why were they attacking her? They all worked for the same team. It didn't make any sense. Then it did. Larson. He knew something. She pushed all that from her mind. Survive first. They had attacked. If they wanted a conversation, Captain Ahab shouldn't have been so trigger-happy.

The Stalkers without weapons were the most dangerous ones. Testing her theory, she hurled the pink box at the woman in front of the butter.

The box incinerated in a flash of sparks three feet from the woman, coating the seventies pea-green tile floor in ash. Yep. These folks were likely going to burn this place to the ground with all the witnesses. If she put up a fight, Gary might make it out of here.

Clutching the harpoon shaft, she gave it a wiggle. It felt breakable. "Gary! Run!" she bellowed, applying pressure on the harpoon. An excruciating stab of pain tore through her as the asshole holding the harpoon gun yanked on the rope to drag her across the floor and keep her from breaking the shaft.

"Run! Now!" she screamed, applying her strength to the shaft of the harpoon, dragging her across the floor through puddles of her own blood. The shaft finally split. Screaming, she yanked the shards from her leg, hurling the pointy end at McFlamey and grabbing the piece still attached to the rope with both hands. The harpoon fragment incinerated before reaching its target.

Captain Ahab continued reeling her in. She stuck her good leg out, jamming it into the grocery racks. Her whole body swung as if on a pendulum as he pulled, her arms stretching above her head. Tilting her head back and adjusting her grip on the rope from the blood-slick shaft fragment, she pulled with all her might. Thank God for all the crunches and core work Rhodes still insisted on.

Captain Ahab stayed on his feet, but he took a few very important steps closer to her and away from his friends. Running a few calculations in her head, she let her eyes fill with rainbow plasma. A frigid moment later, she stood in front of Ahab, realizing she wouldn't be for long. Her leg wouldn't hold her weight. He seemed surprised by her sudden appearance. Recovering quickly, he swung the harpoon gun at her head. She grabbed his shirt, desperate to stay upright and calling it a tactical combat maneuver. It threw him off balance, bringing him with her. At the last moment, she wedged the jagged shaft of the harpoon she still held between them and jerked her head to the side. The harpoon squelched as his face landed at the perfect angle to jam the harpoon shaft all the way into his eye socket. She shoved and pushed on his dead weight as all hell broke loose.

Someone screamed, "Cody!"

Not Ahab. Huh. "Sorry about your frontal lobe, Cody."

Another barked, "Light it up!" He must be the guy in charge.

Gunfire erupted all around her. Blue stopped dislodging herself from Cody's corpse and curled herself inward, using him as a morbid meat shield.

Something exploded. God, she hoped Gary listened and ran like hell. A bullet ricocheted off the floor and lightning surged through her hip. Now she bled from a harpoon wound and a gunshot ricochet. She was soaked in Cody's blood, too.

Snaking a hand around the dead man's waist, she found what she was looking for. Snatching the weapon from the holster, she flicked the safety and shoved Cody's body with all of her might. Before it fully flopped to the side, she pointed the weapon at 'Light it up' and opened fire. No sense shooting at McFlamey. She would just incinerate the rounds.

Two rounds straight to the chest knocked him on his ass, but he wasn't bleeding. Body armor. Shit. Now he was prone, and she didn't have a clean headshot.

Another explosion rocked the building, toppling shelves a few aisles over. Her shoulder lurched as pain radiated through her arm. Emotionally Compromised had landed a decent shot. A harpoon wound and two bullet holes. What a fucking nightmare! Her right leg and left arm were functionally useless. She wasn't worried about the wounds. They would heal quickly, but not if she got shot in the head. She needed to get out of here, but wondered if Gary had time to get away. How long had this been going on? Likely only seconds, but it felt like an eternity.

Firing once toward Emotionally Compromised, she didn't even try to hit center mass. He probably wore armor, too. Instead, she aimed right between the eyeballs and obliterated the right one. If someone didn't know better, they would think she was doing this eyeball thing on purpose.

The air was fetid with smoke and chemicals. Her lungs burned and her eyes watered. This building was no longer habitable. Heat fanned her from all directions.

Commander Body Armor stood and advanced on her position. He no longer had his gun, but she knew he was still dangerous. He chopped his leg down on her right arm, knocking the gun from her hand before she could move her battered body. Gary was on his own. She ran the calculations. Skipping injured took extra effort, extra math, and inconveniently extra time. The more injury, the more effort, math, and time she didn't have. Her opponent pulled a nasty-looking blade from his belt, embedding it in her back, right between her ribs. She screamed. It really hurt.

She was in trouble. That was a serious wound. She may or may not be able to withstand this one without medical intervention. Blood drenched her back like it flowed from a faucet. She would not be conscious for long.

Commander Body Armor stepped away, sneering. He hadn't read the part of her file about enhanced healing capabilities. Knowing Larson, it was redacted. She found the handle of the knife in her ribs, counted to two, and yanked the knife out as cleanly as she could, using only one hand. She should skip right now, but she was pissed. This fucker tried to kill her, ordered Gary's life's work incinerated, and didn't look at all like he gave a shit about either. Dumb fuck even turned his back on her. Couldn't let that slide.

Rearing back, she hurled the knife at the base of his spine, doubting she would hit him. But she might remind him he wasn't all that. Commander Body Armor turned and stooped for his gun at that exact moment. The knife slammed into the side of his face, blade first just above his cheekbone. She swore she wasn't doing this shit on purpose, but the knife ripped right through the side of his eye socket. He stood for a moment, swaying, then crumpled.

The rainbow slid over her vision as McFlamey rounded the corner, taking in her three dead teammates. Rage filled the woman's features and her hands extended. Fuck it. She didn't have time to do this right. McFlamey was going to barbecue her ass.

She lifted her good arm, extending her middle finger, then skipped without finishing the equation, hoping she ended up where she was trying to go.

She hadn't. It took her three jumps and all her energy to get back home.

Her cell phone buzzed, pulling her from the memory. She gulped in a huge breath of air that smelled like pine cleaner, not smoke. Likely the mop water on her pants. Something she could smell. She placed her hand on the chilly wall next to the elevator. Something she could feel. She was safe and in control. Yep. She was in control. She heard the ding of the elevator as the floors ticked by above her. Something she could hear. Her heartbeat slowed, and she slid fully into the present. She glanced down at the little black piece of glass in her hand. God bless Devon. Her timing couldn't have been better.

Mamma Bear: ETA? Harper is texting me now. Make it stop.

Me: 2 minutes.

Mamma Bear: Don't forget. He is an asshole. You like fruity drinks.

The elevator finally arrived, and she dialed Harper. It rang a few times before the perpetually exasperated woman barked, "This is Harper. Start talking."

"I'm here, girl." She stepped onto the elevator and hoped she kept her signal.

"Oh, thank sweet baby Jesus," Harper half-whispered and half-screamed.

"Coming up the east bank of cargo elevators now? Meet me there?"

"I'm on my way. You are my hero." The line went dead as Harper's voice faded away. She put her phone back into a pocket, taking in the silence as the elevator lumbered upward.

The door opened and a five-foot-tall ball of energy all but tackled her. "Come on, girl." Harper motioned for Blue to follow speed-walking away without waiting for a comment. She held two phones clutched in one hand and a tablet in the other. "He has been a bear all night. He insisted on taking the entire crew out for dinner instead of letting them eat the catered meal, and it messed up the entire schedule. What is up with the butter? I want to wring his bloody neck. Talk him down." Harper rattled on.

Blue did her usual and let the woman talk. This was good information. They wandered through the underbelly of the arena surrounded by noise and hustling staff. The concert would start soon. She waved at his hand-picked director of security, Kendra. Kendra glared in her direction. She hated this assignment. Blue suspected doubly so tonight. Soon they arrived at Rhodes' dressing room. Harper didn't even knock. She opened the door even though she had no free hands, put her shoulder into it, and barged in. "Here she is, you big crybaby."

A salt and pepper pug wearing a pink rhinestone collar and a silver doggie shirt turned its little stubby face toward her and yipped excitedly. "How is my sweet girl?" Blue cooed.

The crybaby in question seemed pretty non-pulsed by the general disrespect of his assistant. He turned toward Blue and smiled a smile so big you could still see it through the massive amounts of shaggy facial hair he now sported. She had seen him on four magazine covers this week alone. His beard was trending. She rolled her eyes.

His arms flew open, and he advanced. "Blue!" He wrapped her in a gigantic bear hug that lifted her feet off the ground and squeezed the air from her lungs. There was no way he couldn't feel her holstered gun as tight as he was squeezing. He dropped his face next to her ear and whispered in a more serious tone, "Glad you are here, my sweet angel." Blue tensed. What in the hell was he up to? He held her for a moment more and set her down before she could kick him in the shins for picking her up in the first place.

"Stop it." She slugged his chest hard as she mouthed seriously at Rhodes. His smile changed to something more serious, and he pinned her with a look that always made her squirm. Rhodes and Blue went way back. Too far back. Farther back than most people knew. And he didn't even try to hide it. But he really should, considering what an utter asshole he was. And that is what her semi-glare was trying to communicate back to him. That, and you were the one who couldn't handle me. Why do you keep calling me?

"Stay for the show. Stay after the show." Rhodes reached out and took one of her hands in both of his.

She couldn't keep her eyebrow from reaching for the ceiling. "Have you lost your mind?"

"VIP seats. I will make it happen."

Blue glanced around the room. Harper watched them like a Telemundo drama. She held his gaze for a moment, a question in her own. She didn't like what she saw. Damn it. He had gotten to her. Again. Holding in a sigh and blocking Devon's voice from her internal dialog, she stepped closer and took his hand. "I have a few minutes now."

Rhodes turned to Harper. "Give us the room."

11

RHODES

R hodes was relieved Blue picked up on his message and played along. No matter what face he wore or how long they were apart, he could count on her to listen and see him. A crushing weight of panic and worry lifted off his chest.

He had re-lived one of the worst days of his life on a loop in his head all day, waiting for Blue to arrive. There were moments when he swore he could smell the copper bite of blood in the air. Rhodes turned to Harper, who still stood watching. She had lots of opinions about his activities, mostly because she ended up walking the girls out and dealing with the blackmail threats and press. But she really had an opinion about Blue. She liked Blue. Harper considered her a friend and didn't approve of the way she thought he treated her. Still. There were things she didn't know. And he had asked for the room. So he raised his eyebrows at her, not letting go of Blue's hand.

Harper said nothing, just turned and pointed a finger. "Be at the stage in twenty." The door slammed behind her, leaving Rhodes alone with Blue and Lady Lucille. The smile fell from his face immediately.

"I met a woman this afternoon." He crossed his arms over his chest and waited.

"Straight to the point," Blue responded cautiously. "She must have been something."

"Indeed. She showed up just like you do."

Her features remained blank and careful. "Lonely, drunk, stupid, or horny? Which one? All four?"

Rhodes laughed. He loved and missed her candor. She referred to the only time she had responded to one of his calls that didn't filter through Herne Tactical or her bulldog, Finn Torrin. Apparently, she considered herself stupid for answering his call and joining him in New York, already three sheets to the wind. He tried to apologize for being a complete idiot, but her friend Devon had texted incessantly. The messages consisted of comments like, "Don't be an idiot," and "You are better than this." "Don't forget, he is an asshole," had graced the screen more than once. Followed by, "ASSSSSSSHHHH-HOOOOLEEEEE!!!!!!!!" The one that had sent him over the edge was, "He can't blow your mind like that hottie in Denver."

Rhodes stomped on her phone to make it shut up. She spent the night, left the next morning without a word, and never answered his calls again.

He would never forgive himself for not protecting her. She never forgave him for trying to make up for it. He still remembered making dinner when the sound of glass shattering and wood splintering rang out from the living room. He found Blue sprawled on the remnants of their coffee table, bleeding out from multiple stab and gunshot wounds. One wound was to her kidney. She was ice cold and barely conscious. If he hadn't been trained in advanced combat and emergency medicine during his Zenith training and working with the benefit of her enhanced magical healing, she likely would not have made it. It was the first and only day in his life he had ever prayed. Knowing whoever had attacked her would likely watch the emergency rooms, he made the second biggest mistake of his life. He called the only person he could think of that could help her without tipping off whoever had ambushed her. Because it must have been an ambush or an entire army, perhaps both. He called Larson Battle, his former boss, and a man he had ghosted three years before to care for his ailing father. Blue was still his asset, and he truly believed the man would help. He had been wrong. Larson loaded Blue into a helicopter, then shot him in the chest while he was distracted.

Rhodes shook himself from his walk down nightmare lane and clarified. "One minute I'm alone in the shower in a locked bathroom. Next minute, I have company."

Her face darkened instantly, but she remained silent.

He suspected she would know exactly what he had been dealing with in that room. And judging by her reaction, he was right.

"She had a message," he continued, then placed a finger in the center of her chest, tapping once. "For you."

Her eyes snapped up, and he watched a dozen emotions cross her face: the last being fury. That wasn't the reaction he had been expecting. Concern he wished for. Calculation, certainly. But nothing as strong as what he was seeing now. She was usually calm to a fault. Just like he used to be when they met.

He pulled the crumpled yellow napkin out of his pocket. It was from a cafe called the Canary and the Cat. He handed it to her slowly. It said, I understand why you did what you did. I'm sorry. Do what you do best. Please. Blue took the napkin, and her whole body tensed.

"Did you tell Harper?" she finally asked and met his eyes.

"No." He shook his head. "What is she going to do against one of us?"

"Kendra?" she asked about his head of security, who was an absolute bulldog and hand-picked by Blue because she had no qualms about doing whatever it took to protect her clients. She was also a regular human. No magical ability whatsoever. Kendra was great, but Rhodes intended for Blue to fill the role at least part-time when he hired her company. It still irked him.

"No. She showed up in my bathroom without using a door. What the hell is Kendra going to do? Follow me to the bathroom for the rest of my life? If I can't handle this woman..."

Blue nodded. "You should be safe in the venue tonight. Just don't be alone. I'll be back before your performance is over and stay with you until we figure this out. I'll tell Kendra to stay close and have Finn send extra security." She looked around the room, assessing whether she could turn it into a fortress. "We will come up with some reason I'm staying, or you can," she waved her hand absently and grimaced, "do your thing and I can be groupie of the week." She glared at him. His ability was a sore spot between them. That had to have cost her. This mystery woman must pose a serious threat if she was even considering that possibility. Blue nodded, as if satisfied with the plan she was forming. "What did she look like?"

"Black wig. Ball cap. Big glasses. Lots of makeup. But she didn't come for me. I'm not worried about me. No extra security."

"Rhodes. She found you. Not me."

"Who is she?"

Blue sighed. "I have an idea."

"Are you going to share it?"

"No."

He was quiet for a moment, looking at a spot on the ceiling behind them again. "She found me. And she knew you were someone important to me. She knew your real name. How, Blue? You aren't recognizable. I'm not recognizable. No one at the Cahlad knew about us until Larson, and he is dead."

Blue ignored him. It's what she did when he asked questions about things she didn't want to share. Especially things Cahlad related. Her silence spoke volumes.

"We need to make sure you're careful. She brought that message for you," he insisted. "You can't stay with me, either. I'll be fine. I didn't call you here to protect me." He felt her release a huff. "I'll turn her into a baby if she comes back."

Blue smirked. The mention of changing a dangerous enemy into a squalling infant without bowel control always amused her. The first time she had seen him do it, he had to carry her away because she was laughing so hard.

"If she shows up again, you call me immediately. She wasn't trained like we were. But she could still be dangerous to you. She almost killed me... once." That gave him pause. Blue had been the best of the Zenith, a team of elite magic soldiers, during her time at the Conclave. It wouldn't have been easy to take her out of commission.

"You don't need to worry about me. Let me go with you. If it is Cahlad, we stand a better chance together."

She shook her head. "There is no we. No together. Remember?"

He couldn't stop himself from flinching. He absolutely deserved that, and he regretted saying those words to her more than anything else in his life. It was his single biggest mistake, and she would never let him take them back.

"This? Again?" Rhodes heard the door open behind them and looked over.

"Five minutes, Rhodes," Harper ordered. His assistant looked suspicious.

"Got it," he barked and shooed her away with his hand, but she didn't go anywhere. She just kept watching.

"Stay near Kendra. I've got this." She waved the napkin. "You do what you do best. Get back to normal."

"Blue," he exhaled. That last phrase hurt.

The look on her face was a mixture of hurt, regret, and anger as she reached up and patted his cheek. "Break a leg, love." She turned without another word and walked from the room. As the door shut, he could hear Harper making plans for Margarita Night at a hole-in-the-wall Mexican restaurant they favored. He stood in silence for a moment. Lady Lucile snorted and licked her privates.

The door opened. "Now, princess!"

12

BLUE

Blue pulled her fluffy pink hoodie tighter around her body and buried her hands in her sleeves as she walked down the stairs. She was positive she would never be warm again. She was emotionally drained from seeing Greenlee's statue this morning and her conversation with Rhodes. Exhaustion pulled at her eyes and made her limbs feel heavy. She wanted to drink a cup of hot chocolate, maybe spiked with something that would burn on the way down so she could forget the world and everything in it existed. The house was quiet; Devon and Lexi were most likely already in bed for the night when she emerged from the foyer and glanced toward the fresh flowers Greenlee brought home each week. He always bought lilies and lavender—Devon's favorite. She glimpsed herself in the mirror hanging above the antique console the flowers rested on. Her emotions were raw, and the reflection of a stranger staring back at her was more than she could handle right now. Tears welled in her eyes as she glanced quickly away. She took several deep breaths and sniffled to control the unwanted waterworks.

"Blue? Sweetheart?" Greenlee was in front of her in an instant, hands on her shoulders. She had no idea where he had come from. Probably the benefits of one of his piercings. He probably stole one of her hairs or even snot off a tissue and didn't tell her. He was sneaky that way. "What happened?"

"I'm OK." Blue pulled herself together and met his eyes.

Greenlee just looked at her, not moving his hands. She had to look down again. This man knew her bullshit better than anyone on the planet, even Devon. She couldn't lie to him, even if she could lie to herself. This big goober was really going to make her cry. She needed someone to give her shit and tell her what a dumbass she was. Not this big goober man being all soft and compassionate.

This big muscular goober man. Good grief. The muscles on his chest were huge, right in her face, and covered in sweat. When had he gotten muscles like that? He had certainly not looked like this the last time they all trekked to the beach. How long ago had that been?

He caught her staring at his tattooed-covered pecs that should have been showcased in one of the blockbuster superhero movies. His muscles jerked and made them jump, causing both nipple piercings to flash in the light. Blue looked up as a wicked grin crossed his features, and he raised a pierced eyebrow. She laughed out loud. That was more like it. He always knew when she couldn't handle the hard emotional stuff.

"Greenlee, you stink." Blue wrinkled her nose and took a step back. His long blond hair was pulled back into a man bun and wireless earbuds adorned his ears. The multitude of piercings in each ear was clearly visible. He looked good. But he really stank.

"You interrupted my workout. I haven't showered yet." he shrugged. "Why you crying, darlin'?"

"No reason a hot beverage won't cure." Blue nodded her head to the left, and they turned to walk to the kitchen together. She plunked a hot chocolate cup into the Keurig and leaned against the counter. She looked him up and down. He was shirtless and had on loose sweatpants. He was grabbing a water bottle from the fridge. The man had six-pack abs now, too.

"When did this happen, Green?" She waved at his body up and down. He wasn't quite at Greek god level, but she didn't know many women that would complain about this view. "Does Devon know you lost all your shirts?"

He threw back his head and laughed out loud. He then gave a slow turn. "Think she will notice?"

"Oh, yeah." Blue nodded. She reached into the cabinet and pulled out a bottle of cinnamon. "Spoil me?" she asked, holding it and her mug of hot chocolate toward him.

"Always." He took both items from her hand and mixed the two together in a way only he could. Blue tried for years to do it herself, and it just tasted better when Greenlee did it. "I added some strength training and martial arts on the days we don't run."

They ran at least twenty miles per week together. Had for eight years now. They even completed one marathon and vowed to have the other committed if they tried to do that to themselves again. But they continued to run shorter distances.

"Are there that many days? Sure, it isn't some super soldier serum?"

"You are going to give me a big head. But this is one hundred percent Green." He flexed and handed her mug back with a frown. He grabbed a box of snack cakes from the cabinet and sat on the stool. "Still going to tell me you are fine?"

"I am." Blue sat down next to him and took a sip of her hot chocolate and purred. "So good."

"I'm not fine," he said.

Blue glanced quickly in his direction at his quiet statement, hot chocolate forgotten. "Talk to me."

"Are you going to be here tomorrow night?" he queried, taking a sip of his water.

Huh. That was unexpected. "Probably not?"

"Lexi is staying with one of her soccer friends, right?" He was starting to look nervous.

"Yeah?" Blue replied, thoroughly suspicious. What was he up to?

"I'm going to ask her," he finally spat out after a hot thirty seconds of nervous energy.

Blue slapped her hand down on the counter and stared at him with her mouth hanging open. "Yeah?" was all she got out as a smile split her face. "About damned time, man."

His scruffy face split into a grin as well. For someone so tattooed, pierced, hairy, and now muscular, his smile was just plain goofy. Forever the nerdy kid. "Yeah. I finished up the ring this afternoon."

Hold up. Her sluggish brain took a minute to catch up with her face, which was no longer smiling. A ring? "Bah. What?" Maybe she had heard wrong. "A ring?"

He nodded solemnly.

"Should you maybe ask her out on a date first?" she said before thinking. Her Dev-lee ship had sat in the dock so long, she was elated that it might finally set sail. But she wasn't sure how Devon was going to react to this. Zero to a ring in sixty seconds would cause some serious whiplash. "Just asking." She took a sip of her hot chocolate just for something to do.

"A date?" Greenlee's blue eyes narrowed and his brow furrowed. "I've lived with the woman for ten years."

Blue nodded slowly. He spoke the truth. But. Oh geez. "You have lived with me for ten years."

He actually scowled at that. "What do you want me to do? Take her to dinner and a movie? Buy her flowers? I've done that already. So many times."

Blue nodded slowly again and sat her mug down on the counter. He had a point. But he was missing some context. "Yes, but..."

"I know all her favorites. I rub her feet when she is tired. I held her hair while she puked." He looked at Blue with an expression that could only be interpreted as Duh. "I've bought her tampons."

She wasn't mentioning the fact he had done most of those things for her, too. Leg cramps instead of foot rubs. But still. "OK. But does she have any idea that...?"

"We are practically together already." He plowed ahead. "Both of our names are on the house."

Blue took a big sip of her drink and looked him up and down, trying to decide if she should help him or drop it and make a point to sneak back tomorrow just to see how it played out. "My name is on the house, too," she pointed out.

"I..." He stopped before he started. Like maybe some of the things she was saying were starting to sink in. "Well, shit."

"I get it, Greenlee. I love it. But have you even kissed her?"

He didn't respond. He just looked at her blankly and put his hands on his hips.

"Held her hand?" Blue asked. She had seen them hug each other and lean against each other on the couch or on the bleachers at soccer games. But in fairness, she and Greenlee had done those exact same things. This house was full of touchy-feely people. And while she knew that Greenlee was head over heels for Devon, he had never given any overt sign that marriage was where he intended to go. At least not publicly, and Blue had been watching. Closely. Because God, these two. Slow burn of the century. She owed Finn a C note now.

His shoulders slumped a bit.

"I mean. Those things usually happen first. That's all I'm saying." She was sinking the ship before it set sail. She had to stop. Time to plug that hole back up. Hopefully, Devon would handle it better than she was. "There aren't any official rules, I guess." She shrugged.

"Neither of us has really dated in years. I love her. And..." he gestured around the house. Their house, home to their unconventional little family. A home they built for Lexi, who belonged in some way to all of them.

They sat in silence for several long moments. She was emotionally tapped out and didn't know what to say that wouldn't make it worse. He wasn't fine. He was right about that. She leaned over and bumped her friend with her shoulder.

"Are you going to show us the ring?" Lexi's voice carried into the room as she casually strolled in like she wasn't supposed to be sound asleep in bed and hadn't just heard something she most definitely wasn't supposed to hear. Blue damned near jumped off her stool.

"Shit," Greenlee muttered, following Lexi's movement all the way to the refrigerator. She met his eyes as she strutted the whole way to the fridge in a defiant stare-down for the ages.

They all sat there for a second, just staring. Blue felt a bubble form deep in her stomach. Despite her shit day, looking at those two mean-mugging each other in the kitchen forced a laugh up. She clamped her lips shut and slapped both hands over her mouth, trying her best not to let it out, but she couldn't help it. A half-suppressed, sputtering guffaw escaped, and she laid her forehead down on the cool counter and let the rest of her laughter loose.

She heard Lexi snicker, followed by Greenlee's deep belly laugh. They laughed until Lexi slid to the floor and Greenlee wiped tears from his eyes. That was better than she could have hoped for. She shared a look with Greenlee, his expressions conveying the same relief. Lexi's reaction could have swung the other way. One down. One to go, she guessed.

"Show us the goods, Green." Blue said once she could breathe again. She wiggled her fingers in a gimme motion. "Hurry before we get caught."

Greenlee got up to go grab the ring, and Blue glanced over to Lexi. Lexi looked at Blue with great big eyes, her long arms and hands flying everywhere, and her feet stomping silently on the ground in an excited little seizure dance. She mouthed, "Is he insane?"

Blue mouthed back, "I know!" Lexi grabbed a bowl of something sugary and gelatinous and came to sit by Blue at the island. Blue put her arm around the girl and kissed her temple as Greenlee came back into the kitchen with a small red box.

He opened the tiny case, holding it out uncertainly. "What do you think?"

Lexi gasped. "Tio G," she whispered, bringing her hand to her chest. "It is so pretty. Did you make this?"

Greenlee just nodded. He was a talented artisan. Some custom commissions for carefully vetted clientele integrated his magical talent of infusing single-use or low-level perpetual magical effects into mundane objects, usually jewelry. Blue wondered if this ring was just a gorgeous ring or some kind of created artifact like the bracelet he made for her to give to Lexi for her birthday.

The ring was a tiny, delicate, white gold band. It wasn't a traditional engagement ring. It was a simple diamond and emerald-encrusted band. Devon rarely wore jewelry because she said it was impractical and got in her way. This was as close to practical as a piece of jewelry could get, and emeralds were her favorite. Lexi met Blue's eyes. They were thinking the same thing.

"Green, it's so her."

He smiled in relief and closed the box, shoving it into the pocket of his sweats. He reached over and put his hand on Lexi's small forearm.

"Apparently, I'm all out of order." Blue saw him squeeze the girl's arm where he held it. "What do you say, Lex? Is that a yes?"

Blue melted a little. She squeezed Lexi's shoulders and watched closely. She was surprised to see tears welling up in the corners of the little girl's eyes. She also saw a smile. "Yeah." Lexi nodded and laid her hand on top of Greenlee's. "So cool."

Blue sniffled. This was the sweetest thing she had ever seen. These tears didn't bother her one bit.

The devil board at the top of the steps squealed like a stuck pig. Devon was up. "What's all the noise?" she heard Devon call.

Lexi looked at Blue, eyes wide again. "Oh boy, Git. Both of you. I'll cover for you," Blue uttered as she let go of Lexi's shoulders and the kid slunk off the stool. The girl left, giving Blue another silent O.M.G. before she disappeared around the corner.

"My hero." Greenlee winked and slipped out behind her.

Blue sat alone at the kitchen counter with two drinks, a box of snack cakes and a serving bowl of gelatinous dessert when Devon appeared in the kitchen door wearing a purple fluffy robe and Yoda socks.

"Oh, honey." Devon stopped and looked at the sight in front of her, sympathy crossing her features. "That kind of day?"

"You have no idea."

WEDNESDAY

This Soccer Mom Needs a Beer *@SoccerMomNeedsABeer*

OMG! I need to do some laundry! Did she see those abs!

#LadiesLoveLacroix #washboardAbs #IvanTheIncredible

The Amazing Underwear Company *@AmazingUndies*

We have a job opening in the modeling department.

#LadiesLoveLacroix #washboardAbs #IvanTheIncredible

Senator Nolan Miller *@USSenatorNolanMiller*

Yesterday's disaster is more proof that the Cahlad is inept at executing its tasks. People were hurt! Gross negligence on the part of @CahladPrimeOfficial and @Cahlad Paragon! *#WolfGuardingTheHenHouse #RealMagicRegulation*

Senator Nolan Miller *@USSenatorNolanMiller*

The Senate Magic Regulation and Relations Oversight Committee is convening an emergency hearing to discuss @CahladPrime 's blatant disregard for the safety of our citizens.

#WolfGuardingTheHenHouse #RealMagicRegulation

Cade Rhodes Biggest Fan *@CadeRhodesBiggestFan*

What an AMAZING show! Way to save the day. Thanks for the free tickets @CahladPrime.

#FurtureMsCadeRhodes #AmericasBeard #MagicAintSoBad #EmmettOBrienSucks

13

BLUE

Someone was breaking down her door. Blue reached under her pillow, expecting to wrap her hands around her gun, but it wasn't there. She jerked upright, opening one puffy eye. It was still dark outside.

The pounding on the door continued as the haze of sleep burnt away, and she realized it was more of a knock than a breach. It took a moment for her to remember where she was and that she didn't keep loaded weapons under her pillow when she was in the house with Lexi running around. Only when she was by herself or had other sleeping arrangements. "Blue!" Devon yelled through the closed and locked door. "Blue, I'm late. Get your ass out of bed."

"Have mercy, devil-woman," she yelled back, making her way to the door. Her friend stood on the other side of the door in a soft, creamy ivory turtleneck and black slacks: her college professor uniform. Her black hair was pulled back into a bun at the nape of her neck and tiny diamond stud earrings glimmered in her earlobes. "You look absolutely lovely this morning."

"Oh. Thanks." Devon brought her hands up to her neck and smiled, caught off guard by the compliment from the person she had just roused from a deep sleep.

"Now why in the actual fuck did you wake me up this early?" Blue turned to find her robe and slippers since she was standing there in a tee shirt and underwear.

"There's my sunshine." Greenlee laughed. He stood behind Devon in the doorway, hand resting on the doorjamb. He winked. He was already dressed in clothing that had not come from the dirty clothes hamper, unusual for this time of day. Greenlee was a true slob and didn't put on clean clothes until he had to leave the house. And he never left the house before lunch. Ever. The athletic shirt and shorts that he wore today weren't wrinkled, and she could smell the fresh scent of his laundry detergent from where she stood. Everyone was off schedule today.

"I hate you both," she grunted. "Fucking morning people. This is bullshit."

"Hey, Tia Blue!" Lexi ran by in the hallway, a backpack dangling off of one shoulder. "I'm going to ace that quiz." Blue heard her little feet stomping down the stairs.

"Yeah, you are!" Blue called as she returned to the door. "Love you, smart girl!"

"Love you too, Tia Blue!"

Blue crossed her arms and leaned against the doorjamb, putting them all in very close proximity. "I'm waiting. You monsters."

Devon smiled, amused by Blue's grumpiness. "I should have told you last night, but I forgot. I had to move my office hours to this morning. So, I have to leave early. Then, I've got lecture all day, so I didn't want to miss you. Marilee," she referred to her teaching assistant, "has an early class and her car is still broken, so Greenlee is going to help her get it dropped off at the mechanic and get her to class. I'm going to bring her home. But I'll be late. Lexi is riding the bus here after school and Sophia's dad is picking her up and taking her to soccer practice and they are having a sleepover, so you don't have to pick up or drop off. Her soccer and overnight bag are already by the door." Devon spewed in rapid-fire staccato while she ticked off items on her hand.

"Okay. Okay." Blue nodded and rubbed her eyes. "I knew about the sleepover. Thanks for letting me know about soccer practice." Between seeing Rhodes and staying up half the night, dodging Devon's questions about Rhodes, her eyes were puffy and irritated. She needed a mainline of caffeine. Right. Now.

"There is a trail out by the school I've been wanting to check out. I'm going to run after I get Marilee taken care of. Hope they get her fixed today. I don't like these early morning drives." Greenlee added. "You will probably be gone by the time I get home." He was nodding his head vigorously behind Devon's back. It was more of a strong suggestion than a statement of fact. But if Greenlee wanted a night with just him and Devon in the house, she would absolutely help him out with that. It took everything Blue had not to smile at him, so she settled on scowling.

"Sounds good. Let me know if I can help with Marilee. I remember being broke and having car trouble." Blue raised a finger. "Except early morning drop-offs. Anything after noon I will help with."

"Finn's stopping by for brunch. Don't forget." Devon wiggled her dark eyebrows at Blue, turning to follow her daughter down the stairs. She patted Greenlee's arm as she went.

"Finn?" Greenlee asked.

"Not you too, Green," Blue muttered in exasperation. "She's looking for a warm body at this point."

"He is a very warm body. You do you. I have no dog in the fight as long as I don't find you cryin' after spending time with him." He paused for a moment, letting his words hang between them.

"I wasn't crying," Blue told him. Those were his first comments ever about Rhodes. She was stunned and touched. She grabbed his shirt and pulled his face to within an inch of hers, forcing him to lean over a great deal. "I am the first to know how she answers. Don't fuck this up," she hissed in his face, shaking him slightly with the hand fisted in his shirt. "Do you understand me?"

The smile that spread across his face was enough to take some of the edge off her foul mood. "You know it, darlin'."

"Excellent." She let his shirt go and watched him smooth the wrinkles out. "Coffee me."

"I'll avocado toast you. It ain't healthy not eatin' until after Happy Hour. Coffee is not a food group." He waved his hand in front of him in a motion for her to proceed.

"Never mind." Blue shook her head in exasperation. "Torrin is bringing brunch later. I'm going back to bed. See you tomorrow."

"Tomorrow, sunshine. Sweet dreams." He shut the door as he left.

Blue flopped backward on top of her covers with her fuzzy slippers hanging over the edge of the bed and fell asleep immediately.

A text from Finn woke her a few hours later, asking what she wanted from a brunch hotspot down the street. She sent him a quick text back, warning him she hadn't had coffee and therefore could not make decisions about food, then jumped in the shower.

Piling her wet hair on top of her head in a disastrous bun, she walked downstairs in time to hear his knock at the back door. She found him standing on the back porch holding three huge bags of food. "Wow, Torrin. Who else did you invite?" Blue took one of the bags from him and held the door open so that he could bring the food he still carried inside.

"Just me and you. You forget. I've seen you eat. You take out more food than my guys combined. No coffee, but there is a gallon of mimosa in this bag." He lifted his left arm indicating the bag with the mimosas. His aviator sunglasses were still perched on his nose. "You didn't tell me what you wanted, so I bought a little of everything."

"Let me see. It smells divine." Blue peered into the bags, holding five containers each. Finn removed his sunglasses. The bags under his eyes showed he had slept about as well as she had. She stepped back. "Rough night?"

He nodded and rubbed a hand across the back of his neck. "Up coordinating with Hale and Tanner about our missing persons. There is something off about it."

"You sit. I'll get coffee. We could have done this another time." Blue turned toward the coffeemaker to find a full pot still warming. An index card reading This is not a food group! sat in front of the coffee maker. She smiled at Greenlee's antics, pulled two mugs down, and filled them both. Finn drank his coffee black, so she left hers that way as well. Devon only allowed gourmet coffee in her kitchen, so it was good either way. She placed his mug in front of him at the kitchen island. "Here."

"I owe you, Blue. Least I can do is feed you when I'm in town." Finn took a sip of his coffee.

"You don't owe me anything." She dug through the bags, opening containers as she removed them. "Oh. Stuffed French toast. This one is mine."

"You saved our asses," Finn corrected, popping open containers to find the container of bacon.

"It's what friends do. How is Hale?" Blue reached into his container and snagged a piece of bacon.

Finn snorted and voluntarily handed her another piece. "Everyone needs more friends like you then." He was quiet for a moment. "Hale is fine. This is his first job back. It was good working with him last night." Finn wasn't in mission mode this morning. She could tell he had more to say. Blue waited, tearing into the French toast.

"The surgeon said if we had been five minutes later, there wouldn't have been anything he could do. They had to give him five units of blood." She knew that already. She had been in the waiting room. She also knew how much magic she had hit him with to even give the surgeon something to work with. She was also fresh out of emotional capacity this week.

They hadn't spoken about the incident since she dropped him and his team at a hospital in Texas. Which was fine; there wasn't anything to talk about. She stayed at the hospital with them just long enough to make sure that Hale was stable and the team had caffeine, clean shirts, and four family-sized meals from KFC. Granted, just long enough equaled eight hours. But that was her thing. She kept people safe. She kept people cared for. It didn't warrant discussion.

"How is your arm? Your back?" he asked about the injuries she received getting Hale out. The rubble had protected him from the fire. It hadn't protected her. She didn't realize he had seen her burns. She tried to hide them.

"Just a scratch." She smiled, holding out her unblemished arm for him to see. "Looked worse than it was." It had actually hurt like hell and felt as bad as it looked. But by the time she woke up the next morning, it had healed enough to be manageable.

The man across from her frowned and held her gaze, but he didn't ask questions. "I called you into a nightmare without warning. You were hurt. That wasn't part of our deal. I need to apologize."

"Finn. Don't."

"It won't happen again, Blue. I won't ask something like that of you ever again." He shook his head. He was wrong about all of this. She had received a garbled message from one of his men that equated to 911 Med Evac Finn. Messages like that never originated from a safe place. She hadn't even grabbed her gear. She had thrown on some tennis shoes and skipped straight to him. Of course, he had been standing in a burning building, surrounded by gunfire, and she had immediately been clobbered by a flaming chunk of concrete and shredded with a piece of rebar. That was beside the point.

"Bullshit. Don't you ever spout bullshit like that again at me, Finn Torrin." She slammed her fork onto the counter for dramatic effect. He looked confused and surprised. "Do you think I would have wanted you all to burn to death in that building trying to get to Hale? Get riddled with bullets? Willingham has kids! Would you have rather left Hale to die than call me for help?"

"No. Blue." Finn placed his hands over his face and scrubbed his eyes. "Stop." He was very tired. Tough. So was she.

"You or any of your men ever need me. You call me in. I'm not a delicate flower and that building wasn't the worst thing I have seen. Don't you hesitate if I can keep them safe and alive another day. I can get to them all now. Not just you." Blue placed a hand on his arm. "Finn. It is an honor." When he still didn't look at her, she shook his arm. "Do you know what it means to me that you called me? That you all trusted me with Hale's life?"

"I trust you with Devon and Lexi every day. The most important people in my world," Finn told her quietly. "If you hadn't come back to them and it was my fault." He shook his head again. "Devon can't go through that again."

"I have it on good authority that I will not die in a flaming office building saving a man who belches the alphabet backward as his pickup line. The parameters of my death are very specific, and those aren't among them." She clapped her hands together loudly. "Enough of this touchy-feely emotional baggage garbage."

Finn seemed stunned. "You are serious? How would you know the parameters of your death?" Blue just smiled. She knew because Zella told her while they stood next to each other washing their hands in the ladies bathroom at Cahlad Prime. According to the most accurate oracle in the Cahlad's history, she would sacrifice herself for a soul mate when dragons descend from the sky. Soul mates and dragons were both mythical creatures, so she operated on the assumption that she was unfortunately immortal.

"Get your bacon. We are going outside and handling things the right way so that I can enjoy my food without feelings." Blue stood, taking her container of French toast and his bacon.

"Are you going to kick my ass? Handle this like men?" Finn joked, shifting his voice down a notch as he stood pantomiming a boxer. He grabbed the jug of mimosas and his coffee. She didn't miss the tone of voice. He really didn't think she could kick his ass. Cute. But at least they were back on familiar ground.

"I could. But no." She continued through the door. "We are going to eat. Drink mimosas until we wobble. I'm going to get you a blanket and tuck you in. Then we are going to take a nap on the awesome loungers Devon spent ridiculous amounts of money on last month. You are going to wake up refreshed and less emotionally compromised."

"You want to take a nap? That is how we handle this?" Finn laughed, but continued to follow. "I'm in. A nap sounds good. You keep the mimosas."

"Why, thank you. Such a gentleman. I won't let them go to waste." Blue sat the containers down between the two lounge chairs on the covered back porch of the large old house. The backyard was ringed with an eight-foot-tall privacy fence and shaded by a large maple tree. She retrieved a blanket from the deck box and motioned for Finn to sit in the lounge chair. He sat and stretched out. She draped the blanket across his lap. She retrieved the box of bacon and sat that in his lap, tapping it on the top with her finger. "Eat your bacon and let's get some sleep."

"Yes, ma'am." He smirked as he toed off his shoes and opened the box. "Next time. I promise more fruity drinks and that I will be better company. Maybe even an actual beach."

"Oh no. This is fabulous." She waved at a table sitting in the yard with an umbrella sticking up through the center. "Fruity drinks with an umbrella." Blue settled herself in with her own blanket and poured a mimosa. She took a sip that turned into half the glass. Finn devoured the bacon silently.

"This is the best date I have been on in a very long time." Finn laughed. "How are you still single?"

"Date? I thought this was a food offering born of misplaced guilt." Blue reopened her French toast again.

"Devon has texted me twice already, asking how the date is going." Finn pulled up his phone and showed Blue the text messages.

My Psycho Sister: How's the Date?

Me: What Date?

My Psycho Sister: Ha. Ha. It involves drinks with a beautiful single lady. Definition of a date.

Me: It's not a date.

My Psycho Sister: Denial. It must be going well.

"Oh boy. That woman. Is she constantly trying to set you up with anyone with a pulse too?" Blue sipped more mimosa, reading the rest of the text thread. He nodded irritably.

"She doesn't know about Gabby?" Blue asked about the woman Finn had been seeing for a few months. He thought he was keeping a low profile. The Herne guys had a pool on when he would go all in or down in flames. She had fifty dollars on Finn falling head over heels and admitting it by the end of the year. She handed his phone back

He took it and raised an eyebrow but didn't seem surprised that she knew about Gabby. "Not ready to bring her home to the family."

She sent a mischievous grin in Finn's direction. "Just think. Now we can truthfully tell Devon that we slept together."

His face pinched slightly, then he burst out into a deep rumble of laughter. "You have to wait to tell her so that I can see."

"No promises."

"Maybe I should text her that little detail now."

"Not if you want to get any actual sleep," Blue warned. "But you definitely should as soon as we wake up."

Finn relaxed back onto the lounger and closed his eyes as he discarded the empty bacon tub between the chairs. "We should do this more often."

Blue drained the rest of her mimosa, leaned back, and closed her eyes. "You know how to find me."

14

SAM

"There is a lot going on in your head," Nisha said as she waltzed into his closed office uninvited and shut the door softly behind her. She sat in the chair across from Sam's desk. "And yes, it does look like kid furniture."

Sam frowned. Among the many thoughts that had just crossed his mind was the fact that his desk felt like children's furniture when he folded his six-foot-seven-inch frame behind it.

Nisha turned sideways and threw her legs over the arm of the chair. She sipped on the mug of coffee in her hands, the broken bones from yesterday apparently giving her no trouble. They had all been at the hospital or in meetings since the incident in the park. Political rhetoric was escalating, and the investigation into the surges was ramping up. There had been little sleep for anyone.

Mitch was only now being released from the hospital; the doctors were more reluctant to release the Paragon of the Cahlad without an extensive battery of tests. Zella was still with him. He felt sorry for her. Mitch was in a mood.

"Glad I can amuse you." Sam tried to relax into his tiny chair. Shirley, the administrative assistant in charge of all things at the Cahlad Prime campus, hated him for some reason and always managed to forget to order the specialty chair that had been in the budget for three years now. Sam was known for having a bit of a temper, and short of Nisha, that woman was the only one brave enough to test him on purpose. It seemed to be a mission for her at this point.

"Mmm hmm." Nisha sipped her coffee. Her dark brown eyes wandered innocently around the room as she swung her legs. Her long, straight, black hair hung behind her and swayed opposite the kicking of her legs. She could have been a Bollywood star in a different life, Sam noted, as she wiggled so much she almost fell out of the chair. Maybe a star in those clumsy rom-com movies where the heroine was a hot mess. Nisha caught herself before hitting the floor, holding her coffee high, and scooted back into the seat. "Might help if you talk about it."

"Talk about what?" he asked, rubbing his hand down his jaw. His five o'clock shadow was turning into an actual beard. Some days, he had to shave twice to keep his face from looking like a small woodland animal was resting on his chin. He hadn't shaved since yesterday morning, and it was already starting to bother him. Everything was bothering him.

"Really?" she asked as she took another sip of her coffee and tilted her head. If Nisha hadn't been lying unconscious and bleeding in a heap yesterday, he doubted he would be able to find the restraint to keep from snapping at her.

"You aren't supposed to be in my head, Nisha." She really didn't need to be in his head today, of all days. He was struggling not to utter words that would compel her to leave. Quickly.

"I can't not be in your head, Sam. Your head is screaming so loud I can hear you a mile away." Nisha took another sip of her coffee. "Please. Put me out of my misery and tell me about this red thumb drive so that I can have some quiet. And rom-coms? I'm an action movie star all the way."

Nisha faced the same problems he did. Distrust even among powerful Sovaj and magic users. Their gifts set them apart and made others distrustful and fearful. Very few people wanted to be near someone who could read their every thought or force them to do anything with a single word. It was the foundation of their friendship—being outsiders, even in a group of outsiders.

She stuck her tongue out at him.

She had taken a risk coming here. She had no way of knowing how he would react. And she was fully aware of his temper and his struggle to contain his magic when he was stressed. If he could read her mind, he was certain he would find fear, or at least trepidation. For that, he was ashamed. But she was here, offering to help. Because she was one of the bravest people he knew. To a fault. He still didn't like the fact that she knew about the USB. Not only because he wasn't sure what to do about it. But also because he suspected it might put her in danger. "I don't know who to trust right now."

Nisha frowned. And he didn't need to be a telepath to understand that she had taken his last statement personally. She swung her legs back around and looked straight at him. "You can trust your team, Sam."

She was right. He knew he could trust his team. "Do you need to see the files on the drive? Or have you already seen the files?" He needed to know exactly what his mind was screaming a mile away.

"I don't need to see it," she confirmed, and waited. It was a skill she had honed over the years, knowing what a person was thinking and waiting patiently without comment while they worked out a solution in their head. So, she knew the contents of the drive. And every scenario and suspicion that had floated through his overactive, exhausted, and telepathically screaming mind. She knew, and instead of running to Mitch, she came to him. He relaxed even though he hadn't even realized he was that tense. She smiled knowingly. "I'm on your team, Sam. Always will be."

"Until next week," he grumbled.

Nisha just shrugged.

"Have you ever picked up anything about this from Mitch?" Sam asked. He hesitated a moment because he didn't want to ask. "Or Zella?"

"I can't read, Zella," Nisha stated. "Nothing about project Zenith from Mitch. Just random thoughts about adopting Amber. Dad thoughts. Toward all of us, actually."

Sam frowned. That was strange. How could Mitch be surrounded daily by at least two of his little science experiments and never think of the way they came to be there? His brow creased. It didn't make sense.

"You are right. It doesn't make sense," Nisha agreed with his thoughts, and he frowned more deeply. She stood and placed her hand on her hips in warning. "You are still shouting."

Sam sighed. "Sorry. It's just... never mind."

"While you and Ivan met with the one who smelled like a sweaty gym bag, I strolled down to the archive room and dug around in the stacks to see if I could find something we missed in the digital data conversion." Nisha paced. As a member of Stalker Prime, they often conducted sensitive research on individuals and artifacts. Nisha was the best of all of them, driven primarily by her preference to avoid confrontation and violence. Information was one of the most effective tools in her arsenal. She threw her hands up in an exaggerated show of disgust. "Nothing. Bubkus."

It was likely she would knock a picture off the wall as she talked. Or at minimum bust her knuckle when she accidentally hit it against the edge of a piece of furniture. He could no longer count how many times both of those things had happened. The photo on the wall next to the door sported a cracked frame he had not had the time to fix, courtesy of Nisha. Of course, Shirley refused to get a replacement frame.

"Nothing on anything called the Son Sovaj." Nisha held up a finger. "Nothing on any of the parents' names in that file." She held up another finger. "Nothing on the facility. I even rooted around in the archivist thoughts. He wasn't hiding anything other than a shoe fetish. It's like someone purposefully wiped every trace of this thing off the planet." Two more fingers popped up.

"You have been busy." Sam finally gave in and stood. He was impressed with the initiative.

"What is interesting," Nisha ticked off the last finger on her right hand while somehow holding her coffee in the other, "is there are no files printed on red paper in the archive. Not even in the restricted section. And all the archive files have the DDC sticker on the top. Yours don't." She stopped in front of his desk and turned to face him. He was mildly amazed nothing had fallen off the walls and there wasn't coffee splattered all over his office. "That tells me the files on that drive didn't come from the archives."

He leaned over and placed both hands on his desk so that they were almost eye to eye. "So, where did they come from?"

"Someone close to the source," Nisha finished.

Sam nodded. Wherever that file had come from, it held enough truth to concern him. The pages on him were accurate enough to make him believe the file was legitimate. Or someone had gone to a great amount of trouble to make it seem legitimate.

"Feel better?" Nisha asked, bringing her coffee to her lips and missing. Sam smiled at not only her statement but the spill. That was classic Nisha. A dribble of coffee fell onto her shirt. She cursed as she wiped it away. "This is why I wear black."

Just as Sam opened his mouth to tell her that yes, he did feel better now, a knock on the door interrupted him. What fresh hell wanted in his office now? "It is unlocked."

The door opened, and Ivan's gigantic frame moved through. He held three coffee cups in a drink carrier. He had changed into a sweatshirt and cargo pants at some point during the day. "Figured you needed this." He walked in and shut the door behind him. Sam's door was rarely closed. He only closed it when he was on the verge of telling someone to go jump off a bridge. Few people would be brave enough to knock on it when it was closed for just that reason. But Ivan could jump off a bridge and be just fine. Nisha not so much, which made him appreciate her earlier bravado that much more. He loved this team.

"Thanks, man." Nisha reached for a cup, and Ivan swatted her hand away.

"You sit. I brought extra napkins," he told her, sitting the drinks on Sam's desk. Nisha huffed but did as he asked. He handed her a fresh cup of coffee and a handful of napkins. Sam didn't think she needed more caffeine. If she became any more jittery and spastic, she would become a danger to herself and others.

"You want to tell me why the door was closed? Or do you want to know why I'm here?" Ivan sat in the chair next to Nisha. He left Sam's coffee on the desk in the carrier. There were no napkins left.

"By all means. Tell us why you are here." Sam reached over and snagged his coffee, then settled back into his kid chair.

"My FBI contact is hearing chatter about a group that looks a lot like the goon squad that showed up at the piano bar and the park. They are somewhere near Five Points as we speak." Ivan informed them.

"How fresh is this?" Nisha wondered. "I didn't know you had a contact at the FBI."

"My contact is a tap on his phone. I listened in while I was in line for coffee." Ivan grunted.

"Nice." Nisha nodded.

"We need to move fast and quiet on this," Ivan shared his opinion. His features were even darker than normal. He hadn't slept at all, running back and forth between the hospital and the campus all night. A swath of black stubble decorated his deep brown skin. He looked like a kid in Sam's office chairs as well. Where Sam was too tall, Ivan was just too wide and dense.

Sam looked at Nisha.

"Let's do it. Full quiet. Need to know is in this room. Meet you in the lot in fifteen." She repeated his instructions verbatim. That way, if Ivan had a strong objection, a compulsion wouldn't keep him quiet.

"The door?" Ivan inclined his head backward, indicating the closed door behind him. He looked between Sam and Nisha, a question in his brown eyes.

"Take a look at this when you have a chance." Sam handed over the USB drive, then retrieved a jacket and bag that he still kept under his desk containing his gear.

"Buckle up, Ivan. That's good stuff." Nisha stood to leave. As she turned toward the door, she bumped into the edge of Sam's desk, knocking a cup holding pens over. He managed to snag his coffee before it became collateral damage. She just mouthed oops over her shoulder and continued on her way out.

"In fifteen." Ivan nodded, glancing at the toppled pens and following Nisha out. Sam blew out a breath. He was sending high-level Cahlad resources on an unauthorized operation without the Paragon's knowledge. Just like the last Regent. Only difference was, this Regent was knee-deep in his own dirty work.

He was on a slippery slope right now. And he wasn't sure he would be able to stop the slide.

15

BLUE

Someone was shaking her. Why wouldn't the world just let her sleep? It was warm and cool at the same time. She was comfortable. Blue pulled the blanket over her head and scrunched into a ball. "Go away."

Whoever it was didn't stop shaking her shoulder gently. "Blue. We have something on our missing persons." Another shake.

"Fine!" She sighed and slung the blanket off, in the process hurtling it into Finn's face and over his head. "I'm up."

"Hello, angel." Hale's voice rolled from the speaker of Finn's phone.

"Not an angel, Hale." Blue scrubbed the grit out of her eyes and snatched the blanket back. It was chilly out here, even in the sun. She wrapped it around her shoulders and glared at the world in general. If Hale had any idea who she was or what she had done before he met her, he certainly wouldn't use the word angel to describe her now.

Finn pinned her with an irritated look and tried to smooth his hair back into place. He was not successful. He sat the phone down on the lounger next to him and put on his shoes. He looked rumpled and grumpy, too. He must have been sound asleep when Hale called.

"You are my angel," Hale corrected her. "I have eyes on our targets. They are in a new café in Five Points. We are in position for retrieval in an empty storefront across the street. We have potential hostiles on scene. We need to evac the targets before we have to engage."

The fog immediately lifted. "I can be there in less than ten," Blue answered as both she and Finn stood and sprinted toward the house.

"I'll have more details when you get here. Expedience is appreciated."

"Understood." Blue yanked the back door open and took off at a sprint up the stairs to grab the gear she kept stowed and ready to go. It would take her no time to get suited up and skip to Hale's location. An hour in traffic or thirty seconds with magic Uber. Finn sprinted after her with the phone in his hand. "She is on her way, Hale. Hold tight and report any changes."

"Got it," Hale responded, then the line went dead.

She changed into her work clothes, consisting of a pair of black cargo pants, a black tee shirt, and a black jacket with hidden pockets filled with various goodies. She shrugged into her shoulder holster before putting on the jacket. She strapped a knife to her waist and another in her boot.

"Can you take me?" he asked, standing at the top of the stairs. He was familiar with her abilities, but he didn't have a firm grasp on her limits.

"I can take you." She finished lacing her boots and glancing out of her open door. "Just one person one way isn't a big deal. Do you have everything you need?"

Finn looked relieved. "Let me get my bag out of the car." He turned quickly and went downstairs.

"Meet you in the kitchen." Blue moved through the house, locking up and setting the alarm.

Finn held a black duffel bag when she entered the kitchen. He wore his jacket, so she knew his weapon was holstered.

"Have everything?" she asked, rounding the counter and extending her hand.

He nodded. "I do." He wrapped his fingers around her wrist in a grip just this side of painful. Skipping wasn't an activity Finn enjoyed. He wasn't a natural. It made him nervous. And sick.

"Hold on tight," Blue instructed as she reached up with her free hand and grabbed the back of his neck in a grip just as tight as the one he had on her wrist. She focused on Hale and felt a strong tug that churned her stomach. She gripped Finn tighter, just to make sure they weren't battered apart during the skip, and let the plasma rainbow fall across her vision and the cold seep across her skin and down to her bones. Then they were hurtling across the electric trampoline. Ozone filled her nostrils. Finn cursed.

The world grew still so fast that she fought for balance but managed to land on her feet. She felt Finn stumbling to the side. He bounced off a wall, and she used her body weight to counter his tumble and keep him upright. He retched. Still gripping the back of his neck, she turned his head away from her.

The hairs on the back of her neck stood on end, and she instinctively pushed Finn toward the ground, forcing him into a crouch. He was too busy vomiting breakfast to put up much resistance. She looked around quickly, listening to the contents of Finn's stomach make a resounding splat on the floor. The smell of bile and bacon filled her nostrils, mixed with something else. The room they were in was dim, a sparse warehouse space with a polished concrete floor. It was unnaturally quiet. Too quiet for a room that should be filled with large, loud, boisterous men. Not even the air conditioning or heat unit ran. She positioned her body between Finn and the rest of the room to provide cover while he recovered.

Blue swiveled her head, taking in her surroundings and drawing her weapon. There were no immediate threats to her right because it was a wall. They landed in a corner by a deeply tinted window. Nothing actively concerning on the immediate left. Dead ahead was the short hallway, with two doors on either side. Probably a closet and a bathroom. Lumps shaped like bodies lay scattered across the floor. Counting on the wall he had just bounced off to protect Finn's other side, she started moving forward.

"Hale?" she hissed, and then held her breath to keep from inhaling whatever the other scent was. It smelled familiar. She advanced on a large man-sized lump laying directly in front of her. Eyes still adjusting to the darkness, she kept her weapon raised and reached down to feel for a pulse. It was strong. But this person was out cold. She couldn't get a good look at his face, but thought this was Caesar, the team's medic.

"Finn. Get it together. Something isn't right," she hissed and continued sweeping the room for threats, stopping to check three more downed men. She heard Finn pull his weapon behind her, breath ragged.

She checked on door one. Bathroom. Clear. She opened the other door. Office. She circled the desk and checked any potential hiding spots. Empty. "Clear," she announced. A few seconds later, she heard Finn declare the rest of the warehouse clear.

"Hale? Fucking hell. I can't let you go anywhere," Finn said as he crouched next to a large lump under the floor-to-ceiling tinted windows. "What happened?" The unmoving lump on the floor at his feet did not answer.

While Finn checked on his men, Blue walked to the window. For Lease was written in paint in letters taller than she was. The building had a perfect view of one of the most popular corners in Five Points. She scanned up and down the street and sucked in a breath.

"Blue?" Finn glanced up when he heard her gasp as he continued to crouch over Hale. He held a pack of smelling salts from Caesar's medical kit.

"You got this?" she asked Finn as she turned into the room. "I need to get to the targets."

"Stand down, Blue," Finn ordered. "We need to figure out what is going on. This changes things." Hale coughed as Finn cracked the salts and waved them beneath his nose.

"I'll contact you when they are secure." She ignored him. She peered back out the window. There was no way she was standing down today. She could hear Finn standing and his footsteps starting toward her.

"Damn it, Blue," he barked, moving faster. "You don't know what they look like."

"What in the hell?" Hale croaked from his spot on the floor.

She glanced back just in time to lock eyes with Finn as he reached out to grab her. She mouthed sorry, pulling her arms into her body, and fell backward into the cold plasma rainbow just before he reached her. Because across the street from this empty storefront was a cute little café with a Grand Opening sign tied to its awning. Its name was the Cat and Canary.

It was time to do what she did. Whatever that was.

16

FINN

F inn sprinted through the alley onto Woodland Avenue, a trendy street filled with bars, restaurants, and shops. He knew trying to catch Blue was a futile effort. It took him precious minutes to make sure his team was OK while Caesar filled him in on what had happened.

He said someone tossed a small metal object spewing green gas in through the back door. In less than thirty seconds, the entire team fell where they stood. No coughing. No choking. Instant knockout gas. Willingham had been out back on watch. They found him also unconscious and laying on top of a small metal object. Finn had never heard of anything that powerful before. Whoever was using this gas was dangerous. And they knew exactly where to find his team.

They all suffered from debilitating hangover symptoms, so he gave the order to leave. His men were filing out of the back of the building and driving back to their offices. They needed to assess and regroup in a safe environment. Finn's priority was to keep his team alive. Everything else came second. Which is why he was furious that Blue had skipped out of the room as soon as she figured out everyone was mostly OK. This was one of his jobs, and she was currently his team. Which meant his priority was to keep her alive as well.

Slowing for pre-rush hour traffic and dinner crowd pedestrians soured his mood further. Something out here caught Blue's eye. She was close. But where?

He looked up and down the street. A café across the way filled. It was the last known position of the targets his team was trailing. It was a Friday afternoon, and there were already people everywhere. A florist van and an electric car were parallel parked, obscuring his view of part of the street.

Exasperated, he stood for a moment wondering if he should even bother chasing Blue and the targets or double back and make sure his men got back home. They were tough. They were also smart. He knew they would be fine.

Settling on at least checking on the café to put eyes on the targets, he moved to the crosswalk, passing the florist van on the way. The van's placement seemed curious for a Friday night. If it sat here much longer, it would be towed. There was no street parking after six—the opposite of normal. He let his gaze linger. He didn't see anything unusual, but something told him to pay closer attention. He heard the buzz and hiss of an acetylene torch and stepped closer. Another step and he saw a small spark flicker to life on the side of the van. The metal gave a high-pitched ping as its temperature changed.

The hissing sound grew louder as sparks formed, drawing a molten oval on the white panel painted with oversized flowers. Finn stepped away from the sparks and placed his back against the front quarter panel to observe while keeping most of the street in his field of view. Moments later, the oval encircling an orange rosebud was complete, and two soft thuds reached his ears. A chunk of the van clattered to the ground. An enormous set of feet in neon pink running shoes emerged from the opening. The feet belonged to a man Finn knew very well.

"Greenlee?" Finn asked in a low voice, trying not to draw any attention to the scene.

Greenlee's head swiveled toward Finn in surprise. His hand was circled by a broken set of zip ties and held one of the bar earrings he wore daily. The thing spewed a jet of magma directly at him. Finn danced to the side just before the molten stuff landed on him. The metal of the van where he was standing melted and slagged.

"Finn? What the fuck?" Greenlee sputtered, obviously flustered.

"Shit. I'm sorry." The molten jet stopped at once. "Christ. I thought I was going to have to deal with them again." His shoulders slumped, and he put an arm against the van to steady himself.

"What is going on? Are you OK?" Finn asked, moving toward him to assess the situation. He had just welded his way out of a van with an earring. It was obvious someone had beaten the hell out of him. His nose was swollen, his right eye black, and lower lip busted open. The skin on his knuckles bled. He was in a fight recently. Finn had a lot of questions. And a sudden urge to get off this street.

160

Greenlee rubbed his wrist and eyed the sky. "What time is it? How long was I out? That gas did a number on me."

"What gas?"

"Green gas. I couldn't use my magic." His face was grim and dark.

"Shit." They were too exposed out here.

"There were four of them, man. They were waiting for me at the running trail." He rubbed a knot on the back of his head. "One of them hit me with something hard."

Greenlee swayed on his feet. The man was not OK and needed medical attention. Finn nodded. Four on one were never good odds. "Come on, man," Finn instructed as he threw Greenlee's arm over his own and shouldered his weight. "I'm going to get you out of here. Got to get you back to Dev in one piece. Then we will figure out what is going on."

"Blue told you?" Greenlee asked, leaning heavily on Finn as they plodded down the street.

"She didn't have to," Finn told him, shouldering more of his weight. "But she owes me a hundred bucks."

"How did the date go?" Greenlee grumbled, still swaying.

Finn just smiled and shook his head. Now wasn't the time to stir up trouble. "I'll let Blue tell you."

17

BLUE

B lue landed on her feet behind a large green dumpster in an alleyway across the street from the empty storefront, just down the block from the Cat and the Canary. Thankfully, it was empty or full of non-perishable items, and it didn't stink too badly. The early Nashville evening was crisp, and an almost chilly breeze swept down the street and between the buildings. Blue rubbed her hands together to warm her fingers. Two jumps in rapid succession had drained her body heat. She hoped Finn had enough sense not to follow her. Whatever was happening right now had trouble written all over it.

She composed herself and took in her surroundings, using the dumpster as cover to check the roof line that she could see on the other side of the street. Someone was here and knew enough to take out the Herne team.

She strolled toward the street, alert and ready. She moved casually toward the café. A few pedestrians wandered, window shopping in some of the small boutique shops that lined the street. A florist delivery van sat across the street from the Cat and the Canary. She didn't see a florist shop nearby, so the driver was probably getting dinner.

The café patio was crowded with dinner patrons. The tables fit tightly on the paved brick space and were sheltered by brightly colored umbrellas lit with strings of Christmas lights. The chairs were a mismatched collection of thrift shop dining furniture. Blue approached cautiously. Voices floated along the street, indistinguishable from one another. A chalkboard on the sidewalk in front of the door declared, "Best Biscuits in Nashville!"

She stepped inside. The ceiling was low, making the room feel small. The short line of people waiting to order made the space seem even more claustrophobic despite the bright colors and kitschy decor. She waited her turn, observing the room in detail while pretending to scrutinize the various paintings and metal sculptures that adorned the walls. Nothing seemed out of place so far. She had to wonder what Amber meant by 'do what you do.' She knew the message was from Amber. She was the only other person Blue ever knew that could move between locations instantaneously. Did she mean assassinate someone? Wreak havoc? Steal something? Disappoint people? Lie? Serve as a glorified delivery person? Maybe be a magical Uber? Maybe she meant watch bad science fiction television series while drinking a growler of margaritas and wallowing in self-loathing. That last one was too specific, but she was an absolute ace at all of them.

The timing bothered her. She had only received the message via Rhodes last night. And now here she was.

She reached the front of the line and ordered a plain biscuit, sweet potato fries, and a lemonade. Her food was ready before she was finished paying, so she grabbed her lime green tray and wandered out to the patio. There weren't very many empty tables, and there was a special place in hell for a single person who took up an entire four top. A small bar with stools adorned the brick side of the building to her right. Blue headed that way, dodging diners and a few dogs lounging next to their humans. She almost dropped her tray. At a small table wedged in beside a post wrapped in Christmas lights sat a ghost.

Blue hissed out loud. The girl had blonde, slightly wavy hair, brown eyes, and freckles. She was all arms and legs and smiled at the man next to her with an expression very familiar to Blue. The teenager was Amber's in some way. Possibly a clone. The resemblance was so strong. Her mind screamed daughter, but the math didn't work. The girl was in her late teens, which would have made Amber a young teenage mother. That wasn't a possibility. Blue had seen Amber every day between second grade and when Amber left for college. Sister maybe? Probably. Amber was adopted. Mitch and Zella had never told her about her biological parents. A sister could make sense. Maybe Amber had found her and sent Blue. But to do what, exactly? Surely it wasn't to kill her.

Blue changed course and walked toward the table. Fate, destiny, or diabolical manipulation had brought her here. Might as well see it through. Walking toward the table, she swapped her focus to the man sitting in the chair across from Amber's younger twin. He was a handsome black man with broad shoulders dressed in business casual clothing that screamed money. The shirt he wore likely cost more than everything on her body, including her weapon. A blue and yellow Nashville Predators hat was pulled low over his eyes. He was hiding. Her gut told her these were the targets. And Hale said the goon squad was nearby. She needed to get them out of here.

As she approached, she caught the man's eye. She smiled even as his expression turned suspicious, and he shifted in his seat. "I hate to take up a whole table just for me. Would you mind if I joined you?"

He glanced pointedly around the patio at the number of tables with open seats she walked right by. She didn't give him an opportunity to answer. "Is it really the best biscuit in Nashville? That's quite the claim." She sat her tray down on the table between their plates, noticing that Mini-Me's dish sported the meager remnants of a savory spinach biscuit. Mini-Me's attention turned toward Blue, and she froze. She looked at the man sitting next to her with a question in her eyes. She was ready to bolt. These two were on edge. That couldn't be good. Who was chasing them? And why?

She took a moment to smile at both of them and spread her napkin across her lap. "Thanks again for letting me sit with you." She took a huge bite of biscuit she didn't really want. Oh hell. This was the best biscuit in Nashville.

"Boom Kitty!" she muttered.

"What did you say?" Mini-Me asked her, no longer preparing to run.

"It is... the best biscuit in Nashville," Blue repeated.

"Ma'am," the man to her left began to speak and was quickly cut off.

"No. Not that. You said Boom Kitty." The girl waved a hand. Her tone held an accusation. She turned to the man. "Dad. Mom used to say that. She told us her best friend used to say it when something went right. It was their inside joke."

He was quiet for a moment, regarding them both with sharp eyes. "That she did, sweetheart." He seemed to make a decision at that moment, but he didn't look happy about it. He threw one arm over the back of the chair he sat in and stuck out his other hand. "Ben."

Blue took his hand and shook. "Blue. And this is?" She nodded toward the girl on her right.

"My daughter, Ava," he spoke, a calculating look falling over his face. He was silent again. Blue decided to follow his lead and dug into her food while he determined how this interaction was going to play out. Her back was turned to half the patio, and she didn't like it. She adjusted in her seat to sit sideways like Ben.

"Dad," Ava prompted again.

He watched the rest of the café with sharp eyes. She wondered if he had a clue what he was looking for. "Why are you here, Blue?" he finally asked. He was still suspicious. Good for him. He should be.

How did she answer that question? *My ex-fiancé and co-assassin, who is now a Top 40 music star, gave me a napkin from this café.*

He got it from a woman everyone thought was dead who appeared miraculously in a locked room while he was naked as a jaybird in the shower. But she shouldn't have known it was him or that I'm me because he transformed both of us into completely different-looking people on a cellular level a decade ago. Without my consent, by the way.

She probably shouldn't answer that way. The whole truth wouldn't put him more at ease with the situation. She huffed and sat her fork down. "It's a really, really long story. You?"

"I found a napkin for this place on the driver's seat of my locked car this morning," he replied matter-of-factly.

"Interesting." Blue nodded. What the hell? Maybe a partial truth would work in this situation. Leave out the really weird details. "I too received a napkin from this café just last night. It seems someone wanted us to meet. Here. Where they serve a fantastic version of a very special lady's favorite comfort food."

Ava twitched slightly in her seat and looked around the café in a worried manner. "Dad?"

"It's OK." He reached across the table and put a hand on her arm to calm her. "Your mom told me once if we were ever in trouble, help would come out of the blue. She said help would find us when we needed it." He looked directly at Blue. Almost daring her to contradict him. "I always thought the wording was cryptic. Maybe it was one of those fantastic stories she liked to tell. It's making sense now. You have an unusual name, Ms. Blue."

Emotion welled in her throat. Because Amber had told this man to trust her mysterious friend, he was trusting her with not only his life, but the life of his daughter. What if she failed? And Mom? How could Amber have a teenage daughter? Why had she sent her here instead of coming herself? Of course, she was going to help. Whatever it took. That absolutely was a thing she did on a regular basis, with disturbingly varied degrees of success. But she had no idea what she was actually agreeing to. "I'll help you. But I need to know everything."

He seemed relieved. Ava still seemed nervous. This whole thing was strange. The kid wasn't wrong to keep her guard up. "I don't like being in the open like this. We found each other. Let's clean this up and we can find somewhere less crowded." He stacked all the trays up, including her half-finished biscuit, and stood to take them to the trash can in the corner near a swinging gate in the fence that walled off the patio from the sidewalk. "I'll be right back."

Blue momentarily mourned the loss of yet another meal. One day, she would get to eat an entire meal uninterrupted, and maybe if it was a really good day, still warm. Today was not that day. "So, Ava. Pretty name. Hi," Blue started, not certain what to say now that they were alone. Her kid expertise ended at around ten years old. How much did the kid know? What was appropriate? Jeez, she looked just like Amber.

"Awkward." Ava laughed.

"That's me. Every day. Maybe we can get dessert before we leave?" She waved toward the door to the interior of the café. "I didn't get to finish." She stopped mid-sentence as she turned her gaze to the door and saw another blast from the past step through. A massive man at least six foot three and almost wider than the door he now effectively blocked. He held two bags of food and a soda. His skin was as dark as Ben's, but Photoshop-perfect. He sported short dark stubble and closely cropped hair. His large brown eyes were both beautiful and dangerous in their intensity. He was just as intimidating as she remembered him being. It was Ivan Lacroix, former Cahlad Zenith, and the current heavy hitter of Stalker Prime. He had on more clothes than when she saw him online yesterday, and he was looking right at Ava with recognition in his eyes. "Oh, shit."

"What?" Ava asked as Blue rose from her chair and grabbed the girl's arm. She didn't take her eyes off him as she pulled the girl from her seat. He shifted his focus to her and stared intently for a moment as if he was trying to place where he knew her from. Good luck with that, buddy. Ivan's focus shifted back to Ava. He took several menacing steps toward them.

"Forget dessert. Let's go," Blue ordered, pushing the girl behind her.

She glanced toward the patio exit, finding Ben's eyes immediately. He took in the situation, a frown creasing his forehead. She knew what it looked like. Then he saw the other man moving toward them. The frightened look on his face told her he knew exactly who this was. The video of Ivan taking a fireball in the face without blinking was running on repeat on every major news outlet. His abs, exposed when his dress shirt had shredded during the onslaught, now had their own hashtag on social media. They were trending. The brand of boxer briefs he wore this morning already reported a spike in sales. The times they lived in were weird.

She might not have time to wait for Ben to get to them. She couldn't fight Ivan. Maybe she could drop him in a large body of water and hope he forgot how to swim. All she could do was run.

She felt Ava jerk her arm out of her grip. Shit. She glanced back at Ivan. She was pinned in. She couldn't get to either exit without getting entirely too close to his massive reach. And she just lost her grip on Ava. She would run without Ben. She wasn't going to run without Ava.

She saw Ivan's head jerk up, looking in Ben's direction. She followed his gaze. A beautiful Indian woman sprinted toward them from across the street, ignoring oncoming traffic. She was yelling something and pointing. Blue and Ivan spotted the problem at the same time. A backpack that had not been there before was sitting conspicuously on the sidewalk right next to the metal fence lining the patio. The two tables immediately next to it were fortunately vacant. But there were still people sitting nearby, and the woman was very clearly shouting, "Bomb!"

Patrons started to scatter, pushing Ben through the fence onto the street in the rush. Some ran into the building; others jumped the fence and ran up the sidewalk in the opposite direction. Most screamed.

Blue hurled her body toward Ava. Just as she reached the girl and their momentum directed them toward the ground, a large mass slammed into them, taking them the rest of the way with enough force to rattle her teeth. She did her best to keep her weight off Ava, but the mass of whatever had knocked them to the ground was too great. Just as she registered that Ivan was indeed the thing crushing them to the ground, shielding them with his body, an explosion ripped through the café's patio.

18

SAM

Sam sat on a bus stop bench looking for all the world like a bored commuter, staring at his cell phone. He did his best to stretch his legs after being folded like an origami bird into the cramped backseat of Ivan's fast but tiny sports car. At least in the back, he could stretch his legs across both seats. It was an inadequate space for a six-foot-seven man, even when Nisha graciously scooted her seat as far forward as possible. He made a mental note to lobby to get Ivan a raise. Maybe he would spend the extra money on a bigger car for their next off-the-books endeavor.

He watched the video Ivan secured from a business across the street from the Cahlad's new park. Two hours before the dedication ceremony, two vehicles rolled into the parking lot. Four people got out and looked at the statue before the official ceremony. One of the individuals looked like the artist, who had not attended the unveiling, citing a phobia of crowds. Another appeared to be Finn Torrin of Herne Tactical. His organization was on the Cahlad's watch list, though on the surface it remained outside their jurisdiction. Sam knew they were involved in artifact retrieval, but he couldn't prove it yet. He didn't know who the two women with them were. Ivan was running facial recognition, and it would alert them when it found matches. The gathering wouldn't be suspicious if not for the random bird attack and the presence of a magic treasure hunter.

More concerning, several cameras in the area captured suspicious-looking actors who appeared armed and organized. They surrounded the gathering and were moving into position for something when all hell broke loose with the birds. The local authorities were aware and had shared the fact publicly which was bad for the Cahlad and fed the anti-magic frenzy Nolan Miller was trying to stir up with his press conferences.

He frowned and looked around again. The street was relatively quiet, a cool spring breeze picking up speed as it blew between the buildings. There was no suspicious activity or people since they arrived an hour and a half ago. A florist van sat across the street from a small cafe named the Cat and the Canary, situated in the middle of the block in the trendy Five Points area of Nashville. The outdoor patio was peppered with brightly colored umbrellas and mismatched chairs filling with the dinner rush.

They swept the area in a five-block radius with no results. Finally, Ivan demanded sustenance. He was currently in the cafe grabbing the team's first and possibly only real meal of the day. Nisha browsed through a clearance book rack a few doors down. He wasn't sure where to go from here. This lead was a dead end. His phone pinged with a facial recognition alert. He opened the notification. A partial match to one of the women at the park with a photo from the rooftop brawl earlier in the week. This couldn't be a coincidence. Ivan's program had just found their magic surge problem. Sam studied the grainy photographs. Shouts erupted across the street, Nisha's voice among them.

Sam thought louder as he scanned the area. Nisha?

"Bomb!" she shouted louder. She ran toward a random backpack sitting in the middle of the sidewalk near the crowded cafe patio. Everyone else was heeding her warning and running for their lives. The patio was virtually empty. She was still running toward it. What was she doing?

"Nisha! Stop!" he managed to shout. He saw her body grind to a violent halt, arms flailing forward as if she was caught by a seat belt. "Get out of there!" he screamed as he ran toward her. Just as she turned to face him, taking a few quick steps away from the suitcase, the world erupted in noise and flame. He watched for the second time in twenty-four hours as his best friend's body was pummeled by a shock wave.

He sprinted across the street. The bricks on the cafe's front were gone. Most of the wall was still present, but whether it was structurally sound was questionable. The patio was in shambles. The fence and furniture were mangled. Twisted umbrellas were scattered like morbid confetti. Car alarms blared, and sirens in several of the surrounding buildings drowned the street in noise. He skidded to a stop and dropped to his knees next to her. By the time he reached her, she was already sitting up and shaking her head. Her arms were scraped, and she looked confused. Immediately, his hands flew to her head, and he began a basic first-aid pat down for injuries. He reached her ankles, leaving his hands resting there like he was helping her with crunches, and looked up. "You are going to be the death of me."

A man wearing a Nashville Predators hat groaned a few feet from them; he lay in a heap in the middle of the street. "Sam. Guns!" Nisha uttered, still clutching her head. He hardly had time to react before pops of gunfire joined the other noises of destruction and chaos. Just one or two shooters. He couldn't see them. The gunfire was focused on the remaining occupants of the cafe. "Found the goon squad." Nisha crawled toward the injured man next to them, who was trying to sit up. His nose bled badly, and his arms were spotted in burns. With no concern for her own injuries or the deadly situation unfolding around them, Nisha stood and pulled the man to his feet. "We have to get you out of here."

Sam rushed over to help. They all needed to take cover, but he knew telling Nisha to leave the man exposed in the street would cause more trouble than it solved.

A thump rang out. Someone was lobbing more explosives. Green gas rolled from the destroyed patio.

"Ivan's in there. He needs help." Nisha pointed toward the de-molished building.

"He will be fine," Sam dismissed her comment. Ivan was literally indestructible and genius-level smart to boot.

"No, Sam," Nisha insisted, dragging the injured man with her across the street and pushing him down in an alley between buildings. "He's scared. Something about ghosts. Pain. It's bad."

"You have a head wound," the man finally responded after remaining disoriented and silent while he was hauled off the street.

"Are you guys OK?" a voice asked from behind them. Sam spun and put himself between the two people leaning unsteadily against the alley wall and the speaker. Nisha leaned around him to get a look. A tall man in business casual clothes with salt and pepper hair knelt next to a striking man wearing pink shoes sitting on the ground leaning against the brick wall of the building next to them.

"What are you doing here?" Sam demanded. These were the men from the park before the dedication ceremony yesterday. What were the odds that they would be here, too? Finn Torrin eyed him carefully as recognition crossed his features. The other man rested his head on his knees and groaned.

"Oh. OK. Torrin. And the artist guy," Nisha said, and he knew she was in his head. "It's OK, Sam," Nisha told him. "They didn't have anything to do with this."

The man she helped poked at the cut on her head. "You need to stay still. I need my kit." She swatted his hand away and closed her eyes.

"Ben Hughes?" Torrin asked, stepping closer but stopping when Sam leveled a glare at him. The man in question didn't answer, but turned his dazed gaze toward the street as the steady staccato of gunfire echoed between the buildings.

"They are here for a Nova?" Nisha shook her head. Between her injuries and the barrage of thoughts she was filtering through, Sam could tell she was struggling to stay on her feet. Panicked people were mentally loud, according to his best friend. "Your artwork was beautiful, by the way," she randomly told the injured man behind them.

"Thanks?" the man sitting on the ground answered wearily. He looked like hell. And his shoes were practically glowing. He had never seen that many piercings on one person.

"Are you seeing this?" Torrin nodded toward the street. Sam followed his gaze, and his stomach dropped. The street filled with armed men and women in full urban tactical gear. They were no longer trying to remain hidden, and Sam knew that meant they didn't care who was hurt or who was killed.

"Sam. Get Ivan. Now," Nisha demanded, pushing hard on his arm. "He has two women with him. He won't leave them, and he is hurt."

Sam stood for a moment, unsure. He didn't want to leave Nisha. But if Ivan was hurt, this situation was spiraling out of control quickly. She was in no condition to charge into this. "Go. I'll be fine."

He stood for a moment, looking down at her. He could easily say the words that made her stand down and leave the injured man behind. And she would have to do what he told her. His jaw worked in a tense rhythm while he stared directly at her. He knew she could feel what he was thinking, anyway. He sighed and squeezed her upper arm "Ravi..." He defaulted to her last name in a doubtful hiss, a habit he had when he was trying to separate his friend from his teammate.

"I've got them, Sotach," Torrin told him. "I have transport incoming for this guy. They are two blocks out."

Nisha glared at the man and frowned. She didn't look happy, but she nodded. Sam had to trust her assessment, even if she was likely prioritizing Ivan's safety over her own.

"Medic?" he asked the man Nisha was holding up as much as he was holding her up at this point.

"Doctor," the man answered. His eyes were still glassy and unfocused. He must have taken a hard hit to the head. "My daughter..."

Making up his mind, he pointed at the man. "You take care of her," he instructed with venom in his voice. The man's face registered shock and the usual frustration following a directive. A worried look crossed Nisha's face.

"Torrin, get them out of here safely."

"You didn't have to order him to do that, you know. He offered," the injured man behind Torrin called out even as Sam turned away and sprinted back down the street. "Jerk."

The bad guys seemed to be focused on who or whatever was in that cafe. People running by on the street weren't even on their radar. If Ivan was somehow hurt and had two extras, they were going to need transportation. He scanned the street for something within his skill set to steal. Grand theft auto was Ivan's specialty, but that delivery van would do just fine

19

BLUE

Her ears rang. The sounds of people screaming reached her from the end of a tunnel. She lifted herself and found Ivan's weight no longer holding her down. He was still there, lying across her legs. But she had room to move.

She checked on Ava. The girl seemed fine. Her eyes were wide and stunned, but she was moving. They needed to get out of here. Just far enough away to keep anyone from seeing their unconventional departure.

Blue felt gigantic hands grab her by the waist and lift her like she weighed nothing. She kept her grip on Ava and dragged the girl up with her. They found their feet, and she took in the surrounding chaos. Ivan shouted something in her ear. She wasn't sure what it was, but she was pretty sure he was telling her to run for her life. Or he was going to kill her to get to Ava. Could be either.

Most of the furniture had been blown clear of where the suitcase was. Several people were injured, but miraculously, she saw no obvious fatalities. Pieces of the metal fence were hurled everywhere. One jutted wickedly from the post directly beside them. She saw three bent pieces of metal fence post and a mangled chair at their feet. The fence posts appeared to have hit something but had been unable to impale it. Ivan turned slightly away from them, looking toward an alley that ran next to the patio between the buildings. Her eyes flew to the holes ripped in his shirt: three perfectly formed holes about the size of the fence stakes. The chair at their feet was bent in a curve shaped like Ivan's back. She spared a moment to glance at his face. He looked far better than he had the last time she saw him in person. Any one of those projectiles would have grievously injured her and likely killed Ava. "That makes us even, big guy," she muttered, focusing again on her exit route.

The street was the best way out. Just around the corner for a few seconds with no witnesses, and she would have Ava out of here. She pulled Ava away from the building and toward the sidewalk, keeping an eye out for Ben. She tightened her grip on Ava's arm. She couldn't risk Ava jerking loose and taking off.

Ava screamed for her father and fought to get loose. "Calm down. We are going to find him," Blue assured her, knowing she was lying. She wasn't waiting on the man. Priority one was to get Ava out of here safely. If he conveniently appeared during the time it took her to get off this patio and to a private corner, he could tag along. Otherwise, she would leave his ass and come back and sift through this mess for him.

Ivan reached out from behind her and grabbed her wrist. Shit. She couldn't fight with him right here and now. She turned back to him, not letting go of Ava, and got a face full of chest as he bowled toward them. He wrapped his arms around them both yet again and shoved them behind an overturned cabinet that had once been used for condiments and plastic ware distribution. "What are you doing?" Blue shouted as she hit the ground again. Her question was quickly answered when gunfire erupted from the alley. The post impaled with the fence splintered even more as bullets slammed into the wood.

"Cover her!" he ordered, pushing Blue's head down with force. And that is just what Blue did, plastering her body over Ava, who curled into a fetal position, arms covering her head. The big man stood and charged toward the sound of gunfire with a roar. She heard dull thuds and knew the bullets were bouncing off his chest, just like the ice shards from yesterday. The guy was truly frightening. Blue peered over the cabinet. Two men charged in from the alley. One advanced from the street front. Another blocked the door to the interior of the café. Goon squad all the way. Lovely.

People were pinned inside what was left of the patio, some injured and sprawled on the ground, others taking cover behind whatever furniture or debris they could find. She and Ava were not obscured by the cabinet. She didn't see Ben. She needed to go. Maybe nobody would notice two women disappearing into thin air among the chaos of the explosion and gunfire.

She spotted a middle-aged white man in a bomber jacket and jeans pointing his phone in their general direction. He flipped the camera back and forth between the chaos and himself. Blue heard his raised voice over the surrounding noise. The idiot was live-streaming. What was wrong with people?

All four of the goon squad fired a quick burst above head-level and stepped back in unison. Immediately two individuals stepped into the vacated space holding grenade launchers and wearing gas masks. Ivan was still charging. Blue ducked.

Two booming thumps filled the air, followed by the clatter of metal on concrete. Ivan skidded to a stop on his back right next to them, a large circular burn mark in the middle of his shirt. Another thump sounded as Ivan clambered to his feet, ready to charge again. "Ms. Blue, what was that?" Ava asked from her huddle on the ground.

"I don't know. Hold on." Blue didn't have to look to see what had happened. Gas canisters were rolling through the patio. One rolled right between where Blue crouched and Ivan stood. They inhaled huge lung-fulls of putrid green gas. "No. No. No." Blue cried. She had seen this gas before. This stuff had a starring role in her nightmares.

"Don't breathe it, baby. Don't breathe it," Blue choked out and slapped her hand over the girl's mouth until she nodded. She grabbed Ava's hand, shot the live streamer a bird and... nothing. Nothing happened. What the hell? Her magic was gone.

"We've got to go. Go now. Get up." Blue yanked Ava to standing and shielded her as much as she could. She was not watching another child die. "Stay on me." People not already prone collapsed and slumped over. A twenty-something woman in business casual attire remained conscious where she was crouched behind a trash can. Other than that, Blue, Ivan, and Ava were the only people not wearing gas masks, still upright. Magic had to be the common denominator. That meant Ava had magic. Is that what these people were after? The gas cleared, and the gunmen reemerged, faces covered.

Blue dashed toward Ivan. "Help me get her out of here, Ivan." A momentary flash of surprise and confusion crossed his features when she said his name before it was replaced with a concerned scowl. She could see in his eyes that he knew what this stuff was and clearly remembered their last run-in with it. He nodded.

Blue drew her gun from her shoulder holster and shoved Ava between Ivan and herself, effectively making an Ava sandwich. She could feel Ava's hand on the small of her back as they maneuvered their small group through the chaos. Ivan drew his own weapon and fired at the men in the alleyway. She fired low at the goon, securing the door to the interior of the cafe. He screamed and fell. Shins rarely had armor. She fired again at his arm. Ivan shouted at Ava to stay behind him. The girl didn't respond. She was alarmingly silent.

Another man took the downed man's place in the doorway, immediately aiming a weapon and firing. Whoever these guys were, they were organized and disciplined. Blue adjusted, fired at his head, and missed. But she did force him to take cover. A searing pain coursed through her side, and she couldn't stop the cry she let loose. Just because it was going to heal before she went to bed didn't mean it didn't hurt like a bitch right now. She heard Ivan grunt. Oh shit. How many bullets could he take before he went down? He wasn't used to not being bulletproof. At least he was still firing his weapon.

She pushed backward, making sure she could feel Ava. Bullets pinged all around them. She swore she could feel some getting so close to her that they skimmed her skin. But only one had reached its target so far. She looked down in confusion at projectiles rolling on the bricks where she was standing seconds ago like they were stopped in midair. She didn't have time to process any of that.

She fired low again when the man reemerged. This time, she scored a hit in the thigh. He fell on top of his buddy. A flare of pain shot through her right bicep; nothing critical, but it made her arm hard to use. That bullet came from the street. She cursed and swapped her gun to her left hand. She fired, still pressing back on Ava. The lady on the street was smart and crouched, creating a smaller target, blocking most of the leg shots. She hated the smart ones.

She kept pressing back and glanced over her shoulder to see how close to the alley they were. Ivan dropped the last of the three gunmen in that direction. Damn, he was good. How was he still standing? A light at the edge of her vision caught her attention. Ava's hand pressed hard into the giant man's back, encased in a swirling red light. The girl's head was down, and her face flushed almost purple, eyes closed in concentration. Ava was holding her breath and still had magic. What was she doing? Who cared? It was working.

The florist van that had been sitting across the street earlier took the corner into the alley on screeching wheels, dodging debris and prone bodies as it barreled toward them. It thumped over the bodies of two of the gunmen Ivan dispatched and screeched to a stop, one wheel disturbingly cradled in the chest of a dead man. A dark-haired man Blue instantly recognized as Sam Sotach, Regent of the Prime Cahlad, threw open the passenger door. "Get in!" he barked. Blue felt a pressure on her chest and a sudden urge to do whatever was necessary to get into that van.

A bullet whizzed through the top of her leg. She dropped like a stone. Her leg wasn't having it. This seemed familiar. But she still needed to get in that van. This was utter bullshit. She hated this guy on principle.

"Go. Get her out of here," Blue yelled, firing at the woman who shot her with her left hand, panicking that she was no longer covering Ava's body. One of her shots landed, but the woman didn't go down. She steadied herself to fire again. Black mist crept into her vision as she focused on the crouching woman. She was in worse shape than she had initially realized. She heard heated words behind her and Ava pleading, "Please help her."

She was jerked backward by the collar of her shirt, her butt sliding across the uneven pavers. That definitely wasn't Ava unless she had super strength. She fired her last bullet as she was lifted yet again and dragged bodily into the van and across Ivan's lap. He shoved her between the driver and passenger seat into the back with Ava. The radio blared. The engine revved, and the door slammed in that order. If she weren't already prone, she would have toppled over. She knew this, because Ava, who wasn't prone, flew sideways and banged off the rear doors.

"Oh, my God. You are shot." Ava scrambled back to Blue's side and jerked off her hoodie. She wadded it up and jammed it into the wound on Blue's side. "You are bleeding! I didn't have enough. I tried." Her voice started to raise. She turned to the front of the van as it went around a corner too fast. "You are bleeding too," she wailed when she looked at Ivan. She fell forward, pressing even harder on the wound, causing Blue to groan. "She is bleeding!" she told the two men up front.

Blue grabbed Ava's wrist. "It's going to be all right. Hang in there."

"My dad," Ava whispered. Her eyes found Blue's pleading. "We left my dad. He's a doctor. He can fix you."

"I will find him. I promise. Let's get you somewhere safe first." Blue squeezed gently. "It's what he would want."

"Nisha?" Ivan asked as he turned slightly to face Sam and keep Ava in his line of sight.

"Mostly fine. Somehow," Sam answered, some exasperation leaking into his voice. "She is helping the injured. She told me something about a ghost and that you needed help more than she did," Sam explained.

Ivan grunted, focusing on Ava. His scrutiny made Blue nervous. He had definitely made the connection between Ava and Amber, and she didn't know what he was going to do. His gaze shifted her way, and he frowned. He was trying to figure out where she fits into all of this. Blue waved at him and smiled weakly. She would like to know that herself.

"Is all that blood hers, Ivan?" Sam asked as he gestured toward the back with one hand.

Ivan grunted. "No." Blue watched Ivan point to a spot on his body she couldn't see. Sam glanced between the road and the man in the passenger seat with disbelief on his face.

"No shit," he muttered, glanced in the rearview mirror, and grimaced. "Hold on. We must have something these people want." He jerked the wheel, and the van bounced up onto the sidewalk. Blue and Ava both screamed as an electric scooter swung in through an oval hole in the side of the van. "These things are a menace," Blue groused as she kicked it back out the way it came.

"They had some kind of gas. Killed my magic. Then that one grabbed me and some of it came back. Enough to keep me standing." Ivan jerked his head toward the back of the van. He reached up and touched his cheek. A purple bruise was blooming. If Ava hadn't done whatever it was she had done, Ivan would no longer have a face. Blue was certain Ava had been the target. She and Ivan had just gotten in the way. Those guys were shooting to kill to get to Ava.

A new song started playing on the radio, and Blue groaned louder. She did not want to hear that voice right now. "Can we change the channel?" Ivan peered at her incredulously.

"Aw. "Baby Blue." I love this song. Cade Rhodes is so hot. I love his new beard." Ava protested and sang along. It was Blue's turn to throw an incredulous glance at someone. Ava sounded a lot like her mother when she sang, like two squirrels trying to drown each other in a rain barrel. They were running for their lives, and she was prattling about a country music singer. What was this girl doing?

"She familiar to you?" Ivan asked Sam.

"Which one?"

"The girl," Ivan clipped, still staring in their direction. Here it was. He was doing something with what he had figured out. Outing them to the Regent.

"Look at me," Sam spoke softly. Ava jerked and turned her face toward the front of the van. Ivan and Blue did as well. They had no control over the action. He regarded Ava closely in the rearview mirror, and recognition dawned on his face. "Yeah."

Tension filled the van. Blue could feel her wounds stitching back together uncomfortably. That meant her magic was returning. Still, she whined. "I'm in hell. Please, for the love of God, change the station." Neither man moved to turn the radio down or change the station. She wouldn't be able to math a skip with a passenger and compensate for their current speed safely, though. She was stuck here. In hell.

"I recognize the other one, too. From the roof and the group at the statue." Sam continued as if she hadn't said anything and couldn't hear him, jerking the van to the left to avoid a slow-moving vehicle and slinging Ava onto her butt. Mercifully, she stopped singing and pressing on Blue's side. Maybe the guy wasn't so bad after all.

"She helped me. But she isn't a civilian," Ivan answered in an ominous tone. "We need to keep an eye on her."

As the van jerked again, a burst of gunfire roared from behind them. Metal pinged against the rear doors. "Hold on to something!" Sam ordered. Blue chose to hold on to her gun and pull herself to a sitting position so that she could reload. She skidded to the side, her foot flying out of the hole in the van's wall. Were those scorch marks? She yanked her foot back in.

"Baby Blue" still wailed from the van's speakers. "Did you guys know you have a big ass hole back here? That song keeps playing. I might jump out of it." She slammed a new magazine into place. Another round of pings bounced off the doors. "Ava, honey. I need you to lie flat on the floor and cover your head for me. Just in case." Blue racked the slide of her weapon.

"Oh. OK. OK." Ava quickly complied as the sound of sirens joined the chaos around them and grew louder.

"You stay with me. No matter what happens. Do you understand?" Blue whispered to the girl. Who knew what would happen to Ava if these guys took her back to the Cahlad? Mitch's long-lost granddaughter might not be welcome, considering the circumstances of her mother's disappearance. Ava nodded vigorously into her arms. "Do you have earbuds or headphones?" Blue asked, still whispering. She saw Ava nod again. "Good. Put them in." Ava began fishing around in her hoodie pocket. A pair of cheap wired earbuds appeared.

Tires screeched from in front of the van. "They've boxed us in." Sam jerked the wheel to the side again. Bullets peppered the front of the van this time. The windshield shattered, spiderweb cracks obstructing the view of the road ahead. "Ivan!" he shouted. Ivan quickly leaned forward and used his fist to knock the shattered windshield out of the way. It flew free and bounced down the side of the vehicle. He reloaded his weapon. Both Sam and Ivan fired straight ahead.

A gray town car careened out of a side street and sped up next to them, ramming against the side of the van. Sam was forced to lay his weapon on the console and use both hands to compensate for the wild rocking it caused. Blue slid onto her belly and inched forward, peering out through the mysterious hole in the van's side. The car's rear window lowered. Blue opened fire at once, hitting the backseat passenger, who was holding a grenade launcher in the throat. She fired twice at the driver's side window. The car veered away and slowed.

"They are trying to gas us again." Blue pivoted onto her knees and leaned forward between the front seats. Ivan still fired out of the missing windshield. Sam hunched over the steering wheel. "How bad is it?"

"Completely under control." Sam deadpanned.

"Plan?" she asked, glancing back to check on Ava. The girl was still face down on the floor, covering her head. At least that was going right.

Neither man spoke. Their faces grim.

"There's no plan?" Ava wailed into the floor.

"Sam," Ivan warned, squeezing the trigger of his gun in a slow steady rhythm. Blue followed his gaze. The back gate of the SUV in front of them was open, and a man crouched on his knees, aiming another rocket-propelled weapon at them. Ivan's bullets were slowing him down, but he wasn't stopping.

"Take a deep breath and hold it, people," Sam instructed. Blue and Ivan compulsively drew in a deep lungful of air. Ava seemed unaffected by the directive. The weapon fired ahead of them; Sam jerked the wheel at the last moment, trying to avoid the projectile. It landed to their left. To Blue's surprise, it exploded.

The rear of the van lurched into the air, and everyone was thrown hard forward and right. "Not gas," Ivan grunted helpfully. A spray of bullets peppered the back of the van like annoying flies just to remind them that the goon squad was back there, too.

The gray sedan sped back up, trying to drive next to them. "I have nowhere to go." Sam barked. "Any ideas?"

Making a decision she hoped she wouldn't regret, Blue leaned forward between the seats. "I can get us out of here. But I need you to slow way down."

"I don't think so." Sam shook his head.

Ivan's head turned slowly, and he leveled a menacing glare her way. "How?"

"Almost to a stop. I promise I will explain when we aren't being blown up and shot at."

"Do whatever she says!" Ava screamed, still face-first on the floor. "I don't want to blow up!"

"He's loading another one," Sam barked. Ivan fired again. It did no good.

"Look. I'm getting Ava out of here, with or without you. It will be a lot less painful if you slow the fuck down," Blue warned. She reached back and pushed Ava's jeans up, grabbing her ankle. "I've got you, big guy," she told Ivan. "I promise."

Ivan's face turned hard as stone, and his jaw ticked. He stared straight at her. Blue shifted uncomfortably. Ivan was scary. She cleared her throat but didn't say anything else. Apparently, she said the wrong thing. She didn't want to leave him to the mercy of these maniacs, especially knowing what they could do with that gas, but she wasn't going to beg. She was already regretting her offer. They all looked forward as the SUV in front of them locked its wheels to avoid slamming into a police car that had entered the fray. It hit the police car anyway, knocking it to the side and receiving a complimentary round of police-issued bullets for its trouble.

The man with the grenade launcher pointed the weapon at them again. Ivan reached out and wrapped a giant hand around Blue's free hand. His other hand flew out to Sam's wrist. "Slow down, Sam."

Sam glanced at his friend in surprise. "You are serious?" A flash of fire shot from the gun ahead of them. He jerked the wheel hard and slammed on the brakes. The van spun sideways toward the wrecked police cruiser, slowing as it went.

"Don't let go!" Blue shouted as she let the rainbow fall over her eyes and the cold wash over her. Something was wrong. So much magic flowed through her it felt like holding on to an electric fence. Her hand clamped down on Ava's ankle even harder. She screamed and felt like gravity was suddenly gone. The whole van was floating. Sam shouted, and Ivan was on the verge of snapping her wrist. The colors in the rainbow morphed together. And everything went black.

20

FINN

Finn watched the Regent of the Cahlad, the right hand of the Paragon, hot wire a delivery van like it was second nature to him. Interesting. He turned to the group of injured people he needed to get out of this area. Nisha Ravi stepped suddenly away from Ben Hughes with a horrified and confused look on her face. She looked at Finn with wide eyes. "There is more than one person in there." She nodded to Ben.

"What are you talking about?" Finn asked as he sent Hale a text telling him to be ready for two more, one Cahlad, and one acquired target.

"Oh, they are loud and nasty, and they aren't happy." Nisha took another step back.

"Ben, I'm Finn Torrin of Herne Tactical. Your parents hired my company to investigate your disappearance. I'm sorry we are meeting under these circumstances, but I am glad you are safe." He extended his hand toward Ben, but Nisha's sudden step back drew his attention. She shifted, so she stood partially behind him.

"My parents?" Ben asked, getting Finn's attention back. The man's voice was a low rumble.

"What in the hell?" he exclaimed, also stepping back. The man's eyes were large black orbs with purple flames licking out of the sockets. A dark gray mist swirled around his feet, stretching into tendrils that rose and stretched out. Nisha stepped even further behind him, clutching her head with both hands and grimacing.

"My parents are dead." Ben sneered. "Are you here for my daughter, too?" The flames growing from his eyes grew larger.

"Um." Finn pushed Ravi backward toward Greenlee with his body. He had personally spoken with two people who claimed to be Hughes' parents, and the background check his tech Trix ran corroborated that fact. "Actually, yes, I was hired to find you and your daughter."

"Oh. No," Nisha muttered. "You are so dumb." A sickening smile decorated the man's face. He didn't look much like a world renowned orthopedic surgeon right now. The man looked like a demon. "He is saying, daughter. Energy. There are so many voices."

"Back up. Go with Greenlee," Finn told her as he reached over to unholster his weapon. He didn't want to shoot someone he was being paid to retrieve. But he would if he had to.

"No. He's a soul eater. You won't last five seconds," she told him, and he felt her stop and dig in. Finn stood stunned for a moment, unable to back up because Nisha had stopped. He had only read about them. Soul eaters had magic so feared and powerful, the Cahlad had never allowed a practitioner to live outside of a campus or prison. There were no known living soul eaters registered. "Let's stay calm, Ben." The insane woman moved around Finn and approached the man slowly with her hands out, palms up.

A woman dressed in black, carrying an enormous gun, stalked by on the sidewalk, firing carefully toward the cafe as if she was trying to keep people pinned in the patio area. Nisha's movement drew her attention, causing her to twist and squeeze off a quick burst of bullets in their direction. Finn stepped forward and fired at the woman. His bullets did not reach their target.

Nisha yelped, but not because she was being shot at. Black, mist-like tendrils wrapped around her waist and yanked her until she dangled two feet in the air. A similar tendril snaked around Finn's ankle and pulled his feet out from under him. He fell backward, slamming into the ground. He then was dangling upside down four feet above it. A wall of tendrils batted away the woman's bullets. New tendrils appeared from Ben's feet and flew toward their attacker. Ben pulled her, screaming in terror in their direction as one tendril stripped her of her weapon and threw it, clattering across the street.

Finn, doing his best with the odd angle, took aim. "Don't you do it," Nisha demanded. He glared at her. He didn't like that she could read his thoughts. Ben's victim was gray, and her head lolled to the side. She was no longer fighting the pull of the tendrils.

"Ben. Let's think this through. Let Torrin and I down. We are going to help you," Nisha tried to placate the man. His head tipped to the side in a curious manner. More tendrils wrapped around the woman's limp body. In an instant, they all squeezed violently, causing a chorus of sickening, crunching sounds. She cried out and fell into a limp pile at his feet.

"Sure you don't want me to shoot him?" Finn demanded sarcastically.

Ben's head tipped to the other side. The tendrils drew Nisha toward him. A free tendril shifted to Finn's torso, wrapping completely around his ribcage. He felt a deep ache in his chest and a bone weariness he had never experienced before. Whatever this man was doing to him, he knew it was fatal. Finn tried to stay calm and draw in deep gulps of air. He looked at Nisha as she glided through the air even closer to Ben, effectively blocking any chance he had of getting a clean shot. She looked back and flinched. He must look horrible. He heard her gulp. He thought that was a reaction only found in overly dramatic books. But apparently it was a genuine alternative to pissing yourself out of fear.

"My friend is with your daughter," Nisha said. "My other friend is driving to get them." She reached her hand forward as he got closer. "You saw him leave. He helped you."

"The Regent. What will the Regent do with us?" The man's voice seemed to echo in stereo around them. He locked flaming eyes on Nisha. "The Cahlad can't have my daughter." Another wave of desperate exhaustion washed over Finn, and he felt his eyes growing heavy. It was all he could do to hold on to his gun.

Finn watched the tendrils wrapped around Nisha. They looked like they were constricting but were having no impact. The only thing saving her was Sotach's last directive. That directive was probably what set this guy off, too.

"No. No. I'm going to help you," Nisha told him in a pained voice. Sam's compulsion was slowly fading. The gunfire stopped. The street fell eerily silent. A vehicle door slammed and tires screeched.

"You lie." Ben's voice was deep and rolled between them, almost like thunder. "We will kill you all."

"Oh, God," Nisha screamed. "Don't listen to them!"

"Kiwi!" Greenlee screamed. A small metal object whirled by Nisha's head and hit Ben square in the chest. The tendrils holding Finn and Nisha in the air vanished. They both fell to the ground, hard. Finn landed on his head but rolled quickly, keeping his eyes on Hughes and raising his gun. The man's eyes were normal once again.

"What have I done?" he asked, voice no longer rolling with thunder. Ben knelt and extended a hand toward Finn, who couldn't help flinching away.

"Hold up, Cthulhu," Greenlee demanded, wobbling closer to their group. He was the only one standing. "Back away from my friend, or the next thing I hit you with won't feel so harmless." The man held something small and gold in his hand and rolled it back and forth between his fingers.

"What the hell just happened?" Finn demanded weakly, closing his eyes. He flopped to his back, too tired to breathe right now.

Ben reached for Finn's eyelids, pulling them gently open "I'm sorry," he said sincerely, and placed a large hand on Finn's forehead. He felt warmth rush through his body, the ache in his chest lessened, and some of his energy returned. Ben had healed him in some way. Finn still felt unsettled, and his limbs shook.

"He has thirty people in there, and they all want to kill everything," Nisha slumped.

"Shit," Greenlee huffed out and sat down hard against the wall, still rolling a piece of body jewelry between his fingers.

Finn watched, unmoving, because at the moment he didn't think he could, as Ben looked down at him. "How are we getting out of here?" Sirens wailed as emergency crews swarmed the area.

"My team is meeting me two blocks over," Finn groaned, sitting up and fighting a wave of dizziness.

Greenlee groaned. "Two blocks?"

"Can you do more of whatever that was? Not the soul-sucking. The other?" Finn asked, eying Hughes, who still seemed relaxed or more relaxed than the soul-sucking demon he had just been. He contemplated cuffing the man, but he had nothing that restrained otherworldly mist tentacles.

"All of it," Nisha scolded. "Everything you took."

Ben said nothing, but placed his hand back on Finn's forehead. Finn felt more warmth seep into his body.

"Let's get out of here before we get stopped by the authorities," Finn ordered, standing up and helping Nisha to her feet.

"She is the authorities," Greenlee grumbled.

She nodded and grabbed Ben's hand to direct him down the alleyway. "Let's go find your daughter."

Ben tugged his hand away. "Why do you care? Isn't it your job to deal with people like me?"

Nisha stopped and all the men stopped with her. She glared at Ben Hughes and stepped up until her nose was just below his. "It is. But there is more than one way to deal with a situation, Ben Hughes. Do you think I enjoy killing people? Taking their freedom? Feeling that? I feel all of it. Every time." She placed a hand over her chest. "It's my job for one more week to keep people safe. And you are one of those people, Ben."

"They will kill anybody that gets in their way."

"You've already tried to do that today, asshole," the woman quipped back, and Greenlee guffawed.

"What are your plans after next week?" Finn asked, impressed with her complete lack of fear in the face of what they had just seen.

"I'll consider your job offer," she huffed, then pushed Ben forward, hard. "Walk."

Finn had forgotten for a moment that she could waltz right through his thoughts. "You are yelling!" She called back over her shoulder.

He reached down to help Greenlee to his feet. His friend did not look well. "What in the hell was that, man? Kiwi?" It was the first time Finn had ever actually seen Greenlee use any kind of magic. "You saved our asses. Where did you get that thing?"

"Anti-magic charm. Unregistered," Greenlee told him as they limped behind the Soul Eater and one of the highest-ranking Stalker Captains in the Cahlad. He looked pointedly at Nisha. "I made it. Wasn't sure if it would work. That was crazy as hell."

"What's in your hand?" Finn nodded toward the object still clutched in Greenlee's hand. Finn noticed that one of Greenlee's ever-present ear piercings was missing.

The man was silent for a moment. "I've been holding on to this one for a long time. If I throw it at him," Greenlee glanced over grimly, "try not to be near him."

21

LEXI

Lexi stepped off the bus, waving at her friends. Mom said Mr. Larkin would be here to pick her up about fifteen minutes after she got off the bus. She didn't have much time, and she didn't want to keep him waiting. She bounded up the whiteboard stairs to the front porch. She needed to change out of her school clothes and grab her bag before he got here. Before she left, she wanted to run next door and hug Tio G. But she would be cutting it close.

She skipped across the deck, digging her house key out of her pocket. After practice, she was spending the night at Sophie's house. She couldn't wait. Sophie's mom always made Swedish pancakes for sleepovers. And they had an air hockey table in the basement. Sophie had somehow installed FaceTime on her phone without her parents knowing. They were going to call Eric from science class tonight.

Lexi placed her key in the lock and turned. The door remained shut. She whined in frustration. It was an old door, and sometimes it was stubborn. She bumped it with her hip and wiggled the key back and forth. Finally, the door opened, and she stepped inside.

She dropped her school backpack next to her overnight bag, where it waited by the door, and raced for the stairs. She climbed them two at a time, giggling because no one was here to yell at her to be careful or tell her she was going to break a leg. Having three parents was usually great, but it did ratchet up the nagging exponentially. Tia Blue was usually pretty cool, but she still had her old-person moments.

She stepped onto the upstairs landing and skidded to a halt. A man dressed in black was standing at the back of the hallway near Tio G's room. He had black hair and olive skin. He turned his head toward her in surprise when her foot hit the squeaky board at the top of the stairs.

This was bad. It suddenly struck her she had not disarmed the alarm, and it hadn't beeped at her when she came in. She was so excited to go to Sophie's that she didn't check. The instinct to run took over, and she turned back down the stairs. She took one step down, and panic set in when she saw another man at the bottom. He was also wearing black, and his light blue eyes were scary. Lexi screamed. She raced back up the single step and toward the closest room, Tia Blue's. Both men were running toward her as she threw herself into the room, slamming the tall wooden door behind her. She turned the lock and tossed the deadbolt. Thank heavens Tia Blue was a paranoid, crazy person who really liked her privacy.

She looked around the room frantically. Her breath was coming in gasps, and tears were blurring her eyes. Mom wasn't home. She was going to be late. And Tio G was next door. Where was Tia Blue? Her phone was in the backpack she dropped downstairs.

She looked up at the tiny horizontal window well above her head. She couldn't climb up. It didn't open. And it was a two-story drop. It also faced the backyard. Even if she broke the window and screamed, no one would hear her. What was she going to do?

The men were yelling now. The door rattled as one of them hit it hard. Oh, God! Oh, God! She spun in circles, pushing the beads on her fidget bracelet around manically.

She sucked in a breath, a memory forcing its way into her mind. She looked down at the blue bead with a silver heart Tia Blue had given her for her birthday last year. A gift just between them, Tia Blue said. She said it was only for end-of-the-world emergencies. This seemed pretty close to the end of the world. At least her world.

The door rattled again under another assault. They were no longer yelling, and their silence was more terrifying than their shouts. Everything was quiet except the rattle of the door. They were going to get in. Soon. She pressed her back against the far wall under the window, wishing she could disappear into it.

Lexi wracked her brain. What else had Tia Blue said about the charm? It had been so weird, and out of the blue, Lexi hadn't paid attention. She remembered sitting on the back deck while Mom and Tio G played a game of badminton. Mom won. Only because Tio G let her. Tia Blue had wound the charm onto her bracelet and told her if she was ever out of options to hold the charm tight and say... What was she supposed to say? A tear spilled out of her eyes. Think Lexi. The words were right there at the edge of her brain, but she couldn't grab them.

The door gave way, splintered wood flying into the tiny space, followed closely by a man's foot. Lexi screamed again and stood stunned for a moment, clutching the charm. He kicked the door in. The big, heavy, ancient door with a deadbolt. She couldn't believe it. He snarled at her, and Lexi jerked back. "Baby Blue!" she screamed, and the world went cold and white

22

ZELLA

Zella sat in her usual spot in Mitch's home office, in an oversize blue corduroy chair they referred to as the beast. It sat in the spot formerly occupied by Mitch's desk. A year ago, she hired movers to relocate his desk, so her chair had the best view in the room. The view featured the two campus clock towers and a parking garage with a perfect line of sight in this window. Now his desk set caddy cornered to the window with no line of sight from any point outside that wasn't an aircraft. Mission accomplished. She patted the beast and enjoyed her view.

Her legs were folded up and her chin lay on the high arm of the chair as she looked out over the courtyard. The sun was setting, making the maple tree in the center glow with a halo of light. The office echoed with angry voices from the speakerphone on Mitch's desk. After several suspicious delays in drafting his hospital discharge paperwork, they finally made it back to the Cahlad campus. Instead of going to the office, he had returned to their home. His staff was doing an impressive job of keeping the vultures away so that he could recover from his "grievous" injuries while still valiantly running the Cahlad's operations from his sickbed. Sam's idea. Zella liked the idea a lot. It forced Mitch to at least be near his bed. He might even give in and use it, eventually. She fiddled with her latest notebook, a beautiful leather-bound creation with lotus flowers carved on the front that Mitch had given her for the thirtieth anniversary of their non-marriage.

Today was rough, not necessarily because they ended up in the hospital. The park dedication was going to be hard regardless, but the fact that it went so sideways and civilians were hurt made it worse. It was also Sam's first public speaking appearance, not just as Regent. A man who could compel anyone to do anything with a single word had to be very careful about what he said. It made Sam hesitant to speak in large groups, much less with a microphone. She hoped this hadn't put him off public appearances permanently.

Words have power. Zella understood this better than almost anyone on the planet. So, most days, Zella sincerely wished that her last words had not been, "Eat shit. Asshole."

She observed a young woman scurrying across the courtyard, a precious thing with light brown hair and green eyes. That one was going to have a busy year. A promotion and a son. Both would be a surprise.

Zella smiled and jotted the vision down in her notebook. It was filled with poetic gibberish. Even before she lost her ability to speak or communicate with written words, she had learned the hard way that not a single thing could change what she saw. The inevitable attempts to do so could certainly create a hell of a mess.

Mitch glared at the phone and tried to remain diplomatic with the members of the Cahlad Conclave, or the international cabinet that Mitch was the leader of, and Nolan Miller, chair of the Senate Magic Relations and Regulation Committee. They all wanted a report on the magic surges and the release from the MNPD that another paramilitary group was spotted near the scene of the bird attack. Mitch believed it was a newly organized group of collectors, people who engaged in human trafficking of Sovaj. Zella knew better.

She glanced over her shoulder at the audio zoo and lifted an eyebrow. No women. That was a problem as far as she was concerned, and probably why this had turned into a nonsensical shouting match. She met Mitch's eyes where he sat, leaning back with his hands crossed, resting on his chest. He was watching her intently, ignoring the voices of the men who were vying for his attention. She knew he was on edge; she could feel the vibration in the air. But the men on the call were too focused on advancing their own agendas to notice the impatience in his voice.

She smiled serenely at Mitch as the political animals kept barking and beating their chest. She turned back to the window to catch the last of the sunset. This was going to be messy. But she was fairly certain it would work out for the best for almost everyone. Not everyone. Because nothing ever worked out for everyone.

She remembered this day ten years ago.

Amber burst into Mitch's office, screaming incoherently about her fiancé, Percy. As Mitch and Zella tried to calm their daughter and determine what was wrong, Larson burst into the office, followed closely by Sam. Mitch, unable to ignore Sam's order to get to safety, left Zella frozen to the spot, trying to wrap her head around a vivid but blurred image. It felt important, but she could not pluck out details.

"You knew. You had to know, and you didn't warn him. She killed him. You told her to kill him!" her daughter screamed. Zella barely comprehended the accusations before the girl disappeared into thin air.

"Where did she go?" Mitch demanded as he ripped open the door to the bunker, still following Sam's compulsion. Zella didn't know. She shook her head, trying to force herself to move and process what she had just seen.

"Stay where you are, Larson," Sam ordered as Larson stalked further into the room, his hard eyes following Mitch. His feet stopped immediately, but his hands still glowed. "Nisha told me what she heard in your head."

His lips lifted in a sneer. "Your daughter is quite the troublemaker, Mitch. This was sooner than I planned. But I'll adjust."

She had never liked him. But she didn't see this coming. This asshole planned to kill Mitch and take over the Cahlad. He knew he would never win a fair fight.

A single hazy flash of Larson releasing an explosive burst that disintegrated Sam floated through her mind. She stumbled forward and grabbed the young man by the back of his shirt and hauled with everything she had.

Larson's hands grew so bright that they blinded her as she flung them both back into the door to the concrete stairwell leading to a safe room that Mitch left open. "Eat shit! Asshole!" she screamed as she fell backward. Milliseconds later, a blinding flash ripped through the room as Sam's body crashed into hers and the door slammed shut with a thundering boom.

No one within thirty feet of Larson on the other side of that door survived. When she woke in the pitch-black stairwell, she had a concussion and could no longer speak. No matter how hard she tried, she had never been able to utter another sensical word. Even the words she wrote came out in a code that only she could read. The doctors couldn't explain it. Sam suffered two broken vertebrae, and a shattered femur. If Mitch hadn't immediately healed him, the young man likely would have been bound to a wheelchair.

"Gentlemen. That will be enough for now," Mitch insisted, bringing her from her trip down nightmare alley. "We will re-convene in the morning when we have more information." He stood and extended his arm toward the closed door, although she was the only one who could see him.

Senator Nolan remained on the line when everyone else hung up. "Paragon, if the magical outburst and this new group con-tinue to be a threat, I can't promise the committee will continue to condone a close relationship with the Cahlad."

"Then perhaps you should deal with the new group. The only role Sovaj or artifact users have played in those incidents has been as the targets." Mitch snarled at the man. When the man remained on the line, Mitch glared at the phone. "You should hang up now, Senator."

Mitch's phone pinged with an incoming text.

Nisha: My ride left. But I found a great black hat.

Mitch: Moles of gravy

Nisha: It's very delicate. Can't wait to show you. Call you soon.

Mitch: River's lollipop

Zella frowned. My ride left meant Nisha didn't know where Ivan and Sam were. Found a great black hat meant she had the highest classification of Sovaj in custody. That meant that the situation was handled, and the person was not hostile. A peaceful intake might be possible. If she said gloves, they would need to send in reinforcements. Lots of them for a person of such a high-power designation. Maybe even Mitch, depending on the threat. It's very delicate, meant exactly that. But Zella had faith that Nisha had things under control. She was the best at de-escalating potentially dangerous situations.

It had been a long day, and she had admittedly lost track of time. But Stalker Prime hadn't been gone long enough for something like this to shake out. Had they?

Zella watched Mitch as the silence of the phone call continued. The Senator was a slimeball who hated all magic users and led campaign after campaign to dissolve the government's working relationship with the Cahlad. Only pressure from the executive branch and Mitch's close relationships with several of the other committee members kept the man in check. But political speculation indicated he planned to run for president in two years and would probably carry the party's nomination. They weren't going to have to wait two years for Nolan Miller to be a true and dangerous threat. Zella checked her watch. His true colors were going to show through in less than two hours. "Gladly," Senator Slime Ball finally uttered, and the line went dead. She stood and crossed the room, stopping in front of Mitch.

Mitch relaxed his shoulders. They were almost slumped at this point. The nap she forced on him at the hospital had helped, but he was still running on empty. She walked over to his desk and sat on the corner. He took both of her hands in his, gentle as always. "You don't seem concerned."

She shrugged. "That means you know something, but you are letting me make my own decision, anyway." She wiggled her hand that held his phone.

Mitch took it and read the text from Nisha. "What on earth have they gotten into now?" he asked. She shrugged. Mitch leaned down and kissed her forehead. "Sneak me out of here, my love."

Minutes later, Zella drove her Jeep with Mitch in the passenger seat down an access road that cut across the campus. She kept it parked in one of the employee lots that was a short walk down a dark and overgrown back alley directly behind their fenced back yard. Years ago, Sam helped her install hidden hinges on two of the boards. She could slip through just fine. Mitch had to wiggle.

She stopped, looking both ways before she pulled into the main street. Getting into a wreck drew attention. She didn't need that right now. "Zella?" Mitch asked, leaning forward and looking past her toward the main gates of the campus. A line of cars and vans, some of them obviously police cruisers, drove in. He looked at her with a curious face, raising an eyebrow and pointing. "Did you know about that?"

She smiled and turned left.

23

NISHA

"**S**eriously? He's an asshole?" Nisha asked as she shoved an onion ring in her mouth and swashed it down with a cherry soda. It was the second cherry soda the waitress had brought. The first was absorbed in a pile of wet napkins pushed to the side of the table because she had spilled it almost immediately. It happened so often she wasn't even embarrassed anymore. "You have just shattered my hopes and dreams," she joked with the man sitting across from her, whose murderous inner voices took hangry to a whole new level. So, she insisted they stop and feed the soul eater. His mood had improved greatly once he had eaten. Though he would never be accused of being Prince Charming.

They sat in a greasy diner that might be older than her grandmother. Finn, the angry Viking man, and some guy that worked for Finn and burped the alphabet backward, had scarfed their food like it would disappear if they didn't eat it fast enough and were making the trek to get the car while she waited for Ben to finish eating. Parking and traffic were impossible due to emergency road closures and Nashville's habit of building buildings without parking and scoffing at the idea of a functional public transportation system. Their car was at least ten blocks away.

Everything in this place was repaired in some way, some things more successfully than others. Above the coffee maker that sat behind the counter, an old tube television played a football game. She had finally gotten Ben to talk a bit about his job as an orthopedic surgeon to the stars, using the game as a conversation starter.

"Maurice Bradley. Terrible." He shook his head speaking about a pro football player whose knee he had worked on two seasons ago. "But Kace Graham, super nice." Ben was finishing his third patty melt. All Sovaj found themselves ravenous after a magic discharge. She had seen Ivan devour entire stockrooms of food. Ben wiped his hands on yet another napkin. A small mountain of napkins sat to his right. He used a clean one each time he took a bite of his sandwich. Nisha was curious about how the napkin situation was going to play out when he started on his fries. As it was, between her spill and his copious usage, the napkin dispenser was empty.

"Graham is sexy. And a way better quarterback, anyway. That makes it a little better." She waved to the sixty-something waitress wearing ripped jeans and combat boots. Her hair was dyed pink and styled punk. Despite the attire, she had a soft and friendly face. She dodged the wet floor sign that had been placed after her soda spill next to their table to check on them. "More napkins and a cherry

215

soda, please." Nisha wiggled her drink and pointed at Ben's napkin situation.

The waitress winked. "Sure thing, sweetheart."

When Nisha looked back at Ben, he was staring at her with an unreadable expression. "Are you making fun of me?" She heard a rumble start in his internal thoughts.

"What?" she asked, truly perplexed.

"More napkins?" he grumbled.

Nisha pointed at the empty chrome dispenser. "If I spill again or you take another bite of that sandwich, we are going to have an issue. So yeah. More napkins. Are we in grade school? Am I going to make fun of a guy who has been actively thinking about killing me for the past two hours?"

"I just want to get to Ava. I haven't been..." Ben began indignantly.

"Bull. Shit." Nisha cut him off with a sarcastic tone that came out way more aggressively than she intended. She was really on edge. Ben's mercurial temperament and ability to literally suck her soul out of her body on a whim wasn't helping her stress level. The pink-haired waitress placed a new glass of cherry soda and a full stack of napkins on the table. "Thank you!" Nisha changed her tone even though she was sure the woman had heard at least the last two sentences of the conversation. The women's thoughts veered toward what an odd couple they were and whether the cook had actually cleaned the grill before they opened. Nisha reached out to the cook.

Judging by the things that were on his mind, he probably hadn't. And she wasn't sure she wanted him touching her food. Ew.

Ben crossed his arms over his chest and stared at her. She sipped her fresh soda and stared back, filtering through his thoughts unapologetically now. She could hear him actively tamping down the chorus of voices that had taken over his head. He wasn't having much success. His hitchhikers were a rowdy bunch. She was still unnerved by his thoughts. He was one of the few other people she had listened to that truly had more than one person in his head. Everyone else was singular voices or the same person with different inflections. This guy had more than one person in there. And she still hadn't figured out which one had control.

"My daughter likes cherry soda," he blurted out of the blue. Nisha smiled. He was trying. This guy was not a social animal, and neither were the creepers in his head. Small talk was not a skill he had; she could tell. His bedside manner must be horrible. But she appreciated the effort. It wasn't always easy to operate in a world built for people who didn't have to deal with the things you did. Especially things they couldn't see.

"Yeah? Well, don't bring her here. Their cherry soda game is kind of weak." Nisha continued to smile. Maybe if she could build a rapport, she could get the thoughts about killing her down to once every few minutes instead of a constant mantra.

His brow furrowed. "Do we need to send it back? You should get what you want. Let me..." He turned to wave for the waitress.

Nisha sat stunned for a moment by this bit of normalcy. It was almost endearing. She reached out and pulled his hand down. "Nah. It's OK. Really. Some places are better than others, you know." As soon as her hand touched his arm, she saw his face relax slightly and heard the voices in his head grow quiet, just like they had on the sidewalk in the alley. She could only hear one person now, and it sounded like Ben. He just wanted to make sure she got a good cherry soda. She made up her mind. She stood up without letting go of his hand and walked around to his side of the ancient orange Formica booth.

"Are you sure?" He didn't seem to notice her movement at first, still looking in the direction of the waitress. Then he turned a stunned look her way. "What are you doing?"

"Scoot over, Ben," she told him as she moved her hand down his arm and laced her fingers with his. She sat on the edge of the seat and began scooting his way. It took him a moment, but he scooted further toward the wall. "Here is how it is going to be. We are both having a really bad day. And those assholes in your head want to kill me. It isn't making my day better knowing my dinner date's creepy inner voices have plans to suck the life out of my body even after I fed them. But this." She held up their intertwined hands. "This makes those creeper guys shut the hell up. And I don't think you want to kill me. So we are going to hold hands like lovesick teenagers from feuding families engaged in a forbidden love affair until all of this is over. I hope you can eat left-handed Romeo."

"I—" Ben started, then shook his head. "OK."

"OK." Nisha nodded. His mind had quieted almost entirely, and he seemed somewhat shocked by both the silence and the physical contact. Relieved herself for the relative quiet, she laid her head on his shoulder and allowed herself to relax slightly. She was honestly exhausted. The past twenty-four hours and the stress of sitting near a Sovaj with one of the most lethal and uncontrollable abilities ever documented had taken its toll. Her body ached from being thrown repeatedly through the air despite the magical healing, and she wanted to sleep for days. "They should be here soon. Finish your fries and then we can get back on the road."

He didn't say anything, but she did see him reach for a fry. Just as she suspected, they did need the extra napkins. She watched as he put a dent in both his fries and hers. She checked her phone. She sent Mitch a message as soon as they reached Finn's car, letting them know her status. She had received several gibberish answers and assumed Zella had his phone. He had finally replied with an update. They were leaving the Cahlad campus now, but Friday night traffic was slowing them down. Despite Sam's misgivings after reading the files on that USB drive, she trusted Mitch, and she needed all the help she could get to keep Ben and his daughter safe. At the end of the day, that was her job. She kept people safe, however; she had to do it. Ben and Finn would be pissed. But they would just have to deal with it. She wasn't sure how the angry Viking would react. Probably not well considering he was an unregistered Sovaj crafting unregistered artifacts.

219

"Who were those assholes back there?" Ben asked quietly after several silent moments, careful to make sure the other patrons couldn't overhear.

"I don't know exactly. But they do not have good intentions."

"You do?" he asked bluntly.

Nisha narrowed her eyes angrily, looking up at the man taking up the majority of the booth, and used her free hand to poke him hard in the chest. "For the record, I didn't have to help you. I could have left your ass in the street. I didn't have to tell Torrin not to shoot you. I didn't have to tell you I knew where your daughter might be. I could have called for backup with a detailed description and let a full squad descend on you and not given it another thought. I could be safe with my friends, with a cell phone that's screen isn't cracked, and have complete use of my left hand right now," Nisha reminded him. She was frustrated and sincerely regretted the decision to help this guy. She was getting whiplash from his moods and his hitchhikers. She was well and thoroughly done with it all. Either he trusted her or he didn't. "When I say it out loud, I must be incredibly stupid," she spat. "But my intentions are good."

"Forgive me if I don't trust you. You are Cahlad. Ranking Cahlad." There it was.

"Well, then, good luck, Ben." Nisha stood quickly, pulling on their joined hands. Ben tightened his grip.

"It really is helping." He stopped mid-sentence, looking apologetic and slightly panicked as he shifted to fish his wallet out of his back pocket. He held it out to her. "I'm sorry."

"Holding hands is fine. You being a bipolar asshole, that bothers me," she told him, jumping when someone slammed a hand down on their table. She glared as the giant Viking appeared next to their table and slid into the seat across from them.

"Well, hello there, lovebirds." He smiled and gestured to the diner's front doors, where an SUV driven by a man named Hale sat waiting for them at the curb. "Your chariot awaits."

Nisha hissed as she pulled the money out of Ben's wallet and laid it on top of the check. "I like you the least," she told the man who had successfully annoyed her since he regained his feet in the alley.

"That's because you don't know me yet." He smiled and led the way out. He opened the door for them. The tiny bell overhead jingled. Ben stepped through first and opened the back door of the SUV so she could climb in. They somehow managed to climb in and scoot across the back seat with their hands still attached.

Greenlee got in, forcing everyone into uncomfortable proximity with each other, and closed the door. Hale pulled away from the curb without waiting for anyone to buckle up. She was not surprised by his lack of attention to general safety. He seemed pretty carefree. Finn's phone rang as she struggled to buckle her seat belt one-handed. Ben finally reached over to help. Finn answered the call and sat in silence for a moment, his brow furrowing into a frown. "Dev? Are you OK?"

"Shit," Finn muttered quietly and sent a loaded look at Hale. That look communicated trouble.

Greenlee leaned forward, his goofy persona dropping away in a flash. His face took on a dark, predatory look and his relaxed posture disappeared as a wave of aggression rolled off him. Nisha and Ben leaned away from the man simultaneously. Great, she was stuck in the car with a soul eater and someone who made the soul eater nervous. Everyone grew tense. Nisha tried to filter through Greenlee's thoughts to get a read on the sudden change in demeanor. It was like he turned into a different person. She couldn't hear anything, so she shifted to Finn, his face grim, and winced when the conversation filtered through to her.

Finn issued calm and brisk instructions to the woman on the other end of the line. Nisha and Ben kept weary eyes on the annoying Viking. It felt a bit like being locked in a cage with a lion that suddenly decided he was hungry.

"What's happening?" Greenlee demanded.

Finn just turned and handed him his phone with a shake of his head.

"Devon. Honey. What's happened?"

24

DEVON

D evon turned up the lights in the lecture hall as she finished explaining her last slide. Her last class of the day was a sophomore-level Modern History class with a focus on the Magical Revolution. It may have been a personal specialty, but it was not her academic area of expertise. She was teaching this section as a favor to the chair of the department. It was her least favorite because the required curriculum was heavily biased garbage. It is why she dumped Lexi's homework on Blue the other day.

"Any questions? Comments? Life-altering revelations?" She smiled at the students. They stared in silence for a few moments. Not unusual for a lower-level class filled to the brim with undergrads. She looked around. Some were packing up. Others were looking down at their phones. The silence suited her just fine. It had been a long day. Much longer than usual. She just wanted to go home, put on cozy socks, drink a glass of wine and talk Greenlee into parking on the couch and binge-watching something terrible on television.

A hand shot up toward the back. She mentally rifled through her list of students, searching for his name. Just because it was a large lecture-style class didn't mean she couldn't give them some personal attention. "Deondre. Yes?" She pointed to the student in the back of the room. He smiled warmly. She got the name right.

"What do you think happened to Mullet Roane after the Mandarin Casino Heist? He just disappeared. Like D.B. Cooper."

Devon schooled her features. Why did these classes always devolve into questions about Mullet fucking Roane? It was that God-forsaken documentary series. That was why. She nodded and considered her answer.

She could tell them what had actually happened. But she wasn't going to. Mullet Roane arrived home from that heist, flush with cash and high on power and adrenaline, to find a virtually empty house. His wife, tired of the constant running, drinking, philandering, and exhibitionist nonsense, left with everything in the house except for one thing. That thing being a six-year-old little girl who sat for more than twenty-four hours in the cold dark house clutching a purple stuffed bunny while her mother started a new life with her new boyfriend and her father ran naked down the Vegas strip wearing nothing but his eyeliner.

The woman had even taken their daughter's toys, clothes, and baby pictures. Everything but the child and her stuffy. Mullet Roane dropped off the face of the earth after that, trying and failing to be the parent a six-year-old girl needed. He settled for foisting her off on a never-ending stream of ridiculous girlfriends and business acquaintances that owed him a favor, buying his daughter anything that would keep her quiet and out of his hair while conducting his criminal activities in a more discreet fashion.

The popular theory held that the Cahlad finally caught up with him and spirited him away quietly to atone for his many sins. The theory wasn't far off. Three Cahlad stalker units and eventually an assassin caught up with Mullet Roane over the years. None were successful in bringing him into custody or killing him, but the assassin had come close. They were successful at making him paranoid and mobile. He lived like a vagabond, never in one place for more than a few months. That meant his daughter lived like a vagabond, too. Devon had lived like that until he left her, just like her mother had. Because dear old dad was the most wanted fugitive in the country, if not the world. And had been for the past thirty years.

Devon sighed. Nobody gave a shit about her daddy issues. And only three other people in the world knew who her father was. So, she spouted back the Cahlad theory to the student who seemed satisfied to have her verify the internet theory.

She answered four more questions about Mullet Roane, even one about the size of his penis. She smiled and laughed and fed the eager undergrads a complete line of bullshit. Then she let the class go five minutes early for her own sanity.

She strolled to her office, a converted storage closet, and pulled her phone from her purse. She never took a phone to class. Plopping down in the office chair she had scavenged from the trash pile and patched with pink duct tape, she frowned at the number of texts and missed calls. Three from an unknown number, three from Robert Larkin, and one from her brother-in-law Finn. What on earth?

Nervously, she dialed Robert back. He was supposed to pick Lexi up after school and take her to soccer practice, then to a sleepover. He picked up on the second ring. "Robert. I'm sorry I missed your call. I was in a lecture. Is everything OK?"

"Devon. I'm at your house now with the police," he said with a nervous flutter in his voice.

"The police? What has happened? Is Lexi OK?" Devon shrieked the last sentence. She jumped to her feet, picked up her purse, and ran from her office.

"She's not here, Devon. The front door was unlocked and when we went in to check, one of the interior doors was busted off the hinges. All her stuff is here, including her phone," Robert said.

Devon ran even as her ears rang. This couldn't be happening again. "Is she with Greenlee? Or Blue?" Devon latched on to any type of hope but knew the truth in her gut. How had they found her this time? She was so careful. She rushed down the hallway, the heel of her flat clicking audibly on the polished tile floors. She barely registered the stunned and confused looks of colleagues and students.

"Greenlee isn't answering his phone. Your friend Blue isn't answering her phone, either," Robert informed her. "I don't know what to do here. The police want to talk to you."

"Please, no," Devon whispered, bursting through the door leading to the sidewalk outside the building. She was parked one block over in a small side lot reserved for faculty. She broke into a sprint. Her heart raced. "I'm on my way, Robert. Tell them I'm on my way."

She hung up the phone and dashed the rest of the way to her car. This was exactly what had happened with Alexander and Gage. She couldn't do this again. Her nose burned, but no tears fell from her eyes. "Call Blue." The Bluetooth connected, and the phone rang and rang. Finally, Blue's voicemail greeting kicked in. "Don't leave a message. I won't listen to it." She jabbed the button on her steering wheel to disconnect the call and tried again. Nothing.

"Call Finn," she barked at her phone, throwing her car into gear and peeling out of the tiny parking lot. Finally, the call started ringing. "Come on, Finn. I need you." Devon slammed her fist into the steering wheel, forced to slow down for a person with the audacity to do the speed limit.

The call picked up after three rings. "Dev? Are you OK?" Finn asked immediately.

"Lexi is missing. Finn. She's gone." She finally let herself sob, gulping for air.

Finn's only response was a hissed curse.

"Greenlee is missing, too. They probably think he took her. But the house had a busted door. I..."

"Devon. I have Greenlee here with me. You can't go to the house. Turn around and go the other way." Finn told her.

"What? No. The police."

227

"Are ill-equipped to deal with whoever is behind this. And if you are also a target, you are walking right into their trap. Stop right now and go the other way, Devon."

All she could manage was a garbled "Finn."

Silence hung between them for a moment, but she could hear Greenlee demanding to know what was going on in the background. "Trust me, sister. This is what Herne does. You aren't going to lose another child."

"Greenlee?" she croaked. Somehow, Finn knew what she meant. She heard him pass the phone over, and Greenlee's voice rang over her car's speakers. "Devon. Honey. What's happened?"

Devon had no more words left. Just ragged breaths that filled her car as she found a parking lot to pull into. She whipped the car around and pulled back into the road, going the other direction. She heard Finn's distinctive voice in the background speaking quietly at first, then in a commanding higher voice as he moved away from the phone.

"I'm here, Dev. I'm going to stay on the line with you. I'm here. Finn is already doing his Finn thing. He is going to get our girl, Dev. Our girl is going to be OK. Keep it together."

Greenlee kept talking to her as she navigated on autopilot through rush hour traffic. Her whole body quaked violently. Her mind wasn't in the car. The only thing keeping her grounded was his voice. Her phone beeped and buzzed with other calls from friends and neighbors, but she didn't answer them. She just focused on Greenlee. If she didn't, her mind kept reverting to the day a decade ago when she came home with a car full of groceries to a decimated front door. Those groceries contained two pregnancy tests. Neither was ever used, but they both would have come back positive. Instead, her husband, Alexander, was dead on the living room floor in a puddle of blood. She could still see his bruised face and empty eyes. She could smell the blood. Her son, Gage, was gone. She had never seen him alive again. Standing in shock over her husband, someone had hit her from behind. That day and the four months following had shaped every breath she had taken since. And she couldn't live through it again.

"Devon. Are you with me, Dev?" Her focus returned to Green-lee's voice. Whatever he had said, he wanted a response.

"What?" she asked quietly. "Sorry." Her hands still shook. She needed to pull over. She signaled and turned into the parking lot of a local comic book and used music store.

"Finn wants you to meet us at Lilac." He referred to the location of the Herne offices. "Can you do that for me? Is your phone charged? I'm going to stay with you the whole way."

"I can." She nodded to herself. "You don't have to. I'm OK." She could still hear voices in the background. And road noise. Greenlee was in a car.

"I'm staying with you."

The tears that had dried up as she drove threatened to spill over again. She needed to hold her baby in her arms. She needed to know she was safe. She needed one of Greenlee's rib-cracking hugs. She was alone. Her voice warbled, "Blue?"

"Honey." Greenlee paused. "Have you seen the news?" His voice was full of hesitation.

"No. No. No," she said. More to the thought that something had happened to Blue than to his question about the news. Blue was her rock and best friend. Blue was her family. Blue would be able to get to Lexi anywhere. They had to find Blue. She was their best shot. She couldn't do this without Blue. She didn't want to.

"She was here with Finn. There was an explosion about an hour ago. People with guns. Of course, she was in the middle of it. He hasn't seen her since." Greenlee filled her in. He never did pull punches.

Devon took deep breaths. "Her phone?"

"Last location was dead center of the explosion. But that doesn't mean anything."

"Wait. Green. Are you with Finn? Why?" she asked rapid fire, finally putting those strange circumstances together. Nothing was making sense. And she wasn't able to keep up.

"I was run off the road. Some assholes jumped me. Knocked me out. I woke up in a van in Five Points. Then Finn was there. They had green gas, Dev. It's . . . " He let his words hang as if saying it out loud left him stunned as well.

"Why didn't you say anything?" Devon screeched. They had taken Greenlee, too. They had gas. This was too much like what had happened before. She felt more panic rise. Too much panic. She wasn't going to be able to hold it together. Were they targeting her? Was it because of her? Or her dad? Or Blue?

"It doesn't matter what happened to me. Our girl is missing. I need to take care of you," he answered without hesitation and with utter conviction.

"I swear Greenlee." Devon waited a minute and gripped the steering wheel so hard that her fingers were going numb and turning white. "Green. Finn is going to find Lexi. Then I am going to kill them all. I'm going to kill them."

"I'll help you."

"OK." She knew he would. He always had. And she loved him for it.

"I'm here."

"I know." She placed her forehead against the steering wheel, closed her eyes, and cried.

25

RHODES

Rhodes dropped the enormous load of bags he was hauling onto the hardwood entryway of the small castle he called home and let out a sigh. The realtor referred to it as an "executive" home. He was pretty sure that meant pretentious and disgustingly expensive. He shrugged his shoulders, dislodging two huge duffel bags to free his arms and hands so that he could turn off the beeping alarm. How he ended up carrying his bodyguard and personal assistant's luggage, he had no idea. How did Harper have more gear than he did? She only wore tee shirts and blue jeans. He was the rock star, for God's sake.

He glared at her as she walked in the door behind him without a word, carrying a sleeping Lady Lucille in her arms. Her feet dragged, and her shoulders slumped slightly. She had swapped out contacts for black-rimmed glasses before they left the arena to board a quick there and back flight for a television interview he had scheduled before agreeing to the last-minute Cahlad Conclave concert. Her hair was piled on top of her head in a bun that was starting to fall. The dog was lying on its back, head dangling backward over Harper's crooked elbow, snoring audibly. Harper shot him a bird over her shoulder and continued further into the cavernous house toward the kitchen.

None of them got more than an hour or two of light napping despite the first-class seats. He was dead on his feet, and Harper was so grumpy he was afraid to talk to her. Even offering to carry her luggage and keeping her plied with coffee wasn't helping. Kendra looked refreshed and rested, even though he knew she was running on less sleep than any of them and didn't drink caffeine. She couldn't be human.

She strolled into the house, her long legs covering the distance with half as much effort as Harper's shorter frame. She reached down into the pile of luggage, retrieving her own, and continued walking, casually scanning the house as she went.

"I need a vacation. Somewhere warm. Do you own a bikini?" Rhodes muttered, punching in the code for the alarm and pushing his thumb to the fingerprint pad. The alarm system was over the top and expensive. It also came recommended by both Blue and the company she outsourced his security to.

"I can get one," Kendra answered, checking her phone. Rhodes provided her with a suite in the East wing of the house so that she would have a place to rest on exceptionally long days like this one. Most days lately were exceptionally long days. "Rearm that for occupied Rhodes," she instructed, typing a message into her phone.

Alone in the massive foyer, he looked down at the pile of luggage at his feet and blew out a breath. "You're welcome, ladies. My pleasure." He shuffled toward the kitchen, feet leaden and eyes bleary. He wanted a glass of juice, a Tylenol, and his bed. He hoped the housekeeper had restocked the fridge. She always forgot the juice. She was old and forgetful and couldn't bend over to pick anything up off the ground. He ended up cleaning more than she did. Her cooking was atrocious, so he had Harper order a few precooked meals from a service that he could eat once he threw Nancy's cooking out. The rest he cooked himself when he had time. But Nancy's granddaughter had a heart condition, and she had full custody. The whole torrid and depressing story emerged one day when she cried rivers into the chocolate chip cookie dough she was making one afternoon. Rhodes threw the flat cookies out and offered her a full-time position with insurance that afternoon.

When he walked into the kitchen, Harper stood in front of the coffeemaker, still holding a sleeping Lady Lucille in her arm. The other hand clutched a bottle of red wine. She held the bottle up in front of the coffeemaker and turned her head sideways, trying to decide which she should drink. "Nancy forgot the O.J."

"Wine counts as juice, right?" He shrugged and dug two wine glasses out, then pulled a bottle of painkiller from the kitchen's designated junk drawer. He didn't care how expensive a house was or how executive the kitchen was. It wasn't home unless it had a junk drawer.

"Sure, it does." Harper brought the bottle over to him, and they poured two huge glasses of red.

"Want some?" he asked, shaking the pill bottle and pouring twice the recommended dosage into his hand.

"Nah. Just going to have a second breakfast and go the hell to sleep for a few days." Harper raised her wineglass in salute and took a long sip. Lady Lucille growled in her sleep at the jostling.

They remained in companionable silence while Harper finished her wine. Rhodes took a sniff and decided he couldn't do it. He swallowed the Tylenol dry and gave his glass to her. She could have it. "Let me have Her Royal Highness. I'll put her to bed." He reached for the pug in Harper's arms.

"This one is spoiled rotten. Did you know she won't drink water out of the tap?" She stepped closer to transfer the dog to his arms and yelped when a flash of pale blue light scorched through the kitchen, followed by the boom of thunder. Harper recoiled instantly, pulling Lady Lucille into her chest.

A body flew out of the blue light directly between them. Harper stumbled backward and landed on her bottom with an indignant, "Oh shit. What the fuck?" The body caught Rhodes in the chest like a freight train, and he tumbled backward with a shout. He fell flat on his back and struggled to think fast enough to figure out what was happening.

A sob erupted from the person laying on him. It was high-pitched and watery. He raised his head, catching a glimpse of black hair and a purple sweatshirt. He heard a sniffle, then a wail. "Hey. Hey." He placed his hands gently on the shoulders of what he realized was a child. He was more alarmed by the crying child than by how she had gotten here. He didn't do tears.

Running footsteps echoed through the hall seconds before Kendra burst into the kitchen in a low stance, gun drawn and eyes fierce. She swept the room with both her gaze and her weapon advancing. Her nose twitched like a rabbit's.

Harper sprang up from the floor. "What in the blazes?" Her eyes went from Rhodes to Kendra and back to Rhodes. "You can't shoot a kid!" she barked at Kendra, running toward them and throwing her body between his bodyguard and whatever had dropped from the sky.

"Stand aside, Ms. Kilgarden," Kendra said quietly.

Harper shot her a dirty look and gave her attention to their unexpected new visitor. She crouched down next to them and put a hand on the girl's back. She looked at Rhodes with a muttered, "What the fuck?" before speaking to the child. "Sweetheart. Are you hurt?"

"N-N-N-N-O-O," the child stuttered and sat up. She dug her elbow into his ribs, and he cursed. "I-I-I'm s-s-so sorry."

"It's OK, sweetheart. Let's get you off the floor. What is your name?" Harper sat an indignant Lady Lucille on the floor and helped the child up. She led the girl to the kitchen island and glared at Kendra, who had not lowered her weapon. Kendra, a scowl marring her features, glanced around the room, checking for entry points and coming to the same conclusion that Rhodes had. This kid fell out of thin air. Second woman in a week to appear out of nowhere. He didn't like it.

"Rhodes. Get her a Coke," Harper ordered, sitting the girl down and gently pushing her hair out of her face.

He moved to the fridge, hoping Nancy stocked some sort of soda. She had. He pulled a Coke out of the door and gave it to the kid. She appeared to be somewhere around nine or ten. She had long black hair and brown eyes, red from crying. She glanced at him with fear and confusion. "Where am I? Who are you?" she asked all three of them, recoiling slightly into the chair.

"Kendra." Rhodes shook his head. The kid might be a threat, but hell, if he was going to be a party to holding one at gunpoint. She holstered her weapon and walked around to get a good look at the situation. "I'm Rhodes." He squatted in front of her next to Harper, trying to make himself less threatening. "What is your name?"

The girl's eyes grew big as saucers. "Rhodes? Cade Rhodes? Like "Baby Blue"?" she said in disbelief. "O.M.G.," she whispered and launched herself from the chair, running to the other side of the island. Her hand flew to a bracelet dangling from her left hand. Rhodes placed a hand on Kendra's arm to keep her from doing anything drastic. ""Baby Blue". Oh, my God. She didn't. She did," the girl said as she paced. "She is so cool."

"Sweetie?" Harper tried again. She looked at Rhodes like he would know what to do about this. As far as he was concerned, this was exactly the kind of crazy he paid her very well to deal with. So, he just lifted his shoulders and shook his head.

"She told me to say Baby Blue and I would be safe. Ha! It worked!" The girl crowed and then frowned all at the same moment. "I need to call my mom."

"Who told you to say Baby Blue, sweetheart? We still don't know your name." Harper spoke in a tone Rhodes suspected she would use on a cornered wild animal or a crazy person. She used it on him often enough.

"Tia Blue. She gave me this." The girl waved a hand, sporting a charm bracelet. "And she told me if the world was ever ending to hold this charm real tight and say Baby Blue and I would be safe." She glanced around, eying Kendra suspiciously, then flipped her gaze between Rhodes and Harper. "So, I'm safe. Right?"

"Blue?" Rhodes only managed to sputter a one-word response. His head was spinning. Blue had sent a child hurtling through God knows what to him for safety. She wouldn't even return his calls. She wouldn't let him help her. But she sent him this child to take care of. Why couldn't she keep the kid safe herself? What on earth was happening? Whatever it was, was bad.

Harper quirked an eyebrow. "The world was ending?" she coaxed.

"There were these two guys. Really mean looking. In my house when I got home from school. I locked myself in a room, and they kicked in the door. Like just kicked it with their foot. And it flew open. They broke Tia Blue's door. I was so scared. I think they were going to hurt me." She rambled and slurped the Coke. "Look, lady, I really need to call my mom."

"Tell us your name," Kendra said in a dark voice from behind Rhodes. The girl's eyes narrowed, and she stared at Kendra in defiance. But Kendra was scary, and the defiance quickly left her face.

"Lexi. Lexi O'Neal. And I need to call my mom. I really think Tia Blue might have actually saved my life. I'm going to miss soccer practice."

Harper turned to Rhodes. She looked like she was trying to place a word or remember something.

"Lexi O'Neal?" Kendra hissed. She stepped closer and leaned down to get a better look. "What in the hell?"

"O'Neal." Harper snapped her fingers. "Devon? Is Devon your mom?"

"Is Finn your uncle?" Kendra interjected, pulling her cell phone from her pocket.

Rhodes looked back and forth between the two. He was missing something. "Anybody care to explain?"

"Devon is Blue's roommate. Margarita night," Harper told him. "Get my phone."

"And Finn Torrin is Devon's brother-in-law," Kendra filled in.

"Finn Torrin. Your boss?" Rhodes turned back to the kid who was gulping the Coke like she had just run a marathon through a desert. "Why do I have this kid?"

"Wow. You are kind of slow." Lexi wiped the back of her mouth with her sleeve.

"Am I now?"

"Tia Blue sent me here because she thinks you can keep me safe when the world is ending. You must be a complete badass. Because Tia Blue, well, she is a badass. She doesn't know I know. But I know things." Lexi tilted her head to the side. "I can't believe it is you. My Mom HATES you. Will you sing me that song? Can we listen to it? Tia Blue won't let us play your songs in the house." Lexi sat on a stool on the other side of the island and spun. "Or in the car." She continued spinning. "She makes them veto it at restaurants, too. But I kind of like it. This Coke is great. Can I have another?"

Kid was right. He was slow. He turned to Kendra, who was already speaking softly on the phone to someone. Harper was frantically texting. "I can't get Blue to answer. Devon's is going straight to voice mail."

"Lexi?" Kendra asked, walking forward and holding out her phone. Lexi stopped spinning long enough to take the phone. She held it to her ear.

"Uncle Finn? Yeah. I'm OK." her voice broke, and she looked down at her lap. She shook from her shoulders to her toes as nervous energy coursed through her. "I'm OK," she sobbed, as everything caught up with her. Harper wrapped Lexi in her arms, rubbing her back.

"We need to move. If they heard the activation words for the charm, they might put two and two together. I have a secure location," he spoke quietly to Kendra.

The woman stared at him, hands on her hips, her eyes fierce and calculating. "Mr. Rhodes. I took this assignment as a favor to a friend with very little information. I do, however, know that you nor any of your business holdings own a property that could be deemed secure."

They both turned as Lexi started crying to someone she called Tio G. "You are correct, Ms. Reyes. Neither Cade Rhodes nor his holdings own a secure location. Nor does he have a private pilot's license or a private plane at a hangar at John C. Tune Airport. But I do."

Kendra narrowed her eyes.

"What do you know about Blue, Kendra?"

Kendra didn't say anything for a long moment. Her nose twitched. She looked down, then over at Harper. "I know she works for Finn on high touch or delicate cases."

"Do you know why? Do you know why I sought her out when I decided to get security?"

"You don't screen for crazy before you take chicks back home and a few of them got stalker-y? Because you are delusional and have difficulty letting go of the past?" she clipped.

"Let's just say I knew her in another life. And the man I was in that life has a safe house and a way to get us there."

She nodded slowly. "I need the details if I'm going to do my job."

Rhodes gave her a wolfish grin. "Your job just changed. It's them." He turned and pointed toward Harper, who was now holding the sniffling girl on her lap and speaking into the phone herself. "This is my chance to make something right and that little girl just became the most important person in the world."

"Yes, sir."

"I need a few minutes. Then we go."

"You are going whether I advise against it or not? Whether I'm with you or not? The security system here is top-of-the-line. There is a safe room."

"Ms. Reyes. If Blue sent her to me, the people coming after this little girl will wipe through this security system and crack that safe room before you can blink your eyes. You have never fought anything like them before. And they are probably on their way now. I would rather not be here when they arrive."

She sucked her lips across her teeth in frustration and glanced back over at Harper. "I'll lock us down. Move us to the interior. Keep a patrol until you are ready to leave."

Rhodes nodded. It amazed him that either woman was handling this crazy ass situation as well as they were. A kid literally fell from the sky, and they were trudging on as if it were a matter, of course. He pulled out his phone and dialed Blue's number. She didn't answer. He hit the button to disconnect aggressively. Still peering down at his phone, he noticed a news alert. "Explosion in Nashville hot spot leaves a dozen injured." He frowned, clicking on the link.

"A puppy!" Lexi squealed as Lady Lucile spotted a new person to con scratches out of and trundled over, snorting and snotting.

His stomach dropped as he read the article on his phone. Images of the napkin he passed to Blue flashed through his head. The Cat and Canary, the scene of an explosion and gunfire less than two hours ago, was a war zone. He sent her to that place, and it was attacked. Then a child calling her Tia Blue hurtles out of thin air into his kitchen. A child Rhodes knew Blue should have been able to protect or would die trying to do it. And she wasn't here.

He stretched his hand out, signaling for Harper to cough up Kendra's phone. He placed it to his ear. "This is Rhodes. Who am I talking to?"

The line was silent for a moment. "Finn Torrin." Rhodes could tell he was on speakerphone. He heard a man telling someone that they had found Lexi and she was in Nashville. Even more reason to move her. That information did not need to get out. He didn't know who that was or who else could hear.

"Torrin. Good to talk to you again. I'm moving Lexi to a secure location. I will have Kendra contact you with a meeting point."

"That's not going to work for me. We are coming to you. We are thirty minutes out," Finn replied in a deep voice that garnered no argument.

Rhodes ignored him. "Blue? Do you know where she is?"

"No, man. I wish I did," Finn answered sincerely.

"What is the situation as you see it, Torrin?" Rhodes asked, shifting back into a mode he had been running from for a decade. He felt calm. The world was coming into focus.

Finn took a moment to debrief him in an impressively emotionless and practical manner, given the fact his niece, sister-in-law, and employee were involved. Rhodes was impressed with the amount of information the man had amassed in less than two hours. But none of the information did anything for the lead ball of dread that had settled in his stomach. The more Finn spoke, the more he was convinced he needed to get Lexi as far from this city and any person tied to her as he could. Blue was in over her head.

"I'll have Kendra contact you." He hit the button to hang up as a half-formed shout escaped the phone. It rang again immediately, and he silenced it, tossing it back to Kendra. "Answer that and you can walk out the door." She silently put her phone in her pocket. He wasn't sure what to think of Kendra. But he could use her skills as long as she followed his lead.

"Lexi." Rhodes walked over to the group clustered around his kitchen island. "I'm Rhodes. I've known your Tia Blue for a very long time. She is very important to me and a good friend. I'm going to make sure that nothing else bad happens to you."

Lexi took another sip of her second Coke and nodded. "Tio G says that if Tia Blue trusts you, then I can."

Rhodes sighed in relief. Her cooperation would help.

"He also said that if you make me cry like you did Tia Blue, there won't be any pieces of you left to bury." Lexi smiled sweetly and blinked her eyes rapidly.

"Duly noted," Rhodes acknowledged. This kid was something else. Not only did the kid's mom hate him, but apparently, her uncle did as well. He had never even met the man. The Uncle he did know probably hated his guts now too. "Let's get ready to take a ride. Have you ever ridden on a plane?"

26

DEVON

Devon looked down at her lap. Greenlee was silent, but she heard voices in the background. The longer she sat in the comic store parking lot trying to get herself under control, the more she was convinced she should go back to her house. Trap be damned. The kidnapping assholes and very likely every soul in a half-mile radius of them would be dead and meeting their maker in less than thirty seconds. And they would never know what hit them. She no longer cared about the collateral. These people needed to know she was not a person to mess with. Her family was off-limits. Screw being the good guy. They made the rules. She would play by them.

She turned the key in the ignition. Hell with going the other way. She would deal with this once and for all.

"Hold on, baby. Finn has something," Greenlee said as she eased out of the parking space and pulled onto the road. The traffic was hideous due to the fact it was a Friday night, and she was wedged between two colleges. Cars and pedestrians were everywhere.

"Yeah," she muttered distractedly. She was glad he was occupied. He didn't need to know she was going home. The tone of his voice caught her attention. He was emotional and speaking to someone else. Her heart thundered in her ears and her mouth went dry. Was it news about Lexi? Then he said her name and told someone to calm down. He called them darling. He was talking to Lexi. "Finn! Greenlee!" she yelled into her phone. "Somebody talk to me. So help me, God!"

"Dev," she heard Finn's voice and the noise of a phone being fumbled. "She's safe. She's with Rhodes and Harper. I'm trying to get details. Something about a bracelet."

Tears spilled from her eyes again. She found herself caught between sobs and gasping for breath. "Where? Tell me where."

"Hang tight, Dev," Finn replied, and she knew in her gut that she was being handled and she saw red.

"Now!" she barked into the phone. "Finn Howl Torrin! Right the fuck now!"

"Giving you back to Greenlee." Finn's voice faded away. She pounded on the steering wheel.

"Dev. She's good. She's scared, but she's good." Greenlee breathed into the line, and she heard joy and relief in his voice.

"Where, Green?" she asked again.

"Oh, God. I didn't ask. I know she is with Cade Rhodes. She used the charm on the bracelet Blue had me make for her. I didn't know that was how she set it," Greenlee told her. She heard him ask Finn where she was as his hand covered the phone. Finn's voice echoed in the background with the road noise. "No, man. Tell me where my girl is," he barked at Finn. The frustration in his voice mirrored her own. What was Finn hiding? The muffled conversation grew more heated as Devon chewed her lip. It felt like her insides were shaking apart.

"She's with Rhodes at his house in Belle Meade," Greenlee finally answered. "Finn is sending everything he has that way."

"I'm closer," Devon said, turning on the road in the direction she knew Rhodes' obnoxious house lay. The frustration she felt before at the traffic that kept her from heading toward Greenlee melted away. That traffic meant she was just closer to her daughter. If she ran some people off the road and cut through alleys, she could be there in twenty minutes. Her foot pressed down on the accelerator.

"No. His place might not be secure. Let Finn's team look first," Greenlee begged.

"Uh, huh? See you there." Devon hung up on his curse. A few minutes later, she careened down a residential street and turned left toward the stretch of road that hosted a few dozen of the most expensive homes in the Nashville area, favored by old Nashville money. She knew exactly where she was going. When Blue took the security job for Rhodes, Devon ran every background check and search possible on him. Given her background, there was a lot of possible, both legal and illegal. You didn't grow up in the heart of a criminal enterprise without developing a few skills and contacts that could be put to use later. She peered down the road toward her intended destination and narrowed her eyes. Three black

SUVs pulled onto the small road leading to the gate that sequestered Rhodes' estate from the rest of humanity. Their movements were smooth but aggressive, and her foot instinctively pushed toward the floor. She felt the tickle of hair rising from her head as she struggled to wrangle her emotions and her magic.

Whipping her car down the paved drive, she floored it. Those weren't Finn's guys. Her tiny Honda strained and finally put her back within sight distance of the rear SUV. The lead SUV rammed the fifteen-foot-tall iron gate flanked by a white horse rail fence. The two that followed didn't slow down as they sped through the swinging gates.

She turned off her headlights. Her phone rang. "Answer call," she uttered. She zeroed in on the vehicles in front of her. The lead vehicle was already stopped in the circular driveway. Eight sleek figures in black poured out of it and ran up the steps, fanning out. The other two vehicles parked at either entrance of the circular drive, blocking the way in and out. Devon sneered, a feral feeling spreading through her chest and limbs. That worked just fine.

"Devon. Do not engage," Finn barked as soon as the Bluetooth connected the call to her speakers. "Kendra reported three incoming."

"I see them." She cursed her underpowered, four-cylinder junker. Occupants of the two parked vehicles exited and began flanking the house. Two people stayed with each car. Static sparked off her fingers, and her hair flew around her face.

"Dev?" Finn's voice held an edge of wariness.

"Hmmm. Lined up nice and pretty for me. You should probably send someone to clean this up," she said as one of the guards remaining with the vehicle to her right noticed her. He lifted his weapon, and she floored the accelerator.

Her windshield broke and splintered when a bullet hit it. She hunched down and whipped the wheel. Finn and Greenlee shouted from her speakers as her car veered through the grass in the U of the driveway, bypassing both vehicles and jumped the brick edging. She gritted her teeth to keep them from rattling loose and kept her head down. She had everyone's attention now. And that was OK, because they weren't trying to get into the house with Lexi anymore. Her rear passenger window shattered.

She let off the accelerator as the front tires hit the steps leading up to Rhodes' front door. The car jerked and bumped, climbing the stone stairs and tilting, coming to rest with the front wheels on the large front patio. Devon flipped around, putting her knees in her seat, and peeked around the headrest. Yep, they were still clustered. They had no idea what she had planned for them.

"Devon. Tell me you are OK," Greenlee asked with a deceptively calm and quiet voice through her speakers.

"I'm fine," she answered. She was for now. But she wasn't likely to remain that way. She had her back to the open front door and knew there were at least seven very bad guys in there who heard the racket she made. Twelve people with guns were moving her way. She laughed humorously. She really hadn't thought this one through. Blue would be proud. "I love you, Green. Thank you. For everything. Tell Lexi Mommy loves her."

"What are you doing, sweetheart?" She could hear the fear in Greenlee's tone and Finn losing his mind in the background. Something about not a damned person listening to him today.

She took a deep breath, extended her arms, and released the energy she gathered as she drove. Her black hair flew straight out from her head, tickling her scalp with its weightlessness, then collapsed limply as the charge left her. She slumped, smelling something burnt. Her eyes were heavy as she collapsed forward onto the headrest of her seat. A visible wave of static pulsed outward, little sparks dancing through the air like glitter. The speakers in her car crackled and hissed static.

Each person the pulse touched crumbled to the ground. The ones in the back got wise and tried to sidestep the wave, but it expanded outward and still carried a great deal of power. She knew the ones at the front would never wake up. The ones at the back would be out for a few hours. She needed to find a weapon to make sure they would stay down permanently. She might look like a bookish single mom that took healthy snacks to soccer practice, but she no longer had any qualms about killing people. She lost those when her family was murdered.

Satisfied all the people in the rear two cars were incapacitated, she spun back toward the twenty-foot-tall doors in front of her. The right one stood open, the doorknob and part of the wood shattered.

She saw movement inside, but wasn't sure what it was. She tried to power her phone on. It was dead. The static fried it. Damn.

She escaped from her leaning car and crawled up the stairs. Her energy was drained. She wasn't in control of that burst, and it took every ounce of magic she had. That was the largest blast she had ever thrown. She hesitated and listened, expecting gunfire but hearing none. Furniture crashed and men grunted on the other side of the doors. Suddenly feeling out of her element, she scurried back to the car and popped the trunk, extracting a crowbar. She may not be some Cahlad-trained super badass like Blue, ex-military like Finn, or take weekly Krav Maga lessons like Greenlee, but a girl didn't grow up on the run and surrounded by criminals without learning how to bash a head in when the situation called for it.

She climbed back up the stairs and looked inside. Kendra, the person Finn assigned to Rhodes' ridiculous I'm trying to get my ex-fiancé to talk to me security detail, was fully engaged with two individuals and holding her own. Her nose bled, and a wicked bruise marred her jaw. She wore black pants and a fitted black shirt covered by a black vest. Her black pixie cut topped off the dark and dangerous look. She was intimidating. And she looked like she was enjoying herself.

In contrast, Cade Rhodes looked like a wild man in a seedy illegal death match. A frightening sneer crossed his bearded face, his hair stuck out in tufts, and he crouched barefoot in a pair of old sweatpants and a tee shirt so faded the logo was no longer visible. His stance was aggressive and lethal. He held no weapons. There were no signs of the affable crooning heartthrob the world knew. Four semi-battered men circled him cautiously. He positioned himself to prevent them from leaving the foyer. A seventh man sprawled in the middle of the room, bleeding profusely from a gash in his skull. A large metal sculpture lay on its side a few feet from him. Lexi was nowhere in sight. Strangely, a baby sat squalling in a pile of clothes on the floor in the center of the group.

Devon's heart sank. Pieces of metal floated languidly in the air, as if gravity no longer applied to them. She counted eight guns and a few knives. That explained why she hadn't heard gunfire and why this devolved into a hand-to-hand brawl.

She knew why these assholes were here for her baby. But how had they known when even she, Blue, and Greenlee weren't entirely sure Lexi was manifesting magic yet? Why did it have to be this magic? She was never going to escape her father's shadow. And now, neither was Lexi.

Devon couldn't see Harper, and she knew the woman rarely left Rhodes' side. She hoped that meant Lexi was with her, and they were well away from this mess. She crept closer, feeling a slight pull on the lug wrench in her hand. The magnetic field in the room gently tugged it from her hands. Kendra looked in Devon's direction. Her eyes pinched with pain and her nose scrunched like something smelled bad. She shook her head slightly. Devon gritted her teeth. She hated this, but Kendra was right. A lug wrench-wielding soccer Mom with tapped-out magic wasn't going to help them right now. She would just get in the way or get herself killed. She settled for crouching by the door and focusing on trying to pull in magic. It was slow, like the magic was heavy and thick. That burst drained her, making recharging difficult. She watched in awe and horror as one of Rhodes' opponents got too close and Rhodes let out an inhuman growl. He grabbed the man and jerked him off balance, wrapping his hands around the man's head and twisting violently. The resulting snap echoed through the room, making Devon's stomach lurch. Rhodes' opponent fell limply, narrowly missing the baby, as he danced away with the grace of a panther circling the other three opponents. His eyes turned yellow, and his movements grew even more cat-like. Magic rolled off him in waves. Blue told her that Rhodes didn't need a security detail. That this assignment was a joke. Now she understood why.

The man danced back and reached behind him without looking away from any of the men still circling him. He grabbed one of the men harrowing Kendra and slung him with one arm through the air into one of his own opponents. Both men toppled to the ground with shouts and grunts, the force of the throw causing them to skid across the floor and land directly at her feet. One of the men shrank as he landed on top of his friend. Big baby eyes looked up at her. She stepped back, lifting her lug wrench in shock. When she glanced back up at Rhodes, he winked and glanced down at the tangle of bodies he had just sent her way and nodded. The wink did nothing to ease her fear. The man was terrifying to the point her insides might be liquid. But she understood he wanted her to deal with these two. But she wasn't going to bash babies in the head with a crowbar. Not stopping to think of whether this was a good idea or not, she stepped forward and placed a hand on each of them. She let loose a jolt of the magic she had left, channeling it directly into their bodies and down toward the floor. The last thing she needed to do was knock Rhodes or Kendra unconscious with a wild bolt of knock-out magic. She would like to end these guys, but she refrained to conserve energy. They weren't out of the woods, and another carload of assholes could roll up any minute.

Kendra let out a wild shout and advanced on her lone opponent, taking advantage of the opportunity Rhodes gave her. Rhodes growled again, and Devon cowered. She couldn't help it.

Kendra's foe fell backward in a spurt of blood. She spun to help Rhodes as he flexed his hands, revealing razor-sharp claws. His face now sported fangs that even his bushy beard couldn't hide. His eyes glowed. Kendra stopped, taking a step back, fist at the ready. Devon couldn't blame her. If her daughter wasn't in this house somewhere, she wouldn't even be in the room with him.

Moving so fast, he was a blur; he lashed out with his claws in a circle. A black-clad combatant fell in her direction, clutching his neck and gurgling. The blood from his wound wept past his fingers and joined the ever-growing puddle on the floor. Another man howled and clutched his upper leg where his femoral artery spurted through both hands as he teetered, then collapsed. Rhodes wasn't swinging wildly. Those were precision strikes.

She wanted badly to close her eyes, but couldn't. Kendra took two giant steps back and placed her back against the wall, sending Devon a warning look. Kendra wanted her to stay put. Rhodes snarled once more and leaped at one of the remaining men, landing on top with all fours and lowering his face to the man's neck. Devon screamed as he used his fangs to rip the man's throat out, shaking his head while pieces of muscle and flesh dangled from his mouth. The last man standing wisely turned to flee. Almost in a daze, Devon reached out a hand as he passed, never taking her eyes off Rhodes, and sent a bolt of energy into his calf muscle. His feet stopped while the rest of him kept going. His face landed with a sickening thunk on the hard floor.

Devon's breath rattled in her chest as Kendra circled in a crouch to place herself in between Devon and Rhodes in a defensive stance. Rhodes stood in an unnaturally slow movement from his spot above the body that no longer had a throat, the muscles in his back flexing. His claws wiped at his mouth. Bits of viscera flew to the side as he spat. "I really liked this shirt," he uttered, and turned toward them. The baby wailed. His fangs were gone, claws no longer present, muscles less pronounced.

He looked over Devon's shoulder toward the swinging exterior door. "We had two more incoming, Kendra. Look sharp."

"I handled those guys," Devon told him, standing from her crouch and sliding with her back flat against the wall trying to stay as far away from Cade Rhodes as the space would allow and still make her way toward where she thought her daughter was waiting. "Where's my daughter?"

"Excuse me?" Kendra graced Devon with both a sarcastic tone and an incredulous look. "You took care of those guys?"

"I took care of them," Devon repeated. "Lexi. Where is she?"

Rhodes walked to the open door and looked out, turning his head left and right. He let out a low whistle and raised his eyebrow. "Your daughter says you HATE me. Am I safe?"

"Not if I don't see her with my own eyes in the next thirty seconds, asshole," Devon bit out.

"She is in my office with Harper. Let's get you to her." He wiped his blood-soaked hands on his sweatpants and padded barefoot through the blood puddles down the hallway without a second thought. "Kendra. Can you handle the situation she left in the driveway?"

The two women shared a long look as he disappeared from view. Kendra shook her head and stalked toward the door, muttering under her breath about favors and smells. Devon picked her way around the blood, trying to control her stomach. Baby Jesus on a cracker batman, Blue was going to marry that? She shook her head and looked ahead through the very luxurious and tastefully decorated house for any sign of Lexi. Rhodes arrived at a set of double doors on the right. He knocked twice. "Harper. It's Rhodes. It's clear."

No noise came from the other side of the door. Devon walked up next to him and jiggled the handles. The door was firmly locked, and she could see deadbolts thrown at the top and the bottom of the door. She glanced up at Rhodes' bloody countenance and grimaced.

"Harper?" Rhodes knocked again. "You guys OK in there?"

"What was the name of the hot brunette I walked out of your room in Dallas last month?" a voice yelled from the other side.

Devon glanced at Rhodes curiously as his face folded into a confused scowl. "How the hell should I know?" he bellowed.

The lock on the door clicked, and Harper's eye appeared in the crack. "Oh, my God. You are hurt," she said, throwing the door to the side. Devon didn't wait on any more theatrics. She rushed into the room, calling for Lexi as Rhodes told Harper the blood wasn't his.

"Mom?" she heard Lexi ask from across the room. Devon bolted toward her voice, rounding the large mahogany desk and searching frantically for the source. "Down here, Mom."

A sliver of light under the desk illuminated a trap door propped open a few inches. The top of Lexi's head and eyes were visible. "Come on out, baby. It's OK now."

Lexi lifted the door the rest of the way and climbed the narrow stairs of an underground shelter. She held an elderly black pug tightly to her chest. The dog didn't seem to mind. She ducked as she crawled out and into Devon's outstretched arms. Devon wrapped her arms around the girl and the dog, buried her face in her hair, and let out a dry sob that bordered on a laugh. She might never let her go. "Mom. I can't breathe," Lexi whined.

"Shhhh, baby girl. Give me a minute." Devon yanked Lexi into her lap and rocked, not easing her hug in the slightest. Echoing clatters rang out from the foyer as the floating metal fell to the ground. She looked up at Rhodes. He was standing in the hallway, using the door for cover. His hands were on his hips, and he had a small, worried smile on his face. She realized that he was trying to keep himself out of Lexi's sight. He was a blood-covered mess, and he didn't want to scare her girl. "Thank you," she whispered in his direction. He gave her a curt nod and glanced down at Harper, who was pointing toward a door on the other side of the office.

He nodded and squeezed his assistant's shoulder. "You have her for the moment?" he asked. When Devon nodded and grabbed Lexi's head to make sure she couldn't see the carnage, he moved with an unsettling grace across the room and disappeared into the door Harper pointed to. Devon closed her eyes and loosened her grip on Lexi when she heard the door click shut. She had to admit to herself, for a moment, she was furious with Blue for sending her child to a man that she thought they both despised. She didn't know the whole Rhodes and Blue story. She didn't know most of Blue's story in all honesty, but she did know that her friend still lived with a piece of her heart missing and that man was the person who had taken it and shredded it. Blue shared that much, and Devon couldn't believe Blue would put Lexi in his care. What she saw in the entryway made her anger dissipate. Her friend put the safety of their girl above her own feelings, and it paid off in a big way. She squeezed Lexi tight again, ignoring her whine of, "Jesus, Mom." All she could do now was see it through. Right now, Cade Rhodes was the biggest, scariest person she knew. So, she was going to stay with him and pray that she would be able to tell Blue thank you soon.

27

BLUE

S he was probably alive. Death couldn't possibly hurt this much. She wasn't in Hell unless it had frozen over. Her feet were ice cubes, her fingers were numb, and the tips of her ears stung. Her head pounded with every beat of her heart. Every muscle in her body was stiff and sore. She struggled to open her eyes. Even those muscles protested. She finally got one open and assessed her situation. She needed to find Ava. She was in a bed buried in blankets. Panic set in. The last time she had blacked out and woken in a strange room, it hadn't ended well. People died.

The room she was in was dark. Someone was lying on the bed behind her. Maybe it was Ava. Whoever it was felt small, almost like Lexi, when she snuggled with her. Something roared mechanically in the otherwise oppressive silence. Probably an air unit turned up all the way. A large figure sprawled in the compact chair next to the bed. She heard a single snore. It came from the floor below her.

Blue blinked. Her left eye still wasn't cooperating. She checked her hands and feet as best she could. She wasn't bound. She tried to throw the blankets off. Either she was very weak or there were a lot of blankets. Possibly both. Her eyes focused, and she realized the figure wore only boxers and was familiar. It was Ivan, she could tell by his size and the thick scar that circled his forearm. She tried harder to throw the blankets off and only drained what energy she had woken with.

"Take it easy," he spoke. Blue didn't realize he was awake. He leaned forward, placing his elbows on his knees. The room was small, and the movement put his face within inches of her own.

"Everyone OK? Make it?" she rasped. Her lips were dry, and her throat was parched. The words made her cough. It had been a long time since she felt this bad. Cold. She was cold all the time. Not usually this cold. A shiver wracked her body. That was good, though. Hypothermic people died when the shivering stopped. But she also felt like a truck ran her over after she got the plague, then the EMTs threw her in a frozen lake instead of taking her to the hospital.

"Yeah. All here. No additional injuries." He gestured to a bandage on his chest. He reached over to the bedside table and retrieved something. When he reached up and touched her face, she realized he had a washcloth and was using it to wipe her nose and her chin. "Your nose is still bleeding. But it's slowed down." He pulled the covers up to the nose he just wiped and tucked the blankets firmly in around her shoulders. Blue didn't know what to think. She couldn't remember anyone ever wiping her face or tucking her in. But if he wanted to harm her, he wouldn't do those things. For now, she wasn't in immediate danger. And she couldn't do anything about it, even if she were.

She gave in to the pain, exhaustion, and warmth of the blankets. Ivan placed a massive hand on the top of her head and patted it gently like a dog. She barely had enough energy to be alarmed when he used the name she went by during her time at the Cahlad. "Get some sleep. I've got you, Di."

His voice carried over into her nightmares, an anguished scream, as she skipped out of the crowded cab of the truck and into the hallway in front of door number one.

She landed with a groan as her sliced feet smacked the cold floor. Someone shouted immediately. A man clad in black ran toward her. Shit. Both of the men who were lying face down on the floor when she left were back up and wearing some sort of mask. One emerged from room number one, fresh blood splattering his visible skin saying, "He doesn't know anything." Green gas filled this hallway as well. The old-fashioned way it would be.

She peddled backward and fired. Guard number one fell. She pivoted and fired at the second shocked guard. He fell. Expert marksman by age twelve. Take that, Larson Battle.

She heard a click and swung, placing her back against the window. The door at the end of the hall opened. She waited for a moment, having nowhere to go. A tink rang down the hallway as a tiny metal ball bounced toward her. She ran forward and picked it up, hurling it back at the door. She turned and ducked as the thing exploded.

The heavy metal door slammed backward and titled. A heat wave slammed into her back and knocked her forward, her face slamming into the cold concrete floor. Her ears rang. Where had he gotten that? And why would he throw it into a hall full of his own people? She pushed herself up, thankful she still held her weapon. Behind her, a body lay ten feet down the hallway they fled down earlier. If they didn't know she was here before, they did now. The sprinklers above her head turned on, slinging frigid water. Wonderful.

The man on the table moved slightly, still alive. But Devon said there were three guards in this hallway. She stopped to search the guard that came out of the room for keys. No luck. She paced down the hallway, still shaking her head, trying to clear the ringing in her ears, and turned the corner into the office, weapon raised. The guard inside lay slumped over a gray metal desk, unmoving. She walked up and poked. He wasn't warm. Asleep permanently. She was suddenly very glad that Devon decided to be her friend. Looking around the room, the closed-circuit TV screens showed a quiet lobby above the security guard sitting at the desk. Devon's loop was still working. Meaning she couldn't see if anything was coming at her. She didn't have time to reverse it. She had a mountain to move.

Her eyes landed on a metal and leather contraption in the corner. A wheelchair, strangely out of place, sat tucked between a filing cabinet and a dorm refrigerator. She tugged it loose and took off back down the hallway. Coming to the window, she stopped. How did she get in? She lifted the wheelchair and slung it against the window. It bounced back at her with an unsatisfying thunk. She eyed the lock and the mutilated body in the hallway. What were the chances that the keys survived that, if he even had them? Not likely.

Opening the hand that still clutched the gross little bar Green gave her, she shrugged. Stranger things had happened today. She placed the bar against the door and uttered Mango. She yelped as sparks flew and the ball at the end of the bar warmed up. "Ha!" she whisper-shouted as she moved the bar in a circle. It took almost no magic to make it work. Despite singeing her fingers, she soon had a small hole, just big enough to put her hand through. She tapped the center with the butt of her weapon, and it fell inside the room with a clang. Carefully, she stuck her arm through, hissing as hot pieces of slag fell onto her arm. She turned the lock on the inside of the door and pushed slightly. It opened, and she stepped inside, dragging the wheelchair behind her.

"Please. No," the battered man on the table mumbled through swollen and cracked lips. Blue's heart broke a little. She pulled the chair closer and walked over to him, laying a gentle hand on his cheek below his swollen eye.

"Hang in there, big guy. I'm going to get you out of here." She loosened the restraints as fast as she could. Two for each extremity. When she finished, he flinched away. "I'm sorry. I need you to help me. I can't lift you. Can you sit?"

"I don't know."

"Try for me." She took his hand and tugged with all her might. He cried out, but slowly lumbered upwards. "I promise." She threw his arm over her shoulder and hoped she could hold up his weight.

He had to be six foot three and two hundred and fifty pounds of solid muscle. He screamed as she lifted, and he tried to stand. "I promise," she grunted. With everything she had, she shifted them and let his body weight carry him into the chair. It rolled backward, but thankfully stayed under him. A breath whooshed out of her as she patted his knee. His head lolled back and his eyes rolled. A fine sheen of sweat shone on his forehead. That took everything he had. Which was OK. She could take it from here. She stepped back to the cabinet and fished through. She found a pair of scrubs and tossed them into his lap, covering him. She needed to move him quickly, but she would give him what dignity she could. "I promise, big guy," she said again, digging through the cabinet again for anything to cover the wound on his forearm. It was jagged and ugly and went all the way around his arm. She could see exposed and chipped bone. That wound had not been there when she left. He suffered this wound because she left him here. She opened drawers and glanced at the counter, grimacing. A saw lay next to the sink, blood still coating the blade. "Jesus," she hissed. She found a roll of gauze and wound them around his arm while she tried to push some of her magic into him. She didn't have much and couldn't tell if it was helping. She was hurting him, she knew, because his head fell forward and he wept softly. She had never seen anything like this. "I'm so sorry, big guy."

"Ivan," he whispered.

"Ivan?" she asked, stopping to take a closer look at him. "Oh my God."

"Lacroix," he finished.

Blue stared in horror. Ivan Lacroix was a fellow Zenith. He was indestructible. He was a few years older than her, but they had been on missions together. He was also the unfortunate soul assigned to teach her defensive driving because all the other instructors refused. She didn't even recognize him. They used that saw on his arm while he was conscious. Had the gas allowed them to do this? "What did they do to you, Ivan?"

He just rattled out a wet sob and clutched her hand where it lay on top of the subpar bandage.

She heaved and pushed the wheelchair out of the room and down the hallway. Navigating around the exploded guard, she searched for an elevator bank. There was no way she could get him up the stairs. Pushing him as fast as she could with frequent stops to put his limp feet back into the foot holders, she came to a hallway much like the one they just left. Windows lined the walls next to the doors. She looked into the first one she passed and cursed. She was past being shocked. She was just furious. It was a ward, a line of beds holding small, frail bodies. All but two were attached to ventilators. They were all restrained with leather cuffs. They were still. IV poles stood next to each child with bags of green liquid hanging from them.

She tried the door, and to her surprise, it opened. Leaving Ivan where he was, she stepped in and smelled the familiar acrid scent, like the green gas, but different. Four of the children lay silent with green faces, mouths foaming.

She bit her lip and moved to the other two children. One, a brown-haired boy with freckles across a delicate nose, had an IV in his arm. The green liquid dripped. He wasn't moving. She checked for a pulse and found none. She turned to the other child. He had dark black hair and tan skin. He looked to be four or five. His brown eyes looked at her with hope. He didn't look frightened. "Did my mom send you?" he whispered.

For a moment Blue couldn't say anything, then she nodded through a film of tears. "Yeah, baby." She grabbed the sheet and placed it over the IV to hold pressure while she removed the needle. "She loves you, and I'm going to take you to her. What's your name, sweetheart?" She lifted his frail form in her arms, dragging the sheet with him.

"Gage." He nuzzled into her neck as she rushed him from the room. "I miss my mommy."

"I know, baby. Hang in there. My friends call me Blue." She patted him and sat him in Ivan's lap. Ivan groaned as she maneuvered his arm around the boy. "Ivan, I need you to hold on to him for me." When his arm didn't tighten, she whispered a please and his hand flexed over the boy's hip. There was nothing she could do for the other children.

She pushed the chair hard, charging down the hallway. She glanced in the windows to the other rooms as she ran, thankful that they were empty. She finally found an elevator bank and pressed the button repeatedly, hoping that the service hadn't been cut. The sprinklers in this section weren't on. Finally, she heard a ding, and the doors opened. She shoved the chair into the tiny space and hit floor one. Ivan's head was still limp and lolling forward. His eyes were closed. But he held the boy tight to his chest. "Tell me about your Mommy, Gage."

He coughed, a wet rattling sound that frightened her. "She's pretty. And makes the best cookies."

"That sounds awesome. What's her name?"

"Esde..." He coughed again. "Irving." Oh hell. This kid was Devon's. The Devon who was driving away at this very moment in a bubba truck loaded down with barefoot pregnant women.

Ivan lifted his head. "He's shaking," the big man ground out. His voice was hoarse from the hours he had just spent screaming. The door opened, and Blue leaned out to make sure no one was waiting on the other side to murder them. Nobody. What were the odds? Shouldn't the regular police be showing up? Maybe not, since obviously they were doing things that they wanted to keep hidden.

She pushed them into a hallway. The air was cool and fresh, probably due to the gigantic hole she left in the wall of the lobby. She knelt in front of Ivan and Gage, the boy coughing violently. Ivan grimaced with the effort of trying to hold him in his injured arms. "Hey, buddy. Hang in there."

"Miss." He coughed. "Blue." He coughed again, and she saw foam roll from his tiny mouth.

"Oh no. Buddy." She lifted him out of Ivan's arms and sat with him in her lap. She wiped at the foam and rocked his small, jerking body. She pushed magic into him, letting the cold flow through her until she was almost tapped out. His condition didn't change, and she knew there was nothing she could do with what she had. "Mommy loves you, baby. Mommy loves you," she whispered. He missed his mommy, and every child should hear those words often. Even though his mother couldn't be here to say them. She rocked and rocked. Stroking his hair.

"I miss Mommy," he whispered as he stared at her. His body stopped its erratic movement. His breaths turned to rattles, then eventually stopped. He stared at her with sightless eyes. She stared back in silence. Her chest burned and felt numb at the same time. She gulped to force air into her chest and stopped rocking. Her hair hung down into her face, and she barely noticed it was red again. Maybe this was a surreal nightmare. She hoped it was. She didn't want to live in a reality like this.

Ivan sat silently, a tortured expression on his face, clutching the arms of the wheelchair with his nail-less, bent fingers. She couldn't save Gage. But Ivan might make it. "We need to get you out of here."

"You can't let them do this to anyone else," he rasped so quietly that she almost didn't hear him. "I can make it from here."

"Big guy?" She eased Gage from her lap and closed his eyes. "You can't walk."

"I'll be fine."

Blue let out a bitter laugh. "I'm already responsible for five dead people today. I'm not leaving you to die, too."

"How many will they murder if they keep making that gas?" he asked quietly. "You got me out of that room. I'll go the rest of the way on my own."

Blue let out a huff. He was right. And she felt up for a suicide mission right now. At least then she wouldn't feel the empty pain ripping its way through her chest. "I'll take care of it. But you have to make me a promise. You never mention this. Not the gas. Not me. Not the kids. Not the two pregnant women they murdered in cold blood. You leave here and tell them anything but the truth. If you mention it, they will spend the rest of eternity trying to replicate it. Even the good guys. Do you understand?"

He tilted his head so that his swollen eyes could focus on her. His face was so badly mangled, she knew he couldn't see much. But he nodded.

"Go," he ordered and grasped the wheels, pushing himself with a stifled groan of pain forward toward the exit.

Blue sniffed. The air was cleaner up here, and more magic tingled in her belly button. "Wait up. Let me try something." She walked over and placed a hand on his mangled arm, channeling the magic and forcing the cold through her fingers and into his tissue. He jumped, but stayed in place. Hopefully, she could keep him from losing the arm. Knowing she didn't have much left, she placed her other hand on the side of his face that was the least battered. She channeled the cold into his cheek and watched the swelling reduce and his eye grow wide and bright. It would help his chances of survival if he could see the bad guys coming at him. "That's all I have left. I hope that helps." As his newly functioning eye stared up into her face, she saw a flash of recognition. "Di?"

She took his hand and wrapped it around the gun she took from the security guard earlier. "It has five rounds left."

His expression was shocked as he opened his mouth to speak, but she turned and fled. She was at the end of her emotional rope. If she stayed, she would lose it.

She had been through every corner of the maze that was the basement looking for the elevators. There had not been a lab. That meant it was up here somewhere, and the footprint of the top floor of this building was much smaller than its basement. She navigated carefully, passing dark rooms with locked doors. Most looked like small offices. When she reached the end of the hall, she found a solid metal door, much like the one that had been blown off its hinges in the basement.

She looked up and around, trying to find a way into that room that wasn't through the door. But the wall and ceiling were solid. What the hell, right? Nobody left to kill but herself now. She let the cold rainbow slip over her vision and thought happy thoughts about not ending up bifurcated by a steel door. The happy thoughts worked, and she reappeared in a crouch with her butt just skimming the door.

The lights were bright, and the room was large. It was filled with liquids and equipment. She could hear two men speaking, so she remained crouched and moved toward the end of one of the long rows of equipment. She stood slightly and looked in the direction of the voices.

"Alpha site has been compromised. The primary inmate containment system was deployed, but I've lost video feed. Someone set the system on a loop." She recognized that voice. It was Percy, Amber's fiancé. What was he doing here? She continued slinking forward. His back was to her, and he was talking to a screen. She inched closer to get a look. She bit her lip when a familiar face appeared. It was Larson Battle, Regent of the Cahlad, and technically her boss. How had she missed this?

"Relax, son. I have units en route to your location. Stay where you are, and I'll let you know when it is safe." The wall with the screen plastered with Larson's face held a plethora of computers and screens. This was a command center for something evil and terrible. She could tell by the relaxation of Percy's shoulders that he believed Larson. Dumb asshole deserved what he had coming to him. Blue knew Larson was sending in a cleaning crew. They would retrieve the data and destroy the evidence, including Percy. She knew this because she had been his cleaning crew on more than one occasion. She needed to make sure there was no data to retrieve.

Choices. Choices. She skulked about as the two men continued to talk, Larson obviously stalling Percy to give his people enough time to get here. She worked her way to the corner of the room. If this was indeed the command center, maybe there was more in here than just chemicals and computers. She found a door toward the back of the room and turned the knob. It didn't open, but she wasn't too concerned. She skipped silently to the other side.

She had to wait a moment for her eyes to adjust. Mops, brooms, buckets, and a rack of guns filled the space. Odd combination, but perfect for her purposes. She moved closer and felt below the gun rack. The guard downstairs had thrown an explosive. Maybe she could find one of those. Her fingertips found a bag, and she unzipped it silently. Feeling inside, she was elated to find the entire bag was filled with small metal balls that were likely very explosive. She could work with this. "Boom Kitty."

She grabbed the bag, a nasty-looking knife, and a handgun, and moved back into the room. The boys were still chatting. She crawled along, perusing the shelves of chemicals until she found what she was looking for. These would do. Fuck Larson and his explosives training. She was glad she paid attention now, though.

A few minutes later, she had vials of separated chemicals taped, wedged and rubber banded to levers on little explosive balls. She hadn't seen any paper files, so she was going to focus the explosions around the computer bank and hope that the soup of chemicals in this room caused a big enough fire that anything hidden would be destroyed. Probably not long now before Larson's backup arrived. She crawled closer until she was on the edge of the last row of tables less than five feet diagonally from Percy's unsuspecting back. She tipped the corrosive vials in a way that would eat through the stoppers at their ends, then plunge into the vials below them, making a very volatile, explosive, and loud compound she hoped would pull the arms on the grenades they were secured to. Double boom, kitty. She had four to five minutes now, depending on the quality of the stoppers. She placed one in the corner and another slightly closer before she finally stood behind Percy and looked directly into the camera he was speaking to.

"Sorry for the delay, sir. The facility is contained, and the package is secured." She gave an irreverent salute as Percy jerked her way in surprise. She wanted Larson to know he was caught and his clean-up team was unlikely to have anything they could clean up when they got here. Larson's face registered panic and fury just as Blue grabbed Percy's elbow, placed a hand on his shoulder, and twisted. Bones snapped and crunched, and he screamed. She brought her hand down into his face, crushing his nose and sending his glasses flying.

She looked back at the screen, a silent red-faced Larson staring back at her. She grabbed Percy's other arm even as he tried to crumple to the floor. This time, she targeted his elbow and smiled as the bones broke. He was choking on his own screams now. "Just as you ordered. Nothing will make it out of this facility. Sir."

She saw movement behind Larson's video and stopped short. Amber, holding two cups of coffee, stood just to the right of the frame. Her face twisted in horror as she watched her fiancé's arms snap, crackle, and pop. She let out a blood-curdling scream.

Well, shit. This was going to be hard to explain to her best friend at their next girl's night. She threw Percy to the ground and slung the satchel of Macgyvered explosives across the floor toward the other corner that also held a bank of computers.

Larson turned when Amber screamed, but she was already slinging her coffee at him and running from the room. "Amber!" he roared. His furious face turned back to the screen, and he pointed at her. "You stupid bitch. You think you are so smart? You are cleaning up the mess!"

She shot him a bird and jerked Percy back to his sniveling feet. She leaned in and whispered in his ear, "This is what happens when you murder children." She twisted his neck and let his body fall to the floor.

His body was still collapsing when three rapid-fire bolts of pain seared through her back. A hand grabbed her shoulder and spun her around. Her eyes grew wide, and her jaw fell slack. Light blue eyes bored into her from a face peppered with freckles and framed by curly blonde hair. "Amber?"

Her friend didn't say anything. She lifted an aerosol bottle and sprayed a cloud of green into her face, then calmly plunged the knife she was holding into Blue's abdomen and ripped. Confusion sliced through Blue with the blinding pain. Where had Amber come from? She had just been at the Cahlad with coffee in her hands. Blue's hands fell to her stomach, clutching at the wound to hold it together. She felt the sickening press of inside bits trying to spill outward. Disbelieving, she took two steps in a circle and turned back to the camera, unable to resist one last dig. "Mission accomplished, sir."

She smiled as she fell to her knees, then backward onto her butt. She slumped against one of the worktables facing the computer banks. Looking down, she was mere inches from one of her improvised explosives that would detonate any minute. She gazed up at Amber with rapidly blurring eyes. This had been a bad week. A really bad week. But this was right. She shouldn't leave when all those others hadn't. This was right.

"You killed him," Amber said without emotion as she took a few steps back and further to the side. She was staying out of the camera's line of sight.

"I'm not sorry," Blue managed to say as her body slumped further.

"I'm not either," Amber spat.

Everything was getting warm and cold at the same time. "These things will explode any minute. Run."

The knife fell from Amber's hand and her eyes grew wide and confused. She rushed toward the door, yanking it open, and fled down the dark hallway.

Blue watched as her best friend left her to die from the stab wounds she inflicted. Black filled her vision for the second time in five days.

28

FINN

G reenlee wasn't speaking to him. He didn't know where Devon was. He only knew she drove her car into the middle of a bunch of armed men. Kendra was no longer answering her phone. Blue was unaccounted for. He had a member of Stalker Prime wedged into their back seat with a cantankerous soul eater with his emotionally unstable future brother-in-law. And they were still too far from Cade Rhodes' house because of traffic and potholes.

"Nobody listens to anything I say," Finn groused.

"I do, boss," Hale croaked, still recovering from being gassed. "I've got Paco rolling to Rhodes' estate. The other men are on the way, too." He made a quotation motion when he said "estate" before he continued. "We will have eyes on the situation out there shortly. Trix has patched into the security system. Whatever made Devon's phone crap out must have taken out the cameras and the sensors. Probably Kendra's phone, too. We have no remote eyes on site. But traffic cameras in the area show two more vehicles that could be a problem rolling in about five minutes ago. Whoever we are dealing with has resources."

"Thanks, Hale." Finn appreciated his captain's initiative. Hale might belch the alphabet backward, but there was no one more levelheaded under pressure than the man in front of him. "How are the other guys?"

"No worse than after Willingham's bachelor party," Hale told him.

Finn winced. That was still pretty bad. Tanner had scars from that party. "What is Paco's ETA? He knows about the potential threats?" Finn asked.

"Less than ten minutes. He does." Hale nodded. His phone rang. It was Trix, his computer guru, so he answered it using the car's systems.

"Anything on the situation in Five Points? Anything on social media?"

"Interesting you should ask. I have reports of a stolen florist van containing four people: two men, one woman, and a teenage girl that was run off the road by our mystery men. Still waiting on casualty reports," Trix told him. He glanced nervously over his shoulder at his silent passengers. Greenlee leaned against the passenger side door, staring out at nothing. Nisha sat with a frustrated look on her face, holding Ben Hughes' hand, apparently to keep him from killing them all. She strangely had not insisted on taking Hughes back to the Cahlad and fired off several text messages when she thought he wasn't looking. He needed to figure out why.

Hughes was cooperating for now, but only because they promised to help him find his daughter, and Nisha was somehow neutralizing the man's multiple murder hobo personalities. He really wished Trix would stop using the word casualty about the man's kid.

Finn could hear the click of Trix's keyboard clattering and the murmur of several news feeds in the background. He wondered sometimes if Trix was actually typing that fast or just smashing keys for ambiance. "The teenager, I'm pretty sure, is our target. And I'm sure you won't like this, but those men. They are Cahlad." He really wished Trix would stop referring to the man's kid as a target, too.

"That I knew," Finn told him. He glanced at Hale, who stared forward, guiding them onto the interstate, but his face held a scowl similar to Finn's. They didn't like to tangle with the Cahlad. And here they were, all wound up in the Cahlad's business. He leaned back and looked at the ceiling. This is what he got for taking a nap. "Excellent work, Trix. So our client and a team member are in Cahlad custody." Finn went back to pinching the bridge of his nose.

"If they aren't bodies on the side of the road. That van is a mangled mess," Trix corrected.

"Not helping, Trix," Hale grunted as he eyed the man in the back seat nervously and stepped on the accelerator, going as fast as he dared.

"Please hold," Trix quipped, and the line went silent.

"It's good to be back," Hale deadpanned.

"It's good to have you back," Finn said again sincerely.

"Paco is in contact with Kendra. The situation is not ideal." Trix popped back onto the line without warning.

"Define not ideal," Hale interjected before Finn could. Trix and Hale had never gotten along.

"Kendra is safe, but injured. Rhodes' assistant and dog are with her. They have over twenty dead or unconscious mystery men and six disabled vehicles on site we will need to deal with. And three babies? I don't know what is up with that. Nothing on local police chatter somehow. But somebody is going to come looking soon."

"Devon and Lexi?" Finn nudged. He was glad Kendra was safe, but he really needed to know about Devon and Lexi right now.

"They are with Rhodes. He took them out a back exit while Kendra held off the last batch of mystery men. Something about a demolition derby," Trix informed him. "Hold on. Got something else. There were no bodies in or around the van in Five Points."

"Our girl is still kicking." Hale slapped the steering wheel and smiled. Finn nodded. That was good news. Now they knew Blue, Devon, and Lexi were all still breathing, even if they didn't know where on earth they were. But they did know who they were seen with last. All these things his team could work miracles with. Hughes' daughter was last seen with Blue, which was a good sign she was still breathing, too. Finn threw a meaningful look in Ben's direction. The man had remained quiet and watchful since he overheard the phone call from Devon.

"Where is Rhodes?" Finn brought the conversation back around. Blue could handle herself even against two members of Stalker Prime. He needed to focus on Devon and Lexi.

"Kendra isn't sure, boss. She tried to follow him once the threat was neutralized, but he was gone," Trix answered.

"Cell phones?" Hale asked.

"All fried. It's like an EMP went off at that house. All the electronics are done for. Security system is toast."

"I trust Kendra's assessment. If there was a trail, she would find it. Have Paco evac Kendra and the assistant and the dog. Once they are clear, send in an alert to the local authorities." Finn told him.

"Devon's car is there, sir," Trix informed him.

"Will it still run?"

"Please hold," Trix mimicked in a high-pitched voice, as the line once again went silent.

"God, I hate that guy," Hale grumbled.

"He's one of the best," Finn reminded him.

"The best at raising my blood pressure and making me want to punch him," Hale groused.

"Paco is moving it off-site. I'm sending them to Lilac," Trix informed them, referring to their office that took up most of a warehouse in a seedy industrial district on Lilac Avenue, just south of downtown Nashville. "Oh yeah, have you seen the latest breaking news?"

"There's more?" Hale complained.

"Government officials just raided Cahlad headquarters," Trix informed them. "And I mean raided with guns and stuff. Place is swarming. I'm going to go get some popcorn."

"What?" Nisha demanded from the back, her free hand flying to her phone.

"Oh." Trix chuckled. "Who is that?"

"Don't worry about it," Hale answered, exchanging a look with Finn. All these events weren't a coincidence. But how did they fit together? He eyed Nisha out of the corner of his eye as she quickly fired off a series of texts.

"We will meet you at Lilac." Finn was pleased that his team could predict his preferences in situations like this and act without directive. It made things so much smoother when time was of the essence. Nisha's phone pinged several times, and she looked even more frustrated than she had moments ago.

Ben leaned over, reading her screen. "What in the hell does worry burgers' mandolin mean?" She glared at Ben and jerked her phone out of view.

When he hung up, Greenlee leaned forward. "Take me to the house, Finn," he said in a tone of voice Finn had never heard from the man before. Greenlee was normally goofy and jovial. He was always good-natured. Now his voice held absolute menace.

"We will go to Lilac and regroup." Finn shook his head.

"I need to get to my workshop. I have things there that can help us find Devon and Lexi."

"They are probably still watching your place, waiting for Devon to come home," Finn argued.

The car struck a pothole and bounced violently. They all winced. "Damn potholes," Hale exclaimed in aggravation. "Couldn't dodge it in this traffic."

"I need to retrieve my tools and my gadgets." Greenlee's expression grew mulish, and he crossed his arms over his chest. "Isn't that what Herne does? They retrieve things."

"He's got you there, boss," Hale told him.

"No. We will do this by the book," Finn insisted.

"No magic? Is that how Hale got to that hospital in Dallas?" Greenlee demanded. "Good enough for one of your guys, but not good enough for Devon and Lexi?"

"I'm out." Hale whistled.

Finn pulled his lips over his teeth and seethed. That was not the truth. He trusted Blue. He didn't know anything about Greenlee's magic and wasn't willing to bet people's lives on it.

Nisha's phone dinged twice.

"I can get to them if you get me to my stuff," Greenlee insisted. "You have a better idea?"

"Whatever is happening is big. I would like to weigh in on the validity of your plan," Nisha said quietly out of nowhere as she looked at her phone one more time. "But I can't hear your thoughts."

"Yeah, I know," Greenlee told her smugly. "Now take me home and help me, Finn, or drop me off so I can go myself."

"I'll help you if they won't," Ben finally spoke up. "I know what it's like to have those men after your child. I'll help you. Then you'll help me."

"Done," Greenlee told him. "Much appreciated."

"Did you just volunteer us?" Nisha asked, holding up their joined hands indignantly.

"No," Ben insisted. "I volunteered myself. If you want to go, that's your business."

"Fuck you, Ben," Nisha grumbled. "Killer birds and bombs. Men with fire shooting out of their eyes and creepy voices in their head. Government raids. Renegade artifact hunters. And whatever the hell you are." She waved her free hand at Greenlee. "I didn't sign up for this. I should have quit last week."

Finn exchanged a quick look with Hale, who hadn't flinched when the Cahlad official in their back seat flippantly mentioned the secret objective of their company, but his scowl deepened. Problem for another day.

"Guess she's going, too. Not like she can go back to the office," Greenlee announced. "Turn us around, Hale, or drop us off."

Hale didn't respond, but he did throw a questioning glance in Finn's direction. Finn was going to give the man a raise. He was the only person who had listened to him today.

"You don't have to go. I'll take them," he told Hale, making up his mind. He truly didn't want to sit around and wait on Trix to type some more and pray something shook loose. He needed to do something to get to Devon and Lexi before anyone else caught up to them.

Hale snorted and flipped the turn signal. "Wouldn't miss it, sir."

"What's your plan, Greenlee?" Finn turned sideways in the seat and gave the mutinous lot in the back an expectant look. "The cops will still be there, and we know the mystery men are likely watching. I hope it isn't walk in guns blazing. You've already had the shit kicked out of you today."

"She is going to tell me what she hears and where." Greenlee pointed to Nisha, who sighed in resignation. "I sneak in, avoid them, grab my bag, and meet you guys a few blocks over."

"How are you going to sneak in?" Hale asked, thrumming his fingers on the steering wheel as he guided the car toward Greenlee and Devon's house. "You got some trick up your sleeve?"

"In my nipple, actually," Greenlee deadpanned.

Ben snorted.

"We've had worse plans than nipples," Hale said thoughtfully. Finn pinched the bridge of his nose in exasperation. Hale wasn't wrong. But did he have to say it out loud?

"Sure." Nisha shrugged tiredly and glared at all of them. "Operation sneaky nipple. Why not?"

29

BLUE

She jerked awake, lying on her side underneath something heavy again. No pain, but the phantom smell of blood and chemicals clung to her nostrils. Ivan still sat in the chair next to the bed. She still felt Ava behind her. Her lips were parched, and her body still ached. How long was she out? She should feel better than this.

Without a word, Ivan stood and crossed to the dresser that held the television. He cracked open a bottled water that rested there. He still wore nothing but a pair of boxer briefs, and he was soaked in sweat. It was hot in the room. The air unit must be turned to full heat. He made his way back to the side of the bed and set the bottle on the nightstand. His expression was guarded as he sat on the bed, and she felt the weight of the blankets growing lighter. She tried to help and sighed in exasperation when she still couldn't do it. Even sighing exhausted her. A moment later, gigantic hands rolled her over and lifted her beneath her armpits. She was scooted up the bed and propped against the headboard. "Can you sit?"

"Yeah. Yeah. Sure." She tried to nod and just ended up looking down without the upward movement. He let go to grab the water, taking her at her word, and she slid sideways toward Ava.

Ivan grunted again, and straight-armed his gigantic hand into her shoulder, pinning her to the headboard. He helped her take small sips of the water while he kept her upright. It was the best water she had ever tasted. She had never been this weak and ill in her adult life. What on earth was going on? It felt like magic poisoning. But she had never experienced that before. Why now? She looked around the room as much as she could. They were in a small hotel room with a single double bed. The walls were a terrible blue and cream stripe, and the furniture was maple laminate, popular in the seventies. A tiny door next to the chair Ivan had occupied led to a bathroom. Ava was indeed laying on the bed next to her on top of the covers wearing a tank top. Her pants were rolled up to her knees. She was sweating as badly as Ivan, hair plastered to her face. She could see a bare hairy leg on the floor to the side of the bed and assumed it belonged to Sam Sotach. The Cahlad Regent lay asleep in his underwear on the dirty motel room floor. This wasn't how she expected to end her day. But all four souls made it to the other side of the skip despite the fact she was out cold the second she fell into the rainbow void.

Eventually, she finished the entire bottle and felt marginally better. Her extremities were still leaden and cold, and her head still throbbed. "Thank you."

"Are you still cold?" he asked. Shifting himself so that he was no longer holding her up, he propped her up at a safer angle and reached for the covers in a questioning motion.

"I'll live," she told him. He breathed an audible sigh of relief, tossed the covers lightly over her, then walked to the roaring air unit. He pressed a button several times, and Blue felt much cooler air circulating through the room immediately. She didn't say anything else, just watched as he stepped over the hairy leg on the floor and disappeared into the bathroom. A harsh yellow light streamed into the dark room from the open door. When he came back to the bed, he scooted the tiny chair closer and sat. He handed her two small pills.

"Your bleeding seems to be under control. I think it's safe for you to have these now."

"Thank you," she said again. She was glad he was being nice to her for now. Because if he weren't, there wasn't a damned thing she could do about it. But this was weird.

He remained in the chair, leaning toward her, his elbows once again resting on his knees. They stared at each other for a few moments. Well, he stared. And stared some more. She looked around the God-awful hotel room. Surely, they didn't pay money for this place. The silence became uncomfortable.

"I know who you are."

Blue kept her expression blank as her mind screamed every curse word she knew in all five of the languages she was fluent in and three of the ones she wasn't. She didn't say anything, just watched and gave her magic an exploratory tug. It was there, but she was weak and possibly poisoned by the thing she was trying to use. She needed to get Ava out of here with her. She couldn't do that right now.

He continued to stare at her. She fought her way into a sitting position with an oof. Her arm and leg hurt like hell.

"We aren't even. Not even close," he said after she had righted herself and propped herself up higher with the thin excuse for pillows wedged behind her. Her eyes grew wide. He heard her in the café. "We never will be, Di."

Well, fuck. He did know who she was. She looked at his face, remembering the last time she saw him. It was the day he got that scar. A day the indestructible Ivan Lacroix with abs currently trending on social media was on the verge of death and unable to walk. He couldn't know who she was, though. She didn't look anything like the person he had seen that day. Her hair had been red by the time she fixed his face. She closed her eyes. She still saw his face in her nightmares. If she had helped him or done something more, maybe he would have suffered less. There was so much about that day she would do differently if she could go back in time. "I'm sorry."

"What?" He sounded truly shocked, though she couldn't see him. She was looking down at the shiny polyester bedspread. It was bright red and truly hideous. She rolled it between her fingers. It felt more like cardboard than fabric. The room smelled like body odor from the three sweat-drenched people and possibly years of lackluster housekeeping. The air conditioning unit roared, now throwing cool air instead of hot. Things she could see, touch, smell, and hear. She was right here and not back in that stainless steel hell hole.

"I'm really sorry, Ivan," she repeated, letting her pattern calm her.

"You saved my life."

"They hurt you."

"You said hang in there, big guy," he told her, never moving from his position leaning on his knees.

She nodded. "I should have gotten to you sooner. Before the saw."

"You said I'll get you out of here," he said, voice still even. "I promise. You said, I promise you, big guy."

"You are a really big guy. I had to get them out first." She let out a shaky breath.

"I can still hear your voice. In my nightmares. Sometimes in my dreams. Did you know that?"

"I hear yours, too. I'm so sorry." A strange emotion washed over her as she finally got to say the words. She wished she could say the same thing to all the others she had failed or let down that day.

"Why?" he asked.

"I left you. I should have tried to take you with the rest." She went on staring at the damning scar on his arm. Faced with the evidence of one of her failures, virtually helpless in a shitty motel room in the middle of she knew not where her usual bravado fled. "I didn't destroy all the gas. I told you I would. That I wouldn't let them hurt you again. I really thought I had. But—" She let out a shaky breath.

"No, Di. Why did you help me?"

289

"What do you mean?" She finally looked over at him. He was a big scary guy and his usual scowl frightened small children and grown men alike. But right now, he just looked perplexed.

"You told me not to tell anyone about the gas. That they would just try to recreate it," he almost accused her.

"They would have. I thought I got it all. I blew the hell out of that place. I'm sorry," she told him again, beginning to feel desperate and slightly defensive. The explosion she set off should have incinerated everything near that lab, including her.

"You could have run. They almost killed you. But you went on a suicide mission when you could have run." He was no longer asking questions. He was telling his version of the events. "You saved me, and they made you out to be a monster," he continued. He wasn't wrong. The character assassination within the Cahlad had been brutal and thorough.

"How do you know they almost killed me?" she asked him. They had almost killed her. She remembered choking on her own blood, waiting on her makeshift bombs to explode, and being ready for it to happen. She remembered pain and movement, but nothing else. She regained consciousness alone in a copse of trees to the east of the facility as smoke billowed from its windows.

Ivan didn't answer her. He looked away for a moment.

Blue chewed her lip and eyed him carefully. "You carried me out of there."

He nodded. "I left you in some trees and went to get help. I couldn't carry you any farther. You were gone when I got back." He looked back down at his hands. "They were already rolling in. You were guilty before they got there. I was glad you were gone."

"You never told them?" she asked.

"I promised. You were right. They would have used the research. If I defended you, I risked them discrediting me and hurting others." He glanced at the ceiling and rubbed the scar on his forearm absently. "I didn't even tell them I was there."

They went back to staring at one another. A man of few words and a woman who liked to make people uncomfortable with silence. "You look different."

Blue smiled slightly. This was the most stilted and prolonged conversation she had ever heard or been a part of. "That's a sad and unsatisfying story."

Finally, his expression changed, an eyebrow-raising. But he didn't comment further. "I owe you."

"Nope." Blue shook her head. "You carried me out of there."

"Never. Even," he stated again, his voice firm.

"It's time to tell me what's going on, Ivan," a voice carried upward from the floor. "Sounds like we should have left this traitorous bitch in the desert."

"Damn," Blue uttered. She had completely forgotten that the guy was there.

30

DEVON

Devon followed the shadow of the man in front of her through the damp underground tunnel. There were no lights, just the dim beam of the flashlight. She pushed Lexi in front of her, fearful that their hiding place would be discovered and they would be attacked from behind in the narrow tunnel. The floor was surprising even, but the air was dank, and the sound echoed ominously off the dirt and stone walls with nothing to absorb it.

"This is so cool," Lexi said from in front of her. "It's like in that movie you guys made me watch where the kids were hunting for treasure to save their town."

"Where are we?" Devon finally asked. These were the first words spoken since Rhodes ushered them into this tunnel, shut the door, and shimmied by them in the narrow space. They had been walking for a few minutes.

"I bought this place from a fairly popular Christian artist. She had a little somethin' somethin' going on with a big-time country artist next door, and they didn't want their spouses to know. When she put in the pool, she had this built. It pops out in the music studio next door," he explained, still leading them forward into complete darkness.

"Oh yeah. I heard about that. They both ended up getting divorced and marrying each other." Devon nodded, then realized how silly it was to be talking about celebrity gossip while they were running for their lives through a subterranean tunnel. "The other side is still unlocked?"

"Surely not. New owner." Rhodes laughed. "But it shouldn't be a problem. "

"This is so cool," Lexi reiterated. "It's a secret tunnel."

Devon squeezed her girl's shoulder, glad that she was able to hold on to her natural optimism despite everything that had happened today. Lexi had given her the cliff notes version of what happened before Rhodes burst back into the room and shoved them out the back door. She hadn't thought twice about following him. If that man was running from something, she wasn't sticking around to find out what it was. She couldn't put bullets to sleep. It did worry her that Harper and the other woman weren't behind them. She hoped they were OK.

"Here we are." Rhodes stopped and turned as much as he could in the narrow tunnel. He was already stooping because the ceiling was two inches shorter than he was. She recalled that neither of the artists who had initially used this tunnel could be accused of being tall. He was careful to point his light toward the ground so that he didn't blind them. Devon could see a door behind him.

"Great," Devon whispered. "What now?"

"Is there a water slide? Or a bone piano?" Lexi chimed in.

"No," Rhodes answered. "But there will probably be cameras. I haven't met the new neighbors. And I don't want to meet them today." He looked at Devon and Lexi with trepidation. "I would like to disguise you. So that you aren't linked with whatever is going on at my house."

"Are you going to cover us in mud?" Lexi asked.

Devon shushed her. Then quirked her head to the side because, as usual, Lexi had a valid observation. "Are you?"

Rhodes ran a hand over his face, and when it lowered, his hair had changed to gray and his facial structure was completely different, with a plethora of wrinkles and a scar on his left cheek. He no longer had a beard. His whole build was different. He was leaner and shorter, making his clothes hang loosely. He looked like an actual working cowboy.

"Whoa!" she and Lexi both exclaimed in stereo.

"Oh. K?" Devon drawled. "You can do that to us?"

"Just you. I was going to give Lexi my hood and just try to cover her face. I don't morph kids unless I have to."

"Oh my God, Mom! Who do you want to be?" Lexi jumped up and down.

Rhodes watched her carefully, as if she would defy a werewolf man while she was trapped in a narrow tunnel and nobody on the planet knew where she was. Could she knock him out before those claws came out? Would it even work on him? He had just eaten a man's neck. "We get to the garage and drive out of here. We keep Lexi low in the back seat, so if anyone is looking for two people and a kid, we don't match that description. Put some distance between us and our last known position."

"Yeah, OK." Devon nodded. "That's actually way more solid than my last plan."

"OK?" Rhodes sounded surprised.

"Can you make her super pretty?" Lexi asked.

"Excuse me?" Devon looked down at her mini-me as Rhodes choked on a laugh.

"No, Mom. Of course, you are pretty. But like somebody glamorous, like in the movies." Lexi rolled her eyes and stuck out her tongue.

"Probably not the best choice if we are trying to go incognito." Rhodes chuckled and looked up at Devon in amusement.

"Fine," her girl huffed.

"Let's do it," Devon told him, unable to overcome the fear of someone coming up behind them. One problem at a time was what Finn always said. Survive and we will sort the rest.

Rhodes reached over Lexi's head and grasped her upper arm. Devon looked down at his hand, then at Lexi's startled face. She was pale and her mouth formed a small O shape. "What's wrong, kiddo?"

Lexi took a quick step back, bumping into Rhodes. She turned and looked up at him and closed her eyes, stepping away from him as well. "It's so weird."

"I didn't feel anything." Devon placed her hand on her face. Now she did. Her nose was much larger. So were her lips. And her ears. She felt around some more. Her hair was shorter. Her breasts were flat and... "Oh my!"

Rhodes took off his hoodie, revealing a faded flannel shirt underneath. "You take this and give her that." He waved at Devon's cream turtleneck. He turned and stared straight at the door.

"Sweetheart, is Mommy a man?" she asked Lexi as she pulled her sweater over her head.

"Yep." Her daughter stared at her feet as she took the turtleneck sweater Devon offered her. "Does it feel weird? Like having stuff hanging out?"

"Yeah. It does," she answered honestly, zipping the hoodie up over her now useless bra. She reached down and adjusted herself slightly. It helped. "We are done," she told Rhodes.

"OK. Step back a little. I need room." He flexed his significantly smaller muscles and grabbed the latch, holding the door shut, obviously prepared to rip it off the hinges. He pulled down on the latch and the door tipped open gently. "Huh," Rhodes grunted in surprise.

"Got that under control up there?" Devon asked wryly, loosening her hold on Lexi's shoulders.

"I'll be damned. It was open the whole time." Rhodes muttered as he stuck a hand out in a gesture for them to wait. He disappeared through the open door, returning a minute later to wave them through. Devon stepped out, searching the area. It seemed clear. "There is nobody here," Rhodes confirmed. "Let's move."

Devon pulled Lexi through the door and maneuvered her until she was in between the adults again. They were in a small room with black painted walls and a large audio mixing board facing a window. A couch and various bean bags were scattered around the space. A door Devon assumed Rhodes had already opened was in the center of the back wall, the light flowing in from the outside, making Devon's eyes squint. Rhodes led them out into a courtyard lined with brick pavers and surrounded by magnolia and evergreen trees. At a fork in the walkway, they followed a narrower and less well-kept path to a detached garage that rivaled the footprint of her house. No one spoke as they moved through the slightly overgrown garden.

They reached the wood-sided garage. It was painted white and had green shutters and a black shingled roof. Rhodes tried the lock, and the door swung open gently. "This is too easy," Devon whispered to his back as he once again motioned for them to wait as he entered the dark building. She glanced behind her through the garden toward the cottage-style music studio and the two-story, antebellum-style house with columns and a second-story balcony that ran the entire length of the house overlooking the gardens. She couldn't help but think that Blue would love this place. Every time they drove by a house like this, Blue would mention how it would be her dream home.

"Come on in. Close the door behind you," she heard Rhodes call from inside the garage. It was still dark inside, so she guided Lexi across the threshold and took one last look around. They were alone. Rhodes pointed his flashlight at a valet box mounted on the side of the wall. He plucked a set of keys from the box and moved in the direction of a large red truck with a crew cab. It was old and beat up, likely a work truck instead of a daily driver. Devon helped Lexi into the back seat and instructed her girl to stay on the floorboard. She put the thought of driving on a busy highway without putting a seat belt on her child out of her mind. If they could avoid being pursued, they needed to do that. She climbed into the passenger side of the truck, finding that the extra height Rhodes gave her made that much easier than normal, even if her pants were a lot shorter.

Rhodes joined her up front and pressed a button on the visor of the truck. The garage door creaked up silently. Light from the security lights mounted around the property filtered in. "Where are we going?"

"First order of business. We need milkshakes. There's a great little dive diner up the road that has a drive-thru." They headed down a long, tree-lined, paved drive. White horse fence ran along one side next to the trees. "What flavor of milkshake do you like, Lexi?"

"Are you serious?" emerged from Devon's mouth just as her lunatic child answered.

"Chocolate and strawberry."

"We don't have time for that," Devon protested. How could he be thinking about food?

"Look. I'm running on empty. That kind of shift takes a lot out of me. I need sugar and calories." Rhodes barely glanced at her. "We are getting milkshakes. What flavor do you want?"

"Hot fudge," Devon grumbled. "Extra whipped cream." She crossed her arms over her chest and was startled at the lack of breast getting in the way. She shifted uncomfortably in her seat.

"Chocolate and strawberry and hot fudge, extra whipped cream it is." Rhodes nodded and pulled them carefully back onto the main highway in the opposite direction of his house. Devon glanced in the rearview and saw emergency vehicles screaming up the street behind them. They all turned down Rhodes' driveway.

"What about Harper and that other lady? The dog?" she finally asked, a pang of guilt for abandoning the two women spearing her in the gut.

"Harper's got this. I've never seen a situation she couldn't handle." Rhodes assured her as he turned on the blinker and they drove farther away from the mayhem of moments ago. "She will have that situation under control in no time."

"Harper? Not warrior lady?" Devon clarified.

"Kendra. Oh, she's great. She can hold her own. But Harper. She solves problems." Rhodes reached over and turned on the radio. It was set to a Latina radio station.

"You have a lot of faith in your assistant." Devon scowled at him. She personally thought that faith was misplaced.

"Yep. She'd leave in a heartbeat if I didn't," Rhodes answered, changing lanes one more time. "Here we are. Let's get our milkshakes."

"OK. Rhodes. I really appreciate the fact that you are helping us. And you ate that guy's windpipe. Very chivalrous. Nobody has ever done anything like that for me before. But I need to know what your plan is. I don't wing it. I plan, organize, label, and tag. This whole seat of the pants thing is going to piss me off, and that usually isn't a good thing."

"How have you and Blue stayed friends?" he glanced her way briefly as he pulled into the drive-thru and rolled down his window. The speaker came to life almost immediately, and he ordered three milkshakes and enough food to feed an army.

"She likes my plans." Devon huffed, knowing it was a lie. Blue acquiesced to her plans, typically without complaint. But left to her own devices, she was absolutely feral. She abhorred structure.

"She likes you. She tolerates your plans." Rhodes laughed as he basically read her mind and called her on the bullshit. He pulled to the window, and they waited for their order to come out. She really did dislike him. Momentarily, in the office, she had seen something in him that made her understand why Blue once considered tying herself to the man for the rest of her life. Blue came to her senses, and Devon was quickly coming back to hers as well.

"Tell me what our plan is, and we can argue about who knows Blue better when we have it in motion." Devon chewed on her lip and stared out the window as the headlights of cars passed on the busy road. Every one of them might hold more bad guys. Her mind was going a million miles an hour. Blue hated this guy. But here she sat because her best friend had sent her child via magic teleportation to an ex-fiancé who was an asshole and an actual werewolf. The situation made her uneasy. The only thing Blue told her about Rhodes was that he had done something she couldn't forgive, even if he had had good intentions. She needed more information. She turned back to stare at the man, who changed his appearance more than his underwear.

"Here we go." He handed out frozen drinks. Then he handed her a huge bag of food and pulled away from the window.

Devon fished the straws out of the bag and put them in the milkshakes out of habit. She handed Rhodes his first, then slipped one to Lexi in the back floorboard. "Don't you dare spill that. Leave the lid on," she warned. Lexi liked to take the lid off and lick the ice cream off the bottom part of the straw. It always ended in a mess.

"Fine," her daughter grumbled as she ripped the shake from Devon's hands.

Devon took a sip of her own milkshake and instantly felt better. "This was a good idea. Thank you."

"No problem." Rhodes took a sip of his drink. "The plan is to drive to the airport. We are going to disguise ourselves again, hop on a private plane, and fly to a safe house out west."

"Who is going to fly the plane?"

"I am," Rhodes answered. "Can you hand me the bag? I need fries."

"You are a pilot?" she asked in surprise. "You sing. You dance. You kung-fu. You werewolf. And you fly?"

"Mr. Rhodes?" Lexi asked from behind them, followed by a big slurp. "What were you protecting her from?"

Rhodes and Devon caught each other's eyes in confusion. "What do you mean, Lexi?" She stopped herself from turning to look into the back seat. They were supposed to look like just two men in a pickup truck.

"Well, Tia Blue told you that Mr. Rhodes broke her heart doing something unforgivable for the right reasons." Lexi's little voice carried from the back seat and over the noise of the radio. Devon locked her eyes on Rhodes and studied his reaction as Lexi continued. "She sent me here because she knew you would protect me. And you killed those guys. Which is really bad. But you did it to protect me. Which is a really, really good reason. Totally the right reason. Right? So, you must have been protecting her. What from?"

"How old is she?" Rhodes laughed, a false smile slipping onto his face.

"Nice try." Devon held his gaze, startled by the level of insight and maturity her daughter showed at just ten. More than most adults, she knew. She was so much like her father, it hurt sometimes. "Don't change the subject." Then she glanced in the back seat and saw her insightful and mature child licking the milkshake from the bottom part of the straw. Chocolate ice cream smeared all over her face. "Oh my God, child, I told you to leave the lid on."

"Some very bad and powerful people were trying to kill her," Rhodes sighed. "It's not our car. I'm not worried about a mess."

"Says the man who doesn't do the laundry," Devon grumbled. "Or have to clean chocolate out of hair."

"Why didn't you just kill them like those bad guys back at your house?" Lexi asked as she put the lid back on the milkshake. Devon whipped her eyes back around with a scowl.

"I couldn't kill them all. They would have just kept coming. Sometimes you have to run and hide," he told her daughter gently.

Devon's eyes grew wide as a thought struck her. "Oh buddy," she shook her head, thinking about how Blue didn't like to look at herself in the mirror and rarely took an interest in her appearance. Surely she wasn't right.

He glanced over, a pained expression on his face, but said nothing.

"What did she look like before?" Devon demanded.

He chewed on his lip for several minutes, avoiding her eyes. His silence told her she was right, and suddenly her heart hurt for both of them. "She was perfect," he finally answered. "Auburn hair. Curly. It was a cloud of fire in the sun. Freckles. All across her nose. Hazel eyes with little bits of gold and green. A little scar on her forehead. She tried to cover it with her hair. So fair, thinking about going outside gave her a sunburn."

"You loved her. So, you hid her?" Devon asked, needing more details. "And she didn't want to be hidden?"

"I hid her. And then I walked away. They were looking for me, too. I had to make her a smaller target. Told her there was no us." He stared straight ahead as he navigated the fading traffic.

""Baby Blue" is about her, isn't it?" Lexi dropped another truth bomb. "That line about the cereal aisle. Tia Blue is obsessed with cereal."

"Yeah, kid."

Lexi fell quiet, apparently all out of soul-wrenching truth bombs for the night. The only sounds in the cab were the slurps of Lexi's milkshake reaching the end of its life.

"You are such an idiot," Devon finally uttered. "A complete idiot."

"Yeah, man. You don't leave the people you love. Even I know that and I'm ten," Lexi piped in from the back seat. "Song was pretty cool, though. Strong game on that one. Big gesture."

"You ladies are disturbingly astute and candid." He still didn't look her way.

"You are going to change my mom back, right?" Lexi asked, this time without her typical enthusiasm. Her voice held a tone of trepidation and worry that made Devon wince.

"I promise, kid."

"Wow," Devon said, still trying to wrap her head around the conversation. And possibly the past two hours. "Wow."

"Still hate me?" Rhodes asked.

"Oh yeah. Totally."

"Great," he replied sarcastically. "This should be a really fun trip."

31

SAM

S am sat up from his spot on the floor and looked between a startled woman Ivan called Di and his friend's perpetually stoic face, waiting for an explanation of what he suspected. This was Indigo 'Di' Vale, the woman who helped Larson slaughter a facility full of people, including kids. A woman who completed dozens of off-the-books assassinations on his orders without question. Although there were no records, he suspected she had ended Rhodes Westridge as well. His disappearance was never explained.

Sweat dripped down his back as he seethed, hoping he was wrong. Cold air from the wall unit left him with goosebumps. He was relieved the cool air was finally on. Maybe soon they would be able to breathe in this room, and he could tolerate putting his pants back on.

"You know her?" he prompted when his friend didn't answer.

"I do."

"Is that why you wouldn't leave her in the desert?" Sam asked, remembering the argument they had standing on the side of a dirt road in the middle of what turned out to be the Arizona desert. Ivan carried her dead weight three miles to the nearest town over Sam's objections. They currently occupied one of the shittiest motel rooms he had ever seen, because it was the only motel in town. And the phone and television were busted. "Is that why you have the heat on when it is ninety degrees outside, and I've been sweating my balls off for the past seven hours?"

"It is."

"Ivan. Don't push me," he warned.

"She saved my life." Ivan continued in his Ivan way. He was never a man of many words, but when he wanted to be obstinate, he was brutal.

"When?" Sam prodded. He didn't want a fight with Ivan. But he said the name Di. If she was that Di, it was a big problem.

"Today," Ivan replied dryly. "And April 21, 2010,"

Sam stared at his friend. That was the day of the explosion at the Cahlad headquarters and Larson's hidden facility. "How Ivan?"

"She's an angel," Ivan answered with conviction.

"That's not true, big guy," the woman in question finally chimed in again.

Sam turned to her, fine with having a new target for his surprise and anger. "Since Ivan has so little to say, why don't you tell me why he thinks you are an angel? Because death follows you everywhere?"

She clamped her mouth shut and looked away. "Tell me," he said very slowly.

"Sam. I'm warning you." Ivan stood to his full height. Sam stood as well, not willing to remain on the floor with an angry Ivan looming over him.

"I don't know why he would think that. All I did was fuck everything up, watch five people die, and take too long helping someone who desperately needed it." The words spilled from the woman's lips. Her voice raised into a shout as she pointed at Ivan. "Look at his arm. I'm the reason he has that scar. I'm the reason the alarm was tripped that killed two pregnant women. The reason those assholes had the time and incentive to do. That. To. Him!" She ended her tirade with a high-pitched shout and clasped her shaking hands over her mouth. She had lost it.

Ivan stepped toward the bed where she sat and stopped when she turned her head and put a hand out to stop his approach, a distressed look on his face. His head swiveled menacingly toward Sam. "You are my friend, Sam. But one of us isn't walking out of here if you do that again."

"Is that so?" Sam asked.

"Ivan, don't," the woman asked quietly. "Just tell him the truth."

The big man took a step toward Sam, his nostrils flaring.

"You expect me to trust her? Take it easy on her? She's an assassin. Do you know how many people she murdered for Larson?" Sam asked.

"He's your friend, Ivan," she said softly.

"I fucking know," Ivan rumbled back, answering them both.

"You told me it was a booby trap in an anti-magic field on a mission." Sam accused his friend. He pointed to the woman on the bed. "She fucking betrayed all of us."

"She saved all of us," Ivan bellowed. His voice bounced around the room.

"What the hell?" the still drowsy Ava muttered and edged herself closer to the woman next to her, looking around in confusion.

"Bullshit. I saw the end of that video feed. Right before Larson tried to blow Mitch up. Now she's suddenly back with a bunch of magic surges and a terrorist attack. Disappearing Sovaj. Wouldn't it be easy for her to make someone disappear? You expect me to believe she is some kind of innocent? Some kind of hero? That she didn't participate in Larson's plans? She isn't behind whatever is happening now?" Sam shouted back, taking a step closer to Ivan, using the four-inch height difference to look down at him.

"They captured me. Because Larson told them where to find me. It was a Stalker Unit. They had gas just like today. They cut on me. While I was awake. They cut me everywhere. For days. I prayed to die. But she came when I gave up. I thought she was an angel. I couldn't see her face because they beat me till my eyes swelled shut. Then they burned me with a torch. Do you know what that feels like, Sam?"

Sam stood speechless. He had never seen his friend this worked up. He had never heard him string this many words together. He had never heard any of this in the ten years he had worked with Ivan daily. He was stunned and horrified.

He looked at the woman who caused all of this. Her eyes were closed, and her hand was pressed to her chest. Her breathing was rapid. She was not OK.

"One of them thought it would be fun to use a saw on my arm while I watched. Did you know that you can scream so much no more sound will come out? You can. I have."

"Please stop," Di Vale, Larson Battle's attack dog, and Ivan Lacroix's personal hero, whispered. Ava was sitting up in the bed beside her, watching the two men fight warily, clutching the woman's other hand.

"Ivan. I'm—" Sam started to say, but Ivan interrupted him.

"No. You wanted the story. They were experimenting on other people in that place. Rogue Sovaj nobody missed. Pregnant women. Children. Children, Sam! They experimented on her, too. I remember when they brought her in. And this woman could have left at any time. She didn't. She got people out. Then she came back for me. She got me out and used magic that I know she didn't have to spare to heal my arm and my eye. She gave me her only weapon." Ivan waved a hand in emphasis. "Then she went back into that nightmare again, not even knowing if she could rely on her magic to destroy the place and the research so that they couldn't hurt anyone else like that. But none of that matters, because you saw ten seconds of a video feed and made up your mind. You didn't investigate. You didn't let the team investigate. They rolled onto that scene with orders from you.

Orders they couldn't break. You made up your mind who the guilty parties were in seconds with not even a tenth of the information. You knew which version of the story wrapped up your problem in a nice tidy bundle. Which story you could spin. She was the perfect scapegoat. The perfect explanation for how Larson did what he did under our noses. I didn't tell you because that day I knew exactly what kind of man you were. Not a Stalker sworn to protect the innocent. But a politician sworn to protect the power. And you went right up through the ranks."

"She said stop!" Ava screeched at the top of her lungs. She glared at them, and her eyes flashed. Sam felt his magic surge and watched Ivan's skin flare a vivid bronze. A large golden bubble shimmered away from his body, lifting him off the ground and slamming Sam bodily against the walls. Between the shouting and the sounds of things hitting walls, Sam was sure the cops would be called. Still stunned, Sam tried to say something to calm the girl or Ivan. She leaned against the other side of Ivan's force bubble, and he felt a threatening, uncomfortable pressure on his ribs. "Don't. You. Dare."

Di Vale hunched over on the bed, fighting to draw in air. "Ms. Blue. Are you OK?" Ava asked in a much smaller voice than the one she had just used on Sam and Ivan.

"Blue?" Ivan asked gently, unconcerned with the fact that he was dangling two feet off the floor.

"Ms. Blue. What are you saying?" Ava leaned down to hear what the woman was saying. "You can see? What can you see, Ms. Blue?"

Ava looked up at them. "She isn't breathing right." She pointed at Ivan and waved a hand dismissively. He slid to the floor. The bubble pressing Sam into the wall dissipating. "You. Help her."

"You said she healed." Ivan moved forward and leaned down to look at the place where two bullet wounds had been. It only made the woman's breathing worse.

"I can help," Sam told them quietly. Pissing this girl off with a directive wasn't his best move right now. He didn't want to make Ivan any angrier than he already was. He knew what was wrong. She was having a panic attack. A bad one. And he recognized the technique she was using to try to calm herself. She wasn't succeeding. Sam had seen Mitch use the technique with Zella when she had a particularly bad vision. Ava glared at him.

"Let him help her, honey badger," Ivan told the girl. She eyed Sam suspiciously, then nodded.

"You need to give her space. It's a panic attack." Sam instructed. "She needs air." He walked over and knelt in the two feet between the door and the bed so that he could see the woman's face but wasn't leaning over her. Ava scrambled off the bed and stumbled toward Ivan. He was tall enough that they were eye level. He scowled at her.

"Di? Blue? Tell me what you can see," he said, using a directive and not feeling the least bit sorry about it.

"A sweaty asshole that lost his shirt."

"Tell me what you can hear."

"A sweaty asshole that lost his shirt."

"Tell me what you can smell." Sam was amused, despite himself.

"A sweaty asshole that lost his shirt."

"Tell me what you can feel."

"My lips are chapped."

"Not a sweaty asshole who lost his shirt?" he asked. "We were on a roll."

"Maybe later," she clipped out.

"That's better. Try to take a deep breath and focus on the shirtless asshole, if that helps."

She shot him a bird, rattled in a deep breath, then let it back out. He could see the pulse slowing in her neck. "I'm OK. Just give me a minute." She covered her eyes with her hand. He looked up to find Ivan and Ava staring at him. She looked furious. He looked guilty.

"You." Ava stalked to the dresser wedged against the far wall and pointed at Sam. "You wanted to leave her for dead in the desert after she saved our asses." She snatched up the new shirt he bought out of the lost and found box in the lobby and threw it at him, hitting him in the face. "You are a jerk." His new pants flew in the air behind his shirt, hitting him in the chest.

"You. Drama much?" She pointed at Ivan and chucked his shirt and pants at him. "Think you could let her build up enough strength to sit up on her own before you buried her in your emotional baggage? You almost killed her."

"Take your bromance spat outside and don't come back in here until you've kissed and made up." She placed her hands on her hips and blew a damp strand of hair out of her face. "I'll keep your shoes."

Sam suppressed a smile and caught Ivan's eye. He jerked his head toward the door and pulled his shirt over his head, then hopped into his pants. He waited for Ivan to do the same and headed toward the door. They stepped outside and Ava promptly slammed the door behind them, leaving them on a second-story concrete walkway overlooking a poorly lit parking lot that had once been paved but was now just a mixture of rocks and dirt. Sam heard the deadbolt and chain being thrown behind him. He leaned forward and placed his elbows on the rusted metal railing, then thought better of it and leaned against the wall.

He was quiet for a moment, replaying Ivan's words in his head. He was ashamed. Ivan was not wrong. He had been so certain he was right and handling things the correct way that he had completely missed any signs his friend might have offered about the truth. He looked over and down the few inches that separated their heights. Ivan stood in a similar position to his own, leaning against the wall on the other side of the peeling blue door. His arms were crossed over his chest, and he gazed out at the desert beyond the parking lot, lost in thought. Sam could see the large angry scar that ran all the way around Ivan's arm, between his wrist and elbow. He couldn't even comprehend the reality of the things Ivan had told him. Where were the other scars? What was special about that wound? "I'm sorry."

"It's OK, brother," Ivan grumbled, still looking out into the desert as the sun began to push back the darkness on the horizon. "I didn't know you then. I knew Mitch and Larson were tight. I didn't know who to trust."

"Yet you stayed?" Sam asked him.

"I could do more from the inside. Keep an eye on things." Ivan shrugged.

"I don't think you were wrong. I'm not the man I was ten years ago," Sam told him. "You weren't my friend then. But you are now. And I'm sorry. Will you tell me what happened? Can you?"

Ivan finally looked over at Sam. "Did those vending machines downstairs work?"

Sam shook his head. Ivan did everything in his own way, in his own time. "The lights were on. I'll get us something." He reached into his back pocket for his wallet and realized it was empty. He turned back toward the door in disbelief. "Do you have your wallet?"

Ivan's eyes grew wide as he reached for his back pocket. He let out a belly laugh as he realized it was empty, just like Sam's. "I didn't even see her take them."

32

FINN

F inn sat next to Hale in the front seat of their vehicle, listening to Nisha talk Greenlee through navigating the maze of people surrounding his house. Three squad cars sat in their driveway with lights flashing. Shocked and nosey neighbors gathered on the sidewalks. Nisha heard four extra voices that belonged to goon squad surveillance, as she called it.

Hale seemed calm, but Finn didn't like the fact Greenlee was doing this solo one bit. Especially after what they heard on the radio and the notifications they all received on their phones on the way over. The goon squad was a radical magic supremacy group called the Sovereign, and they were the ones responsible for the well-planned and organized bombing and shooting this afternoon. Greenlee was not equipped to deal with people like that. But he only had one artifact that could make a person invisible, and he insisted he couldn't talk Finn or Hale through finding what he needed in his shop. Seeing the state of the place when Agent Mann showed up, Finn had conceded.

"So, your parents are dead?" Finn asked Ben the question that had bothered him since the alleyway. Trix ran a thorough background on the parents and Hughes before Herne taking the job.

Nisha put the phone on her shoulder to cover the speaker. She still held Ben's hand and was growing surlier by the minute. Everyone in the car had tried to use physical contact to quiet the voices she said she could hear in his brain. But it only worked for her. "He killed them accidentally. I think they are still in there." She jerked her head toward Ben and put the phone back up to her ear.

"Whoever hired you, they weren't my parents," Ben confirmed. His face was unreadable at the moment. "They are probably with the people that tried to grab Ava. I was home from work with a stomach bug or I wouldn't have been there. They killed Anita, our housekeeper, and already had Ava in the car before I got to them."

"What happened after that?" Finn asked quietly, his eyes on high alert, scanning the area for anything more out of the ordinary.

"Slaughter," Nisha interjected. "Oh, nope. Sorry, Viking dude, talking to someone else. You are still clear."

Ben frowned. "I really don't like you being in my head." Nisha rolled her eyes at him.

"I don't like having my soul sucked out," Finn groused.

"Team projects are tough, man," Hale commented, also scanning the area. "Why were you in that cafe?"

"Well, I killed them all. At my house. I thought it was Cahlad at first. I'm not registered. I thought they were there for me. I couldn't register. You understand?" He asked Nisha, whose face softened slightly, and she nodded. "But it wasn't Cahlad. We left immediately. I had an emergency bag with cash, and we left everything so they couldn't track us. Bought a car with cash. But they kept coming. Atlanta, Cincinnati, and Nashville. We moved constantly. Everywhere we went, they sent more."

"The magic surges." Finn put the pieces together and motioned for the man to continue.

"We stayed at a little hotel in Southern Kentucky for a few days. When I went to get more food one morning, I found a journal with a napkin for the Cat and the Canary bookmarking a page inside our locked car. Nothing else had been touched, I assure you. Except that journal."

"What was in it?" Finn asked curiously.

"The last part was gibberish. Abstract poetry? The first half was strange. Almost like one-page stories. But none of them were related."

"He is on his way back. Operation nipple was a resounding success," Nisha hung up. "Do you still have this journal?"

"In my jacket." Ben motioned to the opposite side of the hand Nisha was holding. She unceremoniously fished a small red leather journal from an inside pocket. She handed it up to Finn. He took it and started flipping through. Every page was handwritten. Every entry had a date. Some pages had sketches decorating the text all the way to the edge. Toward the back, a yellow napkin stuck out. He flipped to that page.

The Hounds of Dawn in Blues of Bell
Wild Children War Upon the Dell
Roar of Brothers. Seven and seven.
Vortex Cross a Violet heaven
Splintered Time. Forged Love. Staunch Friend.
Together Stand or All Will End.

Finn frowned. What did this even mean? Agent Mann asked Devon and Blue about the Hounds of Dawn yesterday. This wasn't a coincidence.

"We met a woman in the cafe. Brown hair, undercut, tattoos, a few piercings. A little scary, frankly. She said someone left a napkin for her too. She knew things about my wife." Ben paused. "She was going to help us. Then everything went south, and we were separated."

"She received a napkin, too?"

"That's why she ghosted us," Hale said quietly. "I knew she wouldn't just leave us like that without a good reason."

"So, you guys know this mystery woman?" Nisha demanded. "What does your daughter look like? Clue me in." Hale stirred, fishing a packet of neatly folded papers from his pocket. He handed them back to her.

"This is what we were given," he told her. "Are those photos real?" he asked Ben. Finn understood his question. Since their information was provided by people who were legally dead, all of it was suspect.

Nisha unfolded the paper as gracefully as she could with only one hand and went completely still. Her reaction caught his attention. It caught Hale's as well.

"That's her. That is Ava with her mom right before she died. Sarah died eight years ago." Ben looked down at the photograph with affection.

Before Finn could query Nisha, his phone rang. He swiped to answer, placing the call on speaker so that Hale could hear as well. Trix's voice hit him before he could issue a greeting. "I've got something. Two men and a girl boarded a private plane at John C. Tune. The girl looks like Lexi. I ran facial recognition on the men. Roy and Steele Krantz, brothers who own that big law firm that is on all the buses in town."

"Why is Lexi with them?" Finn demanded. "Where is Devon?"

"Interesting you should ask. Roy is in the hospital recovering from a triple bypass. There is a blurb from two days ago in the paper about it," Trix chimed in. "What I'm looking at: he looks fantastic for a man that had his chest cracked open less than a week ago."

"That doesn't make sense. Tell me something that makes sense," Finn groaned.

"Well, the miraculous Mr. Krantz flew out IFR. Heading West. Flight plan shows a final destination somewhere in Oregon. The plane has a transponder, and the heading is confirmed. But it doesn't have the range. If that is indeed where they are going, they will have to stop somewhere to refuel," Trix informed them.

"What is the range? Get me airports at the edge of that range, generally west and northwest of here. It is the best lead we have unless they call us."

"Yep," Trix nodded, and Finn heard him typing away before the line went dead.

"Good work?" Finn said to the empty line, then turned his attention back to Nisha, who still stared at the photos in her hands.

"Why do you look like you've seen a ghost?" Hale demanded.

Her face screwed up, and she glared at everyone. Her eyes fell on Ben, and she stared at him for a few moments, like she was studying a difficult topic.

"This," she flipped the image around, "is Amber Collins, who is presumed dead as of ten years ago when Regent Battle tried to take over the Cahlad. She died in the explosion."

"What?" Ben demanded, looking at everyone in the car in confusion. "No. That is my wife, Sarah. We married when Ava was one. And she died in a hit and run, walking to work eight years ago."

"Amber Collins as in the Paragon's daughter?" Finn clarified.

"Yep." Nisha handed the papers back to Hale. "That Amber Collins."

"This just keeps getting better," Hale dead panned taking the papers from Nisha and pulling a granola bar from the center console. He reclined sideways in the driver's seat so he could face everyone. He looked like he was settling in to watch a movie. "Keep going."

"Our missing person is the Paragon's granddaughter? One I am assuming he doesn't know about?" Finn queried Nisha.

"Nope. He has no idea. Mitch and Zella think Amber is dead." Nisha tapped the side of her head. "It's still hard to listen to them sometimes."

"Was she a teen mom or something? Their daughter wasn't that old?" Hale asked.

"No, she wasn't." Nisha shook her head adamantly. "No babies."

"That is not Amber Collins. That is Sara Millwood, and her parents are dead," Ben insisted. "Maybe she just looks a lot like this Amber person."

"It's her," Nisha insisted. "Freaking zombies."

Something slammed against the rear passenger side of the vehicle with a thud, followed by a hard slap on the window. Black mist ballooned from the back seat, slamming Nisha against the window and shoving Hale and Finn forward. Hale twisted quickly and barely missed ramming into the steering wheel and subsequently the horn. Finn wasn't so lucky. His forehead bounced off the dash.

Nisha yelped, and Hale struggled to lift his weapon over the mist. Finn looked around and saw absolutely nothing. There was nothing near them.

"What the hell was that?" Ben demanded, eyes growing black and the beginnings of flames emerging from his eye sockets.

"I don't see anything," Hale told them as Finn drew his own weapon.

"Fucker," Nisha uttered angrily, slapping the glass next to her as a laughing Greenlee faded into sight on the other side of the glass, hand suspiciously hovering over his right nipple.

He opened the door, still smiling. "Gotcha. Bet people don't sneak up on you very often. Scoot over."

"I almost shot you," Finn barked, lowering his weapon. "Hughes, drop the soul-sucking mist tentacles. It's just my sister's asshole boyfriend." The mist sucked back toward Ben and his eyes returned to normal, though Finn could tell he was still rattled.

"Ben. My hand," Nisha said in a deathly calm tone as she scooted over to let Greenlee into the car. The man dropped her hand like a hot brick.

Greenlee settled into the back seat, placing a large backpack on the floorboard between his feet and a messenger bag in his lap. "Don't let go of him. He'll go all…"

Greenlee stopped mid-sentence and let out a cry of pain as Nisha's fist flew into his nose with a thud. "Never again," she spat, reaching back and taking Ben's hand again.

"What's the plan now?" Finn re-holstered his weapon and fished a granola bar out of the console. He had seen that look before on Devon's face and he didn't want to deal with hangry right now. He tore it open and handed the bar to Nisha.

She took a bite immediately. "Thank you," she mumbled around a mouthful of food.

"Greenlee," Finn warned. He did not need a war in his backseat. This lot was worse than a bunch of kids.

Greenlee pulled an umbrella out of the messenger bag. "This will get us to Devon," he announced, flipping the bag closed with a huff. "Probably."

"How?" Hale asked doubtfully. He sat in the driver's seat, watching them all with guarded amusement.

"I've been working with Blue. She actually wanted me to make these things for you guys after the Kinshasa incident. But you have to be able to channel magic to use them. So, we ended up making one for Lexi for her birthday and I played around with this one. I'm going to think really hard about Devon, and this should take us to her."

"Wait," Nisha said around another mouthful of snack. "Teleportation magic. That's rare." She frowned. "Blue? As in Indigo? The dead Zenith? The lady in the cafe? Sam and Ivan and Ava disappearing into thin air?"

Greenlee still glared at the woman. "Are we going to have a problem?"

"Freaking zombies," she groused. "OK. Ben's daughter and my best friend are running around with a teleporting zombie. Just another day at the office. No problem. I can handle this."

"Trix called while you were gone," Finn told Greenlee. "We know Lexi is on a plane headed west. A small plane. How accurate is that thing? Are we going to end up in a propeller or something?"

"We?" Greenlee raised an eyebrow.

"How many will it take? Blue can move multiple people."

"Depends on how much magic is available to pull from, I suspect," Greenlee eyed the umbrella. "I really have no idea."

"Either way, let's wait. If Devon is with Lexi, they are on a small plane a few thousand feet in the air." Finn insisted. "Even Blue would have difficulty with that, and she knows what she is doing."

"Yeah," Hale agreed. "I thought she was going to die on that moving van jump in Uruapan. Think I'm going to sit this one out, boss."

"If we have to wait to get to this Devon person," Ben asked, "will that thing take us to this Blue person? Or Ava?"

"Unfortunately, no. It is tuned to Devon." Greenlee looked truly apologetic. "Probably, single use. But I have supplies now. I might be able to come up with something if I can find a space to work." He shook his backpack to indicate his supplies.

"Lilac has workspace," Finn reminded him. "You know, that place I have been trying to get back to this whole time?"

"Who are you?" Nisha asked Greenlee as he shoved the umbrella back into the backpack. Her phone pinged again, and she glanced at it.

"Want to tell us who keeps blowing up your phone, Captain Cahlad?" Greenlee asked. "Is a Stalker unit about to descend on us?"

She kept her head down for a moment and took a deep breath before looking directly at Finn. "I have to ask for help."

Finn crossed his arms across his chest, immediately wary. "Go ahead."

"Trix told you about the raid at the Cahlad," Nisha stated.

Greenlee looked confused. "What? A raid at the Cahlad?"

"Yeah man, keep up. The government stormed the place guns a blazing." Hale interjected.

"They are arresting anyone and everyone ranking higher than janitor," Nisha blew out a breath. "Apparently I'm a fugitive now."

"You want us to hide you from the government?" Finn asked. "That's rich." He noticed that Greenlee had grown silent and was sending Nisha an assessing look.

"No. Well. Yes."

"Which is it lady?" Hale demanded.

"Mitch is the person I've been texting," Nisha said carefully, glancing around the car as if she expected a violent reaction. Other than the floorboard filling with gray mist, everyone else remained stone-faced and silent.

When she didn't say anything else, Finn nodded for her to continue.

"Zella snuck him out a few minutes before the raid happened. Sometimes she just knows things," Nisha sucked in a breath. "And she just drove up to an abandoned warehouse on Lilac Avenue."

Finn couldn't help the look of shock that crossed his face.

"You keep saying Lilac," Nisha rubbed her eyes. For the first time today, she was starting to look tired and stressed instead of just pissed off. "Can they go inside?"

Hale let out a low whistle.

"Oh, how the mighty have fallen," Ben uttered with unhidden disdain in his voice.

Nisha glared over at him, and he held up his free hand. "I know. Fuck you, Ben. You don't have to say it."

Finn stared at the woman, mentally going over what she just said. The Paragon of the Cahlad was asking for asylum from the government at his top-secret magic artifact warehouse.

"Are you seriously considering this, boss?" Hale asked quietly, uncharacteristically nervous.

"I think we should help them," Greenlee interjected, startling Finn out of his thoughts. He had forgotten Greenlee was there, and he was surprised by his statement. Of all the people in this vehicle, he thought Greenlee would be the first to throw the Paragon to the wolves. He studied his friend's face. He was sincere. "I'm willing to help them," his friend reiterated.

"Do you have the authority to negotiate on behalf of the Paragon?" Finn asked her.

"I do." Nisha nodded.

Finn glanced over at Hale and then back to Greenlee, praying to God he wasn't making a mistake that would jeopardize the lives and livelihoods of his employees and friends. He silently asked his brother to forgive him. "Herne will assist the Paragon, but I have a few terms."

She nodded. It occurred to him she likely knew what he was going to ask before he pieced the information together himself. "The Cahlad will transition global research, retrieval, and storage activities of all class four or greater artifacts to Herne by the end of the year. Call it independent oversight." Finn stated his demand, arms still crossed. This is where she laughed at him. He knew the absurdity of what he was asking. But hiding a fugitive from the government, especially one like the fucking Paragon, was a high-risk venture.

Hale whistled again, followed by a colorful comment from Greenlee about the metallic composition of his testicles. Nisha's eyes narrowed, and she stared straight into his eyes. He refused to look away, letting every thought he had about Alexander and Gage and the unit he lost to the effects of a black-market artifact flow through his head.

To his surprise, she neither laughed nor told him to go to hell. She simply replied, "And?"

Hale's eyes grew comically large. Of course, she knew there was more. And she was going to make him say it.

"A Herne representative will join Stalker Prime as a full member, effective immediately. That representative will report to me or my eventual successor," Greenlee hissed in disbelief.

Nisha sat quietly, staring at him for another moment. Finally, she blinked. "If I accept your terms, what is the expiration on this agreement?"

"No expiration."

Nisha snorted. "That's pushing it, Torrin."

"OK." Finn sat up as he thought of a more palatable limit. He leaned forward, noting how silent the rest of the vehicle had fallen. "This arrangement remains in place while any current member of Cahlad Prime's senior leadership remains."

The vehicle hit a pothole, and its occupants jerked violently. Finn wondered if the wheels would hold up. Everyone cursed in surprise and aggravation, breaking the unnatural silence in the car.

Nisha smiled. "Right now, senior leadership is the Paragon, Regent, and Stalker Prime."

"That definition suits me fine." Finn agreed.

"You realize Mitch might lose control of the Cahlad. We have no idea what the government is up to."

"Then I guess it behooves me to make sure he stays safe and maintains his position." Finn leaned back. "Do we have an agreement?"

"Mitch and Zella?" Nisha clarified.

Finn nodded. "Mitch, his wife, and you, of course."

"She's not his wife."

"We will still do our best to help her."

"We have a deal Mr. Torrin," she stuck out her hand. He reached over and took it, expecting a handshake. Instead, a ribbon of light circled their hands, slowly tightening until he felt a mild pressure. A tickle of energy washed over his hand then she shook.

"Fuck me," Hale muttered.

"What was that?" Finn demanded, shaking his hand to remove the tingle.

"That, my friend, was a binding magical contract," Greenlee informed him. "They can't back out now. Then again, neither can you."

"Can I tell them it is safe to knock?"

"Tell them to hang tight until I can inform Trix."

Hale glanced over at Finn with a strange expression. "Lilac?"

"Yep."

"Sure thing," Hale announced. "Just another day at the office. "

THURSDAY

Cahlad Prime *@CahladPrimeOfficial*

The Cahlad denounces the methods and platform of Larson Battle and his organization the Sovereign. The Cahlad does not believe in the supremacy of any group of people magic or otherwise or condone the actions taken by his group of extremists. Our thoughts and prayers are with their victims.

Senator Nolan Miller *@USSenatorNolanMiller*

Where are you @CahaldPrimeOfficial. The Sovereign use magic to terrorize us and you do nothing. Pitiful! Proof that your oversight is theater. We can no longer tolerate overlooking criminals in your own community.

#RealMagicRegulation #WeMustProtectOurselves

Paranoid But They Are Still Out to Get Me

@ShinySilverHats

@USSenatorNolanMiller has been trying to take down @CahaldPrimeOfficial for years. Now he claims they are responsible for the Sovereign even though they haven't used magic yet. Don't be fooled sheeple! This is where he tries to take over the Cahlad. *#ItsAllAConspiracy #StandWithMitch #IvanTheIncredible #FuckNolanMiller #FuckTheSovereign*

Cade Rhodes Biggest Fan *@CadeRhodesBiggestFan*
I just can't. The Sovereign targeted Cade because he played the Cahlad concert. Where are you Cade? *#FurtureMsCadeRhodes #AmericasBeard #FuckTheSovereign #CaughtInTheCrossfire*

Senator Nolan Miller *@USSenatorNolanMiller*
The FBI has executed a warrant at @CahladPrime based on evidence collected in cooperation with the Magic Regulations and Relations Committee. Active warrants have been issued for @CahladParagon and his senior staff.

#RealMagicRegulation

This Soccer Mom Needs a Beer *@SoccerMomNeedsABeer*
Too much bad in the news. Keep the ab pictures

coming. The world needs more beautiful.

#LadiesLoveLacroix #washboardAbs #IvanTheIncredible

33

NISHA

Nisha watched closely as Finn hit a button in his dash and a dented and gratified garage door rolled up on a decrepit warehouse on a dark and questionable street named after a lovely flower. The building looked like it had been abandoned for years. Finn pulled into the dark interior and stopped, allowing the door to close behind them. She looked over at Ben, who appeared apprehensive. She understood. He didn't have the insight into people's motivations that she did. She rooted around in Torrin's head extensively before she committed the Cahlad to his terms. He wasn't a boy scout, but his heart was in the right place. And it was a big one.

It helped that the thought of independent oversight for the Cahlad's most invasive programs made her happy. It was the only reason she had stayed with Stalker Prime so long; it needed a voice of empathy. Someone who wasn't always about the rules and the ideals. Someone who saw the people. She thought Finn could be that person. If she was leaving in two weeks, she would feel better knowing she hadn't left a void. She texted Mitch the terms of their agreement on the way over. Terse would be an apt description for his reply. Best case, he fired her. Worst case, he lost his temper. Either way, the deal was done.

Finn let the car roll forward into the darkness. Bright lights clicked on overhead and the floor lowered slightly beneath them. The room they were in was nondescript and dirty. But the car sat on an elevator, and it was lowering slowly into another brightly lit space. Five other cars sat in neat rows against the walls. The car stopped, and Hale stepped out first. "Let me see what we are dealing with in here." Hale threw an arm up and hustled by quickly, disappearing through the door. Ben opened the door and stood, helping her out, since they needed to remain in contact. She was going to blame the fact she didn't have both hands for the reason she stumbled instead of the fact she was trying desperately to overhear the internal dialogue of the building's occupants. There was a lot of mental activity in this building. She could hear Mitch. Everyone else was tense and unhappy except for two people who seemed cloudy.

Greenlee climbed out with his backpack and messenger bag, took a look around, and followed Hale through the door without a word. "You sure about all of this? I don't see how this is moving us closer to Ava," Ben asked.

"I know you are nervous about Mitch," Nisha told him. "But even in hiding, he is our best shot at finding Ava and keeping you both safe from those assholes."

"But you work for assholes too," Ben told her without an ounce of malice in his voice. "How is it better?"

"Everyone is an asshole if you catch them on the wrong day. But we won't make her a weapon."

"But she will never be free," he muttered, and winced. She heard a spike in the conversation happening in his head, and he squeezed her hand to the point of pain.

Nisha closed her eyes and took a deep breath, wondering if there was any wine in this place. Her paycheck was definitely anemic for this job. "She's not free now, Ben. At least we can keep her safe."

"I promised to keep her safe," Ben told her. His head hung between his large, slumped shoulders. "I promised her mom."

"OK. Then that is what we will do." Nisha nodded and squeezed his hand.

His head jerked up the moment she said we. She felt a wave of emotion wash over him. It was overwhelming. His eyes flamed. The shadows in the room grew darker, especially the area around their feet, which appeared to writhe like a living creature. His nostrils flared, and he pulled himself to his full height. The voices in his head roared briefly, then fell silent.

"You can't scare me away," Nisha told him, wondering what on earth had triggered him this time. She had nowhere to run. Soul-sucking mist, Cthulhu man was never going to trust her. She was in a secret lair in a questionable part of town. And she was tired. Too tired to care right now.

"I can," Ben rumbled in one hundred voices that shook the floor. Nice trick. Nisha looked at him blandly. Why wouldn't he want help? She couldn't imagine how lonely it would be to be on the run with your child, with a terrorist group and a pseudo-government magic mafia on your trail.

Nisha stepped closer. "Either I die helping or I die running, Ben," she said with a resigned sigh. "If I'm going to die, I'd rather do it helping."

The man in front of her jerked his head like she had hit him. He stepped back, but did not let go of her hand. The glow in his eyes suddenly snapped out, and the misty tendrils spooled back into a void at his feet. The voices began speaking quietly, but she no longer heard a discussion about the many ways she could die. "OK."

"OK? You are going to let me help? Or OK, you aren't going to kill me today?"

"I need help. And I'm not going to kill you," he told her firmly. "We aren't a threat to you," he spoke to more than just Nisha.

"How generous of you." Her words dripped with sarcasm.

"Can you leave off your crazy theory that Ava is his granddaughter?" Ben implored. "At least until I'm sure about him?"

"Of course," she agreed quickly. She wasn't even sure how she would broach that topic with Mitch, anyway.

"You got this, Ravi?" Finn called quietly from where he stood next to Hale, who had returned at some point. Both men held their weapons in their hands but had yet to point them at Ben. Hale speared Ben with an intense stare.

"Just a discussion," Nisha mumbled and walked toward them. "Do you have wine?"

"No wine," Hale informed her, sending Ben one last look full of warning. "Two lovely ladies are putting a mighty dent in a bottle of whiskey down the hall. If you hurry, there might be some left."

"Please, lead the way," Nisha told him as they walked down a long white hallway toward the sounds of giggles and laughter. Those must be the foggy brains she was hearing.

Hale turned to Finn. All business. "Kendra is here. We have one extra."

"Who is the extra?"

"Harper Kilgarden, Rhodes' assistant. She's found the whiskey."

Finn grunted and kept walking. "How bad is Kendra hurt?"

Nisha could hear Finn's internal concern. He wanted to put eyes on his injured employee personally.

"Just needed a few stitches. Going to have some bruises. Caesar's already stitched her up. She'll live," Hale filled him in. "The team reports a lot of bodies at Rhodes' place, boss. Trix called it in pretty fast. They didn't have time to deal with all of them. We might have witnesses."

"Understood." Finn nodded as they continued to wander through a maze of hallways.

"The Paragon and his wife are in the break room." Hale's voice held a touch of disbelief. "Kendra tried to put them in your office, but he insisted on staying with the others."

"Thank you." Finn nodded and started to push open a door to the right.

"Finn?" Nisha put a hand on his back. She chewed her lip, looking between Finn and Hale. He paused and turned with a question in his expression.

She made her decision and looked up at the ceiling. Sam was going to kill her. But who better to ask about a mysterious artifact than magic treasure hunters? "Have you ever heard of an artifact called the Son Sovaj?"

Finn's brow furrowed. "No. I'm not aware of anything by that name." He looked at Hale, who shook his head. "What does it do?"

"The only thing I know for sure is it causes cancer," Nisha told them.

"Do you know what it looks like? Where it was seen last?" Hale offered.

"No idea."

"Are you sure it isn't just a piece of radioactive waste somebody thinks is magic?" Hale inquired without an ounce of malice. It was a fair question, but she couldn't go into the details of Project Zenith with them now. Maybe not ever.

"I'm sure," Nisha assured him.

"Would you like for us to see what we can dig up?" Finn offered without demanding any additional information. The look on his face told her he knew she was holding something back, but he didn't ask for any more details.

Nisha nodded. It couldn't hurt to have the best artifact trackers in the world looking for a mysterious artifact referenced in a top-secret file. It was their wheelhouse.

"OK. I'll let you know what we find," Finn told her and pushed the door open to allow Hale to walk through.

A wave of laughter rolled into the hallway. Finn walked in behind Hale without hesitation. She could feel Ben hesitating, and she squeezed his hand reassuringly, peeking around the door frame to see what was happening. She felt a wave of apprehension at the thought of facing Mitch after agreeing to outsource one of the Cahlad's biggest responsibilities to a bunch of treasure hunters. Mitch and Zella sat at a large round table. Mitch relaxed back in his chair with his arms crossed. His bearded face twisted in amusement. Zella sat next to him, sipping a cup of tea with an equally amused expression on her face. When she walked in, Mitch smiled at her warmly. Zella stood, crossing the room to wrap her in a bruising hug. Nisha breathed a sigh of relief.

Across from Mitch, a blonde woman slid a full shot glass of golden liquid toward a muscular woman with short black hair. "Drink up. You earned that today, sugar."

Finn's eyebrows rose in surprise when the fierce-looking woman laughed and actually accepted the glass. She raised it in the blonde's direction. "You killed more of them than I did, Kilgarden."

The other woman lifted her own glass. "To bad ass bitches. And bad guys that leave the keys in their murder mobiles."

They both cackled.

"How long has this been going on?" Finn asked. She wasn't sure if he was frustrated or amused.

"About half an hour. I got Greenlee set up in your office, boss." Hale laughed. The women's names popped in and out of his head. The blonde was Harper, and the other woman was Kendra.

"That bottle was full yesterday," Finn grumbled.

The two women took long drinks of their whiskey. "That was truly impressive driving," Kendra told her and winced slightly.

"That was nothing, honey. I always drove my daddy's entry in the demo derby. They were sitting ducks tonight," the smaller woman laughed and swatted a hand demurely like she was talking about a super simple potluck recipe.

"Sitting ducks, they certainly were." Kendra continued to laugh.

"I really want to hear this story. I need all the intel you can give me," Finn told Kendra.

She was silent for a moment, as if trying to find words. "The initial attack was three vehicles with seven to eight armed men each. They breached the door immediately. Harper took Lexi to a safe room while Rhodes and I secured the entry point to give them time to get there."

Finn looked between Harper and Kendra to see if twenty-one armed assailants made the other woman react. It didn't. She just nodded as she looked at Kendra. "Reyes, enlighten me how you held off twenty-one armed assailants."

"Well, sir. As the first five entered the foyer, all the metal in the house suddenly became airborne. Mr. Rhodes turned out to be very proficient in self-defense. I feel like a great deal was left out of his client profile. We were successfully repelling the attack when a woman named Devon drove onto the front stairs and something that sounded like static happened. Then she came in, Mr. Lane turned into a..." She looked over at Harper, who just shrugged her shoulders. "A werewolf? Some of them turned into babies. He threw a few of them at Devon, and they just went to sleep. He... ate another. We killed a few others using more traditional methods." Kendra stopped for a moment, as if realizing what she was saying, and took a long sip of whiskey. "That was after a kid materialized out of thin air." Kendra hiccuped and slapped a hand over her face. She looked over at Mitch, as if she forgot he was there and who he was. He smiled reassuringly at the woman, who smiled sheepishly back at him. That was classic Mitch. People always felt comfortable talking to him.

"Then two more carloads of bad guys showed up," Harper chimed in. "None of the phones worked. So, Rhodes took the baby girl and her mama out the back. I started to go with them, but I heard Kendra here trying to keep them from coming in. I knew they were going to kill her. She's badass. But ten on one and she was already hurt." Harper made a face as if to say, Duh. "So, you know, I snuck around the side of the house and stole one of their trucks and ran them all over. Just like my daddy taught me. Protect the radiator." Harper finished her story by swiping her hand in a dusting motion and clapping them.

Finn didn't speak for a few seconds. He opened his mouth and closed it again before turning to Mitch. "Welcome to Herne, Paragon."

"Thank you for your hospitality," Mitch said, seeming unmoved by the outrageous story he had just heard. He looked directly at Nisha. "Thank you for taking care of my family."

She looked away. She had come to America to stay with a foster group that took in magic users whose families weren't equipped to handle their abilities. It was an outreach program the Cahlad bankrolled. She had arrived here when she was twelve. It had taken that long for her own parents to grow tired of dealing with a child that couldn't concentrate or perform in school—and when they could no longer handle being ostracized in their community because their daughter could read minds. The straw that broke the camel's back was when she accidentally outed the neighbor for having an affair with a local politician.

Years later, when she officially became a member of Stalker Prime as a favor to Sam, her family reached out. She never returned their calls. Sam and Ivan were her family now. She liked and respected Mitch. She was very fond of Zella. Who wouldn't be? But she never considered that Mitch might think of her as more than an employee and trusted adviser.

Zella nodded her head in agreement as she slipped a leather-bound journal into Nisha's hand and pointed at a page.

Hunger of Souls at Singers of the Mines

A Convergence at the End of Times.

Nisha frowned at the words and looked in confusion at Zella's earnest face. This meant something to her. How did they translate it into normal people speak? Ben peeked over her shoulder. "What does that mean?" Nisha just shook her head. "Is that me? Hunger of Souls? Did you tell her about me?" She shook her head again and shushed him.

"I trust Nisha communicated the terms of the agreement?" Finn asked Mitch.

"She did," was all Mitch said.

"I take it you are in agreement as well?"

Mitch smiled coolly at Finn. "I suppose I do, Mr. Torrin."

"Please make yourself at home. You will be safe here at Lilac. I look forward to discussing the details as soon as things have settled down."

One of the room's three televisions, cut to an image of Senator Nolan behind a microphone. The man was spouting bombastic nonsense about evidence of criminal activity at the Cahlad and bringing the guilty to justice to restore the public's faith in well-regulated magic. Nisha took a second look and hissed. The man was standing on the steps of the Cahlad's main building. She glanced at Mitch, whose face had turned murderous. Ben shifted nervously, and Finn grew alert. Zella scowled at the television. Hale sipped his coffee, seemingly unconcerned with the Paragon's reaction. Kendra seemed to sober up suddenly. Harper did not. She leaned forward and slapped her hand down on Mitch's forearm. "What's got you so upset, shaggy man? Here." She slid her shot glass his way. "Let's turn that frown upside down, sugar."

The whole room waited for Mitch's response. He frowned at the hand on his arm, then looked up at Harper, shaking his head slightly. "You aren't that drunk, my dear."

"You are right. I am not." Harper smiled sweetly at him. Kendra snorted in disbelief.

"Did you not see what this guy did to those birds?" Ben whispered in horror. "Or the last idiot that challenged him."

"I sure did. But that doesn't mean I'm going to tiptoe around him or kiss his ass. I deal with divas all day, every day. I know one when I see one. He needs to get over himself." Harper's smile turned sharp and pointed. "Drink the damned whiskey, Paragon."

Nisha fought a smile. Zella didn't. She fell into a silent fit of belly laughs.

"I like her," Hale uttered from across the room.

They all watched as Zella clutched her stomach, shaking with laughter. A smile showed through Mitch's thick mustache as he watched her, his eyes growing warm. He slowly picked up the shot glass and tossed it back with a grimace.

"Somebody tall, bring me another shot glass," Harper demanded. Nisha saw Finn pinch the bridge of his nose and shake his head.

Then a thought entered her mind that made her gasp. It came from Mitch. He wished Indigo Vale was still on the payroll so he could deal with Miller and make it look like an accident. "Mitch!"

"Stay out of my head dear," Mitch said in a tone of voice that sent chills down Nisha's arms, removing any of the warm and fuzzies that grew watching him humor the drunk woman. His eyes flashed as he stared at her. Sometimes she forgot the kind of person you had to be to retain power in an organization like the Cahlad. And he had just reminded her.

"You know what? Get over yourself, Mitch," Nisha said flatly and watched his face twist into stunned disbelief instead of the anger she expected. Zella seemed shocked as well. She never dreamed she would ever speak to the Paragon of the Cahlad like that. Both because she respected Mitch a great deal, and he would kill anyone in seconds if he really wanted to. Suddenly deflated and tired beyond her limits, Nisha turned to Finn. "Is there somewhere to sleep in this place?"

His face reflected understanding and sympathy. "Yeah, this way. Let's get you settled."

"Ben." Nisha jerked her head toward the door. "You are with me."

34

BLUE

Blue pulled on the clean clothes Ava placed on the toilet seat while she was in the shower. Apparently, Sam made a provision run for clothing not covered in blood while she was passed out. The clothes were too large and neon, but they didn't smell, and they didn't show parts she wanted to keep covered. The shoes were a cheap pair of flip-flops a size too small. She was surprised he had even thought about it. He didn't like her at all. The room was still steamy, and she couldn't see her reflection in the mirror. But she knew she looked horrible.

She rubbed her hair with a paper-thin towel, tossing it into the tub when she heard banging on the exterior door. Alarmed, she yanked open the bathroom door and ran knees-first into the bed where Ava watched TV. Sam yelled, "Let us in!" She felt an overwhelming need to open the door and watched Ava jerk in that direction as well.

"Son of a bitch." Blue vaulted over the end of the bed and landed in front of the door, ripping at the lock and the chain to follow the compulsion. The door burst open with enough force to throw her back across the bed. She hit Ava, who was still trying to get to the door, and they both tumbled in a tangle into the small space between the bed and the far wall. Ava let out a startled squeak, and Blue shouted a curse.

"Get your stuff. We have company." Ivan shouldered his way into the room, stepping directly onto and over the bed as Sam pushed in behind him and slammed the door closed. Ivan continued into the room and snatched his wallet from where it sat beside the television, shoving it into his pocket roughly. He glared at Ava and tossed Sam the wallet that was beside it.

Blue stood. "What are we dealing with? Hand me those." She pointed at her knife and her gun. Someone had salvaged her weapons and their holsters. They were even wiped clean. Ivan tossed her both items, and she strapped them on over her new clothes.

Sam stopped by the window and opened the curtain just a crack. "Eight visible incoming. Armed. At least one vehicle drove around back. We are surrounded." He closed the curtain and stepped away from the window, glancing around the room. It was too small for combat. "They are coming up the stairs."

"How many rounds do you have left?" Ivan asked her as he stepped to the door, placing his body between the entrance and everyone in the room. "You have the only gun that made it."

"Ava, get into the bathroom," Sam ordered, backing further into the room.

Ava did as she was told. Blue checked her weapon. "Three rounds, big guy."

"Fuck," Ivan muttered. "How did they find us?" He ran a hand over his dark hair and squared his gigantic shoulders. His dark arms flexed, causing the pink scar on his right forearm to bulge. His fingers formed into fists. "What are the odds they aren't packing any green gas?"

Sam turned to her and looked her over with a critical eye. "How are you feeling?"

She knew what he was asking, and she hesitated. She still didn't know what had gone wrong with the last skip. It was a miracle they had all made it. Her indecision must have shown, because his expression grew grim. Even with three of the best magical fighters in the world in this room, they wouldn't be able to keep Ava safe in this space.

"We need you to try. If they have that gas, we die here." Sam told her what she already knew.

"Understood. But I can't take us far," Blue told him. "Don't abandon me in the middle of the desert this time, OK?"

Ivan moved away from the door as footsteps echoed off the thin concrete walkway outside. Whoever was coming wasn't even trying to be quiet about it. They knew their quarry was pinned. "Just get us out of this room," he said with more urgency than she had ever heard out of him. "I'll handle Sam."

"Everybody in the bathroom. Stay calm," Sam ordered. Blue stepped into the room and pushed Ava into the still-wet bathtub.

She climbed ungracefully in with her as Sam forced his way into the room, shoving her forward. She thought he was going to climb into the tub with them, but he eyed the short ceiling and placed a foot on either side of the toilet instead.

"What's happening, Ms. Blue?" Ava asked, grabbing Blue's arm. Blue holstered her gun and reached for Sam's hand. He offered it without hesitation.

"More bad guys. We need to get out of here fast. Give me your hand," Blue answered as Ivan maneuvered into the room with barely enough empty space to close the door behind him. Ava whimpered.

"But you almost died last time," Ava implored, burying her face in Blue's shoulder. "Lurch was going to leave you for dead in the desert." Sam's expression remained obstinate. Even if triaging the lives of three conscious people over carrying the dead weight of a stranger through a desert for an unknown distance was tactically a reasonable thing to do. Being the unconscious person in question, he was still an asshole in her book.

"They are at the door. They will breach any second," Ivan announced.

Blue took a deep breath and let the rainbow cloud her vision and the icy cold flow through her only recently warm body. She looked at Ivan's worried brown eyes as he moved toward them. "Hold them tight for me, Ivan," she told him and watched him wrap his gigantic arms in a bear hug around all three of them. She heard a man outside shouting, "Breech! Breech! Breech!" then the reverberation of the motel room's tiny door splintering. Ivan's hands met in a firm grasp at the small of her back, and he placed his chin on the top of her head as they all smooshed together in the circle of his arms. Her face was smashed up against the dark skin of his chest, exposed by the terrible Hawaiian-style shirt he hadn't bothered or wasn't able to button. He had not showered since the room cooled off and Blue wrinkled her nose. Ava screamed as Sam shouted, "Go now!" and she let the rainbow take them all, praying that whatever had happened last time did not happen again.

The skip was rough. Everything turned black for a second but settled for a deep violet that let her remain conscious. She did lose her grip on everyone, but Ivan kept them all in contact somehow. They landed upright and on their feet with a crunch of gravel and muttered curses and grunts. Her knees gave out and her head spun. She opened her eyes to the bright desert sun. They were one hundred yards away from the motel next to a faded and dilapidated laundromat called Sun Washed. The door to their room was open, hanging sideways on only one remaining hinge. Green smoke rolled out of the door. Men in SWAT gear with masks covering their faces swarmed the area. A woman in red leather pants and a black halter top stood to the side, observing.

Sam caught her when Ivan released them from his bear hug before she hit the ground and shoved her to Ava. "Take her," he uttered quietly. Ava took Blue's arm and threw it over her shoulder as Ivan took a place in front of them and Sam moved behind them. Ivan walked them backward so that the building offered more cover. The men were back-to-back with her and Ava in the middle, providing them cover as they moved like they had done this kind of thing before. "I know that one. Most wanted for five years. Petrov. Nasty."

Blue patted Ava's arm to let her know she was OK. She stood to her full height, still dwarfed by the men on either side of her as the dizziness passed. A small pathetic RV park sporting a once cool retro sign shaped like a rounded arrow stood next to the laundromat. The sign once read The Oasis but now just read sis due to fading. It came complete with tumbleweeds and semi-permanent shack structures. Two of the RVs were joined by an enclosed plywood hallway running between their doors. "Do you think any of those things actually roll?" she whispered.

"There's a decent-looking one toward the back," Ava answered, scrutinizing the lots. "Still has wheels. Nothing built onto it yet."

"Everybody in this town drives an RV?" She pulled out her knife, noting the lack of cars and trucks in the area. "Sotach, take Ava and see if you can find some transportation."

"I don't want to go with him," Ava whispered as Sam mumbled, "I don't think so."

"Ivan, help me out here," Blue implored, watching men filing back out of the room. They knew it was empty now and they would search the area. "It's OK, Ava. I'll be right behind you."

"She's right," Ivan rumbled, never taking his eyes off what was happening at the motel. One of the SWAT members tossed an elderly man out of the lobby and into the gravel of the parking lot. The man shouted and pleaded as he rose to his hands and knees and tried to get away. "Take honey badger and get her out of here. We will buy you time. Come back for us if you can."

Sam watched the scene in the hotel parking lot. "Fuckers," he spat as the elderly man took a boot to the ribs.

"Regent. You have two Zenith operatives in front of you. The best fighters in the Cahlad and maybe the world. We fight. You lead. That is the way this works." Blue told him as she stepped up beside Ivan. "Lead us straight to an RV that will roll out of here under its own power. We will keep them off you as long as we can."

The woman on the balcony across the street searched the area with shrewd eyes. The men she commanded filed down the stairs and even more rounded the corner of the building from the back of the motel. She hoped Sam made up his mind soon. She couldn't jump with multiple people right now and guarantee everyone's safety. She was still drained.

The woman on the balcony flicked her wrist. A clap of thunder rolled across the sky, and a bolt of lightning slammed into the tile roof of the motel, throwing fragments of orange clay in all directions. She strolled calmly down the stairs into the parking lot, where her men observed carefully in all directions. More flicks of her wrist sent bolts of lightning arcing close enough to make the hair on the back of their necks stand on end. She and Ivan crouched, and Sam pressed Ava into the building. The bolt hit the roof of the laundromat. Seconds later, the crackling of flame reached their ears. "You have got to be kidding me," she mumbled, flinching with each roll of thunder.

Soon, every roof that wasn't clay tile caught fire and burned. She was razing the town to the ground to flush them out. "It's your funeral, lady. Ivan, stay alive," Sam said with a steely quality to his tone. "Follow me, Ava." Their footsteps crunched quietly away. A wooden lean-to attached to the RV closest to the laundromat parking lot burst into flames with a flash of light.

"They have gas," Ivan said quietly. Blue saw the trepidation on his face. If she had gone through what they did to him, she wasn't sure if she would still be standing here.

"I'll get us some masks. Be right back." She leaned forward and executed a quick skip to the side of the motel, relieved to find skipping just herself didn't drain her as much. She was able to land cleanly. She pressed her back up against the stucco wall of the burning hotel. She leaned out to confirm that the two men that were near the edge of the building were still there. She picked up a pebble and tossed it, then backed up and squatted down to wait. Moments later, both men rounded the corner. She skipped quickly, landing on the shoulders of the first man. She ripped his mask off and slashed at his throat with her knife before he knew what was happening. She rode his body to the ground and came back up. The other man raised his weapon as his partner gurgled his last breaths. He had a clean shot. She tucked, rolled, and skipped at the same time as she heard the gunshot echo off the side of the building. She reappeared directly behind the man, lunging up and wedging her knife into the base of his spine, right below his helmet. She ripped her knife free as he fell and snatched the mask from his face. She ripped the gun out of his hand. She took the other man's gun as one of their friends rounded the corner to investigate the gunshot.

Blue couldn't resist the urge to wiggle her fingers at the woman before the rainbow carried her through the cold to Ivan. "Here you go, big guy." She tossed a startled Ivan a mask and extended one of the handguns. Ivan caught the mask and fastened it carefully over his face and took the weapon, checking it before nodding. She handed him the other as well.

"We need to deal with the lightning," Ivan said as Blue pulled her own mask on and made sure the seal was tight. "Lighting hurts."

"Agreed." She nodded. She glanced toward the Oasis, hoping to see Sam and Ava. All she saw were burning RVs and disgruntled or hysteric residents fleeing into the open areas. Secondary explosions punctuated the chaos. "Let's go."

Ivan moved forward in a slow jog. In seconds, he reached a dead sprint straight into the heart of their opponents, most of whom were still clustered in the motel parking lot. Shouts rang out when they spotted him. Gunfire erupted, making the dirt around his feet burst. Blue let Ivan draw their attention. Petrov was surrounded by three men. Not all of them were looking at Ivan, showing enough discipline to recognize this for what it was, and continue searching for other threats. As long as his mask wasn't compromised, he would be OK. She needed to handle the lightning lady even if her guards weren't stupid like the rest of the bunch. She skipped quickly, landing behind Petrov striking with her knife the minute her vision was clear. Bad math. She messed that one up. She still caught the woman in the side, a deep cut to her abdomen. But not a fatal blow. Petrov screamed and clutched at the wound, rounding on Blue with a crazed and livid expression twisting her otherwise beautiful face.

A strong blow to her back knocked her forward. It hurt, but she used the momentum to carry her toward Petrov, slashing again as she tucked into a roll. She landed only a minor slash on her arm. Leaping to her feet, she rushed back. Petrov's protectors were fully engaged now, so Blue's hands were full. She fell into a rhythm of kicks and punches, ducking blows and skipping randomly in and out of the small circle of fighters. She caught an occasional glimpse of Ivan doing his Ivan thing in a cloud full of gas. His hands were also full, but he was successfully keeping his bunch engaged. It was incredibly difficult to fight a man that you couldn't hurt. Ivan was so large he was even hard to move, and he kept them from coming her way. She saw an opportunity and lunged toward Petrov, stabbing with one hand and grappling with another. Her knife missed, but she managed to grasp the woman at the elbow, throwing them both to the ground. They both screamed, Blue from exertion and Petrov from rage.

Petrov scissored her legs and grappled with Blue while two of her guards piled on. One grasped the wrist that held the knife, the other her left leg at the knee. Petrov unleashed an electric jolt that locked Blue's muscles and caused her to writhe in agony. Her vision went white as she struggled to dislodge herself or find enough focus to calculate a skip. The guards did not let go and weren't suffering any ill effects from the electricity. Petrov had incredible control over her magic.

"Where is she? What have you done with the Nova?" the woman asked in a cold and calm voice, pumping more electricity into their connection. In the distance, a large engine stuttered to life. Blue's muscles continued to spasm in agony. She tilted her head back, and in her upside-down field of vision, she saw Ivan hanging from the ground and charging in her direction. Three men broke away from Ivan when his attention wavered and ran into the RV park. That wasn't good. Time for a bad idea. Fortunately, she didn't care if any of the people currently touching her survived a skip. She closed her eyes and skipped, taking the woman and both guards with her.

They appeared fifteen hundred feet in the air to cold and sudden silence. She felt a flip-flop start to slip and instinctively pinched her toes together painfully. All four of them plummeted toward the earth. Both guards screamed and fell away, unable to keep their hold as Blue kicked and punched. She looked into Petrov's startled face as her mouth formed a scream. The electricity stopped at the same time the woman's hair fully extended over them when she reached zero Gs of free fall, allowing Blue the ability to move her abused muscles.

She only had seconds before they both slammed into the earth. She pulled the surprised woman close, wrapping her legs around her leather-clad waist and arms around her shoulders. She brought her knife up and jammed it into the base of the woman's spine, even as they tumbled end over end. The woman fell limp. Blue pushed away, preparing to disperse the energy of her descent with several smaller skips. Petrov's body shimmered.

"Uh oh," she uttered, pinwheeling her arms frantically to put more distance between herself and the falling body. With a sickening pop, it discharged a wave of electric energy that pushed Blue into a sideways cartwheel and caused her muscles to spasm uncontrollably yet again.

Her downward momentum had not changed. She lost track of where she was in relation to the ground or the fight, the world a blur of white and blue and brown. Even without knowing exactly where she was, she knew she didn't have long. She skipped without calculating. Her only thought was up. The colors in the rainbow morphed together, just like in the car. "No. No. No. No," she gritted out. Everything went black.

She appeared, still tumbling, and focused blearily on orienting herself. Her vision tunneled and something wet dripped down her face. She reached for her magic. She could feel it, but trying to channel it into a jump was like trying to pull something through a clogged vacuum. She could access some, but not nearly enough to get the job done.

She was five hundred feet from the ground. One of the guards lay in a puddle directly below her. Three seconds to impact. She skipped again, almost blacking out. A pain stabbed through her temple. She was higher this time and emerged on her belly, distributing her body to generate resistance. Petrov's body slammed into the roof of the flaming motel, dislodging the tile. It skidded to the edge and fell the rest of the way to the ground. The body no longer looked like a body. That looked excruciating. This was a bad plan.

She oriented herself again, locating Ivan. He stood in the middle of the largest group of mercenaries, a golden bubble of energy hovering around him. Their weapons were drawn, and they fired, somehow missing each other. One of their vehicles sat mangled by a body through the roof.

She only had one more skip left, if she was lucky. She focused around the pain in her temple and mustered her magic, managing one last skip to slow herself down. She landed hard ten feet from Ivan and crumpled to the ground, dizzy. She was conscious and her vision came back slowly, alternating between pitch black and reality like a strobe. She rolled over and retched. Her arms shook as she righted herself and fought her way to standing on shaky legs.

Some of Ivan's opponents were temporarily distracted by the aerial light show and crashing bodies. Not Ivan. He took advantage of the distraction and plowed through the men closest to him.

"Let's run, big guy. The lighting is handled." She stumbled sideways to dodge a swing from a man on the outer edges of Ivan's circle. He quickly drew his weapon, realizing none of his allies were behind her. She let out a strangled "Gah" and threw herself at the ground again, rolling away as the man fired. Ivan roared and charged the man, bringing a brutal blow down on his shoulders. His momentum continued as he ran toward Blue, swooping down and swinging her to her feet without slowing down. She scrambled like an old cartoon thrown off balance by being scooped up and dumped in one motion.

Eventually, she found her stride, and they raced away from what was left of their attackers. The sound of gunfire rang behind them and Blue was once again pulled off balance as Ivan's arm shot out and yanked her in front of him. "Jesus!" she shouted as she stumbled again. Freaking useless flip-flops and jello legs.

The rumble of an engine and a metallic crash drew their attention toward the Oasis RV Park. Gunfire continued. A large vehicle rumbled toward them haphazardly, taking out picnic tables and fire pits as it bounded over curbs, rocks, and everything in its path. Whoever was driving the thing wasn't even trying to stay on gravel paths. Ivan reached out and grabbed her arm, jerking her back in front of him when her path diverged from his. "Stop it!" she yelled.

"Stay in front of me," he grumbled, exasperated. He placed a hand on her shoulder and pushed her in the direction of the RV.

The large bus-like RV lurched to a stop next to the faded Oasis sign. It had an air conditioner and a satellite dome on top. Blue raced toward it. Ava leaned out the driver's window, her blonde hair sticking out in all directions. "Hurry!"

Blue and Ivan reached the open passenger door, taking the steps two at a time. Blue stepped in and got out of Ivan's way. She wiped a hand across her dripping nose and winced at the blood coating it. She snatched a towel from the RV's kitchen and headed to the back. She ripped the quilt off the bed, wrapping it around her shoulders. She shivered and her teeth chattered. She fell to the floor behind Ivan. She didn't have much left.

In one fluid motion, he grabbed the back of Ava's shirt and hauled her out of the driver's seat, depositing her next to Blue. Ava squeaked as her butt hit the carpeted floor. "I'm driving," Ivan said as he looked around. "Where is Sam?"

Ava shrugged, then looked at Blue with horror. "You are bleeding again!"

Blue waved the bloody towel dismissively. "It's fine." She looked past Ava out the large front windshield. Two men ran toward them. "Guys!" She pointed. "That's a problem." A shout and rhythmic bangs moving up the side of the vehicle on the passenger side made them all jerk in surprise. Blue dropped the bloody towel and drew her weapon, aiming at the door while clutching the quilt together with her free hand.

Seconds later, Sam burst up the stairs, sweating profusely and winded. His eye was black, his lip was bleeding, and he lost his shirt somewhere. Ugly bruises already marred his torso. He lurched into the living area of the vehicle with Blue and placed his hands on his knees. "You left me," he wheezed at Ava.

"How does it feel?" Ava turned to Sam with an obstinate and devious look on her face. Blue lowered her weapon and smiled. She really liked this kid.

Ivan slammed his foot down on the gas, and the vehicle lurched forward. "Hold on," he shouted belatedly over his shoulder as he wrestled with the wheel. The warning came too late. Both Blue and Sam were thrown off their feet and landed hard in the kitchen of the RV. Blue found herself flat on her back on the linoleum floor staring up at the ceiling of the RV with a large portion of Sam's body pinning her legs down.

"Get yourself buckled in," Ivan yelled at Ava. He ripped open the window next to him and hung his left arm out and fired his gun. The RV swerved, and she slid across the slick floor, slamming into Sam. She let out a pained "Oomph," and tried to push herself off him, but the vehicle was still turning. She heard a thump, then felt the rear wheels of the RV lift and metal crunch.

"You got him!" Ava cheered, scrambling to the cream leather couch behind Ivan and fumbling with the seat belts.

Blue eyes landed on a television mounted on the wall over the driver's seat. Somehow it still worked despite the fact they were moving and not plugged into power. Fancy. The face on the screen stilled her efforts to free herself. "Oh shit. I knew it. The fucking bastard," she muttered, reading the ticker at the bottom of the screen. "New Sovaj terrorist organization takes responsibility for recent attack. Former Cahlad Prime Regent Larson Battle...."

"What is it?" Sam raised himself up on his elbows, still breathing heavily from his sprint to catch the RVs. "You look like hell," he told her and followed the path of her eyes. He leaped to his feet in one fluid movement and paced toward the television. He placed his hand on the ceiling to steady himself as the RV shifted and lurched. "That can't be."

"Move your head," Blue demanded. "You are blocking the screen." He glared over his shoulder and took a step to the side, re-anchoring himself with his hand at a new spot on the roof.

Swaying wildly with the motion of the vehicle, she walked forward, and lacking anything else to hold on to, grabbed Sam by the waist to steady herself. He hissed and flinched. "God, woman, your hands are ice!"

She ignored him and focused on the television. The sound was too low, and the ticker kept repeating. "Turn it up. I can't reach," she slapped his back.

"Yeah, Lurch," Ava piped in from her spot on the couch. "What happened to your shirt this time?"

He hit the button on the television to turn up the sound. "It got pulled over my head, and I got punched in the face."

"You got shirted. Nice," Ava nodded with a smile, turning her attention to the television. "Who is that?"

Sam looked down at Blue, a grim expression on his face while she listened to the broadcast. Ava started to fidget behind them as the ride grew smoother and Ivan announced, "I think we are clear."

"The woman called Ava the Nova," Blue told Sam. She reached up to his busted lip and placed two fingers on it. He reared back in surprise. "Just hold still." She sent a bit of magic into his lip and watched it stitch up. She was relieved by the result. It felt like the well she drew her skipping magic from was sealed shut. She could normally feel the location or tug of people she skipped with or the tingle of a specific place. She was completely cut off from that right now. But what little healing she had was still working. Moving her hand up to his eye, she did the same.

"That isn't in your file," Sam said quietly as he touched his repaired lip.

"There are probably a lot of things that aren't in my file, Regent," Blue said with some sarcasm as she took care of the ugly bruises on his ribs. "I can't do much right now. But that should feel better."

"It does. Thank you," he told her, pinning her with an intense gaze. "Are you grounded?"

"Yeah, for now." She nodded and wiped at another trickle of blood leaking from her nose.

Sam frowned even more, if that was possible, and looked back at the screen. "Nova?" He shook his head. "Haven't seen anything about a Nova come through the Cahlad."

When the segment wrapped up, they both turned and looked at the girl, who was watching the television with wide eyes as talking heads provided an analysis of Larson's word vomit.

"The anomalies. The spikes." Sam said, looking at Ava like she was a puzzle he was trying to solve. "It's her. Magic burst. Novas." He was right. A person who could boost another person's magic. No wonder Larson wanted her. No wonder Amber wanted to keep her hidden. "You were in Atlanta and Cincinnati, and Nashville recently," he stated, more than asked.

Ava's face grew pale, and she looked like she was about to jump from the moving vehicle. "I don't do it on purpose."

Blue did not know of any documented way to boost magic. Judging by the stunned look on Sam's face, neither did he. They had the holy grail for magic users sitting across from them in a stolen

RV wearing an "I Love Arizona" tank top. An artifact with that capability would cause wars and raise empires. A person with that capability and the possibility of passing on genetics was a whole different level of valuable. Christ, this was worse than she expected.

"I know. It's OK, Ava," Blue assured her. Now she knew why the jump in the van had gone so wrong. She had already pulled the maximum level of magic she could channel prepping to move four people, moving fast while she was injured. Ava's added power overwhelmed her. If her body couldn't heal itself faster than normal, she would likely be dead right now. It probably happened in the air, too. "You boost magic? Does it happen more when you are scared or nervous?"

The girl nodded. "Or angry. I haven't been able to control it since those men showed up and Dad made us leave."

"It's OK. We are going to help you." Blue looked up at Sam, hoping that she wasn't lying to the girl about the we part. He nodded. Blue sat next to Ava on the couch. "I wish we knew where they were planning to take you. We should have kept some alive to talk to."

Ava's shoulders hunched, and she looked down into her lap. "Well." She didn't finish her sentence and continued to look at her hands guiltily. Blue and Sam waited patiently, but it became obvious quickly that she wasn't going to say anything else.

"Tell us, Ava," Sam said gently but directly.

"I stuffed one of them in the storage compartment with the sewage lines. I knocked him out and shoved him in there. He said some really bad things. He had it coming."

Blue let out a laugh, imagining the man lying next to a freshly disconnected and leaking sewer line. Sam looked stunned and slightly horrified. "I told you to hide."

"I did. He found me," Ava replied indignantly. "You were supposed to keep him from doing that."

"There were three of them. They had earplugs again," Sam groused. Ivan harrumphed from his spot in the driver's seat.

"Interesting. That means they knew you were going to be here," Blue pointed out. She turned to Ava. "Does he still have his gas mask?" Blue asked.

"Of course not." Ava seemed offended by the notion. Blue hooted.

"We have an unconscious terrorist in the storage compartment of a stolen RV?" Sam asked. "Did you at least disarm him?"

"Yeah!" Ava rolled her eyes and used a tone of disdain only available to teenage girls. "I wasn't going to trap him in there so that he could shoot us through the floors. The gun is in that map net thingy."

"I see it," Ivan told them calmly.

Sam's lips grew thin, and Blue laughed even harder. Ivan joined in. Sam waited a moment, absorbing what she had just said. "Great. Fine. How did you knock him out?"

"Bounced his head off of a picnic table." Ava sulked.

Still laughing, Blue leaned back on the couch. This girl was a once-in-a-lifetime magic booster. But more than that, she was one hundred percent her mother's daughter.

35

Rhodes

"Mr. Rhodes, is that normal for an airport this small?" Lexi asked from the back seat of the plane, her face plastered to the window as they made their approach to a small regional airport in Southern Wyoming.

"Is what normal, Lexi Lou?" Rhodes asked.

"All those cars and trucks," she answered. "That's a lot of people. Do people hang around airport buildings like that?"

Rhodes, focused more on the runway and landing than the parking situation, shifted his attention and took in the complex as a whole. Any lower, and he would have missed it. Lexi had likely just saved their asses.

Devon pressed her face to the window and looked down. "Hockey Pucks!"

"No. That is not normal," he informed them, pulling up and out of his approach.

"What do we do now?" Devon demanded.

He frowned and adjusted their heading away from the airport. Did he know who all those people were? No. Did he suspect they were the people who attacked his house? Yes. She had an excellent question. And he had no clue.

"Are they going to shoot at us with some anti-aircraft explosive since we didn't land?" Devon wondered out loud.

"No. You watch too many movies," he replied calmly as he climbed away from the airport. But he wouldn't put it past the bastards considering they had blown up a city street.

"We use parachutes and jump out so they can't track us," Lexi chimed in.

"We don't have parachutes."

"Well, we should," Lexi grumbled.

He was exhausted, so he stopped replying to the endless string of questions coming from the two people in his care. He needed all the brain cells still awake to fly the plane. He spent most of the flight engaging in small talk with Lexi and finding out more about her unique living situation. They sang a few songs together. He even dished that Tia Blue wrote the chords for "Baby Blue" learning Devon and Lexi didn't know Blue played the guitar in the process. His silence made Devon nervous. But he needed to think.

"Are they tracking the plane?" Lexi asked from the back seat.

"They are tracking us somehow." Rhodes clenched his jaw and looked back into the backseat where Lexi stretched out. The kid was holding up remarkably well, but her nerves were starting to show.

He had to figure out how to get them on the ground and off the grid.

"Where can we land?" Devon asked. "Do we have enough gas to get to another airport?"

"Of course, we do."

"I have an idea," Lexi chimed in again, leaning forward so that her head was between their shoulders, and she could peer out the plane's front windows.

"Let's hear it," Rhodes responded. He would take ideas from anyone right now.

"Surely, they won't be able to get into a big airport that easily, right? Those things are locked down pretty tight. We pick the biggest one we can get to. Land the plane. Jump into the crowd and poof!" Lexi clapped her fingers and wiggled them. "We disappear."

Rhodes raised an eyebrow at Devon. "Smart kid, you've got there."

"I know," she answered smugly. "I don't even know where we are. Is there a big airport nearby?" She considered her question for a moment and slapped a hand to her forehead. "I can't believe I am on a plane. A plane. In the air. With a man I have never met before, and I don't even know what part of the country I am in. I don't have a phone. Nobody knows where I am. Lexi. Baby. Don't ever do anything like this."

"I think I already have," Lexi mused. "Right? I went to a strange man's house." She held up a finger. "Then followed him through a dark tunnel." The second finger rose. "He offered me ice cream." The third finger went up.

"Well, when you put it like that." Rhodes winced. Kid had a way with words.

"Then I got on his plane." Lexi raised the fourth finger. "But I guess it is OK, since you did most of that stuff with me."

"Oh God," Devon moaned. "I am a terrible example."

"First off, I'm not a strange man. I'm Cade Rhodes, household name. Country music artist of the year five years straight," he flashed them his brightest magazine cover smile. "And I'm Blue's fiancé," he shrugged. "Practically family."

"Ex-fiancé. Could have been family. Chose not to be." Devon insisted with a purse to her lips. "You turned into a wolf thing and ripped out a man's throat. That is strange, even in my world." She held up a finger to halt his response and let out a long breath. "In a plane with a wolf man. OK. Moving on. I know you are trying your best to protect us, and I truly appreciate it. But I still don't like you very much. I will, however, thank Blue for cashing in the world's biggest guilt trip on my daughter's behalf."

"Ouch," he grimaced. "At least you don't hate me. And this isn't guilt." It wasn't. He would have helped anyone who materialized out of thin air being attacked by political extremists, whether Blue was involved or not. However, he wasn't above hoping it earned him some forgiveness points.

"She should have made you grovel. In public," Devon continued as if she could read his mind.

369

"I think that is what he did with the song, Mom. Didn't work."

"Spot on, Lexi Lou. You are a really smart kid," Rhodes told her. "How does Denver sound?"

"I've never been to Denver," Lexi told him. "Everyone says you have to get a brownie if you go to Colorado."

Rhodes looked back at her sincere face, and it made him smile. She was wise beyond her years with a whip-smart wit. He had forgotten how young she was. Genuine naivety was a rarity in this world. Of course, he was never around kids for more than an autograph signing or hospital visit. "I don't know if we are going to have time for brownies."

"But there is a song about the brownies. Rocky Mountain something? High?" Lexi snapped her fingers like it would help her recall the words. "It's an old song. But those must be good brownies."

Rhodes tried to swallow his laugh but made the mistake of looking at Devon, who shoved her fist over her mouth and was trying not to laugh. He was going to lose it.

Lexi huffed, realizing they were laughing at her. "Either way. I like new places. We don't travel out west. Isn't the airport a monstrosity?"

"Why, yes. Yes, it is, Lexi Lou."

"Perfect. Maybe we can find Blue's hottie in Denver," Devon chimed in, receiving a cool reception from Rhodes and Lexi. "What? I wanted in on this cool comedy thing you guys have going on. I feel left out." She looked innocent when Lexi rolled her eyes and Rhodes glowered.

"Mom. I love you. But just stick to being Mom. Let Tia Blue handle the fun stuff."

Rhodes laughed out an "Oh!" as he looked at Devon, who feigned clutching her heart and collapsing back into the seat. She lolled her head forward and stopped moving. Then jerked and announced, "I'm dead. You killed me."

"Rhodes and Lexi. Like Butch Cassidy and Sundance. Smokey and the Bandit. I like it."

"Who? Am I supposed to know who those people are? Is that an old person reference?" Lexi asked, causing Devon to snort and shake with laughter.

"OK, short stuff. Let's go to Denver while I have some ego left. Blue sent you to take care of the rest of it, didn't she? You are her secret weapon."

"Mayyyyybbbeee."

"Lord knows you have enough to spare," Devon murmured under her breath.

Twenty minutes later, they entered class B airspace. Conversation in the plane stalled as he concentrated on communicating with the tower and navigating the busy airport. They landed smoothly and taxied to the private hangars. Devon peered out of the windows, eyes peeled for any sign of trouble. Lexi leaned forward, looking from side to side as well. He didn't see anything, but not all his attention was focused on searching for bad guys. Soon enough, the plane rolled to a stop, and he went about a quick post-flight checklist in case they needed to fly back out in a hurry.

"We ready?" he asked his passengers. He reached over and touched Devon's wrist and focused a little magic on himself. "How do we look?"

"That is so creepy," Lexi shuddered.

"Damn it. I never got to pee standing up," Devon wailed as she looked down at her once again feminine body.

"If it is that important to you," Rhodes chuckled as he opened the door and stepped onto the tarmac.

"No. Mom. Let's go," Lexi demanded from the back seat.

Rhodes scanned their surroundings, not noticing anything out of the ordinary. But every nook and cranny of this place was busy. He reached up to help Devon down, feeling exposed on the tarmac. His gut told him they didn't have much time. He ushered them toward the terminal building. Right now, they looked nothing like themselves, but they were once again their original genders, fitting the profile the bad guys were searching for. The last thing he wanted, however, was to get stopped in the airport because someone became suspicious of two old men traveling alone in a private jet with a pre-teen girl. So, he had to risk it.

"I see one," Lexi whispered. "To our right, coming out of building G." To his surprise, Devon didn't react, but did tilt her eyes to the right. He scanned subtly as well. She was right. Again. There were two. He turned his head in the opposite direction. Two more. They weren't openly armed, but they stuck out and walked quickly onto the tarmac, scanning the aircraft with precision. At least they weren't rolling in with a battalion of heavily armed men, explosives, and RPGs this time. Good to know they had some limits. The four people hadn't spotted them yet, but it was only a matter of time. How on earth were these people staying so close on their tail?

He applied more pressure to Devon's back, and she walked faster. It was time to set the second part of Lexi's plan in motion. He wanted to wait until they were in the building, but they didn't have that luxury. He steered them toward another group of five travelers disembarking from a much larger jet and walking toward the small reception area of the private hangar. They were in full party mode, already obnoxiously boisterous. "I need to disguise Lexi," he whispered in Devon's ear as they drew closer to the other group, who were oblivious to their surroundings.

Her eyes pivoted between the two sets of people rapidly approaching. He was amazed by her calm. This woman was made of steel. "Do it," she whispered back and pulled Lexi so that she walked between them as shielded from view as they could make her.

"Sorry, kid." He reached for her hand and pushed a bit of magic into her. She grew at least six inches instantaneously and took on the appearance of a boy. She stumbled for a few steps, adjusting to her new gait.

"Oh. Oh. That is really weird, Mom!" she barely managed to keep her voice down.

"I know, baby. Roll with it," Devon told her quietly.

"I'm going to create a distraction. No matter what happens, get into the building," he instructed, bumping into one of the men in the approaching group and pushing Devon slightly away. "Oh, I'm so sorry man," he used a bit of magic.

A perturbed man, who could now pass for his less charming twin, turned in his direction. "What in the hell, bruv?" Oh well, wasn't much he could do about the voice and accent. Rhodes smiled.

He took another step as if he were trying to dodge the rest of the group, but actually stepped into the middle of them. He stumbled in apologetic confusion, bumping into each of them. In seconds, the biggest group of country music royalty to ever assemble off stage stood on a private tarmac near Denver's airport. His buddies Jason Daniels. Connor Watkins and Mark Scarlett gazed back at him in aggravation. Even that ass hat Emmett O'Brian joined this party.

"Oh, my God. You are Cade Rhodes," he called out in astonishment, and pointed at the men. "My daughter loves your song. Can I get an autograph?"

"What the hell are you talking about, man?" the newest version of Emmett O'Brian asked with just the right amount of hostility and nervousness.

"Jason Daniels," Rhodes kept going. "Your songs changed my life, man."

They all walked into the small lobby and personnel and other pilots and their passengers were taking notice. The inevitable swarm was forming. He never thought he would be thankful for that aspect of his life. A half dozen people strolled their way, plus two of the bad guys.

"Get away from us, you freak," new Emmett O'Brien told him, nailing the man's terrible personality on the first try.

Rhodes threw his hands in the air and began to back away even as others surrounded the group, blocking their path and requesting pictures. "I'm sorry, man. I know you just want to live your life. Sorry." He spun, hanging his head in disappointment to sell the idea he was shut down by one of his daughter's music idols.

Phones flashed, and voices rose behind him. A harried manager hustled over, moving quickly toward the crowd forming in the lobby. He stepped away but didn't see Devon or Lexi, so he wandered over toward the bathrooms to keep up the facade of a person who had just gotten off a plane. Everybody peed when they got off a plane.

"Did you get your autograph, dear?" Devon spoke from directly behind him. She handed him a candy bar as Lexi stepped up, devouring a bag of cheddar popcorn, looking cool as a cucumber.

"Nah. That Emmett O'Brien guy's a real asshole." Rhodes took the candy bar. "Let's get out of here."

"I hear that Cade Rhodes guy is the biggest asshole of them all," Devon replied with a smirk as she followed him, keeping a hand on Lexi's arm. Shouts rang out behind them. "Yep. I asked them to call for a taxi. It should be here soon. Excellent idea."

He saw a few security cameras, so he shuffled over, putting his body between them and his companions. "Face down," Rhodes told her, giving her arm a tap when she dropped her head. He put his own head down and changed his appearance slightly so that they couldn't be identified as anyone who had been on the tarmac. With the sheer star power that just strolled into the lobby they wouldn't be paying any attention to them which helped.

"Woah. There he is again. I think he's bigger this time," Devon said, looking at her crotch as her features changed quickly back into a masculine form.

They scurried toward the front door of the fixed base operator as an altercation broke out behind them. "If they lock this place down, we are screwed," he told her.

"Oh sh..." Lexi whispered as the noise got louder.

"Don't you dare," Devon admonished. "There," she pointed to the taxi waiting by the sidewalk in front of the building just outside the doors.

"Sugar. I was going to say sugar."

"Sure, you were," Devon took over navigation and led them outside. She walked right up to a taxi. "I wish we could Uber," she said, leaning down to speak briefly to the driver.

"Forgot about that," Rhodes said with some derision. He couldn't remember the last time he was without his cell phone.

"Where are we going, John?" Devon looked over her shoulder, playing along with their multi-disguise escape. This lady was a pro. Where the hell had Blue found her?

"The closest In-and-Out Burger," Rhodes told her and enjoyed the surprised look on her face. But she shrugged and climbed in. When they were all settled into the taxi, it pulled away from the curb.

He glanced out the back window, watching as the Denver airport disappeared behind them. He didn't see a tail.

"How are you folks doing today? I heard that Cade Rhodes was just spotted at the airport with his buddies. One of my buddies that works out here called. Caused a scene." The cab driver merged into traffic. "Glad he is OK after what happened at his house."

"Really? What happened at his house?" Devon feigned innocence.

"That new bunch of magic weirdos busted in and trashed the place. Bunch of them died. Police say they accidentally set off some kind of weapon and took out their own people."

"Oh no. That is terrible," Devon kept playing along. Lexi rolled her eyes so hard Rhodes swore he could hear it.

"Apparently, Cade wasn't home when it happened. He's all good. His people said he was taking a trip and just learned about what happened. Guess he was taking a trip to Denver. I'm glad he is OK. I love that one song of his..."

"I know, right? So glad he is OK," Devon interrupted him and looked over Lexi's head to give Rhodes a hard stare. "And then that thing in Arizona," the cab driver kept talking. Rhodes hated chatty drivers. "Whole town burned. If you ask me, these magic people need to be locked up or shut down or something. Isn't right how they live above the rest of us. Cause chaos. Don't live by the same rules."

Rhodes held Devon's eyes, both of them frowning for a new reason now, and Lexi raised her head to glare at the driver. She opened her mouth to speak, and Devon's hand shot out to cover it so fast Rhodes barely saw it. "Cover your mouth when you cough, sweetheart," Devon told her in a sugar-sweet voice that promised death. Lexi just glared and licked the back of her mom's hand.

He needed to find out more about Arizona, check in with Torrin, and find them all a place to rest for the night. The cab came to a halt in front of the restaurant with a line of cars wrapped around the building and down the block. "Here you go," the driver told them cheerfully. Rhodes pulled his wallet out and handed the man the fare and a tip.

"Ever had an In-And-Out burger, kid?"

Lexi stared at the building dubiously. "No. They don't have those at home."

"Are you sure this is a good idea?" Devon asked. "Shouldn't we keep our heads down?"

"We have to eat. Don't look nervous. Just blend in," he told them both, which only made it worse.

He watched for tails and even drones the whole way here. They had a few minutes. Then they would find a place to sleep and grab some burner phones so they could get in contact with people. He wanted to check on Blue. See if Harper still had Lady Lucille. He knew Devon wanted to call Torrin or that Green guy Lexi told him all about on the flight. She talked about him like he was her dad. She talked about Blue more as a parent than her mom's roommate. It was a weird dynamic. Reminded him of that old My Three Dads movie. Kid seemed OK though, so whatever they were doing he couldn't argue with it.

"I have to go to the bathroom," Lexi announced as soon as they were in the door.

"Do you really?" Devon asked slowly, obvious skepticism lacing her voice.

"Aren't you curious?" Lexi asked her mom in a dramatic whisper. "Just a little?"

"Yeah, a little," Devon whispered back.

"You guys go ahead. Take your time. I'll order the food." Rhodes laughed as they wandered into the bathroom. He placed their order, contemplating next steps. It was unfortunate Devon and Lexi were in this position. But he admitted to himself, it was the first time he felt alive in years.

He ordered two overflowing trays of food and carried them to the tables just as Devon and Lexi emerged from the bathroom. "That is so weird. But very convenient," Devon informed him.

"I prefer it. When we get done here, is there anyone you want to call?"

"Do you think it is safe?" she frowned.

"We will get burners. It will be fine."

"I need to call Greenlee," Devon told him. "He sounded like I gave him an aneurysm before my phone died."

"You mean before you killed it?" Rhodes corrected. "And every piece of electronics in my home."

"Potato. Pototo," Lexi chimed in, pouring herself a water. "She kills two phones a year. I want to talk to Tio G too. I really need one of his silly stories." The last comment elicited a soft smile from Devon as she ruffled Lexi's new hair.

"Then we have a plan." Rhodes remained observant as he ate. He saw a decent-looking non-chain hotel a few blocks down. They would pass a twenty-four-hour pharmacy on the way. "Let's get fed. Procure some wheels. Find a place to rest. And make some phone calls."

"I still want to find some brownies."

FRIDAY

Senator Nolan Miller *@USSenatorNolanMiller*
Under the direction of Senior Agent Richard Mann
the FBI officially seized all US physical and financial
holdings of @CahladPrime. @CahladParagon and
@CahladRegent remain at large. Now we rebuild
with transparency and equality

#RealMagicRegulation #WeMustProtectOurselves #YourReignIsOver

Cahlad South America *@CahladSouthAmericaOfficial*
We stand with all members of the Cahlad Conclave
united with @CahladParagon Collins and @Cahlad-
PrimeOfficial and disavow the actions taken by the
United States FBI that jeopardize centuries of cooperation and peace. Governments have no business
regulating magic.

#StandWithMitch #OneCahladUnited

Paranoid But They Are Still Out to Get Me

@ShinySilverHats

Told you @USSenatorNolanMiller was up to no good. Wonder how much he paid Larson Battle to make @CahladPrimeOfficial look bad. These two are in bed together. Time will prove me right.

#ItsAllAConspiracy #StandWithMitch #IvanTheIncredible #FuckNolanMiller #FuckTheSovereign #FuckLarsonBattle

Cade Rhodes Biggest Fan *@CadeRhodesBiggestFan*

Thank heavens he's OK! Denver spotting. We love you baby!

#FutureMsCadeRhodes #AmericasBeard #FuckTheSovereign #hallelujah

That Sarcastic Them *@ThatSarcasticThem*

@USSenatorNolanMiller are you going to burn them at the stake when you find them. Witch hunt much? Hey Hounds of Dawn, can you make this guy disappear?

#StandWithMitch #FuckNolanMiller #TheHoundsofDawnAreReal

MomsAgainstMagic *@MomsAgainstMagic*

Thank you @USSenatorNolanMiller for protecting us from the magic threat. It was only a matter of time before they showed their true colors.

#RealMagicRegulation #WeMustProtectOurselves #OurSaviorNolan-

Miller

36

FINN

Finn took the seat next to Hale at the break room table. Everyone had gotten a few hours of sleep in shifts overnight. They only had six bunks, so he slept on the loveseat in his office to leave space for the others. Everyone was up and wandering around except for Nisha, who was still asleep, and Trix, who wouldn't come out of his office. When he stuck his head in the bunk room earlier, Ben was awake but sitting quietly, allowing Nisha to sleep. They had somehow managed to sleep wedged in a small twin bunk last night to make sure Ben didn't get anxious and kill them in their sleep.

Mitch and Zella sat together on the opposite side of the table from them, sipping coffee and talking quietly.

Mitch said something last night that made Nisha go pale. It made him uneasy of the Paragon. More so than he was already. One of his best employees got drunk off her ass. Senator Miller still squawked from a television on the wall. Trix was holed up in a locked room and Hale was Hale. His warehouse had turned into a three-ring circus.

Pictures of Cade Rhodes graced the other two screens in the room. Local and online media had gotten wind of the thing at Rhodes' house. The police had not yet released an official statement, but a press conference was scheduled within the hour. Somehow, the country music star's disappearance trumped a bombing and a government raid on Cahlad Prime that sparked an international incident. It seems the other Cahlad Conclaves were supporting Mitch for now.

Hale leaned back in the chair, balancing it on one leg while he sipped coffee from a chipped "We Are Nashville" mug someone brought in after the 2010 flood. Finn was amazed by the fact the man could balance the chair while maintaining a minimum of movement that still allowed him to drink coffee. He was also mildly irked because he knew Hale was about to break another chair. The things had become a monthly expense at this point.

"Do you think the national news is going to pick up the Rhodes story?" he asked Hale.

"There is a lot going on right now. Terrorist attacks. Magical surges. Important stuff with actual consequences. So extremely likely. He's a hot property," Hale answered as one of the screens swapped over to cover the story of the attack at the Cat and the Canary. How was that the filler story of the night? No one was taking credit for the attacks, and law enforcement had no suspects. "Then again, it's been a hell of a news cycle."

Kendra walked in and groaned when she saw the bottle and two shot glasses that still sat on the table. She shook her head at Hale, eying his balancing act. "You are going to break another one man."

"Talked to Trix. Detective from Metro just called. They know Herne handled Rhodes' security. They need a statement," Hale informed him.

Finn sighed. "I was afraid of that. What do you think? Deal with the cops about a bunch of dead bodies or deal with the press because we lost the world's biggest country music crossover artist?"

"Don't forget America's beard," Hale snorted. "There might be riots. I vote police and dead bodies."

"Well, we have our person present and accounted for. The assistant is here." Finn rubbed his chin. "We should say that he has been moved to a secure location. As far as we know, that is the truth."

"They will want to confirm. Probably insist on speaking with him, at least via phone." Kendra brought her decaf coffee over to the table and joined them. "Hale. The leg is bending."

"Maybe we could stall them. Buy ourselves some time. Say he is in the air or something," Hale said, even as he continued to balance the chair on the now warped single leg.

"They will check flight manifest. Too easy to poke a hole in that." Kendra shook her head.

Finn scrubbed a hand down his face. He wasn't sure how he felt about discussing these plans in front of the Paragon. The weight of the bargain he made was starting to weigh on him. His phone rang. He looked down and shook his head in disbelief, then lifted the screen to show Kendra. It was Trix, who was two doors down the hall in his computer cave.

Nisha shambled in, dragging Ben behind her. She eyed the assembly through puffy eyes, her mood obviously less than chipper.

Kendra just shrugged. "Made a beeline for his office when I told him the Paragon was coming. Refuses to come out while he's here."

"Great." Finn sighed. He swiped to answer the call. "Go ahead."

He listened intently for a few moments, still observing the interaction in his break room. Greenlee walked in carrying his backpack and the messenger bag. Both items were lumpy in different places. He slung a thin piece of leather with a silver wire wrapped around it at Nisha, who fumbled the catch and it fell to the floor. "That's for Ben. Skin contact. You are welcome."

Greenlee sent a cold look in Mitch's direction as Harper settled in at the table with her own cup of coffee.

Ben picked up the item Nisha dropped, and she helped him put it around his neck. He slipped it under his shirt and looked at Greenlee expectantly.

"Well, let go of her hand, man. Let's see if you explode."

Harper gasped as Kendra pulled her under the table, and Zella moved protectively toward Mitch. Interesting.

"Shit. Sorry," Greenlee muttered. "I forget who I'm with. Not like that. Go ahead."

Ben reluctantly released Nisha's hand and stood still for a moment. His eyes grew wide, then he closed them. A blissful expression crossed his face. Nisha shook her hand out and stepped away.

"Thank you," she told Greenlee. She looked at Ben intently for a moment, a sympathetic expression crossing her features. "He hasn't heard quiet like that in years."

"Oh. I thought." Mitch waved between Nisha and Ben. "Didn't you, Z?" Zella nodded earnestly.

"Nope," Nisha told them, rushing toward the coffeemaker. "Just trying to keep my soul intact. This job seems to be determined to suck it out of my body."

"Thanks, Trix." Finn sighed and hit the button to disconnect the call. The man was eccentric, but useful. "Trix says that by his best estimates, they should be refueling now if they haven't already," Finn announced to the room.

"That means they are on the ground?" Ben asked quietly.

"It means they might be on the ground," Finn clarified wearily.

"At least it's something real," Hale said.

Greenlee fished the umbrella he showed them before out of his bag and crossed the room to Finn.

"Hold up," Nisha demanded. "How many people will that thing move? You aren't going all Mary Poppins on me and leaving me here with Dr. Cthulhu and Burp-Master-Flash." She sent Hale a disgusted glance, referring to his earlier demonstration of burping the alphabet backward at the dinner. "You said you would help us find Ava AND my team."

Greenlee's movements slowed. "It stores enough for one. If we supply more magic, it might take three more. Maybe four. Blue discharges a ton of magic when she jumps. I've never seen anyone channel so much magic, especially when she has passengers. It's why she is always cold. I don't know how it doesn't kill her. Teleportation isn't for the weak. It will take everything I have just to bring Finn with me and not die. Getting some rest was a great idea, by the way."

Mitch shared a look with Zella and tilted his head to the side, listening intently to the conversation. She scribbled in her notebook.

"I have magic. Ben has magic. We can fuel the artifact," Nisha volunteered.

"You might also fly off into some strange quantum rainbow realm and never be heard from again," Greenlee insisted. "Or drop dead from rapid onset magic poisoning."

"I'll chance it." She shrugged, sounding unconcerned by the gloom and doom Greenlee spouted.

Finn kept his eye on Mitch, shocked that Greenlee mentioned any of this in front of the Paragon. "Nisha, why the blatant disregard for your own safety?"

"To the best of my knowledge, Sam and Ivan are protecting a girl that these crazy Sovereign assholes want badly enough to set off a bomb and shoot up a city block. That's ballsy and means they aren't playing by the rules. Mitch and Zella are safe. Now Sam needs all the help he can get. That Rhodes guy your sister is with wiped the floor with them."

"We don't know that Rhodes will help us," Finn told her. "He's finicky."

"He sure is, cowboy," Harper chimed in.

"No. But he might know where this Blue person is. And she is with Sam." Nisha insisted.

"It's better than sitting around here," Ben interjected. "I'm in."

"You guys have fun with that," Hale weighed in. "What?" he asked in response to Finn's glare. "Dude says four max, and I have zero magic to keep from 'flying off into some strange quantum rainbow realm.'" He used air quotes. "Somebody has to keep an eye on the Paragon."

"Greenlee?" Finn asked. This was Greenlee's show. His call.

"We can try." He turned back and shrugged on his backpack. "Dr. Cthulhu and I have a deal. He definitely has enough juice to get himself there. You OK if Captain Cahlad comes along Ben?"

That made Mitch's wild eyebrows shoot up. Zella smiled again. The woman was enjoying the show.

"Sam is my best friend, Ben," Nisha announced quietly. "I need to help him if I can."

Ben nodded. "How do we do this with four?"

"Oh. Goodie," Hale said dryly. "Transitioning from Operation Ill-Advised Magic Contract to Operation Umbrella. Call me if you get there alive."

"Yeah," Finn agreed grimly. He hated teleporting with someone who knew how to do it. This was going to be awful. "You got this?" he jerked his head toward the Paragon and the women sitting next to him.

"Yep."

"Everybody who is going, grab the umbrella." Greenlee held the cheap polka-dotted object up in the center of the room.

"What exactly are you trying to do?" Mitch demanded.

"That's a really long story," Hale told him. "Hang tight I'll fill you and Ms. Z in if nothing explodes."

"I'm going to go get Sam and Ivan. With an ugly magic umbrella. Then I quit," Nisha deadpanned.

Mitch frowned and eyed the umbrella dubiously. "May I have a word, dear?" he motioned for her to come closer. Zella patted the seat between them. Nisha sat down cautiously, looking uncomfortable. Finn tried to step closer as subtly as he could. He saw Hale turn his head so that he could hear as well. "I'm sorry about my comment last night. Let's clear the air before you use what I assume is an unregistered and untested artifact. I'm not upset about the contract. And I'm not upset that you read my thoughts."

"A woman gave Sam a USB drive at the ceremony, Mitch. It was all about Project Zenith." Nisha said quietly. Finn almost couldn't hear her over the chaos in the room. What was Project Zenith?

"Oh dear," Mitch said quietly. Zella twisted her hands in worry. Finn sent Hale a look and saw the man nod slightly in acknowledgment. He would have Trix digging up Project Zenith as soon as he broke the leg on the chair he balanced in.

"The fact that you kept that secret from me, Mitch. That took intent." Nisha shook her head. "That is why I want to go check on Sam and Ivan myself. And why I agreed to the contract with Finn.

Yesterday, I thought I could trust you. I don't feel like I know who you are anymore."

"Rubbish. There were things I had to keep from you. But you have always known what was in my heart, Nisha," Mitch smiled at her. "You think that your value lies in your ability to see people's thoughts? But I don't think that is your greatest strength. It is your ability to see into our hearts and not lose faith in us, even when you know what is in our minds. That is your superpower, Nisha."

"Thank you? That's..."

"The truth. Give yourself some credit," Mitch cut her off. Zella patted Nisha's arm in agreement.

"You are just trying to keep me from quitting," Nisha accused him.

"Of course I am." Mitch laughed. "But wherever you end up, you should know your worth. And it isn't hearing other people's thoughts."

Nisha looked at her feet, obviously unsure of what to say next. "Go on then, dear." Mitch waved toward Greenlee. "But I advise you to try that outside."

"That's not a bad idea," Greenlee mumbled. "Is there anywhere around here that isn't visible from the street?"

"Roof." Hale pointed up.

Everyone said their goodbyes. The four of them trudged up three flights of steel stairs to the roof of the warehouse. The Nashville skyline graced the horizon behind them; the early morning sun was shining off the glass of the buildings, making the buildings appear to twinkle in the mist coming off the river.

Greenlee stood in the middle of the roof and adjusted his backpack. He held out the umbrella, twisted it back and forth, and popped it open.

"You ready?" He raised it above his head.

"Blue always says skin-to-skin contact. Should we hold on to each other, too?" Finn asked with some skepticism. He was stalling now, and he knew it.

"Sure. Let's all hold hands again," Nisha muttered sarcastically. Everyone shifted to an awkward ring around the rosy formation with an umbrella in the center. Ben hummed the tune softly.

"Really ready?" Everyone nodded quietly. "Oh boy, here goes." Greenlee blew out a breath. "Pomegranate!"

37

BLUE

B lue frowned, listening to the late-night DJ reporting the latest in celebrity gossip. News out of Nashville a few hours ago was a home invasion with multiple fatalities at the home of the country music phenomenon, Cade Rhodes. She had chewed her lip and weighed her options. She couldn't leave Ava. She had reached for her magic and concentrated on Rhodes. She felt a strong tug to the northwest. He wasn't dead. That was all she knew for certain. At the next split on the interstate, she adjusted their course, triggering angry honks from the surrounding drivers. The next celebrity news snippet reported an unconfirmed Cade Rhodes sighting in Denver, which was roughly the direction her magic was leading her. So, she settled in and tried to hang on to the thread without jumping out of the seat and leaving the vehicle driverless.

An hour later, Ivan started moving around, but she dared not take her eyes off the road, especially not driving this behemoth. She couldn't drive a compact car without hitting something. She had no clue why they thought she could drive a 32-foot class A motor home, a.k.a. a damned bus. Surely Ivan knew better. He was one of her driving instructors at the Cahlad.

The man Ava captured in the storage compartment proved extremely uninformative. He knew nothing, even when Ivan stepped aside and let Sam handle the questioning. They dropped him off in the detached restroom of an abandoned gas station with strict instructions not to leave or say anything to anyone for thirty-six hours. Then everyone else went to sleep. That was a few hours ago, and she hadn't wrecked. Yet. There were a few close calls her passengers were blissfully ignorant of.

"Feeling better?" Ivan grumbled with a scratchy voice.

"Much," she told him. She was finally warm, and her magic answered when she reached for it. She needed to be careful while she was around Ava. She spent years practicing pulling more and more magic with each jump, building her magic-channeling muscles, so to speak. It was the reason she could envoy multiple people and large objects now. When she was younger, she could only envoy herself if she wasn't wearing a heavy coat or shoes. She regularly pushed the limits of her magic these days to make sure she could use it if she ever needed it. But the amount of magic Ava allowed her to channel was more than she could ever pull on her own and more than she could physically tolerate, even with her enhanced healing. She had no experience throttling her magic. She never needed to before. She theorized that Ivan and Sam were nowhere near their magic limits and that is why they didn't react as badly to Ava's surges.

"Wrong direction," Ivan ambled up behind her, rubbing his hand across the beginnings of a beard, and sat down in the passenger seat. He still wore the awful unbuttoned Hawaiian shirt. None of the clothes in the camper had fit either him or Sam. She and Ava both scored sweatshirts and pants that were two sizes too big but clean and blood free. Ivan yawned and looked sedately out the window at the passing interstate. "Where are we going?"

"Denver-ish," she replied, and stuck her tongue out as she concentrated on the road. The vehicle wiggled a little. The rumble strips sang beneath their tires. "Shit. I probably shouldn't talk and drive."

Ivan sat relaxed in his seat as she righted the RV. No need to worry about high-speed crashes when you are indestructible. He went so far as to turn the chair around so that it faced into the RV and stretched his legs out. "Without asking?" he finally said.

"Oh. I'm sorry," Blue answered in a perky voice, and moved her head back and forth in a ditzy bobble. "Are the boys in charge? I missed that memo." The RV wobbled to the left this time, and a tractor-trailer blared its horn at them.

Ivan remained silent for so long she assumed the conversation was over. So, when he finally said one word, it startled her. "Why?"

"I heard something on the radio. Thought it might be a lead," she told him. She didn't feel the need to go into the details. Or that she had heard another celebrity gossip report fifteen minutes ago of a Cade Rhodes sighting at the Denver airport. Rhodes, Emmet O'Brien, and a few other hot country artists were spotted departing a plane. She knew it wasn't Rhodes; he wouldn't be caught dead hanging out with O'Brien. They hated each other.

She didn't know of anyone else who could morph someone into a carbon copy of themselves to cause a chaotic fan mob. She did know it was a touch-based ability. There was no way one of Finn's guys agreed to be a Cade Rhodes decoy. That meant the real Rhodes changed some random guy before he got on the plane headed to Denver and said random guy and his companions didn't notice for the whole flight. Or Rhodes was somewhere near Denver. Why? She needed to find out. She didn't have enough going on, anyway.

For the moment, Sam and Ivan were proving beneficial to her overall aim to keep Ava alive and out of the Sovereign's clutches. She was secretly afraid she would overload again if she tried to skip anything more than herself until she figured out how to throttle the magic. Having Stalker Prime-level backup made sense.

She was trying something new with her magic, focusing on Rhodes' location and letting the magic begin to tug. But she wasn't completing the skip when she felt the tug. She was just following it, letting it lead her in a general direction. So far, so good, if a little uncomfortable.

In the periphery of her vision, she saw Ivan nod so slightly that she almost missed it. There was no way he had any idea what she was talking about unless he was feigning sleep and heard the same story on the radio. She appreciated the fact that he wasn't demanding she turn around or trying to wrest control of the vehicle from her.

Because if she had to grab Ava and run, she would do it and die trying.

Ivan leaned his head back and closed his eyes, seeming unbothered by the change of plans. She went over the events of the last two days in her head. They rode in silence for another half hour, which made it easier to stay on the road and think. Thinking wasn't as detrimental to her driving as speaking, apparently. There were a lot of things to think about and work through. But there was one thing bothering her more than most. She generally did not lose consciousness. Before today, she had lived confidently with the knowledge that Rhodes was the first and only person to ever haul her unconscious body anywhere. That single incident was tolerable because they were engaged at the time. Future husbands could do that kind of thing for their future wives. If anyone was allowed to haul your unconscious body around, it was the person you were going to love, honor, and cherish for the rest of your life.

Today, or was it yesterday, Ivan had taken at least a few bullets that were generally whizzing in her direction. He had also, according to Ava, carried her unconscious ass three miles through a scorching hot desert. Not a fireman's carry either, full-on damsel in distress princess carry. Those events alone were bad enough. But the discovery that he had hauled her out of Larson's mad science lab when she had passed out from blood loss—it made her uncomfortable. She had convinced herself that she crawled out of the building under her own steam and just couldn't remember it. That kind of thing was not outside the realm of her experience. Relearning your own history was unsettling.

That made three times she had been unconscious and completely vulnerable. Two times Ivan had carried her. She wasn't just uncomfortable. It made her feel, though she didn't like the word, fragile. She wasn't fragile. Maybe mortal was the word she was looking for. She honestly forgot sometimes that she was. She often did things no sane person would try or survive. Sometimes she did them, hoping that this would be the one that got her. Those were the bad days. She didn't have as many of those lately. Regardless, she wasn't used to being the person needing help or help being available, even if she needed it.

She also felt indebted. Which was much worse.

"What is it?" Ivan asked, sitting up and turning to face the windshield.

"Nothing."

"Try again," he grumbled.

"Fine." She paused, trying to figure out a way to convey her thoughts without sounding whiny or dramatic. "I think of myself as a capable and independent person. I can handle myself. Never had a choice, you know?"

A grunt was all she got in response. Probably a 'Yes, I do know' grunt, judging by the inflection. She was rusty at translating Ivan's grunt speak.

"It occurs to me that you have princess-carried me." She shuddered dramatically to demonstrate just how revolting she found the concept. The vehicle weaved wildly. More horns blared.

"Twice," Ivan said flatly as he reached over and steadied the wheel. When the shaking and weaving stopped, he sat back and resumed his relaxed position, gazing out at the road.

"Wow. You are counting," she groused. "Anyway. Thanks. That's—" She looked over and his expression was distant and blank. She eyed the scar on his arm and looked away again. "Just thanks."

His only response was a grunt. Again. This one she couldn't translate.

"Good talk, big guy."

"What in the hell is going on?" an angry shout erupted from the back of the RV. A loud bang followed the sounds of stumbling. "Ow, who puts a cabinet that low?"

"The asshole's awake," Ava announced grumpily.

"Why are we swerving? Have they found us?" Sam asked as he rushed to the front and knelt on a single knee between the seats Blue and Ivan occupied, alert and ready to fight. He looked out, searching for potential threats.

"She was talking," Ivan informed him.

"She can't talk and drive?" Sam asked sarcastically, still scanning for threats.

"Nope," Ivan replied, popping the p sound at the end of the word with a smack of his lips.

"I would be extremely offended if it weren't true," she told them in her best offended voice. Damned if the RV didn't swerve again. Why could normal people do this, and she couldn't?

"For God's sake, pull over before you kill us," Sam ordered, and Blue felt herself jerking on the wheel. She didn't want to. But she couldn't help it.

"No. No. No. No." She watched in horror as the guard rail grew closer. Maybe it wouldn't have been so bad if she could steer without disaster like a normal driver before he compelled her to turn the wheel. That was not the case, and this was a disaster. She let out a startled squeak as tires screeched. They skimmed the guard rail which was the only thing that kept them from tipping over. The cabinets flew open, and their contents scattered. Sam struggled to stay upright, even kneeling. The left instead of the right side of the camper roared with the rumble strips now.

"Great job, genius," Ava yelled from behind her.

"When it's safe! When it's safe! Get us to an exit and find a safe place to park," Sam corrected, gripping the backs of the captain's chairs to steady himself. "Christ."

She managed to pull back into the lane of traffic and steady the vehicle, blowing out a shaky breath, heart racing, and cut a glare at Sam.

"Watch the damn road," he ordered, and her eyes snapped forward. "Don't talk," he finished as he stood up. "Wait. This isn't the right direction. Did you get us lost?"

Ivan, who had remained stoic through the whole ordeal, continued to gaze calmly out the window.

"Is anyone going to tell me what is going on?" Sam asked in frustration. "That sign says Denver." He pointed at a sign over the interstate. "We are supposed to be going in the opposite direction."

"It's her story to tell, brother. And she can't talk," Ivan told him.

Ava burst into giggles. Blue did, too. Sam hadn't told her not to laugh and her giggles turned into belly laughs quickly. Ivan reached out again to steady the wheel, then put his hands behind his head, relaxing further into the seat like he didn't have a care in the world.

"Oh, that is good. I'm starting to like the scary, grunty one," Ava crowed.

Blue could see in the reflection of the windshield that Sam's head whipped around to look at their charge. "Not you. Ms. Blue is right. You are still an asshole, even if you aren't sweaty. Where is your shirt? You had a shirt before. What did you do with it? The rest of us kept our clothes on," Ava deadpanned, which only made Blue laugh harder. Sam had been nothing but nice to Ava. The girl was just messing with him at this point. It was glorious. She saw an exit ahead and began carefully navigating in that direction.

Without another word, Sam stomped toward the back of the camper. In the reflection of the window, she saw Ivan crack a smile. Worth it.

38

FINN

Finn felt like he was being sucked into a rainbow-colored tornado. Holding hands was a good call because the umbrella brutally bashed them against strange electric membranes. Everyone screamed. Finn was just holding on and praying they could remember to give the umbrella their magic, however a person would do something like that. They landed somewhere noisy. He fell to his knees and felt Greenlee let go of his hand. His stomach caught up with him a moment later, and he fought the urge to vomit. Someone else didn't. A retch and a splat sounded to his right. He jammed a fist into his gut and slammed his mouth shut. People were yelling nearby. He looked around. They were in a narrow, dead-end hallway next to an empty break room. Greenlee lay face down on the floor next to him, shaking his head, his hand still clutching the umbrella. Nisha leaned against the soda machine, and Ben sat against the wall at the end of the hallway. There was no one watching them. He looked up and into the corners, then inspected the ceiling tile. There were no cameras. More importantly, there was no Devon.

Greenlee peeled himself off the floor and looked around blearily. He only made it to his knees. His eyes were bloodshot, and he looked pale. "Everyone make it? Where are we?"

"Denver?" Nisha answered in a weak voice. "Airport? It's so loud. People are excited." Finn looked closer at the group's mind reader. Her hands were shaking badly as she raised them to her head. Blue made this look easy.

"Everybody up," Finn instructed. "We need to move." For the first time, he was not the person who fared the worst from skipping across the nightmare electric rainbow. Greenlee groaned and leaned down to place his forehead against the cool tile. Between the beating he took earlier and whatever had happened during the opening stages of Operation Umbrella, he looked like death.

"Give us a minute." Ben leaned forward and wrapped his fingers around Greenlee's wrist. It took Finn a moment to realize he was taking his friend's pulse. Ben looked up at Nisha, who was still upright, but not by much. "You OK?"

"No." She shook her head, taking long, deep breaths like she was trying to settle her stomach. "But Cade Rhodes is around here somewhere. Small army of paparazzi is forming."

Finn frowned. Why would Rhodes announce his location? Unless it was a distraction. "I need to figure out where we are."

"I've got him. We can't move him right now," Ben instructed as he helped Greenlee shift to sit leaning against the wall.

"If you see someone coming this way, just think really loud," Nisha instructed.

Finn was already moving out of the hallway, pulling his phone from his pocket, and dialing Hale. "Boss! You made it!" Hale answered.

"Mostly. We are at the Denver airport. I'm trying to get eyes on Devon." He emerged into a hallway that led to a concourse and a wall of people. To his right, a long hallway led to a set of people movers. He looked closely at the people heading in that direction. No one was acting out of the ordinary, and none of them looked like any of the people he was looking for. His eyes found two people who did not look like they belonged; they carried themselves differently than a normal traveler. They were methodically looking for someone or something. He didn't know how to think loud, but he gave it his best effort. "I don't see her. But I think I see a few goon squad lackeys."

"Should I send a team?"

"No. I don't know what we are dealing with yet."

"You got it. We will be on standby."

"Thanks, Hale." It was good to have his friend back on the team. Finn hung up and turned quickly, walking casually back to where he came from. Nisha walked out as he drew close. Her walk was stiff, and she looked like she was carrying something heavy. She smiled politely but distantly and walked right past him with Greenlee's ugly messenger bag slung across her body. Finn frowned until he felt a hand that he couldn't see wrap around his hand and squeeze quickly before it was gone. They were disguising Greenlee. "Thanks, Hale. I will keep you posted." He hung up and glanced into the hallway, where Ben fished a candy bar from a machine in the break room. His hat was pulled low over his eyes, and Greenlee's backpack was on his back. His shirt was untucked. He looked generally disheveled.

"Gotta keep her fed." Ben smiled and exited the hallway, falling into an easy stride next to Finn. His head was low as he walked. "She scares me a little."

"The best always do. Let's slow down to put some space between us. Did she hear me?" Finn asked. He glanced over his shoulder. The mob on the tarmac was breaking up, and people trickled into the lobby. He didn't see the goon squad among them.

"Yeah. We thought we should move. And they obviously know who Greenlee is, so we hid him. They are meeting us at the first opportunity for food. We need to get him hydrated and his blood sugar under control or we will be carrying him. I know we need to move, but he needs to rest. She does too. She just hides it better." Ben stepped smoothly onto the people-mover.

"You seem relatively unscathed," Finn noted, taking a closer look at Ben Hughes. His color was fine, and he did not appear to be tired.

"That was nothing compared to keeping these guys under control." He tapped his head and shrugged like it wasn't a big deal. "She says she can hook us up with transportation under a name that won't tip the goons off."

"Squeaky clean Stalker Prime is just full of surprises, isn't it?" Finn asked, thinking the same thing about Ben Hughes.

"I don't know who the good guys are anymore," Ben told him.

"I've seen a lot of things in this life Ben," Finn followed the signs to the car rental area. "There are no good guys. Just people who are less bad in a given situation."

"That's dark," Ben winced.

"No less the truth."

They walked in silence until they reached a small but busy retail area. Nisha already had a large tray of food, and it was spread out across the table. A cup sat on the far side of the table with the straw pointed away, as if she was done with her meal and waiting to clean it up. A leather journal sat on the table as if she might be reading it. Her hair was covered in a floral bucket hat, and she wore a hot pink Denver sweatshirt. She lounged and surfed her phone distractedly. Nisha and Greenlee hadn't wasted time.

As they walked by, she glanced up, meeting Finn's eyes for a moment before looking back down. Finn saw a french fry disappear from the tray. Nobody else would have noticed. He had underestimated this woman.

Finn and Ben got their own food and sat three tables over, not acknowledging Nisha and the still-invisible Greenlee. Finn finished his food and watched the neighboring table out of the corner of his eyes. He was pretty sure Greenlee was eating Nisha's food, too. She wandered away to grab a cinnamon roll and another drink, taking a small bite and placing it in the same haphazard manner on the now crowded table. "She isn't eating anything," Ben mumbled to Finn in disapproval, and he wasn't sure if it was the medical professional speaking or someone who didn't want to deal with a cranky travel companion. They had already been here an hour, and she should have eaten something.

His phone rang before he could respond. "Go grab some food to go," he instructed Ben as he answered the call, expecting it to be Trix or Hale. "This is Torrin."

"Torrin. This is Rhodes. We are safe." Cade Rhodes' voice carried over the line.

"Good to hear it," he replied with relief. He wasn't sure if the umbrella had put them near Devon or just hurled them to a random destination. "Where are you?"

"I'm hesitant to disclose that information. Someone has been one step ahead of us the whole way. I had to create a distraction. They were waiting for us at two airports. Neither was on my flight plan."

Finn made a mental note to think louder so that Nisha could pick up on this conversation. It was both a handy and disturbing ability. But she already knew his most dangerous secret; everything else would just be levels of embarrassment to deal with. "How?"

"I hope you can tell me. I'm flying blind here. I don't know how they are tracking us when you can't," Rhodes responded.

"I wish I could tell you," Finn told him.

"You have a leak," Rhodes replied gruffly.

Finn bristled at the statement. "I don't think so. There is something far more sinister happening here." Finn retorted. "We have a bunch of variables in the mix. It could be anything."

Rhodes was silent for a moment. "Any word from Blue?"

"No."

"Damn." Rhodes sighed heavily on the other end of the line.

"I need to know where you are. Did you see the news? It's rough." Finn glanced around the food court, making sure no one could overhear him. "I'm bringing reinforcements."

"Lexi is on a mission for brownies and John Denver songs," Rhodes told him cryptically. "Until I know what is going on, that is all you get."

Finn frowned. Colorado? How accurate was the umbrella? Feet or miles? "Fine. Let's keep details to a minimum until we figure out how they are tracking you. Report every hour on fifteen." Ben wandered back over with a large bag of food and a milkshake. His face held a questioning look.

"Sounds good."

"Take care of my girls, Rhodes," Finn told him as Rhodes disconnected the call. A moment later, Nisha stood and carried the debris from her table to the trash. She wandered back over after a moment and sat down casually at the table next to them. She pushed the seat across from her out with her foot and pulled her cell phone up to her ear and began speaking. "I've been thinking about how they are finding your people. You are the common denominator."

"Excuse me?" He struggled to keep his voice low and act like he was speaking to Ben.

"Your team calls you, and they are targeted immediately. You were at Greenlee's house before that. They break in and your niece walks in on them. Rhodes calls you about her. They are at his house in minutes." Nisha started gathering the trash from her table. "Trix figures out they are on a plane. Goon squad shows up at the airports. There is no way that is a coincidence."

"You think I'm feeding them information?"

"That's not what I said," Nisha insisted. "I said you are a common denominator. But more specifically, your cell phone is. Tio Viking says it has enough magic in it that it glows like Clark Griswold's house at Christmas."

"My phone has a magical bug? How do you know all this?" Finn asked, laying it on the table in front of him and covering it with both his hands.

"I know everything, Mr. Torrin. Magic bug is the best guess. When was the last time you were away from your phone?"

"Left it in the cup holder with that FBI agent that rooted through my GPS history while I was pumping gas."

"That guy did seem sketch," Nisha nodded. "We should get going. And give Rhodes a new number to call."

"I want to talk to Devon; we need to get phones anyway," Greenlee offered out of nowhere.

Nisha shushed him in irritation. "You are impossible."

"Where are we going?" Ben finally asked.

"The Rocky Mountains?" Finn looked over at Nisha with a question. She didn't look at him, but she did nod.

"And the goon squad probably already knows we are on our way."

39

ZELLA

Zella sat silently in the corner of a conference room next to a lovely young woman named Kendra. So far, her gamble to drive them to the building in her recent vision was paying off. A red leather notebook that had been at the bottom of her bag for years sat in her lap. She sketched the outline of a mountain on one of the few remaining empty pages. Nisha took off with her newest journal, the brown one, in the rush to experiment with the magic umbrella and track down Sam and Ivan. That wasn't an issue other than the need to procure something else to draw in. She knew each of her visions by heart. No one else could decipher anything she had written in the past ten years, anyway. Sam might be able to. But she never let him see her journals. The old notebook would serve the purpose fine.

Her latest vision was fuzzy. It hovered in a blurry mess just at the back of her mind, which was unusual. Typically, her visions were crisp, clear, and full of color. Colorful shadowy figures moved disjointedly across the bottom of this vision, never congealing into an image with details. The number of figures shifted back and forth. Occasional flashes of light and blue sparkles popped in and out at intervals. The only thing she was certain of was the line of mountains in the background. The last time this happened was the day before Larson blew the hell out of Mitch's office. It gave her an uneasy feeling in her gut. She huffed with frustration and turned her attention to the other occupants in the room. At least they were entertaining.

"Chin up, buttercup." The woman named Harper patted Mitch under his chin. Mitch looked flustered and mildly amused. He sat behind a table with an elderly dog sleeping in his lap while the woman tried without success to comb his hair into submission. She insisted Mitch trade in his normal sweater and jacket for a simple black tee shirt on the premise that if he wanted to be intimidating, he had to look the part. He exercised regularly with Ivan. Even at his age, Zella had to admit Harper was on to something.

According to Harper, nobody was afraid of a big, shaggy, cardigan-wearing grandpa. Zella would remember the look on Mitch's face when she delivered that zinger for the rest of her life. The fearless soul then proceeded to practice his scowl with him for twenty minutes while Hale set up a camera and lights.

This all started when Mitch mentioned he wanted to issue a recorded statement asserting his continued control of the Cahlad and stave off any challenges that might arise from leaders in other regions and countries. So far, the Conclave members, who were the most likely to challenge him for leadership, were at least on the surface supportive of Cahlad Prime and its right to autonomous governance of the magical community. However, the sharks would only circle for so long. There was blood in the water, put there by the FBI and Nolan Miller to bring magic under governmental jurisdiction.

Zella was positive he intended for her to record it on his cell phone and have the mysterious Trix upload it anonymously. In the past, Ivan would have handled the technical part, but Hale assured them that Trix was more than up for the task. Harper, however, had hijacked shooting the video and turned it into a full-blown production. She insisted it should look professionally produced to combat the perception they were running for their lives.

"OK, sexy." The woman pointed at Hale. "Tilt that light up about twenty degrees. Let's get rid of the shadows. How is my camera coming?"

The big man named Hale glared at her from his spot in front of a tripod with a camera mounted on it. His head was tilted to the side to hold a cell phone between his ear and his shoulder. He spoke with a man named Trix who was upstairs and refused to come out as long as Mitch was in the building, even though he was the only person who knew how to run all the equipment. "It would be great if Trix would get his sorry ass down here and do his job." He paused for a moment. "I know you heard me," he groused as he adjusted the light.

"I think we need popcorn," Kendra whispered conspiratorially. "You want some popcorn?" Zella nodded her head in appreciation and affirmation as the woman sauntered toward the door.

"Bring me some water, Kay Kay. This hair is something else," Harper called after her. "Do you have any hairspray?"

Kendra quirked an eyebrow and motioned toward her pixie cut. "Fine then. Water will have to do it," Harper conceded.

She stood back and inspected Hale's lighting work with a critical eye. Then she stepped over to the camera, looking at the display screen with a frown. "Would you be opposed to dying your hair? You have a ton of gray. Maybe trim the beard nice and close. Everyone loves a silver fox, but what we have here is The Shaggy Dog."

Hale snorted as Mitch's lips thinned and his shoulders straightened indignantly. Zella clutched her chest in mirth. Nisha, Sam, and Ivan were painfully blunt with Mitch on occasion. She gave him grief in her own way. But no one had ever talked to him like this before.

"What is it that you do again, dear?" Mitch asked her, obviously trying not to be the diva she had accused him of being earlier.

"I'm Cade Rhode's assistant." She strolled over and sat sideways on the table in front of him. "A.K.A. Professional diva wrangler supreme. Thousands of photo and video shoots. It is my job to make him look good and control his image because his manager is useless. And let me tell you honey, sometimes that makes me a miracle worker because the man is a disaster. I've got wings back here somewhere. You'll hear the trumpets soon."

Mitch smiled politely at her as he clasped his hands on the table in front of him and his jaw twitched. That was the face he used when he had to deal with Nolan Miller in public. "You want to convince people you are this big bad man who is still in charge of his precious magic fraternity, and they better not mess with you? You listen to me, and we will have the whole world quaking in its boots. But we gotta make you over, honey. You boys have a razor or some clippers in this place?" she asked Hale.

"Sure, somewhere?" Hale seemed uncertain. "Maybe in the bunk room?"

"Magic fraternity?" Mitch uttered as he nodded calmly and looked imploringly at Zella. She knew her face displayed her amusement at his expense. She wasn't going to save him this time. Not that she could. Harper was a force of nature.

Hale flopped into the seat next to her. "Is Kendra bringing popcorn?" Zella nodded and pointed at the phone in his lap that was still connected. "Oh. Trix still wants to hear the shenanigans, even though he's too chickenshit to leave his cave. You don't think your man will lose his shit and kill us all, do you? I mean, this woman is hilarious, but I don't want to die over it." Zella made a silly face and shook her head. He nodded in satisfaction. "Cool."

"I'll send the clippers down with Kendra," a tinny voice emerged from the phone in Hales lap. "Somebody film it."

"Aw, thanks, sweetie." Harper smiled at the disembodied voice. "You are just a big help."

"How did you come to work for Mr. Rhodes again?" Mitch asked her, rubbing his beard self-consciously.

"Just as a favor to my sweet friend, Blue. She helped me out a while back and asked me to keep an eye on him. I had no idea it would be such a big job. That man was self-destructing. Wonder he didn't kill himself."

"That is quite the favor." Mitch cleared his throat. "She must have helped you a great deal."

The woman's look sharpened for a split second before it passed. Mitch caught it; Zella was sure because his mustache wiggled. "More than you'll ever know, fuzzy bear."

Mitch flinched at the nickname. She seemed to have one for everyone. "Mr. Rhodes must appreciate your efforts a great deal."

"He fires me once a day. But he can't live without me, and he knows it. Hires me back as soon as he has to order his own dinner. Or bottled water for his spoiled little princess. Now run your speech by us and don't forget to scowl."

"My speech?" Mitch sputtered, flabbergasted. "Oh Lordy," Harper threw both hands in the air. "You were going to wing it?"

Kendra came back in, carrying two bags. One was filled with snacks and drinks. The other was a leather case Zella assumed contained a razor. If Mitch allowed the woman near his face with it, her claims of being a miracle worker were accurate. He hadn't even shaved when he was sworn in as Paragon. She only managed to get him to sit still to trim his hair every three months. "A razor and water for the lady." Kendra held up the case and a bottle. "And popcorn for the rest of us."

"Thanks, Kay Kay." Harper took both items and unzipped the case.

"I'm not shaving my beard," Mitch finally challenged the woman. Zella picked up her pencil again, compelled to continue sketching while two unstoppable forces argued. This time, she just let her hand move of its own accord.

"Well, I'm not letting you make a bad video." She popped a hand on her hip and rolled her head. "It will grow back."

"Food me." Hale waved at a bag of white cheddar popcorn Kendra held out. He opened it and passed it over to Zella before taking one of his own without looking away from the spectacle happening before him. "Is that a flag? Colorado?" Hale asked, glancing at the notebook in her lap. "You are really good at that. Nice shading."

"What did I miss?" Kendra whispered conspiratorially, sitting next to Zella on her other side.

"She called him a shaggy dog." Hale popped a kernel into his mouth. "Is she like this with Rhodes?"

"Oh, yeah." Kendra nodded. "Free entertainment."

Zella smiled and looked around her. She hadn't had this much fun in years, despite her inability to get the vision out of her head. People usually tiptoed around her because she couldn't talk or communicate effectively. Or because she was the Paragon's partner. These people hadn't batted an eye. They treated her like part of the team, and Hale even let all the curse words fly without a second thought.

She had noticed someone from Herne had been within feet of her the entire time she was here. It was unusual. Normally, security teams flocked to Mitch, and she was an afterthought. This crew was just the opposite. Despite the hovering, she felt welcome and at ease. Her right hand continued to move across the paper as she ate popcorn using the other.

The Hounds of Dawn in Blues of Bell

Wild Children War Upon the Dell

Roar of Brothers. Seven and seven.

Vortex Cross a Violet heaven

Splintered Time. Forged Love. Staunch Friend.

Together Stand or All Will End.

"What's that?" Kendra asked, also looking down at her journal. She repeated the words out loud and pursed her lips in contemplation. "It's pretty."

Harper used the water bottle and a comb to furiously force Mitch's hair into some semblance of order. The whole time talking to herself and dropping endearments and nicknames.

"Ms. Kilgarden," Mitch began diplomatically as she unzipped the razor case. "I appreciate..."

"Shhh, honey," Harper told him. "Let me work some magic."

Zella glanced down at her notebook and read the words again. The vision was still blurry and for the first time, even she didn't know what the words truly meant. She drew her finger down the page, careful not to smudge the words.

She was startled from her musings by a collective "Ohhhhh!" shouted by the people around her. The dog growled an indignant warning. She looked up, stunned by the sudden noise to see shocked faces. Kendra sat with her popcorn halfway to her open mouth, her eyes wide. Hale had his arm in front of his face, peeking around it with one eye closed. When their voices died down, Zella heard the buzz of the razor. She followed their eyes to the conference table where Mitch sat, missing a large chunk of his beard on the left side of his chin. His face was furious and mutinous as he glared at Harper.

"I should have confiscated his artifact," Hale muttered to Kendra, who sent him a warning look. Zella was sure Finn had issued orders to treat her and Mitch as guests and not prisoners.

"It's started now, sugar," Harper smiled and moved the razor toward the other side of his face. "Might as well finish."

"Tell me you got that on video," Trix's voice echoed from Hales phone.

"Please hold," Hale told him, and ended the call without looking away.

Another buzz of the razor took off the right side of his beard. Zella heard a literal growl from Mitch as she continued to trim the hair on his face. The tiny little pug answered with one of her own. It seemed no one, animal or human, in Rhodes' inner circle had any fear.

"Do I need to save her?" Kendra asked Zella.

She wasn't sure, so she sent Kendra an uncertain look. She extended her hand outward and rocked it back and forth in a motion she intended to communicate fifty/fifty. Often, even her hand signals were garbled, but she hoped the woman got the message.

Harper stepped away from Mitch, switching the razor off. She placed a fist on her hip and observed him. She stepped away and motioned grandly toward her victim. "What do you think, momma?"

To her surprise, Mitch still had facial hair left. Just less. What he did have was trimmed neatly. He was clean-shaven on the sides, leaving dark hair with flecks of gray only around his mouth and on his chin. His hair was combed neatly back. She was stunned. Mitch had been, as Harper so eloquently put it, a shaggy dog the entire time she had known him. She rather liked the change. But knew Mitch would never maintain it.

She gave Harper a huge smile.

She immediately gave Mitch two thumbs up. His face went from murderous to uncertain. She stood quickly and walked behind the table with him, placing a hand on both sides of his face and patting in approval. She gave him a nod.

"It looks real nice, Paragon," Kendra chimed in. "Very sophisticated."

"It will look great on camera, sir," Hale told him enthusiastically, followed by an "Oof" when Kendra elbowed him in the ribs. "I mean, it looks great. Period." "See," Harper preened and plucked the dog from Mitch's lap. "Let's get you some water, old lady."

Mitch put one of his hands over hers and closed his eyes. He took in several deep breaths, and she knew he was trying to stay calm and diplomatic and deal with his embarrassment. Harper was a bit much. But she was right. When his eyes opened, they twinkled. "You approve?"

She nodded and patted the smooth part of his face again. There was her Mitch. She wondered again what their lives would have been like if he had not had to challenge the previous Paragon. He had never wanted this life. But he was one of the few people on the planet who could survive a challenge to the previous Paragon. She was proud of what he had done. She should have told him that more when she was able.

"At least I have that," he grumbled, and tilted his head to the side to speak to Harper. "Do I have your permission to make the video about my precious magic fraternity now?"

"Rehearsal first," she replied, stuffing the clippers back into the bag.

"Lord, give me strength," he whispered. Zella couldn't help the silent laugh that shook her body. Mitch tried to look stern and cross and failed miserably. A rolling laugh fell from his lips as he placed his head on her shoulder. His body shook as they both fell into a fit of laughter and giggles. Things had been so serious and tense for so long, they had forgotten what it was like to laugh at themselves. It used to be a daily occurrence. Before Larson. Before Amber. Tears rolled from her eyes. Ages had passed since they had a moment like this. How strange that it came in the basement of a rundown warehouse where they were seeking asylum. When Mitch finally recovered and stood, readying himself to face Harper once more, he wiped a tear from the corner of her eye. He sobered quickly and frowned as the reality of their situation returned. "What is it they say? If you don't laugh?"

"Let's hear it, fuzzy bear," Harper practically shouted, clapping her hands together. "Don't forget your scowl. I need a thumbnail."

40

BLUE

"Take this." Sam knelt next to Blue, shoving a trash can into her hands. She sat balled in the passenger seat with her chin resting on her knees, pale, shaking, and heaving. He was irritated at the whole situation. They were in the middle of nowhere Colorado. The sky was dark, a storm bearing down on them. They had yet to secure burner phones to make contact with Nisha. Everywhere they stopped so far was sold out or never carried them in the first place. Since they were driving a stolen vehicle, and their faces were all over the news from the bird attack, their shopping establishment options were limited. And this woman was killing herself trying to channel magic she had no experience with.

"You are pushing too hard. This is classic magic poisoning. Your readings probably aren't even right," he argued and glanced at Ivan, who looked grim and upset, hoping the man would back him up. But the man remained silent. He seemed to trust that she knew what she was doing, regardless of how bad the situation obviously was.

The bond between those two was impressive. Sam felt like a third wheel. He had never seen Ivan interact with anyone the way he did with Blue. He was like a protective, playful big brother. She even made him smile. As irritating as she was, he needed Blue on his team. Ava had chosen her as her person, and she had Ivan's loyalty. Better or worse, she was the glue holding this little group together. She was also stubborn and unpredictable. If she didn't give up soon, he had to order her to stop.

For the moment, Ivan drove quietly. The teenager that Ivan now called Honey Badger was sitting on the sofa reading a serial romance novel she found in the cabinets. It was covered in orange powder from the bag of Cheetos Sam bought for her at their last gas stop. It was disturbing how much she looked like her mother. Sam didn't remember Amber being so mean at this age. He pinched his nose and rubbed his eyes. He never thought he would see the day when he wished he could just be Regent of the Prime Cahlad because it was simpler than his current situation. Yet here he was.

"I'm fine," Blue croaked. "Whoa, boy. It's really strong." She stopped on a gag and made use of the trash can he had just handed her. She buried her face in her knees and drew in a deep breath.

"Ava, can you grab her something to drink?" Sam asked.

"Sure," Ava grunted, putting down her book and wiping her hands on her pants. She seemed to believe Blue when she said she was fine. She wasn't concerned by what was happening in the slightest, either. "It's like two hungry toddlers and a monkey went shopping,"

Ava complained when she opened the refrigerator. "No water. Just orange and grape soda."

"Orange?" Blue said weakly.

Ava grabbed an orange soda and handed it to him. "Next time, make them buy water."

He loosened the cap and extended the bottle to the woman, slowly turning an actual shade of green in the passenger seat.

"Thanks." She reached out, barely looking up, and took a sip of the soda. "It's really strong," she retched the soda she had just drunk into the trash can. "Oh, God." She rattled in a breath through her mouth. "I'm dying. For real this time. They have to be close. Do you see anything?"

Sam frowned. She probably was dying for real. He opened his mouth to tell her to stop, but Ivan interrupted.

"There is a blue Toyota about 500 yards ahead of us. Who are we looking for again?" Ivan said, stepping on the gas. The engine surged. Blue groaned loudly and retched again.

"Do we finally have something?" Ava asked, moving forward to kneel behind Ivan's chair, looking curiously out of the window.

"Hey there, honey badger," Ivan greeted her. "How's your book?"

"Trope laden. Forced proximity, arranged marriage, HEA," Ava informed him. "Pretty awesome."

"Cool. I call next," Ivan replied. Sam rolled his eyes. He and Nisha traded romance novels and held frequent movie nights featuring sappy romantic comedies. The camper quickly overtook the smaller car.

"Happily ever afters are such bullshit. How can you read that garbage?" Blue retched again.

"Of course, they are bullshit. That's why it is called fiction," Ava replied in a sing-song voice.

"Three people. One man, one woman, one kid." Ivan interrupted their impromptu book club meeting as they came within feet of the car's back bumper. He honked the horn and pointed to the side of the road.

The vehicle visibly sped up. He didn't blame them, but they would check it out. "You know what to do," he told Ivan.

"Don't hurt ... Oh God," Blue wailed, chucking more into the trash can. "Seatbelt," she retched again. "Ava."

"Please go sit down and put on the safety belt," Sam translated as he observed the car. Ivan moved the camper into the opposing lane of traffic and overtook the smaller vehicle. Sam leaned over an alarmingly pale Blue and looked out the side window. He saw a paunchy, middle-aged couple and a pre-teen boy with a mohawk. "They don't look like much."

Blue wearily set the trash can between her feet and looked out as well. She placed her face close to the glass and started pointing in the universal gesture to pull the car over. The driver glanced up quickly, a stern set to his jaw. His gaze hovered for a moment on Blue's face, and his eyes grew wide. The man said something to the passenger, and the car immediately slowed down.

Ivan slowed the camper onto the narrow shoulder in front of the car and stopped. He flipped on the hazard lights and stood. "You sure?" he asked Blue as he made his way toward the door.

"I've never used my magic like this before." Blue gulped and stood. She was shaky. Sam had never seen someone able to maintain magic once this level of sickness set in. She sucked in a large lungful of air, obviously trying to stop vomiting. "I hope so."

Ivan gave her a disgruntled look and stepped out of the RV onto the roadside. Sam waited for Blue, then followed as she made her way gingerly toward the stairs. "You got this?"

She nodded and put a hand over her mouth. She made it down the stairs and stepped to the side before leaning over and covering the side of the camper in orange soda. Sam exited to the other side, and Ava leaned out the door, her nose pinched up in disgust. "Are you sure you are going to be OK, Ms. Blue? Lurch, you have to buy her some ginger ale or 7up at the next stop."

"Sure," Sam told her seriously. The girl was warming up to him. One cup of fancy coffee with whipped cream and a bag of Cheetos had gone a long way toward the effort. But she still refused to use his name. "Please stay in the camper until we know what we are dealing with. No driving off without me again."

"Ivan took the keys," she pouted, but stayed on the stairs like he directed.

Blue stood and wiped her mouth with her wrist. She watched Ivan approach the car whose occupants still hadn't emerged. Small drops of rain fell from the sky. "Ivan. Hold up," she called and heaved.

"You should let the magic drop. You are killing yourself," Sam said under his breath. Whoever this was must be very important to her.

"I'm afraid I won't be able to do this again if I let it drop. I'll be fine," she told him, walking in Ivan's direction with a hand on the camper for support. "This isn't how I die," she said with utter conviction. What on earth could she mean by that?

"Don't let her fall," Ava watched with a worried face. Blue raised the middle finger of her free hand and scratched the back of her head with it.

"I've got her. Shut the door and lock it." He heard Ava's infuriated "Gah" as the door slammed and the lock clicked. He probably burned through his coffee and Cheetos capital with just a few words.

"You just let me fall. Do you hear me? I'll be fine," Blue told him as they continued and joined Ivan at the rear of the vehicle.

"Not a problem."

Blue ducked Ivan's outstretched arm and approached the car, stopping to place her hands on her knees and empty the rest of her stomach.

The car's passenger side door burst open and an average-height woman with gray-streaked brown hair got out. She wore glasses and had a jolly face. They heard an angry male voice from the car before the driver's side door flung open and a short man with salt and pepper hair stepped out. He slammed the door in a huff. He placed his hands on the hips of his classic dad bod and leveled a glare at his passenger. "You listen for shit!"

They all stood in silence observing, unsure and on edge until a young voice screeched from the back seat of the car, "Mom! Is that Tia Blue?"

Blue whispered, "Thank God." Her body jerked violently as she let go of the magic, falling to her knees, sucking in a deep breath. A tall boy clambered out of the back seat of the car and appeared uncertain. The driver of the car threw his hands in the air and shouted, "What did we talk about? Stay in the car and keep quiet!" The passenger sprinted toward Blue as she fell, causing Ivan to step between them with a scowl, crossing his arms over his chest. Sam maintained cover behind the RV, waiting to see how the situation would play out. So far, they hadn't noticed him.

"It's OK, big guy." Blue collapsed further to sit slumped on the damp ground. "She's family. What are you doing here Devon?" Ivan didn't look happy, and he didn't move out of the way. But he didn't try to stop the matronly woman from running around him and squatting in front of Blue, reaching for her cheeks.

"What have they done to you? Why are you here? We all thought you were dead." A sob ripped from the woman Blue had called Devon as she too fell to her knees and pulled the still-shaking Blue into a tight hug. They rocked together. More like Devon rocked, and Blue allowed it as she used the other woman to hold her up. A thump on the back window of the camper caused everyone to jump. Ava's face pressed against the glass. A muffled call of, "She needs ginger ale and crackers!" reached their ears.

"I've got her, honey!" Devon called as she was tackled from behind by the boy, who had finally decided to ignore the shouting driver and hug-tackle the women on the ground.

"Tia Blue! The charm worked. There were men and they chased me, and I said baby blue," the boy yammered excitedly. They huddled together like football players with their heads together now.

"Wait. Slow down, sweetheart. What happened?"

The driver walked cautiously over, eyes glued to Blue. Ivan blocked his path. Sam heard a low growl from the man approaching. It didn't sound human. "Stop right there," the man cut angry eyes toward him as his body complied. "Arms out. Don't move a muscle."

Ivan executed a textbook pat down. They could eliminate traditional weapons from the equation. The growling continued.

"Put it away, Rhodes," Blue ordered from behind Ivan.

"Who?" Sam demanded, as another piece of the puzzle fell into place. If this was who he suspected it was, his day was getting even worse.

Blue stood with the boy's help and walked around Ivan, standing in between them with her arms out. "Let him go, Sam. Rhodes. Put. It. Away." She pointed a warning hand at the man, who still stood with his arms out, glaring at Sam.

"Fine," Sam muttered. "You are free to go."

"Rhodes?" Ivan asked again, looking between Blue and the driver.

"Yeah, check it out." The boy stood and ran toward the man. "Watch!" He grabbed the man's hand as it fell to his side. "Do the thing!" A moment later, the boy turned into a much shorter girl with long, dark hair and big, dark eyes. Her face held a goofy grin. Yep. That was THE Rhodes he suspected it was.

"I'll be damned," Ivan muttered, and walked toward the man with his hand outstretched. "Westridge?"

"Lacroix." The man stretched his hand out with a begrudging tilt of his chin. Before Sam's eyes, the man shifted to a much taller, muscular body with dirty blond hair and a beard. He didn't look like he had at the Cahlad, but he was familiar. "Heard what happened. Glad you are OK."

"I assumed they got you, too. It's good to see you," Ivan told the man.

"They tried. Three rounds to the chest," Rhodes responded.

Ivan grunted in acknowledgment.

A screech pierced the air, and seconds later Ava flew out of the door sprinting toward the newcomers. "Cade Rhodes! OMG! Is that really Cade Rhodes?"

"Hello there." The man swapped into charm mode and stuck his hand out. Ava didn't stop though and threw herself at the man, wrapping him in a hug. "Oh. OK. Nice to meet you." He patted her carefully between the shoulder blades, looking to Devon with an unsure expression on his face as she continued to squeal. Sam took a moment to really look at the man. It was the country music star that was plastered all over everything right now. Sneaky. Hid in plain sight. He even kept part of his real name.

Sam approached the man slowly. "We thought." He stopped when the man growled at him again and his eyes flashed.

"OK. Enough. Let's get this off the street." Blue sounded disgusted.

"Put me back," Devon demanded, approaching Ava and gently prying the girl's arms off of the missing Zenith Rhodes Westridge. With one swipe of his hand, the woman shrank and morphed into a curvy Latina woman with long, dark, wavy hair.

"Get my stuff, I need to get Blue taken care of," the woman told Rhodes, and to Sam's surprise, the man appeared to be doing as she asked.

"I'm fine. Ivan and Ava are mother hen enough," Blue complained.

Rhodes joined them, holding a few plastic shopping bags. He looked Blue up and down, taking in her pale face, the bags under her eyes, and the nest that her undercut ponytail had become. "I thought you were dead. Again," the man spoke softly and cleared his throat. "You can't keep doing this to me, Baby Blue. I can't take it."

"Baby Blue?" Ava gasped in shock. "Are you THE Baby Blue?"

"I'm going to be sick again," Blue groaned and turned on her heel, an unreadable look on her face stomping back toward the camper.

The little girl that was obviously Devon's daughter leaned toward Ava and shout-whispered in a conspiratorial tone, "It is her. He wrote the song for her because he screwed up big time. They were going to get married, but now they aren't."

"OMG. Spill the rest of that tea." Ava took the girl's hand and dragged her into the camper. "Want some Cheetos?"

Sam remained quiet as everyone clambered on board. He didn't like any of this. He looked up at the sky. The storm was almost on top of them, and it promised to be a bad one. He had a feeling that was true about more than the weather. He climbed the stairs and shut the door.

Blue took a seat at the dinette. "Come here, Lexi. Tell me more about the bad men and the charm." She patted the seat next to her. The girl slid in and leaned on Blue. Devon pulled a water out of one of the shopping bags Rhodes had brought aboard and handed it to Blue with a stern tap.

He leaned back against the counter, too tall to fit in any of the remaining seats. Three extra passengers, one of them a long-lost Zenith, were not in his plans for today. The girl launched into her story of coming home from school to two men in her home and a magic charm activated by the words to an overrated and overplayed country music song. It ended with being stalked by creepy guys at the Denver airport. "Thanks for the charm, Tia Blue. I think you saved my life."

"Wow," Ava whispered, looking between Blue and Rhodes. He looked beyond tired. Dark circles rimmed his eyes as he lounged on the couch with slumped shoulders. Blue was at least beginning to regain some color. He was amazed at her capacity to heal so quickly. That level of poisoning could take months to fully recover from.

Sam watched the woman squeeze the small child's shoulders and turn somber eyes to a man until moments ago Sam thought she had killed. The two Zenith locked eyes and a whole conversation took place in the look they shared. Rhodes finally nodded, and Blue looked away. Devon reached out and took her hand, uttering a quiet and choked, "Thank you."

"Why do I have another Zenith to deal with, and who are these other two people on my hands? Are they your family?"

"Wait," Devon frowned. "Another Zenith? What is he talking about?"

"What's a Zenith?" both Ava and Lexi asked. "Jinx," they shouted.

"She doesn't know?" Rhodes asked in disbelief, looking between Blue and Devon. "Well, at least your propensity for secrets is equal opportunity."

"Blue?" Devon drew out the name in a displeased tone. Sam saw wheels spinning in the woman's eyes. She knew exactly what a Zenith was. When the program was operational, their identities had been closely guarded. But the fact that they existed and what they were capable of was openly flaunted in the right circles to keep members, rogues, and even governments in line. They had not been discussed openly since Larson Battle's attempted coup. That meant she was privy to the right circles a long time ago. This was not a normal soccer Mom.

"You trust them?" Rhodes asked, motioning between Ivan and Sam.

"They are pretty cool," Ava chimed in. Sam could tell she was uncomfortable with the sudden shift in the conversation. "Aren't they Ms. Blue?"

Blue leveled Sam with a look that made his blood run cold and his hackles raise. Up until now, she had been affable and personable. She made Ivan laugh and mothered Ava. She joked around and fought next to them. He struggled to reconcile those things with the look she gave him now. It was the look of a professional assassin appraising a target. Her gaze passed over Ivan before landing on Rhodes. Sam was glad her stare made the man appear as uncomfortable as he felt. "I trust Ivan. He says he can handle Sam," she finally replied.

Rhodes crossed his arms and scowled. He wanted to say something, but wisely stayed quiet. He got the impression that Ivan and Sam weren't on the best of terms.

"Which one of you is a Zenith?" Devon asked. There was no sign of the soft, good-natured woman who had rushed to her friend's side.

"I am," Ivan rumbled from the front of the camper, where he was obviously listening to the conversation.

"I am," Rhodes admitted with a touch of defeat in his voice. Devon's eyes grew wide as she reassessed the man.

"Me too." Blue sighed.

Devon gaped. "There were only three. The program was cut short when Battle died. You are all here?" Her questioning gaze fell to Sam as if she expected him to chime in as the fourth musketeer. He just shook his head. "Which one of you tried to kill my dad?" she demanded.

"I did." Blue seemed resigned now, but she met her friend's eyes.

"Shit," Rhodes muttered under his breath and leaned forward to rest his elbows on his knees. He glared at Sam, his expression telegraphing that he had really stepped into it with the Zenith comment. How was Sam supposed to know the woman wouldn't tell her best friend about something as big as this?

"Her kill rate is 100%," Rhodes cajoled, making Devon's face grow darker. "If he isn't dead, it means she let him go."

"Who is your dad?" Sam asked. Rhodes was right. Di Vale was the most lethal soldier to ever work for the Cahlad. He personally read every sanctioned and unsanctioned mission report. She was the only Cahlad operator with an unblemished record and dozens of confirmed kills. She specialized in making them look like accidents. Which meant Devon's dad hadn't been in the files, or she lied. He was leaning toward the latter.

"You want to tell them?" Devon tilted her head defiantly, hostility rolling off her in waves. "I'm sick of talking about him."

"Mullet Roane," Blue whispered, her expression somewhere between empty and broken.

"Whoa." Lexi scooted away from Blue in the booth, her face taking on a scared and worried look. "That weird dude from the television show?"

"Really, Blue?" Devon huffed. "You let the child watch her grandfather run around naked?"

"I didn't think she would ever know who he really was," Blue defended herself. "She had a quiz."

"Everything was blurred Mom," Lexi tried to smooth things over.

"One thing at a time. But we will be discussing this later." Devon lifted a finger, then rubbed her eyes in exasperation. "You tried to kill my dad? You screwed up on purpose? Then conveniently forgot to mention that for a decade."

"Sums it up."

Sam frowned. Mullet Roane's death was reported far and wide. He looked at Rhodes. The man's expression was shocked. He hadn't known either. This woman was the queen of secrets.

"Why?" Devon asked quietly.

"He was a huge problem for the Cahlad. Everyone else tried and failed to kill him. Mitch gave the order and Larson sent me. He always hated me." She blew out a short breath and continued. "I was only seventeen. He was my first assassination assignment. I think Larson expected Roane to take me out."

"Oh, dear God," Ava muttered, placing a hand over her mouth. "That's my age."

Blue sent her a sad smile. "When I finally caught up with him, he was very drunk. He had just bailed his kid out of jail because she got busted in one of his schemes."

"I remember that." Devon nodded. "I stormed out and met my boyfriend."

Blue observed Devon for a moment, both of their expressions blank. "He should have killed me. Could have then. But instead, he asked me if I had ever been to Disney World. Said he wished he took his daughter there when she was little. And he offered me dinner. Homemade macaroni and cheese and a beer. We played poker and

436

talked for a long time. He told me his kid was amazing and deserved better than him. The eyeliner made his eyes sting. Running around naked required too much time in the gym not to embarrass himself." Devon made a noise that said she didn't want to hear about her dad naked.

"We blew his house sky high." Blue sighed. "He sent you away and went underground. I went back and took credit for killing him. I know it killed you when he left you, too. And for that I'm sorry. I didn't know he was your dad until you told me after Lexi was born. I didn't know how you would react. It's a small fucking world, Dev. I didn't have many good choices back then. I don't regret helping your Dad. I'm sorry I didn't tell you."

"How many others did you lie about?" Sam interjected, astounded. Blue shrugged and stared at Devon, who wouldn't meet her gaze.

The camper fell silent. Sam sat down on the floor in front of the sink, hard. How many off-the-books missions were a double cross? She was a complete wild card. But he knew what he saw on the screen when he walked into Larson's office on the day of the explosion. She had clearly said, "Mission accomplished, sir." He didn't know her at the time and had taken it as the final words of a dutiful soldier reporting to a superior. Now that he had spent the last two days in close quarters with her, he suspected her words were laden with sarcasm and irreverence.

"Why are we here, Blue? Why did you drag us across the state and make yourself sick to get to this guy when you didn't know he was helping your friends? How does he fit into this?"

"He was in trouble. The Sovereign are after him. I've seen what they do to people. I would help anyone with that target on their back. That is how he fits into this."

"Not because once upon a time you were engaged? When did that even happen? The Cahlad would have known about a relationship between two of its top operatives. Especially one that went AWOL." Rhodes ghosted two years before Vale betrayed them. Or supposedly betrayed them. Sam eyed the pair.

"He's a Zenith. Nobody else cared if we lived or died. We had to have each other's backs. Still applies," she told him.

"Amen," Ivan intoned from the driver's seat. Sam was starting to understand the dynamic.

"I thought you killed him." Sam snorted. "But you hid him. And kept working for the Cahlad like you didn't know anything. Have you ever told anyone the whole truth?"

"The Sovereign weren't after Rhodes until Lexi showed up." Devon cut the tension in the camper and redirected the conversation. "He wasn't the target. They weren't prepared for him. At all. Greenlee was kidnapped earlier today while he was helping Marilee with her car. Or was it yesterday? Either way, Finn found him in Nashville after you ghosted him. I think they are targeting us. I don't know if Lexi was a target or if they were there waiting on you or me and saw an opportunity."

"Green OK?" Blue's face grew cold and hard. Whoever Green was, he was important to both women. She looked ready to murder someone.

"He is. Pretty busted up. I talked to him. He was holding up better than last time." Devon told her. "But there have been some developments that we need to discuss."

"I suspect I know who Finn is," Sam told them.

"If you don't already, you will soon," Devon informed him.

The more he looked at the woman in front of him, the more he thought she was the second woman from the park. "I need to know who Green is and why you two were at the park before the dedication."

Devon's hair lifted with static, and she sent a questioning look toward Blue. Her friend gave a weary nod in response. "Enemy of my enemy, right? They aren't Sovereign," Blue told her.

"They are my uncles," Lexi replied. "Well, Tio Finn is. I call Tio G... it's complicated." Blue ruffled her hair.

"Blue and I met Greenlee," Devon paused and glanced at her daughter, "as unwilling guests at a facility that is now a new park a little over ten years ago." Sam sat up straighter, and the camper slowed suddenly. "Finn is my brother-in-law, owner of Herne Tactical." Sam nodded. He already knew that. A moment later, Ivan pulled off the road into what looked like a rundown gas station.

"You mean?" Sam started, then stopped. "How much does she know?" he pointed to Lexi.

"Just be careful how you say things. She will figure it all out anyway," Devon replied as Ivan stood and joined them. He sat in the small remaining space in front of the counter, shoulder-to-shoulder with Sam.

"He was there, too? This Green person. You were there?" Ivan asked. Devon looked closely at Ivan for the first time since they had met on the side of the road.

"That's room one?" she asked Blue, who closed her eyes and nodded. "God. I didn't recognize him. You got him. I didn't think you could. I didn't think he could survive. You never said one way or the other. I can't believe—" The woman cut herself off. "I'm so glad you are OK." Ivan swallowed hard and nodded.

"We are very late on introductions," Blue announced. "I'm the only one who knows who everyone is. How rude of me! This is Ivan Lacroix. Former Zenith operative and current Stalker Prime teddy bear badass with abs for days. That is Sam Sotach, current Regent of the Cahlad and perpetually shirtless asshole. That is Cade Rhodes, formerly a Zenith known as Rhodes Westridge. Just an asshole. This is Devon O'Neal, formerly Esdevona Roane Irving, daughter of Mullet Roane and sister-in-law to Finn Torrin, owner of Herne Tactical. This is Lexi, Devon's daughter. Her aunt and uncles are dangerous people. Be nice to her and don't give her sugar or caffeine. That is Ava, Amber Collin's daughter. I'm still working out that math. Greenlee is my best friend. Everyone involved, except Finn and his team, have, let's call them, very similar qualities. Clear as mud?"

"We are all like magic royalty or something?" Lexi asked into the resulting silence, looking around the gathering for clarification.

"See?" Devon sent a smug look in Sam's direction.

"You are too smart for your own good, Lexi Lou," Rhodes told her quietly.

"That is pretty damned accurate," Sam agreed. The grandchildren of the Cahlad Paragon and its most infamous fugitive sat feet from him. Roane's daughter sat next to them. The red USB drive said everyone else in the camper was custom-made in a Cahlad-sponsored breeding program to be the most powerful magic users to ever walk the planet. This was as close as it got to magical royalty.

"She trusts you. That's obviously rare." Devon gazed at Ivan with an eerie calm. She motioned for Lexi to cover her ears. When the child rolled her eyes and complied, Devon turned to Sam and continued. "Ten years ago, Larson Battle had my husband and son murdered to get to me. My son, Gage, was only four. He loved trains and his stuffed whale named Barry. You unveiled his statue in the middle of a Hitchcock movie."

Sam felt Ivan's arm tense where their shoulders touched. Blue closed her eyes and laid her head against the window. Was she going to have another panic attack?

"He captured me, Greenlee, Blue, and Ivan, among others. He locked us up. He experimented on us. He tortured us. The reason Greenlee and I were caught was because we were running and hiding from people like you. There was nobody to protect us. Nobody that gave a shit about our freedom. If the Cahlad had protected us, instead of treating us like criminals because we can use magic without one of their precious registered artifacts, he might never have caught us. Blue was there because they didn't protect her. A child. You let that monster force her to kill. And when he found out she hadn't, he was furious about Rhodes," Devon trailed off, sending an apologetic glance to her friend. "You can't see her scars because she heals. But I saw through that window. I saw what he did. Four days. It was just as bad as room one." She pointed at Ivan. "They just kept her out of it enough to study how she healed, but keep her from skipping so she doesn't really remember. I heard her screams and his. I heard it all. The scars, the nightmares, the panic attacks. The pieces of our souls that are missing. Those are on the Cahlad. On you." She glared at Sam, her hair floating higher around her head, her eyes wild. He felt electricity charging the air and wasn't sure what to do. He didn't want to make an enemy of this woman by issuing a directive. But the situation was unstable. Ava stood and began pacing.

Rhodes growled and joined her. His hands fisted at his sides. Sam didn't remember him growling this much during his time at the Cahlad.

"It wasn't your fault, Rhodes. You didn't know. I should have told you not to trust Larson. I never dreamed you would risk calling him after you left." Blue said with a shaky breath out without opening her eyes or taking her head off the window. That only made the man growl deeper.

Ivan stood and walked over to Blue. Whatever happened in that facility was a trigger for more than one person in the space. It was like his friend needed to be near her. Ivan placed a hand on her shoulder and leaned down to whisper something that Sam couldn't hear into her ear. It seemed to help. She reached up and squeezed his arm, patting his scar.

"Mom?" Lexi said in a warning voice. Her hands still covered her ears. "You have to calm down. I think you are scaring Tia Blue's new friends. Your hair is doing the thing."

"I'm sorry, morra," Devon smiled tightly at her daughter. She motioned for the girl to keep her ears covered.

"Mr. Sotach, you need to understand something about me and Greenlee and Blue. We got out. We lived. We built a beautiful life full of love and joy and laughter despite the nightmares." She leveled a look at Sam so cold it could freeze a volcano. "We killed everything and everyone in our path to build it. And we have done the same to protect it. If you think for one second, just because you are some big shot at the Cahlad, that we won't end you if you fuck with us, you are sorely mistaken." She motioned for Lexi to uncover her ears.

Sam bit his lip to hide a smile. She had no fear, and he suspected she packed enough power to back it up. He stood and leaned against the counter. Blue had certainly found her people. "Understood."

"Since we are all here and have reached an understanding." Devon glanced around the camper and took a deep breath. "Blue, Finn signed a contract with the Cahlad. He is in charge of the high-power artifacts now. And has oversight of the Sovaj registry." Devon spoke quietly to her friend. "Greenlee told me."

Blue's face bunched into confused surprise. "Damn, Torrin. How did he swing that?" she hissed. "You are shitting me?"

"He did what?" Sam demanded. "With who at the Cahlad?"

"Someone named Nisha." Devon shushed him and talked to Blue again. "In exchange for helping the Paragon with this situation with the FBI and Senate Magic Relations and Oversight Committee."

Sam turned a startled face to Ivan. Why would Nisha agree to something that extreme? He assumed Mitch had it under control when he avoided being taken into custody. He must have assumed incorrectly. Ivan looked as stunned as Sam felt.

"It can't be a coincidence that the ex-Regent rises from the grave and the government storms the Cahlad in the same twenty-four-hour period and on the anniversary of..." Devon trailed off. "Anyway. The man needs allies. I'm supposed to call Finn and Greenlee back in about an hour and a half. This Nisha person is with them. Let's discuss it then."

"Oh, yeah." Blue snapped her fingers. "I forgot to tell you. You got your wish. Finn and I slept together."

Devon's face turned red, and she stuttered, obviously caught completely off guard by the comment. "What?"

Lexi's nose wrinkled. "Tia Blue," she admonished.

"I knew it," Rhodes grumbled.

"Yep. We had a lovely nap on those expensive ass loungers you bought," Blue continued, trying to keep a straight face. "You know how I get after a few drinks." Finally, she winked.

Devon huffed, her expression shifting from shocked excitement to aggravation in an instant.

"Oh, you got her good, Tia Blue." Lexi giggled. "Did you see her face?"

"I wish I had a picture." Blue leaned over and whispered conspiratorially. "Tio Finn wanted to see that in person. You will have to describe it to him."

"You heifer," Devon muttered.

"Stop trying to set me up." Blue laughed as Lexi began practicing an exaggerated impression of her mom's stunned face.

Ivan's lips quirked, and even Ava chuckled. It seemed the only two people in the camper not amused by Blue's sudden change in topic were he and Rhodes.

"What do you want to discuss with Finn and this Greenlee person?" He brought the conversation back to the last topic before Blue made her friend choke. The woman cut shrewd eyes in his direction. Her misdirection had been purposeful. He gave her a tight smile.

"Dev," Blue warned.

"It will be easier if you volunteer the information," Sam told them.

"You remember that part about not hesitating to fuck you up?" Devon purred.

"Look, ladies and gentlemen. I have two young ladies here and a bunch of gun and poison-wielding psychopaths are hunting them. Someone has displaced the fucking Paragon. Global power shift for the magic community. So far, we have been lucky. But they outnumber us and have been one step ahead of us the whole time. They don't care if we have history or not. They are probably counting on it," Rhodes rumbled in exasperation. "We need to get our collective shit together. I don't know this Nisha person, but I agree with her. If you have information that can help us now, spill it. Trust somebody for once, Blue."

Ivan grunted in agreement.

"It's not my secrets," Blue told them. "Greenlee trusts this woman?"

"He spoke very highly of her," Devon confirmed. "I know his vote."

"She is one of the best people I have ever met," Sam chipped in, changing his tactic. Blue didn't miss it. She sent him a sarcastic look. Nisha made this look so easy. He wished she were here.

"Me too." Ivan nodded his agreement. Ivan's words drew Devon and Blue's attention. His opinion of Nisha carried a great deal of weight.

Blue let out a long zerbert and laid her forehead on the table in front of her. "I've made promises, Devon." She grumbled into the table.

"I know," her friend answered softly. "But Rhodes is right."

"Did hell just freeze over?" Rhodes asked.

"Shut up, wolf man," Devon snapped. "Whatever we are up against is big. If Finn is in…"

"Who did you make promises to?" Sam inquired. He was having a difficult time keeping up with this bunch. It felt like watching a ping-pong match being played with a rubber ball.

"This is your fault." Blue raised her head and pointed at Rhodes. "When did you grow a logic bone? Where was this shit ten years ago?" She sighed and looked up at the ceiling.

41

NOVA

Devon smiled. "OK. Since you seem to think everything is your business, Mr. Sotach." She smoothed her hair back into place.

"Magic," Sam reminded her. "Regent." He pointed at himself. "It's in the job description."

She pursed her lips dismissively. "What we were planning to discuss is whether the Hounds of Dawn should throw their hats into the ring with the Cahlad or remain a neutral party."

Rhodes jerked to a stop. Sam's eyes grew wide.

"We are uniquely equipped to assist with things a man who finds himself a fugitive from a large and powerful organization could need," Devon continued.

"What are you saying?" Sam asked.

"I'm saying that the Hounds of Dawn are in the house." Devon giggled. "I've always wanted to say that. The Hounds of Dawn are in the house."

Lexi groaned and rolled her eyes. "Let Tia Blue handle the cool, Mom."

Sam stood speechless. His first thought is he couldn't wait to rub Nisha's nose in this. His second thought veered more toward shock and disbelief.

"Fuck," Ivan grunted, grunted, but didn't let go of Blue's shoulder. His other hand went up to rub the back of his head.

"Explain," Rhodes bit out, glaring at Blue.

"What is there to explain, Rhodes? You've heard of the Hounds of Dawn. Turns out you know them."

"They are an urban legend," he insisted. "They are ghosts."

"Not so much," Devon corrected.

Blue shrugged, as if the information they had just dropped was no big deal. "We find people who need the help we didn't get. People who want to live their lives without quarterly inspections and yearly interviews. People running from the assholes who want to make us live on a campus or in a cell or like to sell us on the black market. They all have a story. But they are all good people in bad situations. We help them. We give them new identities. Ways to hide their magic. Money if they need it. Support while they start over. An ear when it gets too hard."

"How long?" Sam asked, watching Rhodes' reaction closely. The man was upset and not hiding it well. He clearly wasn't part of the Hounds of Dawn. Likely an unknowing client. He seemed more hurt than angry. "How do you find them when we can't?"

"Ten years," Devon answered. "We silo to protect ourselves and the people we help in case one of us is compromised. I just handle the identities, courtesy of growing up on the run from the Cahlad in a criminal organization. Blue and Greenlee never see the identities. I don't know how we find them. Greenlee makes sure they stay hidden when Blue drops them off. How do we find them, Blue?"

"Napkins, post-it notes, menus, playbills, random papers left in odd places. They always had locations and times," Blue answered her. "Someone has been leaving them for me since a month or so after we got away from Larson. Never at the house, Devon. I promise you that."

"Oh sugar," Ava mumbled, looking toward the group with wide eyes. Blue shook her head slightly at the girl. They had a secret. Old habits die hard, it seemed. If it was bigger than this revelation, he needed to ferret it out quickly.

"You are kidding me right now Blue," Rhodes looked like he could bite a steel nail in half. "Some unknown person leaves you unsolicited messages about powerful magic fugitives, and you don't question it. You just show up and risk your life?"

"I thought it was Zella." Blue directed the comment at Devon. "She was the only one at the Cahlad that was ever even remotely human to me, really. Other than Amber. She would leave me notes of encouragement or jokes written on random pieces of paper in my dorm room, or tucked into my books, shoved in my pockets. The handwriting looked the same. She had the means to get the information and to find me if she wanted to. I think she even had the means to deliver the notes. She used to be a Stalker before Larson." Sam frowned. He had not known that. He assumed she was just Mitch's partner. "There was always something up with her. I kept Dev and Green insulated. It was worth the risk."

"But it wasn't Ms. Z." Rhodes' voice rose in frustration. "It was Amber, wasn't it?"

"I know that now." Blue turned toward Rhodes.

"She herded you straight into an explosion. We all thought you were dead." Rhodes' tone held exasperation now. "Again!"

"She herded me to her daughter, who would have been dead or worse if she hadn't had help. I don't care who sent those notes. All those people needed help. And I helped them. Just like you helped Lexi."

"That's different. I knew who sent her. You never stop to think."

"I think if you hadn't given up on me, you would be entitled to an opinion," Blue interrupted him. "But that isn't how things worked out, is it?"

"I absolutely get an opinion," Rhodes insisted. "You didn't tell me any of this! I didn't have all the information."

"Come on, guys," Devon used her mom voice.

"I don't want to have this conversation sitting down. Yet. Again." Blue stood and climbed over the back of the dinette. Ivan took her arm to help her, and she stood next to him. "There was nothing to tell you. The Hounds of Dawn happened after you did this." She waved a hand up and down her body. She poked herself in the cheek. "And this. Without my permission, by the way. You told me to get the hell away from you. And I did. Regardless of your reasons, I don't give a shit about your opinion on anything after that. So, as you said before, let's get our collective shit together and move forward."

Ivan let out a long drawn-out "Oh." Sam caught up with him a moment later. That explained why she didn't look as Sam remembered. She used to have red hair, freckles, and fair skin. If he remembered correctly, she was shorter as well. Rhodes changed her appearance permanently, then dumped her after she was kidnapped and tortured. Damn. The man had guts even being in the same room as her. Sam found himself pissed off on her behalf and amazed at the level of restraint she was showing.

"Mr. Rhodes is a shapeshifter," Lexi spoke to Ava, who appeared confused and nervous. "He can do it to other people. She didn't always look like this."

Ava stopped and turned astonished eyes on Rhodes. Her mouth formed a perfect O. "Dude. Consent is a thing. What the hell?"

"I said I was sorry. I looked for her for years. I couldn't find her."

Ivan put his hands on his hips and looked down, his shoulders bunched. "You motherfucker," he grumbled.

"Ivan?" Sam asked his friend with a warning tone in his voice. Ivan rarely cursed. Hell, he rarely spoke full sentences.

"Under the bridge, Ivan," Blue told him.

"Yeah." Devon nodded at Ivan in solidarity as the man's face grew stormy. "It's pretty messed up."

Rhodes threw his hands out in exasperation. "I thought I had killed you when I found out what happened with Larson. I sent you to him. I was the one that called him. What happened to you was my fault."

"No. What happened to me in that house of horrors is Larson's fault. And I never blamed you. I told you that. What happened to me after that was your fault."

"I wanted to protect you. From me. I fucked it up." He reached and grasped Blue's forearm gently.

"Take your hand off of her Westridge," Ivan warned in a low and dangerous tone.

"Mr. Ivan?" Ava asked nervously.

"She can speak for herself," Rhodes responded.

"But will you listen?" Ivan snipped back.

"Oh, for fuck's sake," Blue huffed in exasperation.

"Back off, Lacroix."

A dark expression that was almost a smirk crossed Ivan's face. It was very un-Ivan-like. "Do you have any idea what life was like for us after you left?"

Ava took a concerned step back.

"What? I thought it was just me?" Blue seemed caught off guard by Ivan's words.

"Let's take a breath," Devon spoke, standing from her seat as she keyed into the potential disaster of three Zenith operatives in a standoff in a closed space. How had they even gotten to this point? She sent a concerned look in Sam's direction. Lexi slunk away, joining Ava and squatting behind the passenger seat. The kid had good instincts.

"Stop," Ava demanded, scooting into the passenger seat in front of Lexi and sitting backward on her knees to keep them all in her sights.

Blue shifted to put herself between Ivan and Rhodes, like she had earlier outside. Sam questioned the sanity of that maneuver. It wasn't where he would be standing right now. "Come on guys," she urged, like she had done this before. Maybe she had. "This isn't middle school."

The three stared at each other, not acknowledging anyone else. Ava fidgeted.

"I'm not asking you again," Ivan warned.

Sam wasn't sure what to say here that wouldn't cause a bigger problem. Directives could be tricky in large groups. Deescalate. That is what Nisha would say. He opened his mouth to try something generic, like calm down.

"Lurch," Ava warned, and he raised both hands in a gesture of peace. He wasn't trying to make things worse. Ava's eyes narrowed at him.

The next second was eerily quiet except for the ever-increasing staccato of heavy raindrops pelting the camper. When the silence ended, the only way Sam knew how to describe the subsequent events was a chaos bomb. Silverware left in the sink sailed upward, forming a metal tornado over Rhodes' and Blue's heads. Devon's hair lifted from enough static that everyone could feel the prickle on their skin. She extended her hand, saying something that ended with "calm down!" Blue looked at Rhodes with huge eyes as he started to grow hair and sprout fangs. His expression mirrored hers as a prismatic aura shimmered around her, just like the one Sam and Ivan observed in the van in Nashville before everything went sideways. Ivan looked down in alarm as a golden glow radiated out of his body. "Honey badger?"

"Oh shit," Ava stuttered. "How do I turn it off?"

Everything metal in the camper's interior buckled. Small items like screws flew loose and zinged through the air. A knife from the cutlery tornado embedded itself in Sam's arm, and he fell backward into the small hallway. Rhodes stepped in front of Blue, jerking as a barrage of screws pelted his back, some hitting hard enough to sink into his skin like buckshot. Devon flinched as a few small metal objects tore through her clothes and skin.

The yellow glow erupted and encompassed Ivan's body. It expanded, pushing everything in front of it out of the way, including Sam, who was thrown through the air, down the hallway, and onto the bed. Devon slammed into the window next to the dining table, cracking it. Claws shot from Rhodes' hands. The gold wave hit him, driving his claws into Blue's ribs. She gave a startled shout of pain and surprise as they both skidded backward, propelled by Ivan's shield. Rhodes' furry face looked conflicted as he tried to both pull his claws from her chest and keep her upright in the skid. Blue screamed in agony now as she and Rhodes slammed into the refrigerator and blood sprayed everywhere. Ava screamed in horror.

Ozone filled the air and a prismatic pulse flashed. Blue disappeared and Rhodes collapsed forward onto the vacant and blood-covered floor.

Ivan "landed" on the ground in the kitchen where Rhodes and Blue were sub seconds before, his body suspended in a glowing golden bubble two and a half feet from the floor. The bubble crushed Rhodes' face first into the ground.

Devon, her hand pinned up and to the side, shot a visible ripple of energy that exploded with a boom that rivaled the thunder outside. Blue reappeared on the ground in front of Ava's seat, bleeding profusely from a gaping wound in her chest, more blood dripping from her nose. She clutched her chest and tried to crawl back toward Ivan and Rhodes. She wobbled, even on her hands and knees, and fell motionless just in time for Devon's wave to go over her head. Ava jerked to the side, but the very edge of Devon's wave caught her shoulder, twisting her body in the air. She crumpled over the back of the passenger seat instantly.

The second Ava hit the floor, the golden bubble around Ivan collapsed. He fell to the floor with a grunt, his weight causing the camper to shudder. Devon slid into a heap, no longer held up by the force around Ivan. Sam leaped over the bed in one jump and ran back to the front of the camper, trying to determine who needed the most help. Everyone was down, and he couldn't see the little girl named Lexi.

Devon righted herself on wobbly legs and one hand, holding her other hand over a puncture wound in her neck. Ivan shifted to his knees and rolled Blue to her back. He placed both hands over the wound in her chest. She was semi-conscious, and her breath rattled in and out in gurgles. Blood flew out of her mouth with a cough. Sam guessed her lung was shredded at minimum. He hoped she would be OK for Ava's sake. The girl wouldn't handle it well if Blue didn't recover.

Sam ran to Ava. She lay eerily still. He pressed his fingers to her neck. Her pulse was weak, and her breathing was shallow. "Is yours OK?" Sam asked Ivan. He searched the area, finding a frightened Lexi hunched behind the passenger seat. She appeared physically unharmed. None of the metal or flying magic had hit her. Her arms covered her head, and she peeked from between them.

"No," Ivan grunted, lifting Blue's shirt to reveal four deep puncture wounds right under the rib cage. "She bleeds too much."

"Is Ava breathing?" Devon asked as she crawled over.

"Breathing," Sam answered, shifting the girl to the floor, straightening her body out to make sure her airways remained unobstructed. "Not well, though. Out cold. What did you hit her with?"

"OK. Everybody stay calm. Work the problem." Sam suspected Devon spoke more to herself than to him. "We keep Blue alive, and she will wake Ava up. Otherwise, Ava is going to die in a coma. If we can keep Blue breathing, she will heal herself. This could have been worse," she said, twisting to grab a hand towel. "Keep her breathing," Devon instructed Ivan, who looked overwhelmed. Sam wasn't sure how she expected Ivan to do that. Rhodes appeared at her side a moment later.

"I didn't mean to. I've never lost control of my magic before." He shook his head and took the dish towel that Devon offered. He placed it over the wound Ivan exposed and applied pressure. The man rocked forward on his knees and locked his elbows, his eyes never leaving the bloody face below him. "I'm sorry."

"It wasn't you. What was that?" Devon demanded. "If your gold thing hadn't hit me, I would have killed all of you."

"It's Ava. She causes magic to surge," Sam told them. "That is why the Sovereign want her. They call her the Nova. The magic spikes are her."

"There she goes. She's healed from worse than this," Rhodes muttered, peeking under the dish towel. "Remember that time in Edinburgh, Lacroix?" Ivan's grunt held both affirmation and displeasure. Rhodes looked over his shoulder, unable to see Lexi from his position. "Lexi Lou, you, OK?"

"Got plenty of practice at the duck and cover," Lexi piped up as she climbed out of the floor and observed the wreckage. Her face was grim, and her hands were shaking as she stared at the blood covering every square inch of the kitchen. She pointedly did not look at Blue. "Me and Tio G practice live drills every month. Mom and Tia Blue get so cranky. You have a knife in your arm, by the way." She pointed at Sam with false bravado. Her lip quivered.

"I noticed," Sam grumbled. Her attention made it hurt worse. It was a very dull knife. But at least she was distracted and calm.

"I'm sorry," she told him, looking guilty. "I didn't know I could do that until yesterday."

"It's not your fault." He reached out to pat her head as he stood up. She was Mullet Roane's granddaughter in the truest sense of the word. Devon needed to keep her away from the eyeliner. "I'll let you pull it out."

"Oh, cool!" Lexi exclaimed, and jumped forward. "On three." She grabbed the knife and yanked immediately.

"Gah!" Sam shouted and slammed his hand down over the hole in his arm. He glared at Devon. "That isn't normal."

"Let's get this one up on the bed and that one on the couch," Devon instructed, ignoring him and climbing to her feet.

"I can get her. You keep pressure on that," Ivan told Rhodes as he reached down to lift Blue.

"Don't you fucking dare," Blue whispered, her eyes still closed. "I'll be fine. Give me two minutes."

"Third time's the charm," Ivan smiled and gently pushed her hair out of her face. "Welcome back. Again."

"You like carrying people. It's weird. Go get Ava if you need to carry somebody. Bring her here. I can wake her up. She's all into that being carried around by a dashing hero bullshit," Blue chuckled, then groaned. "Owie."

"Dashing." Ivan posed smugly. Sam had never seen him joke this easily with anyone, even members of Stalker Prime. Especially not someone laying in a puddle of blood.

Blue laughed at his antics and clutched her side, groaning. She may be healing, but she was hurting. "Don't make me laugh."

"You should save your energy," Rhodes told her, earning himself a middle finger from Blue and a slap on the back of the head from Devon. "Hey!"

Sam motioned for Ivan to maintain his post next to Blue since he was closer to Ava. He knelt and picked the girl up, shifting her so that she was close enough that Blue could reach out and grab her hand. She did with a groan of discomfort. Ava's eyes slowly fluttered open even as the person healing her turned gray and weak. Ava looked up at him with bleary eyes and then looked around at the broken table, cracked window, trails of blood, warped metal, and shattered cabinetry. "What happened? Did a bomb go off?"

"Pretty much. We found out what happens when a nova gets upset around six emotionally compromised Sovaj. Let's not do that again, honey badger." Sam smiled down at the girl. "Can you recharge Blue so she can heal? She got hurt pretty bad. You calm?"

"I'm better. I'll try." Ava nodded and sat up. She wobbled slightly, but eventually held herself still. "God, my head hurts."

"I'm sorry, sweetheart. It's a side effect." Devon patted her back. "Blue will get you fixed up here in just a second."

The color returned to Blue's cheeks as she threw her arm over her eyes to block the light. "You can let go now," she told Rhodes. "Come here, Dev, let me see your neck." The weeping wound on Devon's neck puckered and expelled a small metal pellet, then closed up. "How's your arm? Let me see it," she told Sam.

She touched his wrist and a wave of warmth raced up his arm and the pain subsided. The wound grew shallower and smaller. It was impressive magic, but Blue's color was edging back past pale into blue. "That's enough. I'm OK."

Ivan nodded at him in appreciation and helped her sit up.

"Rhodes?" She offered her hand to the man. His back was covered in oozing blood.

He shook his head. "I'll be OK." She seemed conflicted as Ivan and Devon helped her stand.

"I'll help him," Ava offered. "I saw a first aid kit in the bathroom earlier."

"Thank you, sweetheart." Blue leaned a little more on Devon.

Tapping on his leg made Sam look down. Lexi stood next to him, looking up with concern and innocence. "Who is Nisha?"

Sam squatted, so that he was mostly eye level with the girl. "She's my best friend."

"Is she cool? If Tio G likes her, she must be pretty cool." Lexi frowned. "I don't understand everything that is happening anymore."

"Nisha is the coolest," Sam told her sincerely. "I haven't wrapped my head around all of it myself, kid. But everyone here is doing everything they can to keep you and Ava safe."

That made the little girl frown even more, and Sam sighed internally. He always said the wrong thing. "Who is going to keep you safe?"

Sam didn't know what to say. He couldn't tell her the truth—that likely no one would keep them safe. He had never spent much time around kids. What if he said something that scarred her for life or

in the cup holder. Nothing was sacred anymore. "OK. Thanks for the heads up. I'll tell him."

"What do we have?" Finn asked.

"It was Trix. The FBI agent that tapped your phone, he's real. But he works on a special task force formed by the Magic Relations and Regulation Committee," Greenlee told him. "The government hired you to track down the same people the crazies are after. I don't think that is a coincidence."

Finn didn't respond. The news was very concerning. He made a mental note to speak with Trix about giving out information to people who weren't technically on the team.

"Trix helped Mitch contact the Cahlad Conclave representatives. They are sticking with him so far. They don't want governments up in their business. He made a video. I hope he calls Nolan and his cronies out."

"He is going to blow the lid off this thing," Finn muttered. "It's going to start a war."

"We are already at war. Catch up," Nisha quipped from the back seat.

"Trix say anything else?"

"Magic surge near Grand Junction in Colorado," Greenlee continued. "Unexplained rapid plant growth trapped some hikers in the backcountry of the National Park and busted the glass out of a medical marijuana grow facility."

"Think Devon got caught up in whatever that was?" Finn asked.

"Too close to be a coincidence. Happened around the time they should have checked in. I say we head that direction." Greenlee plunked the phone back into the cup holder in frustration. "We need to find them."

"I know. We will." Finn nodded. "They've got this."

The phone rang once again. This time, Finn snatched it up before Greenlee could. If something bad had happened, he needed to be the one to take the call.

"This is Torrin," he answered, bringing the phone to his ear and waving off a glare from Greenlee.

"Tio Finn?" Lexi's voice startled him.

"Lexi, are you OK, sweetheart?" Finn kept his voice calm as worry tightened his chest. Why weren't Devon or Rhodes making this call? "Where's Mom and Mr. Rhodes?"

"They are asleep. And I remembered that we were supposed to check in every two hours. I didn't want you to worry." Lexi told him.

"That's great thinking. Is everyone OK?" Finn asked, still not liking the situation. Why were they asleep? Was it the gas that took out his guys?

"Not really. That's why they are sleeping. But Mr. Sotach wants to talk to you," Lexi told him.

"What? Lexi honey, Mr. Sotach?" Finn asked and watched Greenlee's head whip around. Nisha sat up in the back seat and leaned forward. The line was quiet for a moment. He heard the rasp of clothing against the microphone.

"Mr. Torrin. Is Nisha with you?" a polished male voice came over the line.

"How in the hell did you find my niece before I did?" Finn bit out. Where was Rhodes?

"Mr. Torrin, I assure you that everyone is safe. We are just trying to stay ahead of this Sovereign threat," the man replied in a calm tone. "No more cookies. Your mom said two. Damn it, Ivan. Stop sneaking her cookies."

Finn frowned and pulled the phone away from his ear. He knew who Ivan was, too. His abs were all over social media right now, and Nisha talked about both Sam and Ivan constantly. He was having trouble reconciling Stalker Prime's reputation with a conversation about cookies. Either way, Lexi felt safe enough to enjoy cookies. Devon was safe enough to have an opinion about it. He could listen to what the man said. "This is a rather long story. Is this line secure, Mr. Torrin?"

"To the best of my knowledge. Call me Finn. I'm putting you on speaker. I have my associate Greenlee Anderson, Ava's Dad Ben, and Nisha with me." Greenlee raised an eyebrow at being called an associate.

"Nisha?" Sam's tone changed. "You OK? Our phones didn't survive, and you know I can't remember numbers."

"I'm good, Sam. And I quit immediately."

"You can't quit now. You have to coordinate this contract with Herne."

"Devon tell you?"

"Yep, and a few other interesting things."

"I still quit."

"We will discuss it later."

"There is nothing to discuss," Nisha huffed and sat back.

"Let's move on. Ivan Lacroix is here with me. Everyone else is asleep. The past few hours have been lively, to say the least."

"Tell him his abs are trending," Nisha called from the back. Finn heard a distant grunt come from the phone.

"Hey Tio G! Our practice paid off. Mom totally lost it and I duck and covered just like you showed me," Lexi chortled from the background. Finn could tell her mouth was full. It sounded like more than two cookies.

"Good job sport!" Greenlee sounded chipper, but the look on his face was dark. It said he wanted to know why Devon had lost it.

"Yeah. The drama was so extra. Like those shows Mom watches. Tia Blue was going to get married to Cade Rhodes? Did you know that? It turns out he is a shape-shifting werewolf person. Super bad A. They used to work together. He wrote a song about her. It was a bad breakup. Capitol B bad. They started arguing. Tia Blue was super chill like always, you know. But Mr. Ivan called Mr. Rhodes a bad name and got upset. Mr. Ivan is super cool. He gives me cookies. Then the silverware started flying. The kitchen exploded. Boom! Except just the metal parts. Mr. Rhodes is still bleeding. Then he stabbed Tia Blue in the chest with these wicked claws. But it was totally an accident, and he feels really bad about it. Mr. Ivan was floating like whoa in the air. Two feet in the air! In this magic bubble.

Mom got hit with pieces of the kitchen, too. She tried to make everyone calm down, but she was super juiced, and it almost killed Ava."

Ben sat forward, and Nisha was pushed to the side by a wave of gray mist. She reached over it and rapped him on the head.

"Ava is my new friend. There are bad guys after her, too. She says Mr. Sam isn't bad and will buy us Cheetos, but we have to call him Lurch so that he doesn't get a big head. You should have seen it all. Tio G. Tia Blue says it was a moment you must stop and appreciate even if you lose a lung doing it since you have two, anyway. It was amazing!"

Finn stared at the phone in shock as the rapid fire of Lexi's voice finally wound down. She obviously didn't have her ADD medication with her and was high on sugar. He felt a brief flare of sympathy for Sotach, especially if Lacroix was still giving her sugar. Greenlee sat dumbstruck. Ben whispered, "What the fuck?" from the back seat as he rubbed the place on his head where Nisha had beaned him.

"I said it was going to be a long story," Sotach mumbled. "But she's pretty efficient. Do not give her more sugar, Ivan. You got me on a technicality with the Twinkie."

"I'd kind of like to hear the long version," Nisha announced from the back seat.

"No kidding," Greenlee grunted and scrubbed a hand down his face. "Blue is with you, too? Is everyone going to be OK?"

"Yes, she is. And everyone is going to be fine," Sotach assured them. "Mr. Anders. May I call you Greenlee?"

Greenlee frowned and sent Finn a questioning look. "Sure?"

"Do Devon and or Blue have your consent to represent the Hounds of Dawn on your behalf?"

"Excuse me?" Greenlee croaked. Greenlee seemed more guilty and caught than confused. Finn slammed on the brakes and jerked the car to the side of the road. He felt Nisha hit the back of his seat with a curse.

"What the hell did you just say?" Finn demanded as he looked at his friend.

Nisha leaned up and speared Greenlee with a scowl. "I knew there was something up with you." They all sat silently for a moment, Greenlee unwilling to meet Finn's eyes.

"Greenlee?" Sam's voice carried into the now silent car.

"They do."

Finn threw up his arms and slammed his head back against the seat. What was this craziness?

"Excellent. Let me fill you in on what is happening here."

As Finn and Nisha stared holes through Greenlee, Sam rattled off a series of numbers indicating their current coordinates. Nisha typed it quickly into her own phone. Sotach launched into a terse debrief of how he found himself the guardian of a cadre of powerful magic users that all seemed to be the target of a radical terrorist group. He filled them in on Zenith operatives and Mullet Roane's progeny.

"I'll be damned," Ben uttered when nobody else said anything.

Nisha looked floored. "He shows me up every time," she grumbled.

Finn didn't know how he felt about it. He hovered somewhere between anger, hurt, and disappointment. He tabled it for the moment and shared their information regarding the FBI agent and Mitch's plans.

"You owe me a twenty Ravi," Sam said smugly. "Ben, do you want me to wake up Ava? The rest of us are pretty beat up, but the girls weren't injured. I'll get her if you want me to."

"I'd really like to hear her voice," Ben accepted.

"Contact me when you reach those coordinates. We are a few hours out. I think we need to run dark. Rhodes says they have been able to track him too easily. If they have a sniffer, our trouble just doubled. There is so much magic in this thing we must be glowing." Sotach told them.

"Got it. I appreciate you looping us in. I know you didn't have to do that," Finn told the man begrudgingly.

"Seems like I do, thanks to Nisha. I have a camper full of unregistered Sovaj here. Aren't you in charge of that now?"

"I suppose I am," Finn sighed.

"If we are going to keep these young ladies alive, we all have to be on the same team," Sam told him. "Besides. Have you ever tried to say no to this kid?"

Greenlee snorted. "I make her mom do it."

"That's what Blue said." Finn heard Sotach sigh in exasperation.

"I love you, Lexi," Greenlee announced into the car. "Tell Mom I love her too."

"Love you too, Tio G. I will."

"Anyway. I've got them until you get here. We will put our heads together then. Let me get Ava." Ben took the phone gratefully and spoke softly to his daughter.

"Nisha, where are those coordinates?" Finn asked.

"A place called Ridgway, Colorado. It's not very big. About a thousand people. Mountain town," she replied.

"Plug that into the GPS, Greenlee," Finn ordered.

"The Hounds of Dawn. You just cost me twenty dollars," Nisha sounded grumpy as she tapped Greenlee on the back of the head. "I still can't read you? Is it your other nipple? Spill. Sam cannot know more than I do."

Finn listened intently, adjusting their course to follow the GPS instructions. He wanted to know the same thing. The fact that Blue was involved didn't surprise him. He liked her and considered her a friend. She was transparent in the fact that she was hiding things. But Devon, she told him about her dad and about her criminal history. He never suspected that she was keeping a secret bigger than that. She seemed so stable, and dare he think it, boring?

Greenlee stared out the window in contemplation, fiddling with one of the many piercings in his ear. He glanced over at Finn with uncertainty. "There are things you don't want to know, Finn. It was bad. You started Herne because of Alexander and Gage." He sighed. "The Hounds started the same way. We help people. Devon and

Blue help and protect people. Not telling you. That was Devon. She wanted to protect you if things went bad. The details need to come from her."

Greenlee looked into the backseat and removed one of the piercings high on his ear. He turned back to stare out the window at the quiet Colorado landscape. Nisha gasped, and Finn felt the shift of the car as she slammed back against the seat. Greenlee flinched and shrank against the door. He watched in the rearview mirror as her hand flew to her heart and her eyes grew wide. "Oh, God. They didn't," she said as tears filled her eyes and her other hand flew to press against the side of her head like she had a sinus headache.

Ben hung up the phone. "Are you OK?" He sent Finn a concerned look when Nisha just shook her head quietly. "Jesus. There are tears. This woman doesn't cry," Ben said. "What are you doing? Stop."

"I'm just letting her see what happened," Greenlee muttered. He reached back for his ear.

"No. I need to see this," Nisha insisted, still hunched in the backseat. "We didn't know."

"Well, you do now," Greenlee ground out, turning away. The car fell into tense silence as Finn drove toward the coordinates.

"What happened to you, Greenlee?" Finn asked his friend softly.

"We all have our nightmares, Torrin." Greenlee sent him a sad smile that told Finn the conversation was over. "Don't worry about mine."

43

BLUE

She fished a water out of the refrigerator, wishing there was a way to heat something. But the camper wasn't plugged into anything. She leaned against the counter and took a sip, rubbing the sleep from her eyes and taking in the scene in front of her. They were parked in a rest area. Everything was quiet except for the quiet rhythm of traffic zipping by on the interstate. Devon slept on the couch. Lexi and Ava were asleep in the bed in the back. Both girls snuggled up next to her at some point overnight and ended up pushing her out of bed. Rhodes sat sideways in the passenger seat to keep pressure off the wounds he had yet to let her heal. His head slumped forward as he snored softly. Ivan and Sam were sleeping as well. Ivan was passed out on the floor. Sam sat in the kitchenette booth with his legs stretched diagonally and sideways under the table into the opposite seat. His shoulders were hunched up, and the side of his face rested against the window. His shirt lay in a wad on the table in front of him. They were all bloody, even Ivan. They looked like extras in a B-rate horror flick.

She contemplated sitting in the driver's seat and decided she would probably wreck the camper somehow, despite the fact it was parked and off. So, she quietly slid into the small empty space in the booth next to Sam and watched the sunrise for a few moments through the window next to his head. "Everything OK?" he grumbled without opening his eyes, voice thick with sleep.

"Yeah, shhh," Blue scooted over as much as possible to make sure she wasn't jostling him. "I didn't mean to wake you up. There's nowhere to sit."

"Mmm hmmm." He sat up and stretched, his arms nearly touching the ceiling of the camper. He looked out the window and rubbed the red spot it had left on his face. His dark hair stuck out in all directions. Her's probably didn't look much better after all the drama yesterday. "I wanted to talk to you anyway."

"Want something to drink?" she asked, since she was blocking his exit.

"Sure," he yawned, plucking his shirt off the table and slipping it over his head.

She climbed out of the booth and grabbed a bottle of water, handing it to him as she slid back into the seat.

"Thanks." He opened it up and took a sip, grimacing. "I wish this were coffee."

"You and me both."

"I talked to your Greenlee last night."

She smiled at his choice of words. "What did my Greenlee have to say?"

"That you had his consent to represent his interest in the Hounds of Dawn. Devon told me the same thing this morning before she passed out."

"Interested in brokering more deals?" Blue asked. "Should I go get Lexi?"

He smiled, fatigue still showing on his face. "She told you?"

"Yeah."

"She's ten?" Sam sent her a sideways glance.

"I know. Right?" Blue chuckled. "But she still sleeps with her teddy bear and," she covered her mouth and looked around quickly before continuing in a whisper, "believes in Santa Claus."

"Cool." He nodded his approval of Santa Claus and crossed his arms, still looking out across the horizon at the early morning sky. "I talked to Ivan and Rhodes too, while you were sleeping off your latest near-death experience. The people in this camper think very highly of you."

"OK?"

"Cahlad Prime needs help right now," Sam continued. "The leaders of the Conclave are holding the line on magic governance. They don't want the non-magical governments involved. But most of the Stalker units stateside have been taken into custody, so we no longer have trained fighters at our disposal to deal with the Sovereign. Herne is it."

"OK?" she repeated, unsure of where he was going.

"The next few days are critical. If Mitch can't reestablish control of the Cahlad, one of the other Conclave leaders will probably challenge him and he will have to concede to stay in hiding or risk being taken into custody by the regular authorities. Mitch isn't perfect, but there are worse options to have in the seat."

"That's a real pickle." Blue nodded.

"We need an army."

"This is what happens in your head when you sleep?"

Sam shifted to lean against the window so that he could look at her. "We need the Zenith back. You can go anywhere in seconds. Survive anything. Be anyone. And you fight like spider monkeys."

Blue choked on her water. The Cahlad had tried to kill them all. Well, Larson had. Regardless, she and Rhodes lost the warm and fuzzies for the Cahlad long before it tried to kill them. "That took a lot of balls, buddy." Blue wiped at the water that spilled onto her shirt. "I'm impressed."

"Hold that thought." Sam lifted his chin. "Because we need the Hounds of Dawn, too. And you represent them both."

Blue gaped at him. Hold that thought indeed. He looked serious. He frowned so hard his eyebrows were practically touching each other. "You are serious?"

"Absolutely." He nodded. "The Zenith combined are a small army. The Hounds of Dawn have connections. How many people? Hundreds? And I bet they are all powerful Sovaj. Why else would they run?"

Blue shook her head furiously. "No. We aren't even discussing that. Those people aren't soldiers. And I don't speak for them. We are not discussing this."

She moved to stand, and he placed a hand on her leg. "Please hear me out."

She stopped and stared at the hand. Her body grew tense, and a wave of nerves washed over her, remembering who she was dealing with. If he compelled her to tell him where the people she had hidden over the years were, it could be catastrophic. Trusting him yesterday suddenly seemed premature. She might have to kill him. "You said please." she quirked an eyebrow and looked back up at him with apprehension.

He pulled his lips over his teeth, and she saw him chew the corner of his lip as he observed the look on her face. He looked almost sad. "I did. Because, as Ava said, consent is a thing. I try very hard to be aware of my language patterns. But I'm not perfect."

"Fine." Blue nodded slowly and let out a slow breath. "I'm listening."

Sam pulled his hand back and tried to put his hands in his pockets. "Thank you." The borrowed pants he wore didn't have any, so he settled on crossing his arms over his chest again. "Ivan is in without reservations. Rhodes is in. But I know that is contingent on you."

"I'm not pledging his life. I have enough blood on my hands. You can't expect me to do that."

"I'm not asking you to," Sam tried to clarify. "I'm asking for two things." He held up two fingers. "Your personal active participation as a Zenith operative in the coming conflict with the Sovereign and whatever faction of the government they have managed to infiltrate." He lowered one finger.

"And?"

"You will reach out to the people you have hidden and ask them if they will help us." he lowered his other finger. "You don't have to tell me where they are. Just ask them. I'm not asking you to pledge anyone else's life but your own. Everyone else gets to make their own decision."

"Isn't that in direct conflict with the promise you made to Lexi last night? Here you are trying to get me to fight when you promised her you would try to keep me safe."

"Ah." Sam tilted his head to the side with a smug look. "I believe you were excluded from that agreement. I said I would do my best for the rest of them. And they aren't safe if we do nothing. Whatever the Sovereign and government are up to, it isn't good for any of us."

Blue smiled despite herself. He was learning. "OK. Two things. In exchange for what?"

"Clemency and lifetime immunity for you, Rhodes, Devon, and Greenlee, for any violation of the Sovaj Registration Act of 1978. The same for any person you have ever hidden to protect them from prosecution or enforcement of the SRA. They will never be required to register and will not be monitored."

"Holy shit," Blue hissed through her teeth. She leaned back and put both arms over her face as the enormity of what he had just said hit her full force. Talk about a golden carrot. She couldn't turn down the chance for people to go back to their mothers or see their children again. The despair on the faces of the people she had helped over the years when they realized they could never go back home would haunt her forever. She pressed her arms tighter into her face and tried to think it through. What about the people she had to hide in the future? The problem would still be there. The Hounds of Dawn would still need to exist, granted with personal immunity. But that wasn't what she wanted.

"If I accept your proposal, I need one more concession."

"What is it?"

She lowered her arms and squared her shoulders before turning toward him. "I want the Registration Act Amended."

"Who has balls now?" Sam snorted, shaking his head in disbelief.

"I know the SRA is in effect by order of the Paragon. The Cahlad isn't a democracy. The last one signed it, but Mitch keeps it in place. As his agent, I need you to agree that it will be amended to only include registration and monitoring of Sovaj convicted of new crimes involving the use of their magic. No fishing for past offenses. It wasn't a fair playing field. You leave the rest of us alone."

Sam pierced her with fierce, obviously irritated eyes. She knew that was a huge ask. But he started it. His expression was hard, and his jaw worked as he clenched his teeth.

"The SRA is bullshit meant to control a public relations night-mare and appease the sheep, and you know it. They threw us away to win back public opinion."

"The last time the sheep panicked, women were burned at the stake," Sam reminded her. "There are more of them than there are of us."

"Excellent incentive to convince them Sovaj aren't the bad guys. You are a sharp guy. You'll come up with something."

Sam looked like he was going to balk. But she found herself unwilling to budge. "Kill the bullshit or lose control of the Cahlad. Your choice."

He rubbed his eyes and dragged his hand down his face. Now he just looked tired. "You are worse than the kid."

"Where do you think she learned it?"

"Clemency and immunity for the Hounds of Dawn, as well as anyone who has ever fallen under their protection. And an amendment to the scope of the SRA to include only Sovaj convicted of crimes using magic after the date of the change. In exchange, you will contact each of those people and respectfully request that they assist us in whatever way they can. And you pledge to fight for the Cahlad in your previous capacity as a Zenith operative until the end of the current conflict."

"Lifetime clemency and immunity just to be clear. And I fight with you, not for you. I am not executing orders I don't agree with anymore. Been there, done that."

Sam nodded, understanding the caveat. "I agree to your terms."

"Christ. I wasn't expecting that. Really?" Blue hung her head and tried to still her racing heart. This was more surreal than standing on a rooftop dodging flying dildos. "You and your friend Nisha are just burning it down, aren't you?"

Sam looked thoughtful. "Maybe Nisha is right, and it needs to be."

"Mitch Collins will be OK with this?"

"He appointed me Regent. I didn't want the job. This is the kind of thing that happens."

"Balls." Blue drew out the word.

"Big ones," he nodded.

They laughed quietly, releasing the tension that had built up over the last few moments, but not wanting to disturb the others. Their laughter tapered off, and they both grew silent, lost in their own thoughts, sipping water they wished was coffee. Ivan snored softly as he rolled onto his side next to them. She felt a pang of guilt dragging Rhodes into this. But she would let him make his own decision, which is more consideration than he had given her. This would change everything. No more hiding. No more secrets. Lexi and Ava would never have to look over their shoulders, at least not for the Cahlad. The world would weigh so much less now. She could feel the weight trying to leave her shoulders, hope she never dared let herself feel trying to lift it. She couldn't believe he had even extended the offer, much less agreed to her extra demand. She had dreamed of this her entire life. It was too good to be true. But she would never know if she didn't try.

"OK, Sotach." She extended her hand. "You have yourself an army."

He took it without hesitation, and they shook. A large blue ribbon of magic twirled around their hands, slowly tightening until she could feel the tingle of electricity where it finally touched her wrist. It zapped and twinkled into nothing.

"Think you could drive us to some coffee?" Blue asked. His face relaxed, and he actually smiled.

"God, yes." He playfully shoved her out of the booth. She stifled a startled laugh and scrambled to catch her footing, surprised by his sudden sense of humor. Who was this, and what did they do with the shirtless asshole? He took a single long step over Ivan's prone form to the vacant driver's seat. He started the engine as soon as he sat down and pointed out the windshield. "To caffeine."

"Blue?" Devon sat up on the couch. Mascara smeared beneath her eyes like a raccoon, and some blood still crusted her chin. She felt the camper shift. Sam wasn't wasting any time.

"Hey mama bear," Blue greeted her friend. "The coffee will be soon."

"Did you just negotiate clemency for my dad? Or did I dream it?"

Blue tilted her head to the side in confusion. "Huh?"

"You are a Hound, and you hid him," Devon pointed out. "He's covered in your terms."

"Damn!" Sam barked from up front. "I should have negotiated with the kid."

Devon smiled as Blue's eyes grew wide. "Oh, my God. I did."

"You sure did." Devon laughed out loud and fell back onto the couch with a wistful look on her face. "I wonder if he will help us."

"Will he keep his clothes on if he does?" Blue mused. He would be the first person she asked for help just to find out the answer to that question.

Sam and Devon both groaned.

She moved to the front and placed a hand on Rhodes' sleeping shoulder. She sent a wave of healing into him as Sam pulled the rolling headquarters of this unlikely alliance onto the interstate. She wasn't sure what would happen next. Whatever it was, it promised to be extraordinary.

ACKNOWLEDGEMENTS

Thank you to my beta readers, Brian Baltz and Caitlin Lebron. You guys are the best.

Thanks to everyone who helped hunt typos.

Thanks to my aviation consultant. You know who you are.

To my editor Beth at Magnolia Author services. I'm so glad I found you.

To my husband who never stopped believing I could do impossible thing even as he witnessed my tumble through the try-fail-learn-repeat cycle of book publishing.

DRAMATIS PERSONA

Blue West (aka Indigo Vale)
Independent contractor/ Former Cahlad Zenith
Faction: Unaffiliated

Devon O'Neal (aka Esdevona Irving)
Associate Professor of Magic Studies and Arcane History/ Mother
of Lexi O'Neal /Step Sister-in-Law of Finn Torrin
Faction: Unaffiliated

Greenlee Anders (aka Anderson Greenfield)
Self-Employed Artist
Faction: Unaffiliated

Finn Torrin
Owner Herne Tactical/Brother-in-Law of Devon O'Neal/ Uncle of
Lexi O'Neal
Faction: Herne Tactical

Lexi O'Neal

Fourth Grader/Goalkeeper/Daughter of Devon O'Neal

Faction: Unaffiliated

Sam Sotach

Regent of the Cahlad and Team Leader of Stalker Prime

Faction: Cahlad Prime

Nisha Ravi

Stalker Prime Captain

Faction: Cahlad

Ivan Lacroix

Stalker Prime Lieutenant /Former Cahlad Zenith

Faction: Cahlad

Cade Rhodes (aka Rhodes Westridge)

Platinum selling crossover country music artist /Former Cahlad Zenith.

Faction: Unaffiliated

Harper Kilgarden

Professional Diva Wrangler

Faction: Unaffiliated

Kendra Reyes

Security Specialist
Faction: Herne Tactical

Christopher Hale
Director of Operations
Faction: Herne Tactical

Trix Carpenter
Intelligence Specialist
Faction: Herne Tactical

Ben Hughes
Orthopedic Surgeon/Father of Ava Hughes
Faction: Unaffiliated

Ava Hughes
High school Senior/Daughter of Ben Hughes
Faction: Unaffiliated

Zella Tyne
Stalker Prime Lieutenant, Retired /Partner of Mitch Collins
Faction: Cahlad

Mitch Collins
Paragon of the Cahlad /Partner of Zella Tyne
Faction: Cahlad

Larson Battle

Former Cahlad Regent/ Former Captain Stalker Prime

Faction: Sovereign

Nolan Miller

United States Senator/ Chair, Magic Relations and Regulation Committee

Faction: United States Government

H.S. Torben weaves urban fantasy tales filled with humor, heart, and whimsy, inviting readers to explore a realm where magic and reality intertwine.

She lives in Tennessee with her husband, two children, and a snoring dog named Pickle. She spends Friday nights dungeon crawling, summers at the lake, and the rest of the year putting up or taking down Christmas lights.

Website: hstorben.com
Facebook: HSTorben
Instagram: hstorben

Also By

The Hounds of Dawn

Hounds of Dawn
Sevens Wild
Flying Fluke
Zenith's Child